The

Marquess

Love Match

JASPERS STORY

LORIBETH DEJOHN

Contents

Chapter 1

Jasper Raventon, Marquess of Bellator, elegantly strolled into the front parlor unannounced on the summons his mother had sent out at first light this morning, demanding his audience. Jasper wore his signature black tailored morning suit that fit him perfectly, enhancing his well-groomed physique. He stood two inches over six feet with broad shoulders, and his hair was black as a raven's wings with a hint of a blue tint. Women swooned in his wake as he walked by, but smart men feared him for his reputation of being ruthless.

The front parlor was the duchess' favorite room in the Devonshire London mansion. She'd decorated the room in mauve and cream colors; the silk curtains were cream, as were four luxurious wingback chairs. The duchess loved collecting paintings of well-known artists, and in this room, she showcased two landscape paintings from a French artist, Theodore Gericault. One hung above the fireplace and the other on a wall behind one of the mauve chaises. Two decorative tables held flower arrangements on them, fashioned by her twin daughters, who enjoyed making them every couple of days. It was a comfortable room. Duchess Viviana, who wore a pale blue muslin morning dress, lounged on a plush velvet chaise, sorting through the daily invites. She was still a natural beauty for a woman of her age, with her golden blonde locks framing her face, and the rest pulled in a modest upsweep to the back of her head.

Jasper said, "Good morning, Mother; I received your letter by my plate this morning. You said there's an urgent matter to come as soon as possible."

When it came to the duchess, everything of the utmost importance was an urgent matter. Jasper bent over, kissed his mother on the cheek, and sat in the comfortable wingback chair beside hers. "Do you care to share with me the problem today to summon me so early," he asked, raising one eyebrow in question.

The Duchess looked up from reading her invites, her emerald green eyes assessing.

"You know the twin's governess Miss Whitman had to retire due to poor health problems. Well, I have interviews set up at noon today for a new prospective governess. With them now being fifteen, you also know that next year will be their coming out to the ton, and we both know that will be of the utmost importance for their welfare. Let alone they are a handful."

"A handful is putting it mildly and a little too high spirited on too many accounts lately," Jasper said.

The duchess agreed, smiled, and then said, "Will you stay and do some of the interviews with me today?" She knew her son, the future duke, had a sharp eye on proper etiquette and could read a person within their first two sentences spoken.

Jasper stood and walked over to the fireplace, then turned and looked at his mother.

"I do have more pressing manners than to stay and interview a future governess for the girls."

"I know, but when it's so important to have someone's second opinion."

Jasper felt irritated but did not show it in his expression. Instead, he sighed, understanding this was important to his mother. "I will stay for the first two interviews. Then I have a luncheon at Whites at half-past one with Cousin Leopold that won't wait." Raising an eyebrow, he said, "Shouldn't Father be here doing this, not I?"

"Thank you for staying. As you know, your father has gone to parliament meetings all day. He never makes time for home matters when they are in session."

Jasper walked back over to the wingback chair and sat. "Where are the twins now?"

The duchess waved her pale, elegant hand to the French terrace doors. "They are in the garden, cutting fresh flowers for new arrangements to put in the front hall and parlors. They do enjoy the garden and the flowers."

Jasper looked impassive, "They should; it's a good pastime for gently bred girls."

A knock sounded on the parlor door. "Enter," the duchess said.

The butler, Wesley, entered with a bow. "Your Grace, the first interview has arrived. Would you like me to show her in?"

The duchess picked up her invites, put them in a neat pile, and laid them on the table beside her. "Yes, Wesley, send the first one in."

As you wish, Your Grace," he said, giving another bow and retreating.

Jasper thought, 'this should be interesting, and sighed.'

A minute later, the door opened, and Wesley re-entered, announcing, "Miss Tinley."

"Thank you, Wesley, that will be all," the Duchess replied.

Miss Tinley, thin and shapeless as a bean pole, entered and curtsied a little too low to the duchess. The Duchess nodded, and Miss Tinley rose.

"This is my eldest son, Lord Bellator," Miss Tinley curtsied again. "You may have a seat," the Duchess said and waved her hand to the chair opposite the chaise. Miss Tinley's coal-black hair was pulled to a single knot on the back of her head. She wore a simple brown walking dress with a high neckline, no-frills, and a matching brown bonnet.

Jasper guessed her age to be about mid-thirty's and one of the most undesirable women he's had ever seen. Miss Tinley sat with hands pressed in her lap, head down, her brown eyes set on the carpet in front of her, and she had no authority about her whatsoever. The woman hadn't even spoken yet; Jasper knew the twins would run circles around her and lead her on a merry chase. Not good at all.

The Duchess cleared her voice and tried to smile. "Tell me, Miss Tinley, who was your last charge?"

She looked up and answered, "For the daughter of Earl and Countess Galemorgan, Lady Audrielle."

Duchess said, "She had married last season to the elder Earl of Dumfriesshire after four seasons."

Miss Tinley answered, "Yes, she did, a true love match."

Oh yes, Jasper thought, he's an old windpipe, and he must be in the late fifties. Dumfriesshire constantly talks about rocks and fossils, plus he had a perpetually running nose. Not his choice to social in his circles in the ton. He shook his head lightly and sat up straighter in his chair.

Duchess continued, "She's a lovely girl, I am sure. How many years did you work for Earl and Countess Galemorgan?"

Miss Tinley answered, looking up again, "Oh, about eight years."

With an impassive expression on his face, Jasper asked in his deep tone, "Did you have any other young lady's that you educated and developed for the marriage market?".

Miss. Tinley's head jerked up, and she gazed at Jasper with a scared expression, looking almost as if she might dissolve into tears. She took a deep breath, then answered, "No, my Lord, just the one."

"I see," Jasper said as he glanced over to his mother.

Then Miss Tinley turned to the Duchess and quickly said, "Your girls and I should become the best of friends."

Duchess asked, "What are your strong suits in education that will help my daughters to broaden their minds?"

"Philosophy and mathematics. I simply adore numbers," she said with a dreamy smile.

Duchess stood and indicated the interview was over, then looked at Jasper. He shook his head no and frowned. With a wave of her hand toward the door, the duchess said to Miss Tinley, "You may leave any recommendation with our butler. I have many interviews today to consider."

The parlor door opened, and Wesley appeared to show her out. Miss Tinley stood and gave a quick curtsy to the duchess and Jasper before leaving.

After the door shut, Jasper said, "I hope you do not consider her in your choice, Mother. If she passed Father in the corridors, she would probably faint on the spot."

"I agree; if I hired Miss Tinley, the twins and staff would have to carry smelling salts to revive her daily," Duchess said, laughing.

Wesley reappeared at the door. "The second interview is here; shall I show her in, Your Grace?"

"Show her in, by all means," the duchess said as she took her seat once again with a sigh.

Wesley announced, "Miss Ledger, Your Grace, my Lord."

Miss Ledger strolled right in, looked over the room like a battlefield, and stopped directly in front of the duchess then curtsied like she was an armed soldier in the military, all stiff and rigid. She repeated her curtsy to Jasper, then stood straight as an arrow. The duchess indicated for her to sit opposite her in the chair. Miss Ledger took her position, sitting in perfect posture. Jasper introduced his mother and himself.

Miss Ledger's gray hair was scraped back into a severe bun, making her look as if she was in her late forties. She was a tall woman with a round face and piercing blue eyes. With one glance, it looked like they could see right through a person into the depths of their soul.

Shivering from her appearance, Jasper stood and walked over to the terrace door to get some distance.

The woman could've been a pugilist boxer. Jasper walked back over to where his mother was sitting on the chaise and stood behind her.

The duchess started the interview. "How many years have you been working as a governess, Miss Ledger?"

With a brief smile, Miss Ledger tilted her chin up, a movement that gave prominence to a considerable mold on her chin, and in a voice almost as deep as a man's, said, "I've been a governess for twenty-six years, all my charges have married."

Then the duchess asked, "Who was your last charge?"

Miss Ledger cleared her throat. "Duke of Cumberland's daughter," she said as her words clipped.

The Duchess started thinking. She knew everyone in the town. She recalled that the Duke of Cumberland family was very reclusive at their country manor. "I believe their daughter's name is Lady Sabrina, and she married the Earl of Radnorshire, a minimal estate."

Miss Ledger, looking insolent, frowned, "Yes, she married, and that is the important part, isn't it?"

Jasper interrupted, "Yes, to marry is an important dream for most girls, but to marry well is even more important to this family." Miss Ledger raised her chin as a challenge. The duchess looked over her shoulder to see Jasper's expression; when she saw his eyes narrowing and his jaw going tense, she realized it was time to call this interview to an end. She knew when Jasper had that angry look in his eyes (just like his father), he was going to lose his temper at any given moment.

The duchess replied quickly, "We heard enough

for today. You may leave your recommendation with our butler Wesley, Miss Ledger."

Jasper walked over to the parlor door, opened it, and said through gritted teeth, "Good day, Miss."

Miss Ledger got to her feet and marched toward the door, stopping right in front of Jasper. She glared up at him, "Well, I never," then marched right out the front door, not stopping or looking back.

Jasper shut the door walked back to his mother, and replied, "You can mark that one off your list with no possibilities."

"Oh, yes, I agree that she will not do. I do hope the next ones are better suited."

A light knock sounded on the door, and Wesley peeked his head in, "Are you ready for the next one, Your Grace?"

Duchess took a deep breath to settle her nerves, "Yes, I hope this one is more fit than the last two."

Jasper started to walk toward the parlor door, having made good on his promise to stay for two interviews, "On that account, it's time to take my leave, Mother."

The door opened wide, and Wesley announced the next governess. "This is Lady Sinclair, Your Grace, my Lord." Wesley stepped aside, allowing the lady to walk in, and Jasper stopped dead in his tracks. He looked down to see the most beautiful violet eyes he had ever seen, a perfect button nose, and lush and kissable lips. She blinked up at him and smiled, and he thought: flawless.

"You are beautiful," he muttered softly before remembering who and where he was. He coughed to cover his faux paus. "I do believe I have time for one more interview. Allow me to introduce myself; I am

Marquess Bellator, at your service," he said with a wicked smile. Jasper decided to stay because if he left now, he might never see her again, and that definitely was not going to happen. Jasper directed her through the room to a chair. "Shall we, Lady Sinclair?"

Jaspers introduced his mother, and Lady Sinclair curtsied eloquently. The duchess nodded with a smile of approval and waved for her to take a seat. Jasper decided to sit beside the duchess on the chaise so that he could look directly at Lady Sinclair with delight and with not so innocent thoughts.

The duchess threw Jasper a look, telling him she knew why he stayed for this particular interview before giving Lady Sinclair a level stare. "Berwickshire Is your father, the Earl of Berwickshire?"

Lady Sinclair nodded. "He's the late Earl, your Grace. He and my mother died seven years ago in a shipwreck whilst traveling to France. I was only seventeen when it happened; I have a brother Lucas who is now the new Earl."

The duchess said, "How much older is your brother, my dear?"

"He is four years older than me. He had looked after me until I turned eighteen, then I started working as a governess to pay my own way, and I do not depend on him or anyone for support. To have one's independence is important."

The Duchess says, "I knew of your parents and remembered the horrible incident. I am sorry for your loss."

Jasper chimed in, "As am I. I believe they would be proud of you."

Lady Sinclair said, "Thank you to both of you. I

didn't come here to talk of my parent's passing but thank you for your kind words. I came for the job as your new governess if the position is still open?"

Jasper looked at his mother, for her to take the lead, and then to Lady Sinclair. "Yes, of course, tell us your strong suits to educate my twin daughters, to get them ready for the ton next year, Lady Sinclair?"

"This is an important year, for it is the last to be ready. We will work on proper etiquette in and around the ton. As for schoolroom lessons, I will teach them reading, writing, mathematics. I speak fluent French, Spanish, Latin, and Italian; I will teach your girls that language with your choices. I believe every young lady should know how to play an instrument; I can teach them to play the harpsichord and the harp."

Jasper knew she had all the qualifications his mother was looking for, but the first time he had looked into those beautiful eyes, she was hired for twin's governess and fleetingly thought she might warm his bed. Jasper looked to his mother, "I do believe she qualifies, Your Grace, and more." Jasper flashed his brilliant smile to them both.

Duchess said, "Do you have a recommendation I could look over?"

Lady Sinclair pulled a sheet of folded parchment out of her reticule and handed it to the duchess. "Yes, Lady Sinclair, very nice, you have been a governess for two families already, for an earl and a duke, and both girls married well. When can you start?"

Lady Sinclair said, "Tomorrow or the next day would be beautiful."

Jasper stood and looked into her eyes and asked, "Where are you staying?"

"At Mrs. Carlyle's boarding house for women, on the south side of London. I travel with my maid personal Sandra; she would also be there waiting for my return. My maid shared my last quarters at my last employers. She looks after me and is a chaperone when needed. I do hope that is not a problem. Sandra has been with me from an early age, and it was a stipulation my brother had made for me to be in London on my own."

"I see no problem in that, as I recall all ladies do have a maid. I will send one of our coaches with a maid to help pack your things and two grooms to make sure all your arrangements are complete in your absence. Your trunks and personal belongings will be here in two hours. If that is acceptable with you?"

Laurentia could tell Jasper was used to directing orders and having everybody follow his commands and do everything correctly. Well, not everybody, because this governess was not one to take orders, she gave them.

Lady Sinclair nodded, "That will be lovely, my Lord" Perhaps just this time, she would let him take control.

Jasper walked out into the hallway and ordered Wesley to carry out what he wanted to be done. Stepping back into the parlor, he told the ladies that everything was rolling on to his orders, and he had ordered a room to be set up for her liking. Not the standard governess room, but one for an earl's sister.

"Now, ladies, I will take my leave. I am already late for my luncheon at Whites. There is one thing I must know before I go, what is your first name, Lady Sinclair?"

She said with a smile, "Laurentia, my Lord."

"That is a beautiful name for a beautiful woman. Good day, Your Grace, Lady Laurentia." Jasper then gave an elegant bow and exited the room.

Chapter 2

Meeting the Raventon Daughters

The duchess looked to Lady Laurentia. "I believe it is time to meet my twin girls. Follow me." As they walked out of the front parlor, down the corridor to the back of the mansion, Lady Laurentia took in the beauty of the vibrantly decorated rooms they passed. The duchess looked back.

"They should still be in the back parlor, arranging the flowers they gathered from the garden this morning. The girls are very fond of flowers and arranging them to lovely vases for different rooms throughout the mansion."

Passing the grand ballroom, Lady Laurentia looked in and noticed a huge crystal chandelier; she never saw one that extensive before, and how the floor shined was impressive.

"Ah, here we are," the duchess said as she turned the handle to the door. The twins were arguing about where to place the floral arrangements. The duchess cleared her throat and stepped into the room, with Lady Laurentia behind her. The girls stopped arguing at once and looked to their mother with big smiles on their faces as if fighting was unimportant to them. Unfortunately, it was not, and more of a daily routine for them.

The duchess walked to the table, "The flowers look lovely as always, my darlings."

"Thank you, Your Grace," the girls said, speaking at the same time.

Duchess smiled then gestured toward Lady Laurentia. "This is your new governess, Lady Laurentia Sinclair. She shall be starting tomorrow after breaking her fast. These are my twin daughters Lady Aurora and Lady Amara."

The girl's curtsy and smile together. "A pleasure to meet you," they said in unison.

Aurora commented, "You are very pretty, Lady Laurentia."

"Thank you, Lady Aurora," Lady Laurentia answered with a smile.

The twins resembled their mother, with elegant features and beauty. The only thing setting them apart was their eye color—Aurora, the eldest, had blue eyes, and Amara, green. Being they were identical twins, it would make things much more comfortable to tell them apart.

With a warm smile, Lady Laurentia said, "I am looking forward to being your new governess, and I think we shall work together, splendidly.".

The duchess was pleased; she could see her girls and Lady Laurentia would do well together. Lady Laurentia started asking each girl what their favorite subject and pastime was. The twins laughed, answering her questions, and asked several questions of their own. They were chatting away like they'd known each other for years.

The duchess interrupted, "I believe it is time for Lady Laurentia to get settled in her new room. After all, she doesn't start as your governess until tomorrow."

Amara said, "Oh, if she must, I was so enjoying getting acquainted."

"So was I," Aurora said.

"You may visit perhaps later after dinner."

"Oh yes, you can meet His Grace and our two brothers. They will love you as we do already," the twins echoed together.

The duchess broke in, "I haven't invited your brothers to dine tonight; they might have other plans of their own."

Aurora said, "You know as soon as they find out that our new governess is a beauty, they will come and seek their curiosity."

Lady Laurentia thought to herself, 'Lord Bellator was quite handsome; I wonder what the other brother will look like. Perhaps, he shall be as stunning as the rest of the family?

Duchess said, giving the twins a shake of her head, "We shall find out later." Duchess walked over and pulled the bell-rope, summoning a maid. When one appeared, she directed the girl to show Lady Laurentia to her room.

Walking back to the front of the mansion to the main staircase, Lady Laurentia asked the maid, "Are we not to use the servant stairs?"

"But, your brother is an earl, and we must show you the respect that is your birthright."

Lady Laurentia asked who gave that order. The maid looked up into her eyes and said, "Mr. Wesley told all the servants that it is a request from Lord Bellator, of course."

Laurentia, not pleased, said, "That most certainly

is not going to do. I am hired to be the twin's governess, so that is how I should be treated." They walked up the stairs then turned left.

The maid said, "Servants for His Grace and their family, follow orders given to us, with no questions asked." Laurentia would have to deal with Lord Bellator later and tell him to stop interfering with her work relations with the other servants, she thought to herself.

Halfway down the corridor, they stopped. The maid opens the door to their right. "Here we are."

Lady Laurentia entered the room and stopped in the middle of the bed chamber, looking around in bewilderment. The room was far too big to be the governess room. Laurentia asked the maid her name.

"My name is Jennell," she answered with a smile.

"That is a lovely name. I think you and I shall become good friends with us both working for this good family."

"Yes, they are a good family to work for, and we servants are very loyal to them," Jennell responded.

Laurentia asked, "Now tell me, is this the regular governess room?"

Jennell twitched a little bit. "Well, no, it's the room his lordship ordered to be ready for you. It's a grand room, is it not?"

"Yes, it's grand, I would say, but too much for the governess to stay in," Laurentia said with a sigh.

Jennell said, "Let me know if I can get you anything else. I have been told that your trunk and belongings should be arriving soon." She curtsied then took leave.

Laurentia looked over her room; it had a large canopy bed with lavender curtains that matched the ones that adored the windows, a dressing table with a mirror, and a large dressing room. This room is not the governess' room, Laurentia thought as she walked over and sat in the comfortable wingback chair in front of the fireplace to relax. But one should be happy with a little extra comfort.

Ten minutes later, there was a knock on the door, and in walked Jennell with a tea tray. She set the tray on the table beside Laurentia, "Her Grace thought you would like some tea and finger sandwiches for refreshment while you relax before dinner."

"Thank you, that is wonderful of Her Grace to have it sent up to me."

Jennell walked over to the window and opened the curtains. "This time of day, the sunshine is nice for extra warmth and brightness."

Laurentia smiled at her. "Yes, that is lovely, thank you."

"You have a view of the back garden out your window."

Laurentia stood up and walked to the window, and looked out. "Oh, how lovely the garden view is from here. Is that a rose arbor over there?"

"Yes, the duchess designed the garden, and you can find her working out their right along with the gardeners to oversee every little detail."

Laurentia replied, "It's truly rewarding just to look out and breathe in the beauty."

Jennell walked to the door. "I better let you get to your tea before it cools.

Laurentia walked back to the chair, sat down, and poured some tea, adding one lump of sugar. She sipped her tea, thinking about how handsome Lord Bellator was, with his sapphire blue eyes, straight nose, high cheekbones, and strong chin. He had the face of a warrior god with black hair that had a hint of blue dusting his shoulders. Then she recalled his introduction, that wicked smile when he bowed and said, 'at your service.' At my service indeed, she thought, he's a true rake of the ton, I am pretty sure. Still, he was charming. She couldn't help noticing the way he glided eloquently across a room, like a panther on the prowl. She picked up a mini sandwich, took a small bite, then thought that man could put a scar on my heart if I let him and to consider the twins said there's another brother too. To think about what he's like.

A loud knock on the door brought Laurentia back from her daydreaming. "Yes, come in." The door opened to reveal two footmen carrying her huge trunk and several large boxes after that. Laurentia directed them to put them in the dressing room. Sandra, Laurentia's personal maid, came in behind the two footmen, carrying a few hat boxes. 'Thank goodness, her maid is here, to help dispense everything else to its new places, and make her room feel more like home for her comfort,' Laurentia thought when she saw Sandra's smiling face. Putting her things away took the rest of the afternoon, right up to dinner time. She had half an hour to dress. Good heavens, that's not much time, so she hurried.

Chapter 3

Late for A Luncheon

Lord Bellator walked up the steps, after handing his horse to the groom outside of Whites, a short ride from his parent's residence in Berkeley Square. As he entered through the door, he ran into one of his best friends Earl Jesse Kingsley. They grew up together, for their parents' estates bordered each other's; his father was the Marquess of Cornwall.

Shaking his hand, Jasper said, "Kingsley, old man, it's' been quite a while since I've seen you last." Jasper shook Kingsley's hand, then continues. "When did you arrive in London?"

"About a fortnight ago. I am staying at my townhouse in Grosvenor Square. And you, are you at your parents' mansion or your townhouse?"

"I am at my townhouse and have been in town for two weeks. Where are you off to?"

"I told my sister Lady Brittany that I would take her for an ice down on Bond Street this afternoon. Then she Shall want to stick her head in a few shops to buy a new bonnet or two."

"I believe my two sisters could fill a whole room with all the bonnets they have purchased or open a hat shop of their own," Jasper said, shaking his head in disgust. "I am meeting Leopold for lunch. Is he inside still waiting? I hope as I'm a little on the late side."

Kingsley walked by a little, then stopped. "He's inside having an ale waiting for you. He is not too happy you're late; we both know how he is a stickler on certain things."

Jasper replied, "I've better get in there then; I'll see you later. I say, would you want to ride early tomorrow morning in Hyde Park?"

"That sounds good. About seven in front of your place, Bellator?"

"Yes, that works for me. See you then, and we can catch up." Jasper continued walking into the club, putting his riding gloves into his coat's inner pocket.

Walking into the club, he nodded to a few acquaintances as he passed. Leopold was lounging in a leather chair, talking to the Earl of Surrey. He was a friend they shared from Eton and had known each other since their youth. Jasper walked up to their table and said, "Good afternoon, gents," showing his brilliant smile that does not happen too often, hoping Leopold would not say anything about his tardiness.

Leopold glared at him. "You're a little late, Cousin, aren't you!" he said unpleasantly, his blue eyes flashing. Leopold had the fairest color of all the Raventon men; he also had the best gentlemen quality of the younger generation. Throughout the ton, every hostess adored Leopold; they always put him on the top of their guest list as a must-have to attend their ball or soiree.

"Her Grace kept me, conducting some interview

for a new governess. She had summoned me extremely early to come and assist her with a second opinion. His Grace was not helping due to his session in parliament. I felt obligated to assist."

Leopold replied, "I wouldn't want Her Grace in distress. It was most likely important to her to have you there." Leopold still studied Jasper's face. "What's with the smile on your face that hasn't faded since you walked in. Did you find a new chit that you're planning to dally with or a new challenge that has you fired up?"

Jasper pictured Laurentia's lovely face, and he grinned then said, "You know me too well. It has been a couple of weeks since I ended my affair with the Widow Countess Angelique; she was getting too clingy for my taste. So, I gave her a lovely ruby bracelet as a farewell gift and said goodbye."

"I knew by the look in your eyes that a new female has sparked your interest," Leopold quipped.

Jasper raised an eyebrow, then said, "You really wouldn't think I'd stay celibate for long."

Jasper suggested they go in for lunch in the dining room. Then he would share who his new female interest is. The gentlemen strolled to the dining room, and the maître d escorted them to a lovely table in the corner so they could talk without too much disturbance. Jasper and Leopold were both thirty, though Jasper was three months older. They were more like brothers than cousins and had each other's back always. They could talk, joke, and tell the other their problems and never worry about any secrets ever going beyond their lips. As they sat down, a waiter hurried over, made a bow, then took the order. Jasper was quite hungry, so he ordered a half-roasted chicken and potatoes, and Leopold the same.

Leopold raised an eyebrow, then said, "Are you going to tell me who is the chit that has you in such a good mood, dear Cousin?"

Jasper knew he must tell as he could not fool Leopold about anything. "I agreed to stay for two interviews with mother this morning for a new governess. The first two were dreadful, so I was about to leave when Lady Laurentia Sinclair walks in. She is a sister to an earl, and mother recognized her surname." He surveyed the room to make sure no one was listening.

"So, she a sister to an earl and doing governess work? They must be in dire straits." Leopold questioned.

"I had not heard the complete story of why she was working, but she was a gorgeous one, who was hired this morning," Jasper explained.

Leopold knew his cousin too well; he knew Jasper was behind having this specific earl's sister hired for the job as the twin's new governess. "Does Her Grace believe the hiring was all her doing?"

"I let her give the final word that she was hired. Then I took over to order a room for her and sent a coach with a maid, two footmen, to fetch her belongings. And I bet as we are speaking, she is in her new room unpacking her trunk now."

The waiter returned with their food, and the two paused their conversation. Jasper started eating his chicken, and he looked up, seeing Leopold staring at him. He swallowed and asked innocently, "What?"

"You are telling me there's a beautiful young woman now living at your parents' residence that you are planning to dally within the very near future."

"Her name is Lady Laurentia Sinclair, and she does not know it yet, but she will be warming my bed soon. I am stating my mark on her." His wicked smile appeared now.

"I have no doubt that's your plan, Bellator."

Jasper's brother Drake entered the room, spotted his mark, and walked over to their table. The waiter hurried over with another chair for him. Drake gave them a nod and said, "Good afternoon, gentlemen," then took a seat at the table. The waiter asked if he would like lunch?

Drake answers, "no lunch, but a glass of white wine would be grand, a Chardonnay, if you would, from the stock I have supplied here recently."

"Yes, as you wish, my Lord."

Drake was the middle child and shared many of the same features as his older brother, though his eyes were emerald green like their mother. "So, what are we discussing today for a topic? Have you figure how to save the world of yet?" Drake asked, looking at both of them for an answer.

Leopold said casually, "About the new young governess you're Grace has hired today for the twins. I've heard she is charming."

Drake looked straight at his cousin and raised an eyebrow. "Do tell."

"It's Bellator's story. I haven't seen her yet." Jasper told Drake the same as he just shared with Leopold a few minutes ago.

Drake said, "I believe it's time to have dinner at our parents' residence tonight, dear Brother."

Jasper motioned for a footman to request a pen and parchment. Then, writing a quick note, he returned it to the footman and said, "Deliver this to the

Duchess of Devonshire on Berkeley Square at once."

As the footman walked away, Jasper said, "Drake, I wrote Mother to expect us for dinner tonight."

Drake said, "I'd like to see what this governess looks like, especially since you keep smiling every time you talk about her."

Leopold chimed in, "I cannot help noticing the smile myself. You haven't smiled that much in a long time or ever to think about it."

Jasper said, "Oh come on, do I not get to relax a little around my brother and cousin for a change?"

Smirking at Drake, Leopold said, "If you say so, but smiling has never been your strong suit."

Annoyed, Jasper changed the subject. "I ran into Kingsley on my way into Whites. I asked him if he wanted to go riding early tomorrow morning in Hyde Park. We're meeting at seven in front of my townhouse. Do you two want to join us?"

Drake said, "Sounds good. Zeus needs a good workout. My stable lad informs me he keeps kicking the hell out of his stall. They are replacing new wood every day."

Jasper said, "Just let me know when you're away, and I'll take him out here and there for you."

Drake said, "That shall be brilliant. My stable hands won't ride him, way too much horse for them." He smiled.

"What about you, Leopold? Are you up to it?" Jasper asked.

"I'll be there; it will feel like the old times when the four of us rode at Devonshire."

Their cousin Victor walked into the room, and he saw his cousins gathered around the table. He nodded to them as he walked over.

"What, do we have going on here, a little family reunion?" Victor asked.

"It seems that way. Pull up a chair," Jasper said.

Victor was twenty-six, tall like his cousins, with black hair, gray eyes with a hint of blue specks, and the Raventon good looks.

As Victor pulled up a chair, Jasper asked, "Have you been in London long? It's still early, and the season has only begun, Cousin."

"Just came in two days ago. Gabrielle came with me. We are going to open the manor for our parents, and once they arrive, I'll move to my place. Cannot leave Gabrielle without a chaperone."

"Your sister is in town. I'll have to tell Her Grace; she shall have her over for tea," Jasper commented.

"She shall like that," Victor said, smiling. Victor and Gabrielle were close, and they shared the same interest in art. Victor dabbles in mainly painting, which has been his favorite pastime since his youth. He owns an art gallery in London. And has been teaching his sister his craft of the art world for a few years.

Leopold said, "After lunch here, I am going over to Jackson's Boxing Salon to watch some warm-up rounds between Tyler Hopkins and that Jarvis Snyder. I heard they are actually going to go nine full rounds in the ring next week."

Drake said, "I'll have to put some wagers on that one."

Jasper said, "I'll put ten pounds on Snyder if anyone wants to meet my bet."

"I'll match you and take Hopkins," Victor said.

Drake smiled then said, "If your pocket is deep, Bellator, I'll match that bet too and take Hopkins for ten pounds. Who's your man on this one, Leopold?"

"I'm with Bellator taking Snyder. I am willing to bet you four rounds, and there shall be a knockout. Anybody wants in, and I say ten pounds sum it up?"

Victor said, "You are quite sure of yourself on that, are you?"

"Oh yes, I have been down there the last two days watching. Snyder, I know, he shall take it in four rounds."

"Alright, ten pounds you're on," Victor said.

The waiter returned with the food and ale Victor ordered. "Let me eat my lunch, Leopold, and I shall go with you to Jacksons. I must see how my man Hopkins is shaping up and get in some more bets. I say easy money on this one."

Leopold says, "I don't think so, but a fool and their money soon part, dear Cousin." Drake decided to accompany them to Jackson's also.

Jasper said, "I have to go home; there is a stack of papers on my desk that need my attention. His Grace has been delegating the Devonshire estate business to me lately to learn the ropes of the dukedom. I have a couple of hours of work to do," Jasper stood and bade his family farewell. "Don't forget, Drake, dinner at the parents' tonight."

As Jasper stood outside, waiting for his black stallion to be brought around from the stable, his mind wandered to those vibrant violet eyes that he remembered in his mother's parlor earlier that day. Then he wondered what her lips would taste like and feel like against his. Yes, he thought, this new challenge to seduce Lady Laurentia Sinclair is very intriguing. The groom walked over with his horse, and Jasper flipped him a coin then mounted quickly. He rode off to his townhouse to get his work done. As he rode down the streets of London, he said to himself, "Step one to make my claim on Lady Laurentia, and then my seduction game shall begin." Jasper's wicked smile appeared again.

As Leopold, Victor, Drake headed out together, Leopold offered his cousins to ride with him. Leopold owned a company that built luxury coaches. "I'm parked across the road over there."

Victor whistled, then said, "That coach looks as if the king and queen are here to grace us with their presence." The coach was a beautiful chestnut brown, with a high gloss finish, brass trim, gold leaf designs, and four large brass lamps.

"No, it's my coach, one of the newest models I just designed. You could have one too, just like this one, just put in an order, and in a month, I'll have it delivered at your door," Leopold answered with a huge grin.

"No thanks, too flashy," Victor and Drake said at the same time.

Drake then said, "But we shall take that ride to Jackson Saloon to see how it rides."

"This way, gentlemen, wait till you see and feel the comfort inside." Leopold smiled, then waved his hand in the direction of his coach. His coach had a driver and two grooms. One groom leaped down from his platform and opened the door. Leopold called out to the driver telling him where they were headed. A click of the reins and the four beautiful chestnut horses that matched the coach to perfection were off to Jackson's Boxing Saloon.

Chapter 4

Devonshire Mansion, Family Dinner

Duchess Vivianna walked down the main staircase when she heard her daughter's descending just behind her, giggling. Duchess stopped so the twins could catch up. "Good evening, girls, tell me what is so funny?"

The twins said at the same time, "Good evening, Mother."

To avoid answering, Aurora said, "Mother, your gown is lovely." The duchess was wearing a gown of rose pink, with a low-cut neckline and with little pearls sewn in.

Not one to be dissuaded, the duchess said, "Thank you, darling, but do share with me on what is making you giggle so much."

Aurora and Amara looked at each other, then shrugged and looked back to their mother. Amara answered first. "Oh, we made a bet, that to which brother will come here first tonight to see Lady Sinclair."

Aurora blurted, "I said Drake because he hasn't met her yet."

Amara said, "My maid told me she overheard that Jasper was very smitten with her and was the one to order the better room for our governess. So, I say Jasper shall be here first."

The Duchess sniffed, then said, "That is amusing to think about. Jasper and Drake always do try to outdo each other in all things. I do hope they behave themselves and be gentlemen this evening. Lady Sinclair may be the sister of an earl, but she is still a member of our staff, and I do have strict rules about that sort of behavior." The duchess continued down the stairs with the twins right behind her. Wesley was at the bottom of the stairs, and he bowed good evening.

The duchess asked, "Has anyone arrived, Wesley?" She moved toward the parlor door then stopped.

Wesley hurried over to open the door for her, "No one, Your Grace."

The duchess said with a light laugh, "I guess we shall see who wins the bet together."

The twins followed the duchess into the parlor.

Amara asked, "You're not mad at us for betting? You did tell us at one time that it's not ladylike to make wagers."

"No, not this time," Duchess said as she walked over to the wingback chair and sat down. Aurora was wearing a lemon-yellow gown with a modest neckline, with flowers embroidered along the neckline and hem. Amara wore a mint-green gown with delicate lace along the neckline and puffy short sleeves. The twins followed suit to the chaise to sit together.

Duchess looked over to the girls and said, "I also like to laugh sometimes, believe it or not."

Twins said together, "You do have a beautiful laugh, Mother; we would like to hear it more often."

Duchess thought about what her daughters said and agreed. "I must start working on that, life is too short, and you are right, my darlings," she said with a smile.

All of a sudden, the door burst open. Jasper was arguing with Wesley that there was no need to announce him at his parents' home; his family knew who he was. He walked around Wesley, shaking off his irritation, and continued across the room. Jasper wore his signature black silk evening coat with tails, gold thread embroidery trimmed around the collar, down the lapel, and a matching waistcoat. His cravat had a perfectly crafted knot, his breeches tight fitting to show off his muscular thighs.

The duchess told Wesley, "It's alright," then nodded for him to leave.

Wesley bowed and said, "As you wish, Your Grace."

Jasper strolled over to his mother, kissed her on the cheek as always, "Good evening, Mother."

She smiled and kissed his cheek. "Wesley has been our butler for thirty-five years and took over the position when his father retired after forty-five years of service for this family. Wesley takes his position very seriously; his father trained him and drilled proper etiquette into him to be displayed at all times. Jasper, why do you fluster Wesley all the time? He's just doing his job."

Jasper smirked, "I guess because I can, Mother."

Duchess shook her head, thinking he is just like his father, in so many ways.

Jasper walked to his sisters. "You both look very lovely this evening. Have you met your new governess today?"

"Yes, we have; she been settling into her nice new

room most of the day," the twins echoed at the same time.

Amara smiled all too brightly when she turned to face Aurora and whispered, "I won" in her sister's ear. Then she looked back to Jasper. "She is quite lovely. What do you think, Jasper?" Amara asked, smiling.

Jasper was wondering what his sisters were up to now. With an impassive expression, he said, "She is lovely, yes. Is she not coming to dinner?"

The Duchess answered, "She shall be down shortly." Duchess noted that Jasper was showing interest in Lady Sinclair, an earl's sister, and from a wealthy family. He was at the age to take a bride and start a nursery. She smiled to herself; Jasper did seem very pushy to have her hired and make sure she moved in today. Maybe she's the one. Jasper walked to the fireplace, leaned against it to support himself, as he looked over the room.

A knock on the door sounded, and Wesley announced Lord Drake had arrived. Drake entered all smiles.

"Good evening, Mother and family," he said as he strolled across the room and kissed his mother's cheek first. Of all her three children, Drake had the best sense of humor and the most exquisite gentlemen qualities. He wore a forest green evening suit that made his eyes sparkle more brilliantly. He then walked to his sisters to kiss both their cheeks, his smile infectious.

"Drake, you're in a good mood tonight," Amara said.

"Yes, I've have had a perfect day, dear Sister. Now, I'm here to dine with three lovely ladies. What better luck could I have?"

Aurora said, "There shall be four this evening. Mother has hired a new governess today."

Drake replied, "Four, you say, things are getting better by the minute." He loved to tease his sisters. He walked to where Jasper was standing by the fireplace and said, "Good evening, Brother."

Jasper nodded then replied, "Good evening, Drake, how was Jacksons?"

Drake smiled, "Very prosperous if all my bets pay up on the same day."

"You still feel Hopkins can win the fight?" Jasper asked.

"Not feel, but I know. The man was looking excellent in the ring today. I guess that time shall tell on the big day."

"I shall still stick with Snyder."

"I thought I was late. Where is the new governess and Father?"

"I do not know, and I have just arrived myself."

The door opened, revealing Lady Sinclair. She walked in, then hesitated as she looked at both brothers watching her, then continued walking over to the Duchess. Laurentia was wearing a simple light blue silk dress, with delicate lace around the modest neckline.

Even in the plain dress, Jasper noted she did not look like a plain frumpy governess, more like an angel with beautiful blonde hair. She curtsied to the duchess, then apologized for being late, explaining the cause of her delay.

Duchess assured her it was alright. She moved to the twins, then curtsied, and with a warm smile, said they looked lovely.

Drake and Jasper both moved closer to Lady

Laurentia. Drake was closer; she curtsied to him first, then said, "I haven't had the pleasure of your acquaintance, my Lord?"

"The pleasures are all mine, my Lady," he said with a wolfish smile. "I am Lord Drake, your charges' middle brother. You are a breath of fresh air to look upon, and to add to the Raventon circle." He winked. Drake was known for being the biggest flirt among the ladies, and they were always swooning around him. Drake asked, "What is your name, my lovely?"

She answered, "I am Lady Laurentia Sinclair, but as your sister's governess, I prefer to be called, Lady Sinclair."

"As you wish, Lady Sinclair." Drake smiled.

Jasper made a cough to break up the awkwardness he felt in front of him, then stepped forward. Laurentia curtsied and said, "Good evening, my Lord."

Jasper nodded coolly, but then with his deep seductive voice, said, "Lady Laurentia, you look ravishing tonight." That gave Laurentia shivers, Jasper noted with satisfaction, with a wicked look in his eyes.

The duchess chimed in, "You may take a seat beside me, my dear. His Grace should be along any time now, and then we shall go into dinner."

Laurentia smiled as she sat down, then thanked her for the tea tray and finger sandwiches the duchess had sent to her room earlier. Duchess nodded.

Jasper and Drake both walked over to the chaise and stood behind it. Drake liked teasing his little sisters to get them squeaking in protest and then laughing loudly. This behavior, of course, had made Jasper more irritated. Drake proceeded in agitating and instigating both siblings at the same time. He had a big smile on his face, knowing how easy that was to do.

Laurentia looked over at the Duchess and whispered, "They don't even see what Lord Drake is doing. Do they not?"

"No, it's so easy for Drake to get them going. He's a big tease, as you have seen."

"I can see that, and it's most amusing to watch," Laurentia said with a smile.

"Oh yes, it can be," Duchess smiled, watching her children.

The door burst open with the Duke of Devonshire standing in the doorway, telling Wesley to find something else to do. He insisted that he does not need to be announced in his own mansion or castle. Then he walked in and shut the door.

The twins jumped to their feet and ran over to him, "Father," they both exclaimed as they hug him all at once. You could see the love and pride in the duke's eyes as his daughters hugged him fiercely.

"Good evening, my lovely daughters," Duke said with a laugh of joy, then kissed the top of their heads.

Pouting, Amara said, "Father, I do love the country better than London, but when we do not get to see you all day, it's truly tiresome." Aurora agreed as they walked their father over to their mother.

"I know my beauty's, but England cannot do without me. To be a part of parliament takes long hours to uphold." He bent down and kissed the duchess, "Good evening, Your Grace, and you look beautiful tonight."

She looked up, kissed him back, then said with a loving smile, "It is good now that you are home."

"Ah, yes, I have been missed, which makes me happy after a busy day of listening to grown men bicker back and forth." The duke beamed with happiness. The duke was a large man with broad shoulders, and one could see where his sons got their good looks. With his black hair that held just a hint of gray at the temples and his sparkling blue eyes, he was a handsome man for his age. When he entered a room, he clearly commanded it.

He looked over at Laurentia, then asked, "Ah, who do we have here tonight?"

She stood, then curtsied, "I am Lady Laurentia Sinclair, your new governess hired today, Your Grace." She did not rise until the duke nodded for her to do so. The Raventon family was a very old family, at fifteen generations of the dukedom, and they were quite wealthy.

Duke said as he looked her over, "You're a lovely little thing."

She looked up, then smiled, "Thank you, Your Grace, it is kind of you to say."

"Sinclair, you say? I remember that name. Ah yes, went to Eton with a Thomas Sinclair."

"That was my father, Your Grace."

"Your father was a good man, well missed."

"Thank you, Your Grace," Laurentia answered.

Wesley knocked then entered, announcing, "Dinner is served."

Before leaving the room, the duke walked over to hugged his sons, saying it was good to see them, and he was pleased they had joined them tonight for dinner.

Laurentia was noticing that this family showed

love, with embraces and kisses. She had not witnessed this in years. When Laurentia's parents were alive, that is how she remembers her childhood, a lot of love through the home. It was so warming to see that and comforting; perhaps if she was lucky, she might have that one day too in her life again. However, the life of a governess was often a lonely one. They walked to the dining room, Duke and Duchess leading the way. Jasper came over and offered his arm to Laurentia, and she placed her hand on his sleeve. They walked together to the dining room.

Drake came around to the chaise, putting out his two arms, then said, "I am a lucky man to escort two of the loveliest ladies in London. Shall we sisters?" They giggled when they stood, taking Drake's offered arms to walk into the dining room together.

As they made their way to the dining room, they walked past a gallery of paintings. Jasper noticed Laurentia looking up to see them as they passed. "They are my grandparents and great-grandparents."

"They look so lifelike in the portraits. The artists captured them well, truly wonderful work."

Jasper asked, "Do you enjoy art, Lady Laurentia?"

Laurentia looked up to his eyes and said, "Please address me as Lady Sinclair, I am your sister's governess, and I have not given you permission to address me by the first name. And yes, I do enjoy artwork, my Lord."

Jasper dismissed the part of calling her by her first name. "I shall have to show you the art gallery at the family estate in Devonshire. After the season, we all go there. The castle is huge and has a lot of private wings."

Laurentia wondered why he was making future plans when they just met today and hadn't conversed much. She just kept walking and smiled, not knowing what to say.

On formal occasions, the Duke and Duchess sat at the head of the table, but for a family gathering, they would seat together. The duke pulled out the chair to his left so that Duchess could take her seat. "Thank you, Your Grace," she said.

"You're always welcome," Duke answered before he walked to his position at the head of the table and sat down.

Jasper went to the table's right, taking his place by his father's. Before seating, he held out a chair for Laurentia beside his. Laurentia looked down the table's length, twenty-eight chairs in all, counting the two head chairs.

Above them hung an enormous chandelier with beautiful crystals shone overhead. She recognized the large flower arrangement on the table as one of Aurora and Amara's creations made earlier that day. She then commented to the girls and told them they have the right eye on making floral arrangements.

Aurora and Amara glowed with pride, and they were all smiles. Then, Aurora said, "Do you really think so, Lady Sinclair?"

"Yes, I do," Laurentia said.

The duke smiled inside, as he thought, 'that gives the new governess points in praising his daughters in his book.'

Laurentia's gaze moved around the room, taking in a vast sideboard for serving, with a footman on each end, waiting for the nod from the Duchess to start serving the first course. Still looking around, she saw priceless paintings hanging on the walls and double French doors that look like they led to a terrace. On the table in front of her, she noted the gold trim china plates with an eloquent floral design, crystal water goblets, and crystal wine glasses, and the silverware so shiny one could see your reflection in them. A table set so perfectly as if the king and queen were to attend.

The Duchess gave her nod to the footmen to start, one served soup and the other served wine, to begin with, then after the soup, five more courses were served, without any flaws. The conversation was light, with laughter and smiles all around the table. Laurentia missed this kind of family bond, and it did feel good to be a part of it, if only for a short time as their governess, she realized. When dinner was over, the gentlemen excused themselves to have some brandy in the library. The ladies went to the front parlor to take tea.

Laurentia told the Duchess dinner was lovely after a long day of unpacking and thanked her for letting her be a part of the family gathering. The twins always sat together, talking away and giggling as usual. Duchess figured this time she could get to know the new governess a little better. The tea tray came, and the Duchess took the liberty and offered tea to Lady Laurentia, then to her daughters, and poured one for herself. The Duchess knew her servants could do the chore, but she enjoyed doing this little task independently with a small family gathering at times. She joined Laurentia in the wingback chair beside her, took a sip of tea, then smiled and said.

"Tomorrow morning, we shall go over a schedule

for the girls' studies and activities. Tonight, let's talk and see if we can get better acquainted."

"That sounds lovely. Where would you like to start?"

Duchess started with, "Tell me a little about your brother and yourself."

Laurentia took a deep breath; she didn't like talking about herself or caring to talk about personal matters. "I grew up in Berwickshire Estate. Although, when I was a young girl, my family stayed mostly in the country, I had the opportunity to travel to London for shopping on occasion and go to the theater and see the museums. Mother loved lace, bonnets, and beautiful gowns. I do share that habit with my mother if she was still here," she said, all that on a sigh.

"You'll have to go with myself and the girls when we go to Bond Street. Shopping is one of our favorite pastimes. The twins love bonnets."

"I would enjoy that very much," replied Laurentia. Then the two talked back and forth about fabric, lace, and the latest fashion. The men return from the library; they enjoyed their brandy and catching up with what's new in their life

The Duchess smiled up at her husband when he walked in. As he entered, Jasper surveyed the room, thinking about how to find alone time with Lady Laurentia. Jasper frowned when he saw Drake making his way over to the Lady's side and started talking away. He knew his brother was trying to charm her, no doubt. Jasper walked over to the fireplace, then leaned against it, his favorite stance. The Duchess started talking to the girls about all the invites that are coming up. They were excited because the twins could go to picnics, musical recitals, family dinner parties, and a couple of family balls this year. Laurentia and Drake added into the conversation with the Duchess, and the twins, all of them shared laughter and talking with excitement.

The duke was over with Jasper, looking on his family. "This is bliss to see your family together, to hear laughter. It warms one's heart. I hope one day you shall have this too, son."

Jasper replied, "So do I, and I know what you are hinting, Father. That it's getting time to settle down."

"I am more than hinting. You have a duty to uphold, to give me a grandson and yourself an heir. The season shall start soon, and this needs to be your year to find a bride. Love is important for a happy life. I wish what your mother and I have, you shall find the same."

Jasper did not realize he was holding his breath and exhaled before saying, "Yes, I'll make this my year to wed, but I do not want all the mothers of the ton throwing their daughters at my feet. So please, Father, do not tell Mother, I need to find my bride on my terms and ways."

Duke agreed and wished him, "Good hunting Jasper, it shall be our secret," with a smile, he then walked away to his wife's side to join in the conversation.

Jasper walked over to the terrace door, wondering how he got roped into agreeing to wed this year. Lost in his thoughts, he didn't sense anyone walking up beside him until he smelled her perfume, honeysuckle, on a summer breeze. It warmed his senses again.

Laurentia looked up into his jewel-tone blue eyes, smiled. "It's a lovely evening, is it not, Lord Bellator?"

"Yes, it is. Are you settling into your room, and were your belongings delivered to your liking?"

Laurentia nodded. "Thank you for arranging it, all." She turned back to the room, and he followed suit so they could continue talking. But they noticed Her Grace was telling his sisters it was time to be off to bed and that she would be up in half an hour to say goodnight. His sisters protested at the early bedtime hour, but mother was not having any of that and waved them to say goodnight to everyone else. So, the girls came over to Jasper, hugged him goodnight. Jasper kissed them on the cheek and said goodnight. Then bid Laurentia goodnight and said they couldn't wait to have her as a governess officially starting tomorrow.

Laurentia said, "We shall have a big day. To have good rest is important." Then, they walked over to Drake to hug and kiss him goodnight. Next, they walked to their father, whining that it was too early for bed.

Duke, not having it, said, "No, we shall see you tomorrow morning," and kissed them goodnight. With big boo-hoo eyes, they left the room in the dramatic exit.

Duchess told her son's goodnight and admonished that they must come for dinner more often. She kissed them goodnight and bade Laurentia goodnight. Laurentia said it was a lovely evening and thank you for making her a part of it again. Duke said he be up soon to his Duchess, that Drake brought some paperwork to look over for a second opinion. Drake has an import shipping company. He had always loved the sea as a child and could not find a better way to fill his past time. Drake mainly dealt with fine wines, brandy, scotch, and different cognacs. He imports from France. The Duchess went upstairs to look in on her daughters and retire to bed herself.

Duke said to Drake, "it'd be easier to look over the papers at my desk in the library, shall we." They excused themselves from within, and in a few moments, everyone had left the room, leaving Jasper and Laurentia alone. She stood in the middle of the room, looking lost. Jasper was near the door to the corridor, so he quickly closed the distance between them.

"Would you care to take a stroll in the gardens, Lady Sinclair?"

Though she very much wanted to, Laurentia knew how improper it would be. Still, perhaps since he was her employer and not a suitor, it would not be as inappropriate as all that.

Seeing her hesitation, Jasper said, "Rest assured, I shall be a gentleman."

Smiling, Laurentia said, "I never thought otherwise, my Lord. A walk in the garden would be lovely."

Jasper offered his arm to escort her to the terrace door leading to the gardens. "The gardens are extensive here, but you won't see the true beauty of them in the darkness. We could stroll to the water fountain. It's a full moon," he said, gazing up, "so that she gives us some light."

They made their way down to the fountain, walking past well-manicured hedges and lovely flower beds. She could not wait to see them in the daylight, for the flowers smelled beautiful, and she could only anticipate their colors and textures. The fountain held a statue of a mermaid riding two dolphins and holding a large seashell. Water poured from the seashell, glistening in the light of the moon.

Laurentia said, "Oh, how beautiful this all is."

Jasper turned to her, putting both his hands on her face. "You are beautiful," he said, bending his head down, kissing her softly. Jasper lifted his head to see if she would pull away or slap him as he half expected her to do. When she did not, he retook her lips, this time more demanding, and she kissed him back just as demanding. He slipped his tongue into her warmth, then circled her mouth to taste her. She tasted like honey, so sweet. Sliding his hands down her throat and past her shoulder, he lay one hand on her back, the other on her waist, drawing her close. Laurentia put both arms around his neck, leaned into him, and ran her hand in his hair.

Jasper could tell she had been kissed before, and she was enjoying this just as much as he was. He pulled away, kissing down her neck and then back to those lush lips again. 'Oh, she tastes so good,' Jasper thought. His groin had grown hard as a rock, and pressing against her soft body, he heard her soft moan of pleasure. That slight sound made Jasper's senses come alive; he must push his demons back down. After all, it was only their first kiss. But, Lord helps him; if she had this much passion with just kissing, he couldn't wait to be inside of her, to awaken all her pleasures, feeling her pant beneath him in passion as he takes her into a never-ending climax.

Jasper raised his head, looking down into her

blinking eyes. She forgot herself for a couple of minutes, lowered her arms, and tried to take a step back, but Jasper didn't let her go.

Clearing her throat, "That should not have happened. I am your sisters' governess. It shall not happen again, my Lord."

Jasper smiled down at her then answered, "You are that sure of yourself, are you?"

She broke free of his embrace, took a step back, and then another.

"Yes, I always I'm," Laurentia said with a slight frown. She decided to change the subject back to him or the evening. "Your title, Marquess of Bellator. I believe Bellator means warrior in Latin, my Lord." She thought, 'warrior most definitely fits his built.'

Jasper was intrigued; Laurentia knew Latin and was correct, "Yes, Bellator is Latin for a warrior. Unfortunately, not too many women study Latin as an additional language. Bravo on your accomplishment."

"When my brother was tutored at home, I had sat in with him in many studies, and Latin was one of them. I enjoyed the family dinner this evening. It was nice to be a part of it."

"I'm glad to hear that you enjoy the time. My sisters seem to be looking forward to having you as their governess, my sweet."

Laurentia stiffened, saying, "Do not call me 'my sweet.'"

Jasper had a smirk on his face, "I like Laurentia instead anyways."

She snapped back, "I haven't given you permission to address me by my first name, my Lord." With a bit of fire in her eyes.

He took a step closer, and she stepped back once again to keep the distance. "No, you have not, but I have," Jasper said, looking impassive.

Laurentia knew of what little time they spent together; Lord Bellator gave the order and did as he wished. But he met his match to think he will push and bully me around.

"Lady Sinclair, if you please," she said again with gritted teeth. "And another thing, I do not want any more special privileges."

Jasper folds his arms taking his arrogant stance. "And what pray tell does that mean?"

"My room, for one. You and I both known that the room I received is not a governess room with the extras."

"Shall I have your things moved to a different room?"

She knew he was playing with her, "No, I'm, unpacked now. No, thank you."

"Do you have any more problems I should be aware of?" He raised an eyebrow.

She remarked," "As pleasant as it was, I should not dine with the family. That and the room are my only complaints, my Lord."

"I see. Shall we return to the house? It's getting late," Jasper said and offered his arm to walk her back, and she took it. They walked in silence for a moment, and then she thanked him for the walk just as they reached the mansion side door. Jasper opened the door for her bade her, "Good night Laurentia." With an eloquent bow. Jasper then pivoted and strolled to the stable to collect his horse, not looking back. She stared after him until he disappeared into the darkness.

Chapter 5

Jasper rose at 6:00 am. Between a restless night's sleep, picturing violet eyes in his dreams all night, and the stiff pain in his groin, it was better to rise. Lord Kingsley, his brother Drake, two cousins Leopold and Victor, would join him on his daily morning ride in Hyde Park before the ton cluttered the park with their coaches, carriages, and curricle phaetons. Jasper's valet, Farrell, knocked on this bedchamber door, poking his head into the room to sees if Lord Bellator was up. Then he inquired if he was ready for his shave.

"Yes, come in," Jasper said in a clipped voice. He was sipping his coffee, reading the morning paper, and still in a robe.

Farrell asked, "Are you riding today, my Lord?"

"At seven, bring out a riding suit and my Hessian boots."

"Yes, my Lord, and which riding suit is it you prefer today?" he rambled on as always.

Jasper glared at Farrell, for he damn well knew black was his signature color, which meant everything in his wardrobe was black, though some evening wear might have a touch of gold trim or gold buttons. Besides the point, Farrell had been his valet for eighteen years and should not have asked that question. However, Farrell could read Jasper's mood and immediately went into his dressing room, returning with one of his black riding suits and Hessian boots. Jasper stood, then walked to the bed where Farrell laid out his clothes to get dressed. He then returned to the same chair, with his breeches and boots on, ready for his shave. Farrell was a master of tying the perfect cravat knot; his valet took pride in making sure Jasper was dressed eloquently at all times.

As Jasper walked down the stairs, he saw Pierce Turner, his secretary, walking in the hall below.

"Good morning, my Lord," Turner said.

Jasper nodded and stopped on the last step. "Good morning, Mr. Turner. I shall be back at eleven, so we can meet to go over the estate ledger then and some other papers of importance."

"Yes, my Lord, as you wish." Turner bowed and headed to the library.

Jasper continued through the front hall, and his butler Everett appeared, opened the door to announce his stallion has been saddled and was waiting out front.

Jasper nodded. "Very good, are there any matters I need to know about before I leave?"

"No, my Lord, all is well," Everett answered, then bowed.

As Jasper walked down the steps from his townhouse, he saw Jesse and Drake sitting on their horses talking. A groom held Lucifer at a tight rein, his black coat shining in the early morning sun. Jasper took a deep breath of fresh air, thinking that a long ride in the saddle would get rid of his tormented dreams out of his head and groin.

"Good morning, gents," Jasper said as he mounted his horse.

Drake smiled at Jasper, then said, "I do believe it is a good morning, with no rain in sight, making for a good ride." Zeus, Drake's chestnut stallion, stomped his front legs and began snorting, showing he was ready for a run.

Jesse looked at Zeus then asked, "What do they feed your horse at your stable? He is tearing at the bit to go."

Drake patted Zeus on the side, "He knows when his saddle is on, and I'm sitting upon him; I will give him a good run and work out. He was anticipating that as we waited."

Jesse was riding a red Star Stable Daily; he was a gentle breed, a smooth ride, easily trained horse, and his name was Zeph.

Here came Victor and Leopold now. Victor was riding a dark grey horse, a Holstein; he had bought him from his brother Sterling last summer. A beauty full of muscle and strength, the breed has been around since the 13th century. Victor named him Smokey from his grey coloring. Leopold was riding his white Andalusian stallion, another stunning horse. He had bought his horse also from Sterling two years ago; he calls him Magnus. Sterling is Victor's elder brother; he breeds', trains,' and sells' horses. He was well known throughout England and Wales to have the best horses and stables.

"Good morning," they all bellowed to one another.

Jasper said, "Now that we're all here, shall we

go?" He took the lead, riding down the empty streets of London. They rode side by side, just like in their days of youth, when they all had no responsibilities. They chatted with one another as they rode down London's streets until they journeyed through the main gate of Hyde Park. Not a soul was around; they hit the first carriage trail they saw and took off like lightning so that all one could see was a trail of dust in their wake. Drake was in the lead, letting Zeus have free rein. Leopold was behind him; Jesse was in third place right on his tail, while Victor was half a horse behind Jesse. Jasper was last by choice, and he was letting them have the leg up for a while. Jasper always outrode, outshot, outboxed, out fenced all of them, and all the gentlemen from Eton. It was sometimes nice to let someone else take the lead, he thought to himself, not that he minded being in the lead all the time.

They raced around the bend; you could hear them whooping and hollering, like when they were young lads in the country cutting loose and having fun. It was fortunate that the park was deserted at that hour, for they did not need to read in the morning scandal sheet that the future Duke of Devonshire and his friend and relatives were seen racing through Hyde Park like a bunch of wild banshees, so uncivilized. Jasper thought with a snort, even as a grown man, his mother would go through the roof, read something like that, and see the family name in the paper (his father would say that's my boys). But, within an hour, the Duchess of Devonshire would have all rumors shut down and no further inquiries on the subject. His mother, the Duchess, was not a force to be reckoned with; the ton looked to the duchess for acceptance and guidance.

Now they were going down a straightaway, and Leopold was passing Drake. Jasper decided it was time to join the race, and he passed Victor and Jesse. They were turning around another bend, dust from the dirt road flying everywhere. They did not see her at; first, someone walking along the curve. Then, a woman screamed and twisted her ankle as she fell from the scare. Leopold and Drake did not see her; they were concentrating on who was winning the race. Jasper saw her first on the ground, and he reined into stopping. Jasper jumped down from his horse, who was now snorting in disgust because his race was ended, and Lucifer wanted to beat the other horses. Jasper let go of his reins, then he walked over to help, apologizing for the confusion and her falling. Jesse and Victor stopped also; they stay on their horses at first. Jasper took two steps toward the woman on the ground and saw who it was. In three long strides, he was standing above Lady Laurentia, holding her ankle in pain.

Getting onto one knee beside her, Jasper asked, "Are you alright, my Lady?"

She glared up at him and said, "Do I look as if I am? You could have trampled me or, worse, killed me," she yelled.

Jasper looked at her in amazement; nobody ever yelled at him. EVER! So, he raised an eyebrow and apologized for not seeing her. "No one is usually walking in the park this early. I am sorry we startled you, Lady Sinclair."

Laurentia continued to grasp her ankle in pain.

"Are you hurt, my lady? Could I be of any assistance to you?" Jasper saw Laurentia holding her ankle.

Still angry at them for the predicament she was in, "Yes, my ankle is hurt. I twisted it when I fell. No thanks to all of you." Laurentia waved her hand toward Jesse and Victor, who were dismounting to see if they could be any assistance. Victor, not knowing who she was, asked if she lived far from here.

Jasper stood up, bent down, grabbed Laurentia by the waist, and lifted her to standing. "This is my sisters' new governess, Lady Laurentia Sinclair."

Laurentia fell forward into Jasper's chest when he let go of her; the weight she put on her ankle hurt too much. She cried out in pain, and Jasper's automatic reaction was to pick her up, so she was no longer putting weight on her ankle and feeling the pain. She wrapped her arms around his neck for support, feeling a little overwhelmed by being lifted so fast.

Laurentia looked Jasper in his eyes, then said, "This really isn't necessary, you may put me down, and I could take your arm for support, Lord Bellator."

In the meantime, Victor realized this is the chit; that was Jasper's new interest. Victor smiled his approval with a nod.

Jesse asked, "Can I be of any assistance here?"

Jasper said, "Yes, hold Lucifer, as I put Lady Sinclair on first, then I can mount."

Jasper walked over to Lucifer, and Laurentia's eyes went as large as marbles. She gripped Jasper's neck hard and said, "I do not think so. You're not going to set me on that beast you call Lucifer. I shall not have it; you may put me down now if you please, my Lord."

Jasper looked her in the eyes, "He is one of the best stallions in all of England. I can assure you, my Lady."

"That's not the only problem."

Jasper, still looking in her eyes, said, "What is the problem then?"

She babbled, "You really do not think that I am going to ride on that horse of yours, with you in that saddle behind me where the whole world can see. It is not ladylike or proper."

"Yes, I do," Jasper said. Jesse held the horses as Jasper lifted Laurentia, putting her side-saddle, with her legs dangling off the left side before mounting behind her. As he was doing that, he said, "It's the fastest way to return you to my parent's residence. So as I see it, this must be done."

In the meantime, Drake and Leopold returned from the race, questioning them about what happened. Why did you stop?

Jasper said, "You may fill them in. I need to take Lady Sinclair back to Berkley Square." Jasper spun Lucifer around, and off they went in a slow walk to take her to his parents' mansion. Oh, how he was going to enjoy this nice leisurely walk. He had her perfectly snug against his chest with a firm hold to keep her there.

Laurentia could feel his firm, muscular chest through his riding coat, and she wondered what he would feel like with no shirt on as she ran her hands over his chest. She shouldn't think these thoughts, she told herself. He was so handsome but a little too arrogant for her taste. She also wondered if black was the only color he wore?

Jasper cleared his throat, partly to get his thoughts back from having the woman he desired constantly rubbing against him for the next half hour or so. He started with, "Do you want to tell me what you are doing walking alone in Hyde Park at this early hour of the morning?"

"If you must know, I like to take early morning walks before I break my fast. I've done it for years."

"Alone?" Jasper asked, feeling too pleased.

"Yes, alone, I enjoy the quiet time before I start my day," Laurentia replied. "You do know; this does not look like proper etiquette for an unmarried earl's sister and a future duke to be seen riding on a horse like this. Tongues shall be wagging."

Jasper smiled his wicked smile, "I know, but this is pleasant to have you so close. Besides, there are not that many people up and about this early in the morning. Your virtue is safe today, and you smell good." He leaned forward to smell her hair, sweet as he remembered, honeysuckle in the springtime.

She was silent for a moment, then turned her head and looked him in his sparkling bright blue eyes. "You are enjoying this far too much, my Lord. I do not think I shall fall from this horse of yours. You may loosen up your arms around me now."

Jasper smiled that wicked way of his. "That I am. It turns out to be an excellent start to my day, with you so close, my arms around you. Quite pleasant, I would say, my Lady," they continue riding down the quiet morning streets of London. Laurentia then forgot that Jasper's arms were still around her to keep her from falling off his horse.

'What a suitable name for his horse, Lucifer, or should the master have that name, not the beast of a horse underneath me,' Laurentia's mind wandered lost in thoughts.

They reached the front of the mansion, and a

groom came running to take Jasper's horse. He dismounted first and then grabbed Laurentia by the waist to lower her down to her feet. Jasper saw it hurt too much to put weight on her ankle still, so he quickly lifted her again and carried her up the steps and into the mansion. Laurentia tried to protest, but Jasper gave her a look that said it does not matter how she protests. He shall do as he pleases. Wesley opened the front door as they approached the entrance.

Jasper said as he walks in, "Lady Sinclair has been hurt. Her ankle shall need some tending to."

Jasper took Laurentia into the front parlor, setting her in one of the wingback chairs. The duchess came in to see Jasper standing over Laurentia and wondered what happened here. Jasper quickly gave his account of the story. The duchess called for Jennell to fetch some ice to take down the swelling on Laurentia's ankle. Laurentia maid Sandra poked her head into the room to see if she could help her mistress in distress. Jasper decided, with all this female fussing around Laurentia, it was time to take his leave.

"I can see you are in good hands here, my Lady. I shall check on you later this afternoon to see how you're faring." Jasper bowed and bade them a good day.

Chapter 6

Laurentia's Untimely Incident

The duchess tells Sandra to bring an ottoman and some pillows over to elevate the governess's ankle. Jennell returned with a bowl of ice and some towels. Meanwhile, the twins came in from the dining room. Their eyes were as big as saucers when they saw their new governess in distress and everyone around her in the same state of mind.

"Mother! What happened to Lady Sinclair," the twins asked?

"She was walking in Hyde Park this morning and twisted her ankle." Duchess took the bowl of ice and towels from Jennell. She set a towel on the ottoman first and then placed the bowl of ice down. Sandra took Laurentia's walking shoe off her foot and gently put her foot in the bowl. Laurentia winced a little at first from the shock of the coldness. Then she thanked them all and told them that her ankle felt much better already. Thank you.

Laurentia then decided that with Jasper gone now, she could tell her version of what happened. Jennell and Sandra were dismissed, and the twins sat on a chaise nearby with the duchess seated in a wing-back chair beside her. Laurentia told them her story of what happened and began with, "I always enjoy an early morning walk before I break my fast. I decided Hyde Park would be a lovely, pleasant place to stroll, that it was so early, and no one would be around. I thought it would be quiet and peaceful until I heard this thunderous roar of hoofs and a cloud of dust that was dirt flying in their wake. Five huge horses were running around the bend behind me. I was startled, so when I turned around quickly to see what was coming, I twisted my ankle, as you can see. Only three of the riders stopped to see what harm came to me, and here I sit."

Duchess asked, "Who else was there besides, Lord Bellator?"

"The only other person I knew besides Lord Bellator was Lord Drake. He and another were head-in-head racing to be first. They did not stop at first; they continued and came back as I was leaving with his lordship." Laurentia thought for a moment, 'Jasper was acting very protective over me, almost possessive. Why? We only kissed once.' "To think about it, two of the gentlemen did resemble Lord Bellator and Lord Drake quite a bit. And the other one was tall with light brown hair and hazel green eyes."

Duchess knew only two of her nephews were in town, and she had four Raventon nephews. "I believe that would be my nephews Leopold and Victor, the two who resemble my sons, and more than likely the other was Lord Kingsley, Lord Bellator, and nephew Leopold's childhood friend."

The twins were excited to hear who was in London this early in the season.

Amara said, "Lady Sinclair, you shall adore our cousins when you met them properly. Our brother sometimes can get so absorbed in important priorities, such as your injury; he would more than likely forgotten introductions."

Aurora chimed in, "Yes, that does sound like Bellator." They both giggled.

"Do not sell your brother so short-minded you. He has been remarkably busy, learning the roles to take over as the duke one day. You can excuse him on simple things." Said the duchess.

"Yes, Mother," the twins echoed.

Laurentia wanted to change the subject. "That is what happened. But I can still start the day as your new governess, just sitting down activities."

The duchess asked, "Are you certain? We could let you have rest for a few days."

"No, I am perfectly fine to start today."

Duchess said, "I believe you have not had anything to eat yet this morning."

"That is right. Some tea and toast would be lovely if it is not too much of a problem, Your Grace."

Duchess rang for Jennell to come, so the new governess could break her fast and bring tea for her and the girls. Jennell came in with a tray with tea and some sweet cinnamon rolls for Laurentia. Duchess and the twins had eaten already, so they were having tea while Laurentia ate.

The ice had melted, and it appeared the swelling had gone down; what a relief, Laurentia thought, looking down at her foot. Laurentia asked for Jennell to take the bowl away. Duchess insisted that she keep her ankle up on the ottoman to keep the swelling down and stay off it today.

After her final bit and a sip of tea, Laurentia said, "Let us get to work. Lady Amara and Lady Aurora,

I need to find out your likes and dislikes. That shall make my teaching a lot simpler." On this note, the duchess took her cue the classroom had started. She is fine that today's teaching was in her front parlor in the circumstances. Tomorrow they would be back upstairs to the girl's classroom in their wing. Besides, the Duchess had some calls to make, so she excused herself.

In the front hall, the duchess told Wesley to have the coach brought around in a half-hour. Duchess went upstairs to change her attire. In her room, she pulled the rope to summon her personal maid, Myra.

"Yes, Your Grace." Myra curtsies.

"I need to change my attire. I'm going out to call on my sister-in-law, Lady Louisa."

She changed into a light green silk gown, a modish neckline, and a matching bonnet, perfect for making the call. She never traveled alone, so she informed Myra that she would go with her, plus two groomsmen and her coach driver. Myra had been with Vivianna since the duchess was fifteen. Her mother hired her as a coming-out gift. Myra knew how to do the latest hairstyles and to dress in the best fashion. It worked perfectly; she did marry one of the wealthiest dukes in England. And one of the most important things was that she did marry well, but Conrad and Vivianna were madly in love, the kind of love you would call 'head over heels in love,' and their love grows stronger every day. Duchess wants that for all her children. Love was so important; she hoped they pick well.

Duchess hadn't seen her sister-in-law Louisa in a month. This visit was long overdue. They had a lot to discuss for the new season; after all, they were the

Raventon women. The ton followed what they did and said, and that made them the leaders of the ton.

Duchess was eager for this visit, and it was noon when they pull up in front of the manor. One of her grooms opened the coach door, taking her gloved hand as she stepped down, and Myra followed behind her. Her groom knocked on the door, then stepped back. The butler Reginald, answers the door. He acknowledges the Duchess of Devonshire' and informs them his mistress is at home with all smiles.

"Your Grace, do come in." Reginald led them to the front parlor so that he could inform Lady Louisa of her visitor. Five minutes later, Louisa came in, and the duchess stood with her arms out. Louisa swept in and hugged her sister-in-law.

"Oh, Louisa," the duchess said as they embraced and kissed each other's cheeks, "It's been too long."

"Yes, it has, and how I missed you," Louisa said. "Can you believe another season is to start soon? We each have a son of thirty years. They may not think it, but I, for one, think it's time they marry."

"I most certainly agree with you but, our sons do not. I shall bet on that one."

Louisa was Leopold and Kelsey's mother. She was married to Conrad's brother, Charlton. Louisa had sandy blonde hair with a bit of gray in the front and gray eyes. She was a charming woman, and the duchess was quite fond of her.

The Duchess said, "His Grace keeps telling me they like sewing their oats, that my son and yours had plenty of time. But they need heirs, and we need to start pushing some eligible girls in front of them this season to start the sparks to fly." The two decided to put their heads together and plan their strategy. Louisa rang for tea as they plotted.

Back at Berkeley Square, the twins shared their favorite subjects with Laurentia, and French was one of them. Laurentia spoke four different languages fluently. She thought this was good, to begin with, for she still needed to go over with the duchess on what subjects she wanted to be taught to her daughters. After an hour of going over basic phrases, she realized they needed more rolling their R's and grammar. Wesley knocked on the parlor door at 1:00 to tell them lunch was being served in the dining room.

The girls asked if Lady Sinclair needed assistance in walking to the dining room. Yes, she decided that's a good idea. Aurora and Amara each stepped to one side of their governess. Laurentia put her arms around the girl's shoulders for support to keep her weight off her ankle. Laurentia and the twins strolled slowly to the dining room. Laurentia tried to put more pressure on her foot at first; it hurt a lot trying, so she decided it was a bad idea to walk on her ankle. She was finding out the hard way. The twins helped their governess to her chair at the table, and she smiled up at them and thanked them as they went around the table to sit across from her. Wesley was watching them from the doorway, shaking his head. He did ask to be of assistance, but the twins waved him away saying, they had it under control and needed no help. He thought to himself, not if the duke and duchess were here. It would not be done this way with the girls exerting themselves like that so improperly.

They enjoyed an excellent luncheon, chatting about the entertainment they liked in London. Then Laurentia decided they would have to tour some of the museums when her ankle was better.

Jasper returned to his parent's residence at two-thirty to check on Laurentia's ankle. He walked past Wesley at the front door, going directly to the front parlor, but found the room empty. He turned around, of course, and Wesley was right behind him. With an impassive expression, Jasper asked, "Where is everyone?" Frankly, he was disappointed not to see Laurentia sitting with her foot up.

Wesley answered, "The duchess went out on some calls and should be back anytime now, and the other ladies are in the dining room. They have been in there since lunch was served at one, my Lord."

Raising one eyebrow, Jasper said, "Is that so, do tell how Lady Laurentia walked in there?"

Wesley hesitated at first and took a swallow before answering. "Your sisters helped, Lady Sinclair. They walked with one on each side of her while Lady Laurentia put her arms around the young lady's shoulders for support. I had asked to been assistance, and they refused my help, my Lord."

"I see." Jasper dismissed Wesley, then walked to the dining room.

Jasper leaned against the door jamb, listening to his sisters and his beautiful desire to talk about Greek philosophy. He had never seen his sisters so interested in a subject; the looks on their faces told it all. But, then, to think Greek philosophy was not something Jasper would imagine that would keep Amare and Aurora interested in and not fall asleep on Laurentia. He smiled, thinking, she is brilliant as she is beautiful.

Suddenly, Laurentia looked up and saw Jasper leaning there at the door with his legs crossed, watching them. She did sense him there before she looked up as he watched.

"Good afternoon, my Lord."

"Jasper," the girls chimed at the same time.

Amara said, "Have you come to join us? Lady Sinclair is teaching us Greek philosophy."

Aurora said, "She has a way of making us feel like we are there, in Greece where it all happened. I would say it's a fun way to learn."

"Yes, I, for one, would have never thought my sisters would like the subject, as I have seen just now and witness."

Amara asked, "Have you learned of Greece, Jasper?"

"Yes, I did indulge in a couple of courses when I was at Cambridge a few years back and have been there," Jasper answered as he uncrossed his legs, then stood up straight and strolled into the room eloquently. He came over to the table, behind his sisters, and looked Laurentia in the eyes.

Tilting his head and studying her, he asked, "How is your ankle, Lady Sinclair?"

Laurentia, who was still extremely mad that it was his fault, plus the other gentlemen on horseback, said, "As for my ankle, it is still very much sore, but the swelling had gone down. So it shall be fine in a couple of days. Thank you for asking."

On that note, the duchess came sailing through the door. "Good afternoon, my children. It's a lovely day outside to be cooped up indoors all day. So, what have we been studying?"

Aurora said, "We do love Lady Sinclair, Mother.

We had a French lesson this morning, and before Jasper came in, we were learning about Greek philosophy."

The duchess was surprised to hear the second subject and how her girls seem to enjoy it. "I think it's' time for some fresh air. How about a carriage ride in Hyde Park?" Duchess asked.

"Oh yes, Mother, that a grand idea," Amara said.

"We can wear our new lovely bonnets we bought two days ago," Aurora said as she stood and started bouncing with joy. Then Amara stood and started bouncing also.

"Yes, my dears, go upstairs and change, and I shall order the open carriage so the world can see your new bonnets," The Duchess said with pride.

The twins started to run out of the room, yelling with excitement.

Jasper commented, "Mother, how you do encourage their awful squealing and squeaking is beyond me." The twins stopped just before the door, turned around.

Amara said to Jasper, "Is it, not so long ago, that you have forgotten already what it feels like to be a young, Brother!"

Jasper raised an eyebrow, glared at them, and responded, "For your information, I have not."

Duchess cut in before a battle started between her children, as she knew they were all strong-willed and did not back down easily. She told the girls, "Go on now, do get ready, and do not forget your parasols."

With a matching smirk, the twins giggled and ran out of the room and upstairs to get ready.

Japer then glared at his mother. "Don't look at me like that," Duchess said.

Jasper replied, "Maybe this governess can work on some of their bad etiquette behaviors that need improvement."

"Jasper, I, for one, am glad they can battle wits with someone as strong as you and won't back down. That shows good character." Duchess nod.

Jasper commented, "That shows poor judgment, I say."

Laurentia chimed in, "I say a little of both. They need to know their boundaries in the ton and private wars. So that, we shall work on."

"Well said, Lady Sinclair," Duchess said, and Jasper nodded in agreement. "It is lovely out; would you care to join us?" Duchess asked Laurentia.

"I think I prefer to have a rest in my room and keep the weight off my ankle today. But thank you," Laurentia said with a smile.

"Is the ankle feeling any better?" Duchess asked.

"Yes, much better. A few days off it, and in no time, it shall be right again and good as new," Laurentia answered.

The duchess started to leave, then said to Jasper, "What are your plans, son?"

"I thought maybe Lady Sinclair would like to sit out in the garden instead of her room since it was partly my fault her ankle is sprained?" Jasper said. He looked over to Laurentia and asked as if he didn't care what the duchess said, "Would you like the fresh air and sunlight or the confinement of your room, my Lady?"

She thought, since it was the middle of the day, she would be safe from his advances in the garden. So, she smiled and said, "That would be lovely to go out to the gardens, and yes, it is your fault."

"Very well, I shall see you both later," and duchess continued out of the room, knowing in her house, Jasper would be a gentleman.

Jasper came around the table to help Laurentia walk. He pulled out her chair and put out his hand out to help her up.

Laurentia took his hand to stand, putting some weight on her foot. "Ow," she said, then sat back down quickly.

"That shall not do." Jasper then lifted her out of the chair and carried her to the garden.

Laurentia started to protest but changed her mind and said, "You would think this is going to be a habit with you carrying me like this." She put her arms around his neck to steady herself.

Jasper thought, to my bed would be the habit he was looking forward to; ever since the first time, he looked down into those beautiful violet eyes of hers. But, instead, Jasper said, "That seems to be the predicament of this fall you had." Then he walked to the terrace door, stopped, and looked down at Laurentia, and said, "My hands are full at this moment, could you…" then motioned with his chin at the door.

"Oh, let me get that, there you are," Laurentia said, reaching out to turn the handle to open the terrace door that led from the dining room. Laurentia's eyes grew big and bright with excitement as they step out onto the terrace.

Jasper saw Laurentia's reaction and smiled to himself to see her so overwhelmed, and he drank in the beauty. Jasper stopped at the edge of the terrace, "I can tell that this was a much better idea than the confines of your room, Lady Sinclair."

Laurentia waved a handout toward the gardens, "Oh yes, you did tell me last night on our walk that the garden would be more beautiful in the daylight. But this is so much more. Your mother has accomplished a work of art out here. If I were to visualize the Garden of Eden, this would be my vision of what it would look like."

Jasper then walked to the steps to descend so Laurentia can see more of the garden up close and smell all the different fragrances. He walked past rows and rows of flowers, every color of the rainbow. There were also hedges carved into sculptures, and two rose arbors.

"Her Grace loves to work out here, and it's also something she can share and do with my sisters. As you can tell, it's one of her great accomplishments. In the country, our castle in Devonshire, the garden there are three times larger than you see here. I hope you shall see them someday soon."

Laurentia was suddenly feeling a kind of heat by Jasper's passionate words about the gardens and the talk of the future. Plus, being carry so close to his heated body was enough in itself, and she could feel her face growing flush.

Jasper noticed her blush as he carried Laurentia, and he points out some of the exclusive perks in the garden as he strolled. Jasper thought, 'I would like to see if her whole body blushed from my touch.' He came to a bench and sat her down, sitting close beside her.

"Thank you for bringing me out here. It was kind of you, my Lord. I shall have to tell her Grace that her gardens are magnificent."

Jasper looked down at Laurentia, "It's my pleasure to be the one to accompany you here first, and I am glad you are enjoying the surroundings. And I hope my company."

"Yes, as I am starting to get to know you a little better, your company isn't so bad," Laurentia said with a smirk.

"Am I to find that little smirk of yours to be offensive or the words you just said," Jasper said with a rising eyebrow. Laurentia looked up into his blue eyes; they look like sapphires sparkling in the sunshine.

"I realize that one day you shall be the Duke of Devonshire, and you do take your role very seriously. So, sometimes you are a little rough around the edges, and I haven't seen you smile much." Laurentia cringed a bit inside, hoping she was not being too bold but didn't look away.

Jasper was still looking at her straight in the eyes, the corner of his lips twitching a little. "If I keep sharing your company more often, I promise to work on smiling for you. I would like to get to know you, on a personal basis, and much more."

Still looking in his eyes, she thought to herself, you can see some of his raw emotions, only if you can look deep in his eyes, and I bet that not too many people do that.

"I believe it shall be nice to try a friendship with you, as long as you remember that I am your sisters' governess."

Ah, he thought, 'I need more than friendship. I can start with that and seduce Laurentia into my bed. I do love a good challenge.' Jasper tilted his head and said, "Yes, I shall remember you are my sisters' governess, as you keep reminding me so." He did not mean it, but he knew this would not make a difference at all to him.

For an hour or more, they sat and chatted to get to know each other better. Jasper asked questions about her brother. She told him that Lucas, the Earl of Berwickshire, ran the family estate where he lived almost all year and did not travel to London too often. They wrote letters weekly and shared with Jasper that she did miss seeing her brother and thought of him daily. Then she asked Jasper about his time at Cambridge, asking him what he studied. He'd studied Latin, Greek philosophy, history, geography, and natural sciences. He asked her where she learned her studies.

Laurentia shrugged and said, "My parents paid for the best tutors for me, then when they passed away, my brother made sure I still had the best education."

"Why do you work as a governess? Surely your brother's estate cannot be that poor."

Laurentia hesitated, then said, "I do not receive my trust fund from my parents until I am twenty-five. Working is my way of being my own person, I don't have to answer to anybody, and I am not under my brother's thumb for anything. I like it that way. I do receive a small monthly amount from the estate. My brother had kept the Berwickshire estate running just as smoothly when my father was alive."

Jasper started to ask more about that, but then he saw his sisters walking from the Mansion toward where they were sitting.

Laurentia spotted the girls and thought, what a shame, for her time she shared with Jasper was feeling quite pleasant. The twins were chatting away with excitement as they walked over to where Laurentia and Jasper were sitting. They are still wearing the clothes they had on from the carriage ride. Amara was in light pink, her two-piece dress had little opal buttons, from the high neckline to the bottom of her jacket, and the skirt was pleated. Her new bonnet was stunning, pink to match her dress, with white daisies, around the rim. Aurora was in pastel yellow, and she was also wearing a two-piece dress; the jacket had delicate lace that lined the modestly cut neckline and lined the bottom hem of the jacket and skirt. The new beautiful bonnet she had on matched her dress's color, a wide rim, with cream color tea roses all around the rim. They both look much older than fifteen. Laurentia and Jasper were almost thinking about the same thing. This family would undoubtedly have their hands full when the twins hit the ton next year.

The girls stopped in front of Jasper and Laurentia bench they were sharing. They both twirled around with huge smiles, "Do you like our new carriage dresses and bonnets?" Amara asked.

Laurentia smiled, "Yes, you both look very grown-up, and your bonnets are fashionable."

They then looked to Jasper for his response. "Adorable" is all he said.

Amara said, "Mother said we could come and show you our new splendid carriage dresses. Then we are to return to our room for a rest before dinner."

"Jasper, are you staying for dinner tonight?" Aurora asked.

"No, I have other engagements this evening to attend."

"Too bad you do," Amara said sarcastically. They both bade Jasper farewell.

Aurora said: "We shall see you at dinner, Lady Sinclair." Turning on their heels, they marched to the terrace were gone just as quickly as they came.

Laurentia commented, "They can be very dramatic at times, can they not?"

"You haven't seen anything yet. Let's just say at times they can be more than a handful." Jasper shook his head in disgust. "Would you also like to retire to your room for a rest before dinner?

"Yes, that is a nice suggestion. Shall we go in?"

Jasper stood, then bent down to pick up Laurentia. He took two steps, and she asked if she could try to walk on her own. Jasper gave her a glare that said no and continued walking until he reached her bedchamber door. He looked down at her then said, "The door, please, my hands are a little full at this moment."

"Oh, yes, forgive me, my Lord." Laurentia turned the handle and pushed the door open. Jasper walked in, surveyed the room, then noticed the chair in front of the fireplace. He walked over to the chair and sat her down comfortably.

"There you are, Lady Laurentia, in a comfortable chair." He looked around the room for an ottoman; he then found one and lifted her legs, placing the ottoman under her feet and nodding with content. Jasper looked down to see her smiling at him.

"Thank you. You are very thoughtful."

"You are welcome, is there anything I can do for you before I do take my leave?" Jasper asked, looking into her beautiful violet eyes that he loved to gaze in a little too much.

She sighed then said, "If it isn't' too much, I would like to read for a while. My book is on the end table by the bed. If you, please, my Lord."

Jasper walked over to fetch the book, reading the title as he walked back.

"Sense and Sensibility by Jane Austen. I have read that one as well."

Laurentia was intrigued that a future duke read Jane Austen. A love story. "You like this author?" she asked.

"Yes, she is a friend of the family, my aunt Lady Louisa's, dear friend. We are worried about Jane, for her health has been failing these last few months. Have you read Pride and Prejudice yet?"

"No, this one is the first I read of her books so far."

Jasper continued, "If you like this book, I have her next three novels. You may borrow them if you please. They are Pride and Prejudice, Mansfield Park, and Emma."

"Yes, I would enjoy the chance to read her other books."

"Would you like some tea as you read? On my way out, I could have some sent up for you."

"If it is no bother, that would be lovely, my Lord" Laurentia smiles.

Jasper bowed then said, "Your wish is my command." He looked her in the eyes, giving her that wolfish smile of his, the same smile as when they first met at her interview. He took her hand in his, and instead of kissing the top, he turned it over and kissed her wrist, ever so slowly still looking into her eyes. Then he straightened and said, "I shall call on you tomorrow to see how you are faring, Laurentia."

She shivered when he kissed her wrist like that. No one had ever done that to her before, she must admit it that was so seductive, and those sapphire blue eyes of his, they did make her melt. He turned on his heel and eloquently walked out, not looking back.

Jasper was smiling to himself as he walked down the corridor. This game of challenge to seduce Lady Laurentia Sinclair is on. The way she shivered and the look in her eyes tells me all. I am looking forward to feeling that same shiver when she is underneath me and being pleasured by my very skilled ways. Now downstairs, Jasper ordered Wesley to send a tea tray and some delicate cakes to Lady Sinclair's room before exiting the mansion.

What he needed was a hard ride on Lucifer to relieve the stiff pain in his groin thanks to thoughts of Laurentia nude and looking so beautiful lying beside him in his bed. He kicked Lucifer, then galloped down the street and decided to take a long way home.

Chapter 7

Berwickshire Country Estate, Unexpected Guest

The Earl of Berwickshire sat at his desk in the library, looking over his estate ledgers with his secretary Mr. Gibbs. Gibbs was his father's secretary for many years before his death. Lucas kept him on as his secretary, feeling that he could trust him since he'd worked for his father for many years. Gibbs had brown hair with a touch of gray on the sides and brown eyes. He was fifty-two in years and well-liked by all.

Lucas said, "I have seen with my last ride that the west field fencing needs repair soon."

"Yes, my Lord, the fence has a few areas that need mending. I shall write the order if you wish."

Lucas replied, "Sims can start that tomorrow morning."

A knocked sounded on the door, and Lucas called for whoever it was to enter.

Carlson, his butler, walked in, and with a quick bow, he said. "My Lord, there is a Mr. Hughes here who requests a meeting with you."

"Ah, yes, you may show him in," Lucas said, sitting up a bit higher in his chair.

When Mr. Hughes, a tall man of medium build,

entered, the earl stood, saying, "Do come in, have a seat." He pointed to the second chair in front of his desk. "This is my secretary, Mr. Gibbs. Mr. Hughes is that investor I mentioned to you last week."

"A pleasure, sir," Gibbs said.

Hughes nods then pulled out some papers from his inside coat pocket and handed them to Lucas. "These are your copies of the investment papers you signed last week."

Lucas took them with a confused expression. "I do remember talking about what you offered as a new investment. But signing them, I did not," Lucas said and dropped them on this desk before sitting back down.

Mr. Hughes sat up, straighter in his chair, "Is that not your signature, my Lord?"

Lucas looked down to where Hughes was pointing to, looks back up, "Yes, but I do not recall signing this paper or any other papers you have," Lucas shouted.

Gibbs grabbed the paper to see what was being discussed and scanned the documents. Gibbs looked to Lucas then said, frowning, "My Lord, they look to be legal documents, and the signature does look like yours, I'm afraid."

Lucas looked at Gibbs with confusion and disbelief and said again, "I did not sign them, I swear, and that is the end of this discussion!" The last part, he yelled and looked back at Hughes's smug face.

"Your first payment, we agreed on, is due Thursday. I shall have my man come around noontime to collect if that's good for you, my Lord." Hughes said calmly, not being phased an ounce with the earl's outrage.

Lucas glared at Hughes, "No, it is not. I will not pay this ridiculous jest."

Hughes stood and stepping back from the desk, said firmly, "This is not any joke. You were offered a deal to invest in my company. You did sign the papers before you, and we shall be here Thursday to collect the first payments as indicated. Good day, my Lord." On that, Mr. Hughes's bowed and departed the room.

Lucas looked to Gibbs and said, "Send for my solicitor, right now. I want to see him within the hour. Do you understand Gibbs?" Lucas stood and began pacing. He looked to Gibbs, still standing there, looking confused. "Now, if you please, Gibbs."

Gibb went quickly to do as asked. He had never seen the earl this upset, and this was the worst situation he'd ever seen happen to this family, but for the loss of his parents seven years ago. The curricle was brought out front, and Gibbs was off in a blaze, leaving nothing but dust in his wake.

Back in the manor, Lucas went to the front parlor and started pacing there too. In the meantime, Carlson walked into the room, he had been working for the Sinclair family long before Lucas and Laurentia parent's fatal day years ago.

"My Lord, is there something I can do for you, anything?"

"A brandy would be nice. And how I miss Lady Laurentia in times of crisis like this. She has her way of making everything that was wrong, to the right again." He took a seat in a wingback chair, saying, "I just miss Laurentia not being around."

Carlson handed him a brandy, saying, "I and all the staff, I will speak for them. We all missed Lady

Laurentia and that beautiful smile of hers. Yes, my Lord, she is truly missed here."

"Yes, she is," Lucas said. Then he dismissed Carlson, so he could think before his solicitor arrives.

He thought back to the day he discussed the investment deal. He'd been having an ale in a tavern, next door to the Inn he was staying at, on the way back from a trip from Yorkshire. He was sitting at the table, sipping an ale, when a man asked if he could join him. As Lucas was alone and did not mind some company, he waved a hand for him to have a seat. The man introduced himself as a Mr. Hughes; he looked and acted like a gentleman. They chatted about the nearby lands, and that's when Hughes brought up his new company and that he was looking for investors.

Hughes suggested they have dinner together, so Hughes could show his new investments to see if he was interested in becoming a part of the new company. Lucas remembered the meal and some of the papers that were shown to him. But he awoke in his room fully dressed, sitting in front of the fireplace at about three in the morning, and could not remember how he got there. Lucas left the following day after breaking his fast. He also remembered asking the Innkeeper if Hughes was still on the premises. The Innkeeper told him he'd left at first light, heading south.

And that was it, until today when Mr. Hughes walked into the library. He thought, that's all I can remember, he was sure about it. There must be some reason for all this, but what? Lucas sipped his drink and waited for Gibbs to return with his solicitor.

Chapter 8

Second Day for The New Governess

Laurentia was breaking her fast, sitting in her bed-chamber drinking tea, and eating a delightful Eccles cake. She could not take her early morning walk due to her sprained ankle, so she opted for a quiet time in her room instead. Last night she also had dinner sent up to her bedchamber. Laurentia sent a note to the duchess, apologizing for not coming down to attend dinner.

In the note, Laurentia said she wanted to stay off her ankle so she would more than likely improve her sprain for the next day. The duchess agreed; she stopped into Laurentia's' room to check on her and said no apology was needed. She understood completely.

Laurentia slept heavenly, with Lord Bellator demanding blue eyes staring at her and his black hair shining in the sunlight with a hint of blue in her dreams. He was so handsome and with his deep seductive voice. She was thinking and wondering why he had shown so much interest in her, for London was a big city, and there were many eligible and beautiful women in the ton to entertain him. She imagined that they swamped around him everywhere he went. Plus, he would want someone younger to be his marchioness in the near future, not her at twenty-four. She did enjoy that first kiss they shared by the fountain, her first night here. Then she told herself to stop overthinking this; he was kind to her because he felt obligated, for it was his fault she had sprung her ankle. That was is it, and nothing more, she told herself with a firm nod.

"Sandra comes in was 8:00, Laurentia has a meeting at 9:00 in the duchess private bed-chamber sitting room. Her maid brought out a yellow muslin morning dress to start her day in, then helped Laurentia dressed and pinned her hair up in a simple twist with little wisp around her face and back neckline.

Looking lovely, Laurentia heads to the Duchess room at 8:50; she Knocked on the door, heard "Enter," and then walked in. The Duchess looks up from a pile of letters and invitations, smiles, wave her to the chair beside her.

"Good morning, Lady Sinclair, I hope you slept well, and I see you are walking today."

Laurentia curtsied, "Good morning, Your Grace. Yes, the extra rest and not walking around last evening have done wonders. Of course, it hurts a little still, but I can walk somewhat better on my ankle today, as you have seen." She took a seat that was indicated.

"Then, staying off your ankle last evening was for the best. Now, then, I have all these invitations to look over—balls, recitals, picnics, garden parties, afternoon teas, and the list goes on and on. The girls are allowed to go this year to family balls only and perhaps a few daytime parties by my choice, of course."

"I have a lot of work to do." Laurentia smiled, then looked around the duchess's sitting room. It was an exquisite, chic room in pastel pink and cream. The room held one chaise, two plush comfortable chairs with a table between the chairs. To the side of the room by the wall was an oblong-shaped table decorated with miniature portraits of the family members. The table had a lacy, delicate tablecloth under the pictures. The room was comfortable and feminine.

The duchess cleared her throat, "Let us begin, shall we?"

Laurentia nodded. "Where would you like to start with first?"

"I have invited my niece Lady Gabrielle for tea this afternoon and a few friends. Then after the tea, we have a fitting for the new gowns for the season. Tonight, we have a recital at the Earl and Countess of Surrey on Audley Street. Thursday, we have a garden party at my sisters-in-law Lady Louisa. Then on Friday, we will take the girls to their first ball. It is also at Lady and Lord Charlton's manor. Oh, how Louisa loves to entertain. Since it is so early for the season, this ball shall be family and some of our closest friends. It shall be a nice start for my girls. On Saturday, we shall go to the Theatre Royal. We have a private box there. On Sunday, I am hosting a dinner party here."

Laurentia said, "This morning, I think it shall be a grand idea to go over proper etiquette to be used when we are among the ton."

"Amara and Aurora are well trained, but improvement is always well received."

Laurentia agreed. "Yes, my goal is to brush up

your two lovely daughters and outshine all around us."

The duchess clapped her hands together, "Brilliant, let's get started. My girls are more than likely, still finishing with breaking their fast. Shall we go down to the dining room?"

"I have a couple of books to pick up in my room. I shall come down after I retrieve them." Laurentia stood, then curtsied.

On the way down the corridor, Laurentia was humming with excitement; how she loved to be a part of a new season in London. She'd only had one season of her own due to her parents' untimely death at seventeen. Then a year of mourning, and after that, she became a governess. Laurentia entered her room to pick up the books she wanted and saw a package sitting on the end of her bed.

"Now, who on earth would send me a package?" She noticed as she picked up the package that it was addressed to her, but there wasn't a return address. "That's odd." Well, the only way to find out was to open it, to see what it was and from whom.

Laurentia sat on the end of the bed, untied the brown string, and removed the brown paper to find a card on top of three books.

Laurentia said happily, "It's the Jane Austen books. Lord Bellator said he had them."

She smiled down at them and opened the card to read out loud.

"I hope you enjoy these books, as I have. They are now yours to keep.

Sincerely Lord Bellator."

I never was given such a sweet, thoughtful wonderful gift before from a gentleman or a future duke.

He must have done this as soon as he went home yesterday. I love this gift even more because I know they were his, from his collection, out of his library.

Laurentia hugged the books to her chest and thought, 'he doesn't know my love for books, and I haven't told him yet.' A tear rolled down her cheek as she remembered her father gave her a book the morning they left for France, and she never saw her parents again. It was not their death that was bothering her. Laurentia had gotten over the loss. It was that no one had given her a book since that day, and she did love books so. This is better than a piece of jewelry or flowers; I have received from many suiters in the past. She thought as she wiped the tears from her cheeks. She lay the books and card down on her dresser table. She then checked her face in the looking glass to make sure she did not look like she had been crying. She took a handkerchief and dabbed her eyes, took a deep breath, and told herself she was fine. She grabbed the books she came for and went downstairs to work with her charges.

Laurentia saw the girls sitting at the table in the dining room as she entered.

"Good morning, girls," Laurentia said as she sat down. They were still eating, and the footman asked her if she cared for something.

"Tea would be lovely."

"Have you eaten Lady Sinclair?" Amara asked.

"Yes, in my room earlier. Has the duchess come down yet?"

"Mother is in Father's library. They went there a few minutes ago to talk," Aurora said.

"The duchess and I had a meeting this morning. She informed me of some of the social engagements you have coming up in the next four days. So, this morning, we shall go over proper etiquette," Laurentia said.

Around mid-morning, Jasper came strolling in the front door, in a good mood. He even let Wesley announce him to the duchess in the front parlor.

"Good morning, Jasper. It's nice to see you in such a good mood this morning."

Jasper bent down to kiss his mother's cheek. "Yes, I had a nice ride on Lucifer this morning in Hyde Park. The weather is warm, it makes for a nice day, and I hope the rest of my day goes as well. What project do you have going here, Mother?"

Duchess smiled up at Jasper. "My seating chart for Sunday's dinner party. Are you bringing someone? You didn't RSVP to your invite, but I know you shall be here."

Jasper walked over to the chaise to sit across his mother. "Is Lady Sinclair going to be among those attending?" he asked with forced nonchalance.

"Yes, she shall be joining us. Why do you ask?"

Jasper said casually, "I would like to be seated beside her, for I am coming alone this time."

"I could seat her next to you if that makes you happy, my dear, although having a governess sitting next to you may raise some eyebrows."

"That would please me, thank you. And since when do I ever care for other's opinion of me, Mother." Jasper said with an impassive look.

Trying to read Jaspers' motives, Duchess said, "She is a very pretty young lady, is she not?"

"Yes, she is lovely and can hold an intelligent conversation, perfect for sitting by at a dinner party instead of hearing boring dribble from someone undesirable."

He realized his mother was trying to fish around why he requested her for a dinner partner. He changed the subject.

"Is Father in his library? We are going to Whites for lunch."

"Yes, he is; he's finishing some paperwork when I left him an hour ago."

Jasper stood. "I shall go let Father know that I have arrived. Good day, Mother."

As the duchess watches her son leave, she knew he was leaving her presence, so he didn't have to answer any more questions about Lady Sinclair. She laughed to herself at her son's behavior.

Jasper was walking down the corridor when he heard female laughter coming from the dining room. He stopped just short of the doorway to listen. He recognized his sisters' laughter, too loud for his taste, but the other is soft and gentle sounding, lovely, he thought to himself. Jasper moved closer to lean on the door jamb, watching his sisters and Lady Laurentia as they discussed the weather.

Laurentia hadn't looked up yet; she can sense Jasper is near. The girls were laughing; they both were saying there was a better thing to talk about than the weather. Jasper now knew why they are talking of weather; they were going over dining and ballroom etiquette for a gentle lady to converse with a gentleman.

"Let's ask Lord Bellator his opinion on the subject, shall we?" Laurentia looked up with a smile and saw Jasper watching them in the doorway.

The sisters turn around to see him.

"Is this really what you talk about, Jasper?" Aurora asked.

Jasper walked toward the table. "Yes, at first, you do make small talk and be polite. Even if you don't care for the person, you were introduced too, just say a few words, then excuse yourself. If you do like the person, you may find after a few polite talk words if they like you too. Then you may talk about some-things that may interest you and the other."

Amara said, "That's what Lady Laurentia said earlier. So, it must be true."

Laurentia and Jasper both said "Yes" at the same time. This time Laurentia giggled softly and smiled at Jasper. "You must forgive me, my Lord."

"There's nothing to forgive. We answered at the same time, the right answers. And your little giggle is quite delightful to hear, I may add."

Laurentia could feel a blush forming, and she looked down for a moment. Then she cleared her throat, trying to take control. She looked to the twins and said, "The reason I apologized to your brother is that he outranks me. Let me explain; your brother is marquee a future duke, and I am a governess."

Amara said quickly, "you are a sister of an earl, are you not?"

Laurentia said, "Yes, I am. But either way, he outranks me. One does not speak over someone in a higher status than your own." The girls nodded.

Jasper liked her ways of teaching but not to use him as an example in the classroom. It was unnerving to him.

Then Aurora said, "But you told us earlier that in the privacy of your own home, you can let your brother have your business if needed. That you have an elder brother too, and you tell him as it is when needed. Correct?" Aurora and Amara looked to Jasper and smiled.

"Yes, in private, you can speak freely to each other, that is correct."

"It seems that your lessons in proper etiquette are going well here. I was on my way to Father's library if you excuse me, ladies." Jasper bows elegantly as usual and exited. All three ladies laughed when they knew Jasper was gone.

Amara said, "I don't think Jasper liked being used as an example in our lesson today, did he not?" They all laughed again.

Laurentia then said, "No, he was not amused. Now, where were we?" They laughed some more and continued with their lessons.

Jasper continues to his father's library, thought to himself to remember, he should not go into a room ever again if his sisters are studying in an ethical classroom setting. He knocks on the library door, heard this father yell, "Enter," and walks in.

"Good day Father, are you ready for our luncheon at Whites?" The duke looked up from his work.

"Yes, I had just finished; that was the perfect timing." He stood up, came around the desk, hugged Jasper, then said, "Shall we go, Son."

The duke stopped at the front parlor to kiss his duchess goodbye, let her know he was leaving for the afternoon, and see her at dinner this evening.

Chapter 9

Duke of Devonshire and Marquess Bellator Excursion

Outside the Berkeley Mansion, awaited is the duke's gleaming new coach, a birthday gift from his two brothers last month. The coach was black, the family signature color. The family crest was on the door, and a gold pinstripe lined the doors, windows, bottom trim, and top lines. A team of four beautiful black horses, snorting and kicking the ground, were ready to go. He rode with pride every time he entered the coach.

Jasper usually rode horseback, but to ride with his father was always a pleasure. They chatted about the latest laws being passed through parliament on the short ride to Whites. As they pulled up to the club, people craned their necks and heads to see who stepped out of the magnificent coach. The duke stepped down first, as one of his grooms opened the door and then Jasper behind him. Father and son walked up the steps side by side. The Raventon men were all known for their impeccable gentlemanly style and grace. But the Duke of Devonshire and his heir, when one saw them walk together, one could see and feel their power, possession of control, authority, their influence over others. The genuine respect they earned and received from all around them was truly remarkable.

The doorman bowed to them before he opened the door for them to enter. The duke enters first; he nodded to acquaintances as he walked through the rooms, as had Jasper. They walked to the dining room door and stopped.

The maître d' scrambled to the door, then bowed. "My apologies, Your Grace, for keeping you waiting. Shall it be two for lunch?"

"Yes, Fredrick, my usual table."

"Of course, Your Grace, it is ready for you, right this way," Fredrick said, then led the way, telling their waiters to be prompt, to make sure the Duke of Devonshire and his son receive the best service.

A waiter took their drink order as they sat down, then hurried away.

Jasper asked his father, "What are you in the mood to eat?"

Duke answered, "Something fried, I think. Your mother insists fried food smells up the entire home and shall not let cook prepare it. What shall you have?"

Jasper laughs, "Sounds like mother. I am in the mood for a good steak."

The waiter came back with two cold ales. The waiter looked to the duke then asked, "What your pleasure for lunch, Your Grace?"

"Fried chicken, roasted potatoes, and pickled beets. My son here would like a two-inch, your best cute steak medium rare, with same sides as mine."

The waiter bowed, then said, "Yes, Your Grace, my Lord, right away." Then he rushed off in a flash.

As they waited for their food to arrive, Duke

started talking about estate matters, mostly the castle improvement done when they were in London for the season. Duke told Jasper he wanted him to check the progress that is being completed at Castle Raven-crest in a month. Jasper said he would make the trip in a month. The break from the ton would be well received, he thought. Jasper realized when the actual season started that the mothers of the ton would start pushing their daughters toward him constantly, hoping he would wed them.

The waiter returned with their food and asked if he could get them anything else. They both ordered another ale.

Duke said, "Do not tell your mother I'm eating fried chicken. I shall never hear the end of it."

"It shall be another secret we share." Jasper laughed, knowing they shared a lot of them.

They ate their meal, jesting, talking about family matters and upcoming events that they would attend this season.

Then the Duke cleared his throat; the expression on this face turned serious. He looked Jasper in the eye, "I know we talked about this the other night, my Son. But your mother is on the warpath about you finding a bride and marrying this season. I'm telling you this again, for I know she would ask me later if I brought it up at our lunch today. So now I have."

"Father, you did say I could pick my bride, did you not?"

"Yes, that is what I want for you, to be happy with your choice and find love is most important for good, wedded life together."

"Good, then we are in accord," Jasper said with a smile.

"Yes, give a little show you are doing so, that's all. You, your brother, and your sisters know if your mother is not happy. Nobody else shall be."

Jasper hesitated then said, "I shall make an effort."

"That's all I need to hear." His smile said the subject was over. They enjoyed their lunch, especially the duke having his fried chicken and then a delectable dessert.

When they finished their lunch, the duke said, "Let's go and enjoy one of those French-style brandies Drake has been telling me about, he supplied here last week. The lounge has a big overstuffed chair. I will take pleasure in sitting in it to relax after a good meal."

"That's a brilliant idea. Shall we go, Father?" Jasper thought anything to change the subject of marriage is good with him.

Entering the lounge, they nodded to everyone as they passed, not wanting to be bothered with dull conversation. In front of the fireplace, Duke and Jasper saw the two chairs the duke had described earlier and took a seat.

"This is nice to relax, with no work for the rest of the day. Parliament has kept me busy since I arrived in London, and having this break today is much needed," Duke said.

"One would think England would crumble without you, Father. They all seem to follow your views and arguments on just about everything. I have observed your colleagues."

"I'm glad you have been taking the time to watch; I know you are a quick study. The gentlemen that sit with me at Parliament have taken some years to earn their respect, and even more important is to keep it."

A footman walked over, and the duke ordered two brandies

Jasper was telling his father about the scheduled fight at Jacksons in a few days when Lord Charlton walked up.

"I'd know those two voices anywhere." Charlton held out his hand to the duke. "How are you, Brother?"

The duke stood to shake Charlton's hand and pulled him into a hug.

"I have heard you arrived in London. It is good to see you. I'm doing well. Just had lunch with my eldest son here."

Jasper stood to embrace his uncle. The Raventon family was not scared to show their love and affection to one another, and they were a fiercely loyal, loving family.

The duke looked to a footman standing to the side of the room and nodded for him to bring a third chair over.

The footman returned with brandies, "I took the liberty of bringing a third glass, my Lord." He held it out to Charlton.

Duke said, "It's the new French brandy Drake recommended. It's supposed to have a smooth and rich flavor."

Charlton took the glass and sipped, as do the other two. They all nod their heads in agreement; it was excellent. For the rest of the afternoon, they stayed and chatted about the events that would be taking place in the next two weeks and so on. But Jasper's mind drifted to a certain blonde with the violet eyes, that he anticipated holding in his arms soon. Very soon!

Chapter 10

Devonshire Mansion, Wednesday Tea

The women had gathered in the front parlor for tea and to tell and catch up on the latest gossip when Lady Gabrielle was announced. She lit up when she sees her family. Duchess stood up and held out her arms to her niece for a warm hug. The younger women then hurried to the twins to hug them simultaneously and then started chatting away.

The duchess cleared her throat, and the three looked to her. "Have we lost our manners, ladies?"

"No, Mother, no Aunt Vivianna," the twins echoed and did her niece.

Duchess looked at Laurentia, "Good. Lady Sinclair, I would like you to meet my niece Lady Gabrielle. Lady Gabrielle, I would like you to meet my new governess Lady Laurentia Sinclair."

Gabrielle said, "It is a pleasure to meet you, Lady Sinclair."

"I have heard from my charges that you enjoy the artwork. We shall have to share on that subject, for I also enjoy art as well. It is a pleasure to make your acquaintance Lady Gabrielle."

"Yes, we shall have to. My brother Victor is a sponsor of an art gallery in London. They have such beautiful pieces. Perhaps you would enjoy an outing to the gallery."

"I would enjoy that, yes, and I bring your cousins with me. To be educated in art always makes a good topic in the conversation for a ballroom or a soiree."

Gabrielle said with a smile, "I cannot agree with you more, my Lady." She likes Laurentia immediately.

Gabrielle is a natural beauty. She had raven black hair, green eyes, and ivory white skin. She was eighteen and could charm everyone she meets.

Wesley appeared and announced, "Countess Harrington and her daughter Lady Sabrina."

The countess was the same age as the duchess; they attended finishing school and were close friends. Countess, who was quite tall for a woman, had light brown hair, blue eyes, and high cheekbones. Her daughter Lady Sabrina had blonde hair, brown eyes, and was tall like her mother, and she was sixteen, a lovely girl. Next, announced was Lady Louisa. She walked to the duchess, hugged her, then greeted her three nieces. The duchess introduced Countess Harrington, Lady Sabrina, Lady Louisa to Laurentia since they all arrived simultaneously. Duchess rang for the tea tray to be brought in, with finger sandwiches and little cakes.

Once everyone was seated, Aurora and Amara did the honor of pouring tea, then serving their guests. Beautifully, Duchess gave them a nod and smile of approval when they finished, and then they took their seat. Laurentia gave them a wink and smiled that they had done well without any mishaps. The twins were pleased with themselves; it was their first time serving at a formal tea. The ladies started chatting about the first ball of the season, which would be held at Louisa's manor, on Hanover Square. With excitement, Amara told Gabrielle that they had a fitting that afternoon for their gowns, and they would be finished by Friday. They asked if Lady Gabrielle had gowns made for the new season.

Gabrielle said, "Yes, I have mine already. There were finished weeks ago. Mother wanted them done early, so there would be no rushing. Being I'm eighteen this season; I'm hoping to be engaged and marry soon."

Aurora said with a giggle, "Oh, how exciting it is. Do you have your sights set on someone special yet?"

"I do like the Earl of Cumberland. He is most handsome, but he does not know I exist yet," Gabrielle answered.

Sabrina said, "We shall have to do something about that, won't we." All four girls giggled.

The duchess looked over to her daughters and arched an eyebrow. "Perhaps you should refresh our tea, Lady Aurora and Lady Amara."

"Yes, Mother." They rose to serve. Laurentia was charmed by the little circle of family and friends she met today and felt as if she had fitted in perfectly.

The tea party lasted a little over an hour. After the last guest had gone, Duchess told the twins to change, and she would have the coach brought around in half an hour to go to their fitting. Duchess asked Laurentia to join them.

"Yes, that shall be lovely, and perhaps I could have a couple of gowns made for myself." On the way to her bedchamber, Laurentia wondered if she would see Jasper this evening. She did not thank him yet for the books he'd had delivered that morning to her room.

The four of them rode in Duchess's lovely coach. The outside was deep mahogany with a high gloss finish, and the interior seats were in rich cherry blossom pink leather. They headed for Bond Street as the twins chattered non-stop about the new gowns that the duchess had made for them and wondered if they should add lace or beading to the attire. Duchess assures her daughters that the modiste will help them make the best decision, and with pride, knows her daughters will be à la mode.

Meanwhile, Laurentia could not help herself; she looked out the coach window, daydreaming about Jasper and the way he looked into her eyes when he kissed her wrist yesterday. It had been a long time since any gentleman had made her feel that way. If she thought about it, no gentleman had toyed with her heart. She had kissed a gentleman or two, but she had never let them stay close for long enough for her to get hurt. She did know a man like Lord Bellator was a rake and would break her heart. Well, she thought, nodding with confidence, I must put a wall up and not let that happen. Then she heard her name, shaking her out of her dreaming.

Amara was asking, "What color gowns shall you have made today, Lady Sinclair?"

Laurentia turned back from looking out the window. She smiled, "I like pastel colors for spring and summer."

Amara continued leaning forward and whispered, "Lord Bellator's favorite color is blue," she winked and smiled.

Laurentia wondered what the wink and smile were about? She had not shown her feelings for Lord Bellator in front of anyone. Or had she? She thought

I better be more careful, not too.

Aurora said with cheer, "We are going to Mademoiselle Giselle, she is wonderful, and I love her accent, so sweet and French. Mother has been using her for years, and you shall love her also, I'm sure you shall."

Laurentia said, "I have heard of her, seen some of her fashions. I do like her work, and it shall be lovely to have her design something for me."

As the group departed the carriage and headed through the door, Laurentia hesitated on the street. She looked around, feeling as if someone was watching her. The groom holding the front door to the shop asked, "Is anything amiss, my Lady."

"I feel that someone is watching me."

The groom looked around too. "I don't see anyone but shall keep a lookout."

Laurentia nodded, then continued inside to join the rest. The duchess stepped four steps into the shop and stopped. Mademoiselle Giselle came running out from the ordering desk, with her arm wide open saying in her thick French accent.

"Ah Duchess Devonshire, there you are, oh so beautiful you look. I have the gowns ready for your lovely daughter's final fitting. I have yours finished as requested, your Grace."

Duchess clapped her hands together, "Good, do come along, Lady Aurora and Lady Amara. Time is a wasting." Two young seamstresses come forward, curtsied, and took both girls to the back of the shop for their last fittings. The twin giggled and bounced with excitement as they left.

Mademoiselle Giselle saw Laurentia standing behind Her Grace. "Who is this beauty you have here?" She walked past the duchess to Laurentia.

"This is my new governess, Lady Sinclair. She would like a few new gowns made also."

"Ah, lovely blonde hair, violet eyes, and a perfect figure. Come, let us look at fabric; I have many ideals this way, my Lady."

Laurentia picked out fabrics, lace, jewel beadings, and patterns for three new gowns. She picked out shimmering blue silk for a ball gown and asked if that could be finished by Friday early afternoon, she would pay extra to have it completed. Though the price was dear and would deplete her meager savings, she felt she needed something more appropriate to wear than her serviceable dresses.

Giselle said with a wink and a big smile, "Yes, we shall have it done for you by Friday, and I shall you send the bill."

"You can have them delivered to the duchess's address if you please."

"Of course, my Lady, the blue ball gown can be delivered along with Lady Amara and Lady Aurora's gowns on Friday, and the others shall be completed by Tuesday afternoon at the latest. After all, Duchess Devonshire is one of my best customers."

As did Laurentia, the twins finished up, and a groom came in to carry the Duchess's finished gowns and accessories to the coach. They bade Mademoiselle Giselle goodbye, and off they went to the coach and back to Berkley Square. On the way back, Laurentia thought to herself, 'what was that wink about, and I will send the bill?' She asked the Duchess, "What was that about, the wink and all?

Duchess answered, "Oh, that is just the French way," and left it at that.

Chapter 11

Earl and Countess Surrey, Recital

The Duchess helped her daughters with their final touches to their attire for the first outing of the ton, and of course, they were thrilled to attend.

"Mother, do I look appropriate for the recital?" Amara asked, looking at her reflection in the full-length looking glass.

Aurora, sitting at the dressing table having her maid finishing her hair, said, "Do we, Mother?"

Duchess smiled at them. "Oh yes, I am so proud of you, and you look so grown up tonight. Maybe too grown up." Duchess held back her tears to see her girls growing up so fast in front of her eyes. It seemed like only yesterday they were just babies in their nursery. This recital was the first event of the early season; it would be well attended and should be a crush.

Aurora was wearing a taffy-pink silk gown with a scooped neckline and delicate lace and puffy short sleeves. Her hair had been curled, then pull on top of her head, with a pearl pinned in place to hold each curl. Amara wore a jade-green silk gown with a modestly cut neckline with emerald beading along the edge and puffy short sleeves. Amara loved all shades of greens, for it enhanced her eye color. Her hair was almost the same as Auroras' but had emerald pins in the curls instead of the pearls.

"Well, my darlings, you look lovely; we better go downstairs. His Grace is waiting for us, and you know how impatient he can be," the Duchess said and headed for the door.

Laurentia had just started to descend the stairs but stopped when she saw her charges coming and smiled with approval. All four women walked down the stairs together in a row. The duke smiled and said, "I am one lucky man to arrive with four beautiful women tonight to the recital." He took his wife's hand, raised to his lips, and kissed it. Duke bowed to the three ladies standing before him, and they all curtsied to him and giggled.

Duchess was wearing a peacock-green silk gown with a low-cut neckline to enhance her breasts. Her hair was piled high on her head, with thin wisps down her back and around her face. Two peacock feathers adorned her hair to match the gown. The duke wore a midnight-blue silk evening suit with silver trim, and his waistcoat had a silver paisley design embroidery with silver buttons. He was a picture of elegance, arrogance, and power. Laurentia could see now where Jasper received this from, and it could be exciting to see and feel it in a man. She shook her head and told herself to stop with those thoughts of a certain lord.

The duke said, "Are we ready, my beauties?" He put his duchess's hand on his sleeve and headed to the door where Wesley was waiting to open it for them.

Down the front stairs was the duke's new coach.

Laurentia had not ridden in a coach as extravagant as this one and felt a little overwhelmed with it.

The duke said to Laurentia as no big deal, "It was my birthday gift from my brothers."

The twins laughed, and Amara said, "Father loves his new toy, don't let him fool you."

The duchess smirked, then laughed with the twins. Laurentia felt much better with the laugher in the coach, for this family could make it extremely easy to be a part of, and she giggled along with them. During the ride, they talked about their day, and before you know it, they arrived. Laurentia sat by the window; she looked out and saw the coaches lined up in front of them. They were slowly easing to the front door, one by one, the coaches ahead of them stopping to unload.

When they pulled up to the front of the manor, the twins looked up to the entranceway, and they saw a long line of well-dressed people ambling to go inside. They never saw this before, and their eyes were as large as saucers.

Amara said, "Mother, is it always like this with so many people?"

Duchess gave them a reassuring smile. "Yes, the ton does enjoy being seen in their best; it can be a lot of fun once you are inside."

Aurora said, "I cannot wait to go inside. Look, there are Aunt Louisa and Uncle Charlton." She said excitedly.

Duke said, "You shall see a lot of Raventon's here tonight, my darlings, and many friends."

Laurentia reminded the girls to be ladylike and act with decorum.

Duchess nodded in agreement. "I only expect

your best behavior tonight, and remember who you are at all times."

Aurora and Amara smiled sweetly and echoed, "Yes, Mother, we shall, and we do."

The coach door opened, and the duke stepped out first, then he turned around to help his duchess down the steps. Duchess descended the steps and fluffed out her gown as she took a couple of steps forward. She waited for the rest of her party as they departed the coach.

The duke smiled at his daughters. "Are you ready to give them a show, my darlings?" He winked at them and put his arm out for his duchess to take, and they walked up the steps together, their head held high, and everyone bowing to them or curtsying as they passed by. The duke and duchess nodded to acquaintances and commanded the crowd as they walked proudly.

Laurentia told the twins they were next, for they were higher station than she was.

"I am right behind you for support." Giving the twins one last word of confidence.

They walked up the steps and waited with their parents to be announced as they walked in the entrance and stopped. Once the butler announced them, they greeted the host and hostess and continued into the gala.

Duchess stopped inside the first salon, "Well done, and keep your giggling to a minimum, remember and head up you are a Raventon's. Your Father and I shall continue in and make our rounds. I see some of your friends, and you may visit them. When the recital starts, we shall sit together then." Duchess smiled at her daughters.

They both echoed, "Yes, your Grace."

Laurentia stayed close to her charges in case if they needed her. She was sensing Lord Bellator was nearby. The twins chatted with friends they have known for a long time from the country estates.

From behind, Lord Bellator appeared. "Good evening, Lady Sinclair."

Laurentia turned around slowly, and she smiled up at him as she looked into his brilliant blue eyes.

Laurentia curtsied, "Good evening, my Lord."

He took her hand, kissing the top as he elegantly bowed over it. "Now it is that I have found you for company. You look incredibly beautiful this evening, my Lady." Jasper noticed Laurentia's lovely gown; it was a pastel yellow with puffy shelves, and a delicately laced v-neckline that showed some cleavage. Her hair was in ringlets, piled on top of her head, with a few curls cascading down her back. She looked like an angel to him.

Jasper wore a black evening suit with tails; there was gold embroidery along his cuffs and lapel. His waistcoat had gold buttons, and under it, he wore a crisp white shirt with a black cravat tied perfectly. He looked most eloquent. Jasper put his arm out, "The music shall start in another half hour. Would you like to stroll with me?"

Laurentia looked to the twins, then back to him.

Jasper cut her off, "My sisters shall be fine for a while. They are talking to some of their friends. Besides, I see about ten or so Raventon's watching over them." He pointed out his cousins. "That is Leopold, Sterling, Victor, Gabrielle, Kelsey, my cousins. You know Drake. Plus, mother and father are keeping a close eye on them, believe me, and there are a few more around."

Laurentia smiled. "Are you sure they shall be alright?"

"Watch this! Lady Amara, Lady Aurora, I'm taking Lady Sinclair for a stroll around the room. Shall you be fine for a little while?"

They both beamed smiles up to him. Aurora said, "Of course. We see many family eyes on us. We are perfectly fine."

"Now, you have seen." Jasper held out this arm for her to take, smiling his wicked smile, and said, "Shall we, Lady Sinclair."

Laurentia lay her hand on his sleeve. "Very well, Lord Bellator, lead on."

Surrey Manor was a large home. In the first salon, she saw chairs lined up for the music part of the evening. Jasper took Laurentia's hand; he wrapped her arm through his and placed his hand on top of hers. She looked at his hand, then up to his eyes.

He tilted his head, smiled, "I preferred your hand that way." As if they have always walked together like this, she let it go and continue walking.

As they strolled the outer room, Jasper nodded to some of the guests as he walked through the crowded room. Then he stopped and introduced Laurentia to a few different acquaintances, talked of the weather, and moved on.

Then they stopped to speak to a group; he introduced her to the four gentlemen, saying, "I'd like you to meet some of my cousins, Leopold, Victor, Kelsey, they are all Raventon's and my close friend Lord Kingsley. We all grew up together and went to Eton."

She did not say anything but remembered all of them from the morning she had twisted her ankle in the park. She curtsied to them, and they bowed over her hand as she rose. Leopold asked Jasper if he would play cards later in the cardroom, for that is where he would be when the music starts. Jasper nodded and arched an eyebrow at him as a signal for his answer. His cousin knew when Jasper walked around with a lady on his arm, and he takes time to introduce her to them, he was staking a claim on her.

Drake walked up to join the group, noting Lady Laurentia on Jasper's arm. He smiled, bowed good evening to her, and she curtsied. Drake said with a wolfish smile, "You look lovely tonight, Lady Sinclair. I hope my sisters are behaving themselves; they can be a handful at times."

"Thank you, my Lord. As for Lady Aurora and Lady Amara, they have been a delight so far, but I have been warned about their high-spiritedness, yes."

Drake said, smiling, "Do not let their dear smiles fool you, just a word of advice, my Lady. You also can call on me for help any time of day."

Jasper glared at his brother to back off. Drake loved to flirt, even if it irritated his brother a little, so he just smiled, knowing he was succeeding in doing so.

Jasper looked to Laurentia. "Would you care for something to drink, Lady Sinclair, before the music starts?"

"Yes, that would be lovely, my Lord."

Jasper said to the group, "If you would excuse us." He bowed and took Laurentia into the next salon.

They walked to a refreshment table. Jasper asked, "Would you prefer punch or champagne, my sweet?"

"Champagne, please."

He handed her a glass and took one for himself. This room had a large crystal chandelier, royal blue tablecloths, matching drapes on the windows, several large tables filled with finger foods, pastries, cakes, pies, and different beverages. Jasper held his arm out; Laurentia took it and hooked it through, this time on her own. He led her to the open terrace doors, and they walked outside, stopping at the edge of the terrace.

Jasper spoke first, "It's a nice evening. Is it not?"

"Yes, there is a lovely breeze tonight and warm." She took a sip of champagne, then said, "Thank you, for the books you sent me this morning. I shall enjoy reading them immensely. I have to say reading is my favorite pastime. Thank you again." She smiled, looking up into his eyes.

"I am pleased that they made you happy. The books are yours to keep."

Laurentia, still looking in his eyes, "I shall cherish them, as they are a gift from you, my Lord."

Jasper looked around them and saw some steps, took her glass, and set their drinks on a table. Jasper took Laurentia's hand, and he asked, "Do you trust me?"

Laurentia nodded her head, "Yes, why do you ask?"

"Comes with me." He led her down the steps. Then, seeing a large tree to the far-right side of the terrace, he walked her around to the backside of the tree quickly, out of view. Jasper pushed Laurentia's back against the tree; he held her face with both his hands and captured her lips with his, kissing her hard and demanding. She kissed him back, not holding back at all.

Jasper let go of her face and started kissing her neck and back to her lips again. She wrapped her arms around his neck and leaned into him, giving him free rein to touch her as he pleased. Jasper ran his hand up and down her body, feeling her curves through the fine silk of her gown. She was a real woman with fully developed curves, oh so perfect, he thought as he touched her.

She kissed him passionately and made a little whimper sound of pleasure. That was a noise that drove Jasper over the top crazy with more lust for her. He must stop this and shut his desires and demons down before this gets out of control. He pulled his lips from her, looking down into her sparkling violet eyes.

"As much as we both are enjoying this, my sweet, I don't think it's the right place to be doing this. I do not want to tarnish your reputation; I care for you too much to hurt you."

Laurentia smiled up at him, relishing his words that he cared for her enough not to hurt her. "Yes, you are right, and the night has not even started yet. We should go back in before someone starts looking for us."

Jasper smiled down at her. "You are so beautiful. I do desire you and must have you soon, very soon." He kissed the tip of her nose.

"I like it when you smile at me that way. I can see happiness in your eyes like it's just for me."

"That's because you bring it out of me so easily, and it is just for you." Jasper took a piece of her hair from her cheek and twirled it around his finger. Her smile broadened.

"Your lips look well kissed. The rest of you, I haven't messed up. You look perfect to me."

Laurentia patted her hair, then touched her lips with her fingertips. "I do like kissing you and would not mind a little more."

Jasper raised an eyebrow in surprise. "We shall have more at a later time, and I can promise you that." He stepped back, letting her go from their embrace, and put his arm out for her to take. "Shall we return to the party, my sweet? The music should be starting soon."

Laurentia smiled. "Yes, that's a good idea before we are missed, my Lord," she said, taking his arm.

They walked back up the steps to the terrace, which was empty of guests. Jasper looked down at Laurentia; he smirked and whispered, "I do not think anybody saw us disappear in our short moment of togetherness we had shared."

Laurentia smiled brightly, "I think you are right. But where is everyone?"

Jasper heard some instruments starting tune, and through the windows, he saw the guests moving toward the recital room. "I believe the recital is going to be starting, and the guests have all found seats by now or have gone into the card room. We should go in and find a seat for ourselves." They walked back through the refreshment salon to the next salon.

The guests had taken their seats with a few still standing around talking, for the music had not started yet.

Laurentia looked around for the twins, and she saw them in the second row with the duke and duchess beside them and two empty chairs by the twins. They headed in that direction. Laurentia noticed that when Jasper walked through a room, heads turned and it seemed a path magically opened as he walked through the crowd. As she walked by his side, Laurentia wondered what they thought of her? These people did not really know who she was or who her family was. Laurentia started feeling vulnerable and tried to pull her hand free from Jasper's arm. However, he had his other hand on top of hers and won't let it free.

He looked down at her and saw a slight panic in her eyes. He then realized she's not used to everybody watching her so closely. He tilted his head a little toward hers as they walked, then whispered. "Take a deep breath, my sweet; when you've seen on the arm of a Raventon, everyone watches. You shall get used to it in time. Just show that brilliant smile of yours, and all shall be well."

She looked up to those big blue eyes that were telling her, I have you, not to worry. She loosened her tension and glided through the room with him. They walked to the second row, where the family was sitting.

It was Jasper's first time seeing his parents that night, so he bent down, kisses his mother's cheek. "Good evening, you look lovely tonight, your Grace."

Duchess looked up. "Thank you, Bellator; it's good to see you this evening." She saw he had Laurentia on his arm, and she looked at both of them with a curious expression. Jasper greeted his father. Then they took the two seats by his sisters, letting Laurentia sit by Amara, then he took the outside aisle seat.

Amara and Aroura leaned forward to look their brother in his eyes; they smiled and said, "Thought so," in unison. He lifted his chin a little higher, then ignored them. Laurentia started to chat with the twins, asking who was performing this evening, whether they had heard them before to take the interest off Jasper and herself.

Smart woman, the duchess observed, as did the duke and Jasper.

Earl and Countess of Surrey were standing in the front of the platform in front of the musicians. They were ready for the performance to start. The hostess cleared her throat.

"May I have your attention, everyone, please." Countess waited for silence and for those who had not taken their seats to do so. "Thank you for joining us this evening in our home. I am pleased to see you again, for this is our third year of having the recital in our home. I must say, the turnout this year is a bigger one than the past years." She looked to the earl, then says, laughing, "My Lord, I think we shall have to get a larger home if we keep on like this?".

He took her hand. "We shall have to add on. And for those who have not heard yet, we are expecting our first child this early winter." Everyone started clapping and congratulating them.

The earl said, "Thank you all. My Countess has organized a nice lineup for you this evening, so do enjoy." Countess announced the first singer.

Jasper whispered to Laurentia, "I do not usually come to recitals. But Earl Surrey and I went to Eton and Cambridge. He has been a close friend of mine for years. So I find myself obligated to attend this one. I shall congratulate Lord Surrey later. Perhaps his countess is carrying his heir."

"The countess and the earl look like a lovely couple. You can see the love in their eyes for each other, and a child will bring more love into their home."

"They are well-matched, and it's nice to see my friend happy."

Laurentia asked, "You are usually in the card room when you come to things like this, are you not?"

Jasper looked her in the eyes, "Yes, that is true. That's why Leopold mentioned that earlier."

Laurentia, still looking in Jasper's eyes, said, "If you wish, you may go in the card room at any time, Lord Bellator."

The corner of his lip twitched. "Is that what you wish, my Lady?"

Laurentia looked down. "I do not want to keep you from your usual entertainment, my Lord."

Jasper wished she would call him by his first name; he would love to hear his name float from her lips. "I shall sit here for a few songs if you don't mind my company, my Lady."

She looked over at him, trying not to smile. "Your company is not so bad. You can be quite charming at times, my Lord."

"That's good to hear. But we should stop talking. I believe we are supposed to listen to the music now."

She looked up at him again, smiling, then giggled lightly, for he was actually making a jest. Jasper loved the sound of her giggle and liked she got his jest, and that made him laugh inside, for he would not show feeling or emotion in and around the ton, only in private, as he had been trained many years ago on doing so.

Two different performers sang, and the last one played the harp. Jasper saw his chance to leave, for the next performer was telling the pianist what song she would sing. Jasper stood, excused himself, and the duke was right behind him.

When they reached the doorway, the duke said, "Cards and brandy would suit me right now."

"That was my thought exactly, Father." They entered the card room together, found the other Raventon gentlemen already there, and that was where they all plan to stay for the rest of the evening until the music part of the night was over.

The duchess, twins, and Laurentia were standing in the refreshment salon two hours later. The twins were sipping punch, and duchess and Laurentia were sipping champagne. They chatted with Lady Louisa and Lady Gabrielle.

Amara said to her mother, "I do feel tired. When can we go home, your Grace?"

The duchess said, "Let me have your father called upon." She looked to a footman and nodded.

He came over, bowed, then said, "Yes, Your Grace."

"Tell the Duke of Devonshire that his duchess requires his presence. Therefore, he should be in the card room."

Ten minutes later, the duchess saw the duke strolling into the refreshment salon. He walked to his duchess. "I take it you are ready to leave?"

She smiled at the duke. "Yes, our girls are tired, and it has been a long day. We could go and have the coach come back for you if you wish to stay and play more cards."

The duke put out his arm, "My luck tonight has not been in my favor. I'm ready myself, shall we go?" They bade everyone farewell in their circle. They told the Earl and Countess of Surrey goodnight and congratulated them on the baby and hoped it would be their new heir. On the way home, the twins talked about the evening and saying how they enjoyed themselves. The duchess told them they did well.

Laurentia said with a smile and a nod, "I saw no errors that need to be mentioned."

Chapter 12

Berkeley Square, Midnight

It had not taken long to return to Berkeley Mansion.
The coach pulled to the front of the mansion, one of
the grooms from the back platform open the coach
door, and they walked up the front steps to the entrance. Wesley greets them at the door; he bowed
and asked if he could do anything for them before
they retire.

The duke answer for everyone. "No, you may
lock up and retire yourself for the night, Wesley."

They all walked up the main staircase, climbing
to the top landing. They bade goodnight to one another and continued to their bedchambers.

Laurentia opens her door walked inside. Sandra
was waiting for her and walked out of the dressing
room to help her mistress undress. Laurentia saw her
pale blue nightgown lying on the bed. Sandra walks
to Laurentia to helps her unbutton the gown she was
wearing, and then Laurentia slips into her nightgown. Laurentia sat down at her dressing table in
front of the looking glass. Sandra was standing behind Laurentia, helping her take her hair down.
When the pins were out of her hair, Laurentia picks
up the brush and start to work the brush through her

hair. She then tells Sandra to hang her gown up, and she may go to bed herself.

"Goodnight, my Lady," Sandra said as she exits the room for the night.

"Goodnight, Sandra, and thank you."

Laurentia continues brushing her long blonde hair that fell to her waist. As she brushed her through the hair, she sighed as her thoughts drifted to Lord Bellator, about the conversation they shared and how he'd stayed by her side when the music started. And not to forget the passionate kiss they shared behind the tree away from all eyes. Plus, sadly, she did not have the chance to say goodbye to him tonight. Laurentia wondered if he was still playing cards. Perhaps he had gone to another place to chase women, or maybe he'd gone home. She sighed again and wished he was here with her instead, which she knew was impossible. A girl can wish, can she not?

Still brushing her hair, she sensed Jasper was nearby. She looked up in the mirror to see him standing right behind her. He bent over her, touching, and smelling her hair. Laurentia blinked a couple of times to make sure she was not seeing things.

"Since the first day I looked down into those beautiful violet eyes of yours, I have been wondering how long your blonde hair was. Exceptionally nice, Laurentia." He continued to smell her hair and ran his fingers through it. "Your hair smells like honeysuckle."

"J-Jasper," she stuttered. "How did you get in here? I locked my door."

"That's a good idea; I should lock your dressing room door. We would not want a maid coming in tonight." He locked it and came strolling back.

Laurentia turned in her chair, watching him. Jasper pulled Laurentia up to her feet, so she stood before him, then stepped back to see all of her.

"Ah, I like the whole picture in front of me. You are beautiful, and did you know you are wearing my favorite color?" He saw her breasts through the thin blue nightdress, perfectly round, full. He could not wait to touch them, taste them. He already knew she had lovely curves, but to see them in just a nightdress made his mouth water, and his groin grown even more hard.

Still in shock, Laurentia asked again, "How did you get in my room, my Lord?"

Jasper took up the distance between them. "You do remember that I was the one who said what room you should take. Did I not?"

"Yes, you did."

"This room has a secret passage in the wall; the door is behind that bookcase." Jasper pointed to the bookcase.

Laurentia looked Jasper straight in the eyes, then angrily asked him," You had this planned all along to seduce me, did you not?"

"Yes, but it did depend on you when I kissed you to find out if you could be seduced."

She did not like him, admitting that he had planned to seduce her.

"You get out of my room right this minute and do not come back here."

Jasper said innocently, "My sweet, you wanted me here. You said earlier this evening you wanted more. Well, here I am."

He wrapped his arms around her waist and pulled her closer, then kissed her demandingly and licked her bottom lip with the tip of his tongue. He then smiled down at her and raised her chin with his index finger so that she would look him in the eyes. He asked her seriously, "Do you want me here with you tonight, Laurentia?"

She sighed. "I do, but you could have told me about your plans this evening."

Jasper tilted his head. "That would have taken the whole fun out of the surprise that I have come to you like this. It was priceless, the look on your face when you realized I was here, my sweet."

Laurentia smiled, for she did wish he was with her tonight. She rose to her tip toes to reach up and kiss him lightly and wraps her arms around his neck.

"You are a bad seed, my Lord, one that I have found most intriguing. What shall we do now you are here."

"I first would like to hear you call me Jasper, and after I hear you say my name, I am going to pleasure your body in so many ways, Laurentia."

She licked her lips then said, "Jasper," very softly and all so sweet to him.

That ignited the flames inside of Jasper; he must have her now. He scooped her up in his arms, then carried Laurentia to the bed. He placed her on her feet again before the bed, then he lifted her nightgown up over her head and dropped it on the floor.

"You have on too many clothes on, my Jasper."

Laurentia reached up, untied his cravat, and dropped it to the floor. His coat came off next, and then his waistcoat dropped to the floor. She unbuttoned his shirt and slid it off his shoulders. She'd never seen a man, so well built, with no shirt on before. She took the tips of her fingers and traced the muscles, the ridges on his chest and stomach. She was amazed by his broad shoulders that tapered to his narrow waist. She leaned forward and kissed the spot where his heart beats heavily in his chest.

Jasper grabbed her hands, then kissed each finger one by one, looking into her eyes. If he let her continue touching him like this, her first lovemaking would be over in minutes. He didn't want to lose his control, and he must make this last as long as possible to make Laurentia's first time memorable. "My turn to show you and share with you my lovemaking skills."

Laurentia shivered with the excitement of what was to come next.

Jasper scooped her up, then lay her onto the bed. Laurentia's head rested on one of the pillows, and she watched Jasper take his boots off, next his sword and breeches. Wow is the first response that came to Laurentia's mind, seeing Jasper standing in front of her nude. She thought, 'he keeps telling me I am beautiful, his body is perfection, all muscles everywhere a work of art, like the statue of David.'

Jasper crawled onto the bed like a black panther after his prey. He hovered over Laurentia, just looking down at the beauty beneath him. She saw that all too familiar wicked smile on his face appears. He bent down and kissed her lightly at first, and then it built up deeper, his tongue skimming the inside of her mouth as he tasted her for the first time. Her arms went up around his neck. Jasper grabbed them both, putting them over her head so that she couldn't touch him.

"Keep them there, over your head, my sweet. I want to pleasure your whole body, then make slow love to you."

Laurentia frowned a little, "I want to touch you too."

"After I am finished with pleasuring your body, relax and take it all in. Do you trust me?"

Laurentia smiled. "Yes, I do, but I want—"

Jasper cut her off. "Just feel the pleasure I am going to give you and keep your arms and hands here," he said again.

On that, Jasper kissed her deep and long, then he kissed a trail down her neck, to her breasts. He nipped one nipple at first, then he licked and circled his tongue around one nipple then the other. Her nipples turn hard like delicious buds from his touch, full of feeling, and very sensitive. He took one nipple in his lips, sucking on it like he was feeding, then Jasper played his tongue around, around her nipple, flicking it with his tongue, then took it in his mouth again and sucked more. He moved to the other breast and done the same.

Laurentia moaned in delight, lifting and arching her back from the bed. Jasper looked up at her face and saw her starting to pant. He dallied a little more with her breasts, his tongue on her skin, so perfect, he thought. Then he moved down her body to her stomach, licking and kissing as he went side to side. Laurentia was in ecstasy. She had never felt anything like this before, and it was so wonderful. Her body sang with his touch. She was overwhelmed and loving everything he was doing to her. Laurentia's mind was going crazy with excitement over what he would do next.

"Oh, Jasper, that feels ahhh," she moaned.

Jasper loved to hear his name off Laurentia's lips; it made his desire for her pump harder through his veins, giving him more fuel to pleasure her even more. He stopped at her navel, taking his tongue and circling round it, and he kissed then sucked the middle. He noticed she liked that, and now he wanted to taste her body in the most sensitive, intimate place. Jasper trailed kisses down to her womanhood. Spreading her legs, he took two fingers to spread her folds, smelling her sweet scent first, and then licking her slowly, first up then down with his tongue.

That just about made Laurentia sit up straight. "Jasper! What are you doing to me?" she asked in shock.

"Relax, my sweet. You did say you trust me."

"Yes, but this? Is this…?" She doesn't know what to say.

Jasper looked her in the eyes. "You have liked everything I have done so far. This is going to get better as we go. Just lay back and feel the pleasure, Laurentia."

"I shall trust you." She lay back down and took a big deep breath and blow out.

Jasper smiled up at her, and she was looking down at him now. He dipped his head down between her legs again and started over again. Spreading her folds, licked her softly, then licked and played with her delicious bud. This time she shivered when he did that. Jasper continued licking, pushing one finger inside of her. He feels she is so wet and tight for him, and he knew this is her first time. Jasper loved the fact that he is her first. He knew he must give her an orgasm to relax her more, so she could take him when he entered her for the first time. With one finger inside, he stroked her slowly, still licking and tasting her sweet nectar. She moans as Jasper pulled out the one finger and entered two fingers, so tight. He flicked his tongue around her bud, then licked with a little more rhythm faster and stroked inside with two fingers, on and on.

Laurentia was starting to feel this strange flutter below, and it was building up more. "Oh, Jasper, that feels so good," she said on another moan. Then her body quiver shakes, and she let out a beautiful cry of pleasure. Jasper came up over the top of her, spreading her legs wide for him. He kissed her lips slowly, then deepened their kiss, and he whispered in her ear.

"This may hurt at first, but I do promise it will get better as we go."

Laurentia nodded, and he kissed her long, pushing the tip of his penis in, then stopping, then pushing halfway before stopping again. Laurentia made a squealing noise this time when he moved. Jasper was holding his breath, for he wanted to go all the way in, but he did not want to hurt Laurentia too much. He whispered.

"Are you okay, my sweet? Tell me." He was looking into her eyes.

"Yes, I'm fine. You feel so big, and it does hurt some. How far are you in?"

"Only halfway, my sweet. Are you ready for more?"

She nodded yes but was unsure. Jasper kissed her again passionately to take her mind from the first-time pain, slowly he pushed more. Then he went all the way in, and he breathed out in a sigh. Holding still, letting Laurentia get used to the fullness, the pressure of him stretching her, he moved out slowly, then back in all the way. Jasper kissed Laurentia passionately, moving out slowly, then in. She feels so good and tight around him. He moved all the way out and then all the way in. Hearing a low moan from her, he picked up the pace a little more this time. He wanted her to come again, so he grit his teeth to hold himself back from letting go of his seed. Jasper felt Laurentia's body doing a little shiver, his rhythm picking up some more until she was panting.

Jasper looked Laurentia in the eyes. "Come with me, Laurentia. We will soar together this time. Keep looking into my eyes; I want to see your passion and glory."

She felt her body start to shake, and she went over the top in a long orgasm. Jasper let go of his seed in a long, hard orgasm, moaning, and he filled her. It felt like they were floating above the clouds, and they were in their paradise together.

Jasper hoped he did not hurt Laurentia too severely. He must have her once more before he left her bed. The second time will be better for both of them, he knew. Jasper had also decided she was his from this day forward. No one would touch her ever like he just had; Laurentia was his.

Laurentia was feeling all so good, and she never knew her body could do that kind of thing, and he did give her pleasure, tremendous pleasure twice.

Jasper kissed her, pulled out, and rolled to his back, taking Laurentia with him. She lay on top, and he wrapped his arms around her to hold her close. He kissed her forehead then said, "How was that, for your first, my sweet Laurentia?"

Laurentia hugged him. "I did not know that could feel so good, thank you."

Jasper cannot recall ever being thanked ever, perhaps how good it was, and so on. But never thanked. "I'm glad you enjoyed it. We shall have to do it again in a few moments if I have not hurt you, and you are not too sore, that is.

Laurentia looked up into his eyes, smiled, and said, "I think once is good, don't you think?"

"No, once I had you, I have to have you more. Only I shall have you ever and touch you in this way."

Laurentia props herself up to look him in the eyes. "Well, that is not in my plans, my Lord!"

Jasper did not like she was back to calling him my lord again. For when they were in private, he wanted to hear her call him by his name. "Call me, Jasper, when we are alone. And what is your plan, may I ask?" He arched an eyebrow, quite interested.

Laurentia became serious. "When I turn twenty-five next year, I shall receive my trust fund, and then I shall travel, Rome, Paris, Egypt, and more. I want to see all the places I had read about, and that is my dream. This work as a governess is just temporary, so I can do as I please and not have my brother telling me what I can do and not do." She shrugged like it was no big deal.

This was not what Jasper wanted to hear after he'd just made love to the woman, and it was amazing. He felt she would be his perfect bride, someday, his marchioness. Of course, that sparked his temper, but he wouldn't let her see that.

Jasper looked down at Laurentia with an impassive expression. "We shall have to see about that. Things do change from day to day, as you know."

Jasper rolled Laurentia to her back quickly, kissed her passionately before she could say another word, and that made Laurentia forget she said earlier once was enough, which would never be with her. Jasper decided he would keep making love to Laurentia daily, which would make her fall in love with him, and she would not leave him ever. Jasper made incredibly intense, passionate love to Laurentia, and she cried out his name. He held her close after the second time, feeling the afterglow. Then Jasper kissed Laurentia's forehead and rose out of bed to start getting dressed. He looked down and could tell Laurentia did not want him to leave.

"As much as I would like to stay with you, hold you while we sleep, it's not a good idea for us to be seen like this." He waved his hand over the bed. She nodded in agreement.

"You need to remove the bed linens after you get up later. You shall see some blood on the sheets. Have your maid banish them from the mansion." After Jasper finished dressing and put his sword back on, he bent over the bed, kissed Laurentia long and deep, making her want more of what they just experienced together. Then he disappeared through the secret passage, the same way he had come in.

Laurentia sighed when Jasper left, he was so much to take in. His presence was so powerful, and she did wish he could have stayed. Was this wrong tonight? Should he have left when he asked if she wanted him to stay? She admitted to herself that she was drawn to him. She could sense his presence when he entered the room before she even saw him. Then she smiled, thinking about what they shared tonight. Oh my, what have I done? Laurentia thought. Shall it be awkward being around him now? It was late, so Laurentia decided to worry about that tomorrow. On that thought, Laurentia closed her eyes, and she dreamed about a certain Marquess with black hair and blue eyes all night long.

Chapter 13

The Unwanted Guest

The Earl of Berwickshire was in his front parlor having tea and reading the London Gazette. He enjoyed keeping up with news from London. He received the paper two days late because of London's distance, but all the same, it was a good read. Lucas had not changed anything in this room since his parents' passing. The room was decorated in light blue, with cream color curtains. A large fireplace dominated the main wall, and it was comfortably furnished.

A knock sounded on the parlor door and Carlson, entered, "A Mr. Kent says you are expecting his visit, my Lord. Should I show him in?"

Lucas had a feeling this had something to do with that last visitor Mr. Hughes and his claim that he had made investments. "Have Mr. Gibbs come in first and then wait five minutes before showing in Kent."

So, this is it; let's see how this plays out. It should be interesting, Lucas thought. When Gibbs entered, Lucas said, "Let's see what happens with this visit today, shall we?"

When Mr. Kent entered the room minutes later, the earl stood to feel more powerful and in control. "Do come in, Mr. Kent; you may have a seat."

Mr. Kent was an unusually large man who looked like a giant sitting in the small chair indicated by the earl. Lucas took a position in a plush wingback chair.

"I believe Mr. Hughes has sent you here today on false pretense."

"You are mistaken. Mr. Hughes has indicated you must pay today fifteen hundred pounds."

The earl looks to Gibbs for strength, then looked at Kent and said, "I have no intention of paying Mr. Hughes. Not even one pound. This whole investment deal is a farce, and you are wasting my time."

Kent's expression turned angry, and he stood and took a couple of steps closer to Lucas. "Mr. Hughes had a feeling you would say that, so here is the ultimatum. If you don't pay today, we shall hurt your family. We have located one Lady Laurentia Sinclair in London."

The earl was outraged but kept an impassive look on his face. "I have no family. They all drown in a shipwreck years ago. So, do as you please. Get out of my home." On that note, the parlor door opened, and two large footmen walked in. The earl ordered the footmen to ensure this unwanted visitor was escorted off his estate immediately. They walked Kent out the door and made sure he left.

Lucas felt his whole world has fallen out from under him.

He said to Gibbs, "We must go to London today." He immediately rang for Carlson, telling him, "Have my trunk packed. I am going to London. I need my best wardrobe packed. Order my coach to be brought around with my finest horses. I want to leave within an hour. Send word to my sister that I am coming and that I shall be opening the Portman

Square manor. Tell her I am staying for the season. Also, we need the full staff to follow as soon as they can."

Carlson knew his job, "As quick as lightning, my Lord."

Lucas started toward the door but stopped and turned to Gibbs. "What are you waiting for? We must pack papers, ledgers, and whatnot from the library. And yes, you shall join me on this trip."

"Yes, my Lord, I'm right behind you," Gibbs said as he stood and rushed out of the parlor door behind Lucas.

It would take two days to travel to London, just stopping to change horses. In the meantime, he could only pray nothing happened to his beloved sister.

Chapter 14

Lord and Lady Raventon, Garden Party

"It is a beautiful day for a garden party. Is it not Leopold?" Lady Louisa said to her son as he strolled out onto the terrace that overlooked the extensive gardens with a large pond. Louisa stood at the end of the terrace, giving orders for what needed to be finished before the guest arrived.

"Yes, it's a splendid day for your party, not a cloud in the sky. Things out here do look festive. I must say, Mother."

"Thank you, darling, for the staff, and I have been out here since dawn working to make the gardens look perfectly wonderful for our guests when they arrive. I do have high standards."

"That I know, and the whole ton is aware of that. That is why your gathering are always a crush." Louisa smiled at her eldest son, then turned to the footmen directing.

"Move those tables a little more left, yes, that's better."

A maid walked by with a tray of pastries, and Leopold snatched one. Louisa frowned at him, "Haven't' you eaten today?"

"Yes, but I cannot resist one of Martha's pastries,

and it's been a while since I had one." Leopold flashed his golden smile as he bit into it. "Mmm, just as delicious as I remember."

Lord Charlton walked out to the terrace. "I thought I heard your voice, Leopold. Did you just arrive? Your mother has been out here since the crack of dawn."

"Yes, I arrived about five minutes or so and had to relieve one of Martha's pastries from a tray."

"I can see, and still, you harbor a sweet tooth thing never change." Then Charlton turns to Louisa. "Darling, you should go change before the guest starts to arrive. I shall check on the rowboats and make sure they all have their oars and whatnots. You better get going; everything looks lovely." Charlton winked at his wife before he strolled down the lawn.

Louisa told Leopold as she left to change for the party, "I shall be back shortly. Tell them over there that I need more chairs in the shade."

Leopold walked down to the lawn to give the orders to organize the chairs.

At one, the first carriages pulled up to the front of the Raventon home. Footmen helped the guests exit their carriages, curricles, phaetons, coaches, and showed them the direction they needed to travel around the mansion's side to enter the garden entrance. Lord and Lady Raventon were greeting their guests at that spot. Soon, the Duke and Duchess Devonshire arrived with the twins and Laurentia.

The duke looks around to see who had arrived before them. Then he put his arm out for his duchess to take. "Come, long ladies, this way," Duke said as he started to stroll to the garden entrance. Louisa and Charlton greeted them with usual hugs, kisses, and handshakes when entering the garden gate. Then, Aurora and Amara saw some friends they knew, and they turned to ask the duchess if they could go on to visit.

"Yes, my girls, but do use your parasols to keep the sun from your face. I hate the thought of freckles appearing upon your complexion." Aurora and Amara open their parasol together, lifting them over their head, smiling as they glided down the lawn to where a half dozen young ladies are standing, talking, and laughing.

Laurentia saw a refreshment table set up and excused herself from the duke and duchess to have something cool to drink. It was a warm day; something cold to sip on would be refreshing. She approached the table, searching for something she likes. Laurentia suddenly sensed Jasper was nearby, and he appeared from around a hedge, then he came up behind Laurentia.

Jasper smelled Laurentia's hair, then bent down to whisper in her ear, "My sweet, you smell even better than last night. Your hair smells of honeysuckle on a spring day."

With him being so near, whispering in her ear, his soft words made Laurentia shiver, and she knew he felt it. That pleased Jaspers, making the corners of his lips twitch, to know he could arouse her so easily.

Damn him, Laurentia thought, for she knew he did that on purpose. She turned around to face him slowly with a genteel smile on her. "Ah, Lord Bellator, how it is a pleasure to see you again. It is a lovely day, is it not?" Laurentia was trying to put on a show that being this close to him did affect her. She curtsied to him, and Jasper bowed over her hand. He turned her hand over, looked into the eyes, and kissed her wrist ever so slowly, smiling his wick smile. Another shiver, Laurentia leaned in and whispered, "Stop that, my Lord."

Jasper made two points and counting, he thought to himself.

"My Lady, stop what, may I ask?" He said casually.

"You know what you're doing, and it's not funny," Laurentia sniped.

Jasper smirked and changed the subject. "I see you haven't chosen a beverage yet. What looks good? Do you like lemonade, my sweet?" He picked up a glass as he said it, and sipped it then smiled. "It's delicious, like you. Would you care for one?" He lifted another glass and handed it to her.

Laurentia sipped the lemonade, then said, "It's lovely, thank you, my Lord." She hoped no one heard what he'd just implied.

"Shall we take a stroll of the gardens, Lady Sinclair? My aunt has outdone herself this year." He waved a hand toward the gardens and held out his arm to her. Laurentia felt she must take his arm, for everyone was watching them, and it would be rude to decline him.

She smiled, took his arm, "Lead on, my Lord. I do enjoy seeing the flowers."

They had only gone a short way when Leopold stopped them.

"Good afternoon, Cousin and Lady Sinclair. It is a grand day for a stroll in the gardens. Is it not?"

"Ah, it is a lovely day and even lovelier when you have a beautiful lady on one's arm," Jasper said.

Leopold raised one eyebrow to Jasper. "Yes,

Lady Sinclair is as lovely as a rose, and you are a lucky gentleman to be strolling with her."

Laurentia wondered what these two were saying in a code; she could sense a hidden meaning.

Jasper retorted. "I have picked a couple of petals and chose the right one."

Leopold said, "So, I see. We shall talk later, dear Cousin." Jasper nod and Leopold continued on his way. Jasper led Laurentia down a trail with a flower bed on each side.

"What was that about?" Laurentia asked, looking up to Jaspers as they walked.

Looking impassive, Jasper said, "Just talking about flowers. They are lovely throughout the garden, as you can see, nothing more."

At the end of the trail, Laurentia saw a large hedge ahead of them. When they reached the barrier, Jasper took her hand, pulled her through an opening so that a tall hedge wall surrounded them. It was like a room and entirely private. Jasper turned to face Laurentia and grabbed her by the waist, pulling her close and kissing her demandingly. Laurentia surrendered to his lips and kissed him back just as forcefully. She wrapped her arms around his neck, pulling him closer to her body. Jasper raised his hands to her breasts, round perfect in his hands, and rubbed her nipples between his thumb and forefinger. She moaned against his lips, and then he trailed kissed down her neck to one of her breasts. Somehow with his quick hands, the top of her dress was loosened, exposing her breasts. Jasper held her perfect globes in his hands the slipped her nipple in his mouth. He suckled it at first, then ran his tongue around the nipple, flicking it, and licked and sucked.

Her nipple swelled to his play, and he feasted. Laurentia put her hands in Jasper's hair to anchor herself as he had his way with her.

Laurentia's head fell back. "Oh, Jasper, that feels so good." Jasper heard this name from her lips, and he loved to listen to her say his name and kissed his way back to her lips.

Laurentia felt his hard groin pushing against her stomach. She swayed back and forth, thinking that was what she should do, being new at this game. Jasper broke the kiss and looked into her violet eyes.

"My little vixen, if you keep doing that to me, we shall have to find a more suitable place to explore each other better." Jasper's eyes sparkle with desire.

She smiled; the thought of exploring Jasper's god-like body sounded all too delicious, and here was not the right place for that. "I do like that idea to explore you more, but you are right. We cannot get caught like this."

Jasper helped Laurentia's dress back to right before someone should hear them.

"We better get back before we are missed, my sweet." Jasper kissed Laurentia one last time, long and seductive for wanting more that would come later in private. They went back out from behind the hedge to the flower trail and strolled back to the party, which was in full swing.

They stopped and said hello to a few acquaintances that Jasper knew, introducing Laurentia to them. She felt that everyone was staring at her, for Jasper had not left her side all afternoon. Laurentia looked around for her charges, and she saw the twins talking in a group of girls about their ages, which made her feel content to see them not so far away if they needed her.

Lord Kingsley walked up; he bowed a good afternoon to Jasper and Laurentia and the rest of the group that had been growing around them.

Jesse said to Laurentia, "Lady Laurentia, you have the most beautiful violet eyes I have ever seen."

She smiled. "Thank you, my Lord, that is kind of you to say." Laurentia was feeling a little uncomfortable with Jasper standing beside her, that someone else would say something so bold to her of her appearance.

Jesse smiled back, "You are welcome, my Lady. May I say you are a gem brighter and more beautiful than the flower in this garden."

"Thank you—"

Jasper turned to Laurentia, cutting her off. "I believe that you haven't seen the swans down by the pond. Shall we have a look, my Lady?" He put his arm out for her to take. "If you all shall excuse us." Jasper bowed to the group as he pushed his temper back in check as they walk away. Then, with an impassive look, Jasper said, "There are rowboats to take out. Perhaps you would enjoy a ride in one?"

Laurentia looked up to Jasper's blue eyes and could tell he was not too pleased with Lord Kingsley's advances toward her. "I have not ridden in one since I was a girl."

"We must and shall rectify that, my sweet." He looked down at Laurentia with the corner of his lips twitching. She could see his mood was changing for the better.

Jasper wondered what the hell was Kingsley doing back there, trying to provoke a challenge out of him. In the past, being a close friends, they had sometimes chased the same women, but this was not acceptable today. He would set him straight later.

When they reached the pond, two white swans swam toward them. Laurentia beamed with joy. "Oh Jasper, they are beautiful. Look, they are swimming right for us, they are lovely. Are they not?"

Jasper smiled after hearing her say his name, and it sounded so natural for her to say it. He turned toward her, took her hands, then raised them to his lips and kissed ever so seductively. Laurentia looked up to his blue eyes; the sunlight was making them sparkle like jewels. She sighed, then thought for the first time, she could so easily fall in love with this beautiful man, a future duke.

Japer could not believe him about to say this, but it felt so right to speak with her.

"I have read that swans mate for life. When I made love to you last night, that was how I felt afterward, and when I was holding you in my arms, that is when I knew you were mine. I want you to be my marchioness, my future duchess, and my wife, Laurentia."

Laurentia would not believe what Jasper just said. It was so sweet, wonderful, and she felt the same way. But he did not say he loved me. Oh, how she dreamed someday, a handsome gentleman would sweep her off her feet and ask for her hand in marriage. She was no different from any other young lady to want that for herself. But she wanted to be in love; he had to love her too, and she must hear the word from him to accept his proposal.

Laurentia hesitated at first, then said, "It was truly wonderful the first time we made love, but when you or any man asks for my hand, I want to hear he loves me. You did not. I shall not go into a loveless marriage. So, no, I shall not marry you at this time."

Jasper raised an eyebrow, "So you are telling me no for now. Is that right?"

"Yes, that is what I am saying."

He was still looking into her eyes, trying to read what she was feeling; he could sense she wanted to say yes, but did not.

"I shall have to keep asking you, till you say yes, Laurentia. You are mine. No other man shall ever touch you as I have. I would kill him, mark my words." He was still holding her hands firmly and kissed them again. Suddenly, they heard the twins calling out to them, and their little time when it felt like it was just them in paradise was ended.

"Lord Bellator, Lady Sinclair," Aurora and Amara stopped in front of them, bouncing from foot to foot. "Mother said we could not go into a rowboat unless we have an adult with us. Oh, please, will you take us?" The twins said together.

Jasper started out saying, "I do not-" then Laurentia cut him off then finished, "That sounds like fun. Shall we all go together, my Lord?"

Jasper gave her a look that said, 'you are crazy.' Laurentia took Jasper's arm.

"We were just heading to the dock. Come along, Lady Amara and Lady Aurora." The twins followed in their wake as they headed to the dock that had several boats tied to it. Jasper was not too excited about riding in a small boat with his sisters. But if Laurentia wanted this, he could not say no. He must please her to win her heart.

Jasper waved a hand to the second boat by the dock. "This one looks like a good choice to ride in."

He stopped in front of the boat, stepped in first, then turned around to help Laurentia in next, suggesting she sit on the bench where he shall sit to row. Next, he assists his sisters, directing them to sit on the front bench. Finally, after untying the boat, he took up the oars and set off.

Seeing that she could help Jasper row, Laurentia asked. "Lord Bellator, perhaps I should help row with you, as it seems I am sitting beside you and the oar."

Amara said, "Oh, you should; it looks like fun. I would not mind trying some rowing myself."

Jasper cleared his throat to get their attention. "Rowing a boat is a man's job if one is in the boat with three women. I shall not look foolish to the eyes watching us from shore. So please, relax, and I shall do the work to take us about the pond here today."

Laurentia looked up at Jasper and giggled a bit. "I see your point, my Lord. You may row for us."

Amara said with a pout, "It would have been fun to try, maybe some other time, dear Brother."

Jasper started rowing across the pond. "When we go to our country estate, I shall take you out on the lake there and teach you to row a boat if you wish, Amara."

Amara smiled, "I would like that; thank you."

Laurentia had not seen Jasper's soft side to his sisters until now; she thought his offer was genuinely lovely and showed he cared for their feelings. She smiled and nodded her approval to him. Jasper then winked at Laurentia.

Aurora perked up, saying loudly. "Look at all the ducks over there," pointing to them. "Bellator, go closer, so we can see them. They are lovely and so many."

Amara said, "I counted fourteen ducks."

The twins stood up in the boat, rocking it back and forth. Jasper and Laurentia yelled at the same time, "Girls, Sit Down!"

They were still standing, and the boat was rocking harder. Aurora lost her balance, then fell into the water. Amara screamed, trying to catch her sister but tipping the boat over altogether. Jasper and Laurentia went flying into the water. Jasper swam to Laurentia first to help her. She came up to the surface and started treading water

"I am okay. Go to help your sisters."

"Are you sure, Laurentia?"

"Yes, go and help them. I can swim."

Jasper swam to his sisters, who were flapping around, going underwater; they did not swim well. Jasper grabbed Amara first as she was closest to him. He told her to stop struggling. "I have you, Amare, all is well." Putting an arm around her waist. Jasper then swam to Aurora, grabbed her from going under again, then told her to put her arms around his neck so she could cling to his back. With Aurora's arms still around his neck, he had an arm around Amara's waist, with one arm free. "We will all swim to the shore together."

The twins stopped panicking, for they knew Jasper had them, and he would get them to shore safely. They made it to the beach, and he asked if they are alright.

In the meantime, people who saw the boat capsize came running to their aid. He looked out to the water and saw that Laurentia had only swum halfway in. He took his boots, coat, and waistcoat off quickly and swam back out to help Laurentia. Jasper reached Laurentia once again, and she was thankful he came back for her, for swimming entirely dressed was quite exhausting to do. Jasper wrapped an arm around Laurentia's waist from her back, telling her to relax against him, that he shall get them into shore.

Laurentia did as Jasper said, and he took her to shore as promised. Jasper's arm felt like a steel bar around her waist, and she felt all his chest muscles through his wet shirt. It was not the right time to think about how wonderful they felt against her, but it was a nice feeling. So she sighed, tried to relax, and not make more work for his lordship.

Once they were sitting on the beach catching their breath, Laurentia looked up into Jasper's blue eyes, "Thank you for coming back out for me. I did not realize how far the shore was; thank you again, my Lord."

Jasper grabbed Laurentia's hands. "Are you alright, my sweet?"

She could see the panic in his eyes. Perhaps he did have real feelings for her. Laurentia smiled at him, "Yes, my Lord, I will be fine. I need just to catch my breath. As I said, that was a much longer swim to shore than I thought it was."

Jasper's expression changed to almost angry; he grabbed her shoulders.

"I asked you if you were sure for me to leave you. You said yes, save my sisters. You were not fine to leave by no means!

"Jasper, they needed more help; I can swim. You could see your sisters could not swim, and our clothing made things worse for all."

Jasper was surprised she said his name in front of

everyone who'd gathered around them. But at this moment, he did not care who heard it. He loved it when she said it. His expression softened.

"This whole ordeal had me frightened for your safety and my sisters'. I am sorry to have raised my voice to you, my Lady."

"The whole ordeal was stressful. But I do understand, my Lord."

Jasper stood, then put his hand out to help Laurentia to her feet. She took his hand to rise.

"Thank you, my Lord, for your help. I did not plan for a swim today. I must look a fright." Laurentia patted her hair with her free hand.

Jasper did not let go of her other hand; he lifted it to his lips, kissed her fingers, looking into her eyes, whispered, "You do mean everything to me, Laurentia, never doubt that ever." Then he stepped back and let go. They were surrounded by half the party now. The Duke and Duchess of Devonshire were at their daughters' sides, all in a panic, making a fuss and hugging them.

The duke walked over to check on his son and Lady Sinclair. "What happened out there, Son?"

"The girls stood up in the boat; they were over-excited over the damn ducks. Lady Aurora lost her balance and fell in, and Lady Amara tried to catch her and capsized the boat. Lady Laurentia and I told them to sit down, but they did not listen, as you can see. So, here we are, soaking wet, Your Grace." Jasper and Laurentia were still dripping water.

Louisa came over and handed Jasper and Laurentia a towel to dry off. "Oh, I am so sorry this happened here today, Your Grace."

"My dear sister-in-law, this is not something that

you could control. Not if this involved my daughters, as the family knows by now. All is well, and no one is hurt. Now, if you would excuse me, I have two very wet daughters to take home."

Duke bowed eloquently, then walked back over to his duchess and daughters. The girls walked with their heads down behind their parents as they headed for their carriage. After collecting his soaked clothes and putting his boots back on, Jasper put his arm out for Laurentia to escort her to his family carriage and to leave himself. Jasper must admit he had never left a party soaked to the bone.

Jasper walked Laurentia to the carriage, and just before they reached the carriage, he whispered to her, "I shall come to you tonight if that is what you wish."

Laurentia smiled then said softly, so he only could hear, "I shall be waiting for you, Jasper."

Jasper helped Laurentia up into the carriage; he bade everyone good afternoon, turned on his heel, and strolled away elegantly. Even soaking wet, Jasper walked perfectly. He was looking forward to seeing his love alone in her bedchamber that evening. That thought made the rest of his day full of anticipation.

Chapter 15

Whites Gentlemen Club

Jasper strolled through the salon. He saw Leopold talking to a waiter as he sat in a comfortable leather chair. He walked over, taking the empty seat across from his cousin.

Jasper said, "Not my ideal way of exiting a garden party today."

"That was not your style, Cousin, but made the conversation after you left perk up some, I may say."

After giving the waiter his drink order and they were alone, Jasper said, "I asked Lady Laurentia to marry me today. Unfortunately, she turned me down."

Leopold looked at Jasper with surprise. "I did not know you were that serious about her. I'm shocked, for you have only met."

Jasper looked around to check double no one was listening to them. "I went to her bedchamber last night at my parents' residence. Laurentia is magnificent, her curves, breasts, lips, hair, and those violet eyes. She is the perfect package. She is funny, feisty, brilliant, bold when needs be, and she can handle herself in the ton to be my marchioness, I am sure."

Leopold tilted his head, "That was rather foolish

of you to go to her bedchamber at your parents' home. What if someone saw you, the servants? If you are seriously going to marry the lady, think of her reputation being tarnished."

"Do you remember the secret passageway we played in when we were young? Laurentia's room is connected to them, and I went through the passageway last night, not seen by one soul," Jasper said with a shrug.

"That's very convenient for you. Who decided Lady Sinclair's room when she was hired?"

Jasper gave his wolfish smile, "You know I did, of course. No other man shall touch her as I have if they wish to live. She shall be mine, and you may mark my word on that, dear Cousin.

"Correct me if I am wrong. You did say the lady said no to your proposal."

Raising an eyebrow, Jasper replied, "Yes, she did reject my proposal. Laurentia has this idea that when she turns twenty-five, she shall receive a trust fund from her parents that they left her, and she plans to travel to the continent and other places. Being a governess is her way of being independent of her brother, so she can do as she feels free."

"She turned you down. I am a little shocked by that. Are you losing your touch with the ladies?" Leopold said with a big smirk.

"You know I love a challenge, and she is definitely giving me one. It makes the game of seduction more fun, as you know. She shall be mine, you shall see. I never give up on something I want, and I want Lady Laurentia Sinclair as my wife."

"That, dear Cousin, I do not doubt whatsoever. I am hungry. Shall we have a bite to eat in the dining room?"

Jasper waves his hand. "Lead the way. To think of it, I somehow missed lunch today." They both laughed as they strolled toward the dining room.

Once they had given their order—oyster stew, a fine merlot, and a thick slab of beef—Jasper looked toward the door and watched as Victor walked in. When he saw his cousins, he joined them.

"I thought I'd find you here tonight, after that disaster at the garden party today. Mind if I join you?" Victor smiled. Jasper, waving a hand to an empty chair at the table.

"By all means, please do," Jasper said, frowning when reminded of the day's mishaps. Then, when the waiter came to take his order, Victor asked, "Has the chef-prepared duck this evening, my good man?"

The waiter said, "Yes, roasted with a bourbon sauce, and new potatoes served with it."

Victor, almost laughing, "That sounds divine, and whatever the soup of the day you are serving tonight, I shall have that too." The waiter bowed, hurry away.

"Amusing," Jasper said, clearly not amused.

Victor, still trying to hold back laughter, said, "Come on, in a rowboat with three chits, and it turns over because of counting ducks. You were all soaking wet. What a sight that was, Bellator."

"If you remember right, two of the passengers in the boat were my sisters, and I would hardly consider them as a chit. They could not swim, so I took them to shore first and helped Lady Laurentia half the way into the shore also. Not my idea of a good time."

Victor, still smiling, said, "Amusing or not, you were the talk for the rest of the afternoon."

Jasper knew the guests would talk about the incident. But no one would say anything to his face out of respect for his status. So instead, his family would jest for a while and put in a few jabs.

After the waiter came with their food, Leopold looked at Jasper's oyster stew with disgust. "I don't know how you can eat those slimy things."

"In a stew, they're cooked, and they give an excellent flavor. You should try it."

Leopold wrinkled his nose. "No, thank you, it is all yours." As they ate, they talked about upcoming events.

Jasper said, "The first ball of the season at your parent home on Hanover Square, Leopold. Lady Louisa amazes me, putting on two events back-to-back like that, an incredible woman your mother."

"She loves the challenge! Mother told me in the past that she likes having her events first, so she can go to all the other balls and parties to see if they could measure up to her own. Nobody can come close to outdoing mother's galas."

"That's for sure," Victor agreed as he ate his soup.

Leopold said, "There is a soiree at Lord and Lady Wilmore's tonight. Either of you going to that one?"

Jasper finished his oyster stew, "No, I am going to pass on that one but, after I finish my steak, I shall see if there is any action in the card room here tonight."

Victor said, "I shall join you at the card table. I'm feeling lucky tonight; I hope all the gentlemen's pockets are full this evening, for I tend to take the winnings from the table, Bellator."

Jasper nodded, "I feel luck shall happen in my

seat also, Victor. Let us both clean the table tonight, Raventon style."

Victor replied, "Brilliant idea!"

Leopold said with a wicked grin, "I am going to the soiree to meet up with Countess Ashworth. I have an itch to fulfill."

As their entrees were delivered, Jasper said to Leopold, "Be careful with that one. She likes to leave teeth marks."

Leopold laughed. "Yes, I've felt them already; she is a lioness for sure and very frisky in the bedchamber."

They all laughed and started on their entrees. Victor said to Jasper with a smirk.

"The duck is excellent tonight, Cousin. Would you care for some?"

Jasper glared, "Not tonight."

"So touchy are we. I shall stop," Victor replied.

After they finished their meals, Leopold bade them good-night, and Jasper and Victor remained and headed for the card room.

Chapter 16

When the Raventon family and Laurentia reached home, the duchess ordered hot baths to be sent up for Amara, Aurora, and Lady Sinclair.

"Yes, my Grace," Wesley said. "Anything else for them? They do look a little wet and cold."

"Yes, trays of hot tea and finger sandwiches also. And have a spread put out for the Duke and I. We missed lunch today at the party."

"As you wish, Your Grace, right away," Wesley hurried to the kitchen to see that the tasks are done.

Laurentia and the twins walked up the main staircase to their bedchambers to have their baths. As Laurentia entered her room, she was thinking about Jasper, of all that transpired between them today and last night. But then, a knock on the door brought Laurentia out of her thoughts for a particular dark hair Lord.

She called out, "Enter," four footmen enter carrying buckets of hot water.

One footman said, "Hot water for your bath, my Lady. Where would you like your bath set up?" Laurentia tells them to go ahead into her dressing room and fill the tub there.

Her maid Sandra appears, "Oh my dear, my Lady, you are soaking wet. What happen?" "It is a long story. Let's just say I fell out of a rowboat and into the pound. Not by choice is all." Sandra ushers the footmen to fill the tub and exit. Then follows her Lady into the dressing room to help her get out of the wet clothes she was wearing

Laurentia stepped into the tub and sat down. "Oh, this feels wonderful after my cold ride back from the garden party. Sandra, help me wash my hair, please; I smell like pond water."

Sandra picks up a vase to rewet Laurentia's hair, then adds soap and rinses. She then picks up a sponge to wash her back with, finishes and hands the sponge to Laurentia to do the rest of her body. Laurentia washes everywhere else, then leans back to relax in hot water.

"Sandra, I am going to relax in the tub for a while. You may leave me."

"A tea tray and little sandwiches have arrived for you; I shall pour you a cup and bring this small table over so that you may reach

Laurentia sipped the tea and ate two finger sandwiches, and it was nice to be alone. Now her mind drifted back to Jasper. He is so handsome; those sparkling blue eyes are breathtaking. The way he looked at me and his wicket smiled when it appears to give me beautiful shivers, for I know he is thinking naughty thoughts, and even worse, I do want him to touch me. His raven black hair that dusted his shoulder, his body was a temple with muscles. He's so wonderful, and what am I going to do? Then on top of it all, Jasper asked me to be his Marchioness today.

I never thought this would happen to me. His

lordship is well respected, wealthy, and shall be a future duke one day. Oh, I do love him. I cannot deny that. This whole affair is all happening too fast. But I want love, and Jasper has not said he loves me yet. I shall refuse to marry anyone if he has not said or declared he loves me. I must stand my ground on that, so it shall be up to him to say it. But if I marry Jasper, my dreams to travel the world shall be gone. She sighed again and wished her mother was still alive to talk to. I really do not have anyone to confide in; it saddens me to think about that. Oh well, it has been that way for many years, and one does get used to it after a while. Laurentia sighed.

A knock on the door, then Sandra pecks her head in. "You should get out of the water, my Lady, before you prune your lovely skin."

"Your right; bring me a towel, Sandra," Laurentia said as she stands.

She stepped out of the tub and wrapped a soft towel around her to dry off. Laurentia put a long robe on for comfort, deciding only to dress for dinner. She chose to read for a while and walked to the end table by her bed and saw the books Jasper had given her. She picked up the book Sense and Sensibility, then settled into the chair by the fireplace. Looking at the book in her hands, she said to herself, "Maybe reading this book might help me figure out my future a little better. The title is appropriate for the situation in hand." She opened it to the first page and began reading.

At dinner time, Laurentia walked into the dining room, smiling at everyone as she entered. She curtsied to the duke and duchess, "I hope I am not late. I fell asleep reading in my room."

The duke said, "Not at all; we all just arrived not long ago. Would you like some wine, Lady Sinclair?"

"Yes, that would be lovely, Your Grace. Unfortunately, I cannot seem to warm up since we returned from the garden party."

The duchess asked, "Would you like some hot tea to warm you?"

A footman set a bowl of soup in front of Laurentia. She saw the steam coming off the soup, "The soup looks plenty warm, it should do the trick. Thank you, Your Grace."

Amara cleared her throat to have everyone's attention on her, took a deep breath, then said, "Do you think Jasper will be angry with Aurora and me, Father? We did embarrass him today."

The duke looked to his daughters, who were looking down for his answer. "Jasper probably is not too happy with either of you right now. But he does not carry grudges for long, do not fret, my dears."

Aurora looked up, "I hope so, Father, it was my fault. I stood up first in the boat."

Amara chimed in, "No, I stood; first, I am to blame."

The duchess stopped them from arguing by saying, "If you apologize to Jasper for your actions, all shall be well again."

Amara said, "But it was an embarrassment to have been seen soaking wet. Appearance is important to Jasper. I can only imagine the talk after we left."

The duke said, "your mother will shut down all that conversation tonight when we go to the soiree at Lord and Lady Wilmore's. Lady Laurentia, would you care to join us?"

Laurentia answered, "I have had my fill of excitement for today. So I prefer to stay in this evening, Your Grace. But thank you for the invitation."

The duke said, "You are becoming like a family member, being a part of our household and all. Your parents were well received in the ton, and it should be only natural that you are too, my dear."

Laurentia smiles, then wiped a tear from the corner of her eye. "That very kind for you to say, Your Grace, and I am honored to be referred to as a family member."

The duchess said, "You have fit in with us nicely, and the girls adore you."

Amara and Aurora nodded in agreement. Amara said with a smile, "I believe Jasper likes you, too. When he appears, it seems he likes being around you mostly."

The Duchess raised an eyebrow as she looked at Laurentia, thinking, Amara is right, my son is buzzing around Laurentia as if he's the bee and she is the nectar from a flower. Interesting thought.

Laurentia reassured them, "He is just kind is all, for I am new among the ton." She did not make eye contact with anyone, so they wouldn't think anything was happening between them. Then, Laurentia changed the subject by asking the twins if they should go to Bond Street tomorrow to pick up some last-minute accessories for their first ball.

They perked up, and Aurora said, "Yes, Mother, we must. I would love a new fan."

Amara said, "Oh, could we, Mother? I know there is something I would find that I must have."

The duchess thought, 'intelligent girl, changing the subject from her and my son. I shall watch those two a little closer.'

Duchess answered her daughters, "Yes, my loves, we could go after luncheon. Being it is your first ball, we have to make sure we have everything perfect for the event." The rest of the dinner conversation was about the ball for Aurora, and Amara dominated the conversation throughout the meal.

Not too long after dinner, the duke and duchess left for the soiree. The twins and Laurentia stayed in the front parlor; they decided to work on some embroidery. The night was going by fast. Before she knew it, it was ten o'clock. Laurentia looked to the girls to see them yawning.

Laurentia suggested, "It's almost ten, I think we should start for bed. I am feeling tired myself, plus tomorrow night we shall be out late, with the ball and all."

They stood, as they all agreed, it was a good idea. Walking up the main staircase, the twins told Laurentia once again that they were excited about the ball and giggled as they entered their bedchamber and bade good night. Laurentia continued down the corridor to her bedchamber, stepped through the door, and saw the fireplace's fire burning.

Sandra came from the dressing room door to help Laurentia undress for the evening. Laurentia told her maid she would like the light blue silk nightgown tonight. After dressing, Laurentia sat at her dressing table to take down her hair and brush it out.

"Thanks, Sandra. I shall not need you anymore tonight. You may retire too."

Laurentia continued brushing her hair and wondered if Jasper was still coming tonight. Her wavy hair fell to the middle of her back. She stood then walked over to the window, pulled the curtain back, and, looking up at the moon, she sighed. Laurentia did not hear or sense Jasper walking up behind her. She was too lost in her thought.

Jasper whispered in her ear, "You look beautiful by the window with the moonlight shining through your lovely golden hair." He kissed, then nibbled on her ear.

Laurentia turned around slowly, looking up into Jasper's blue eyes. "I was thinking about you."

Jasper tilted his head, trying to read her, "I do like to hear that, my sweet. I do hope you were thinking of how my lips felt against yours."

He took her into his arms, kissed her deeply and demandingly. Laurentia stood on her toes, wrapped her arms around his neck, then leaned into him. Jasper started kissing down her neck. "Tell me what you were thinking, my sweet, sweet angel."

"Mmm, I was thinking of you if you were coming tonight, and I like this togetherness."

"You taste so good, but from when the moment I walked into the room, one of the things I desired to do is to undress you. It would be a real pleasure to undress you myself, and it would be like unwrapping a gift, just for me alone."

She looked up to him, "I would have to tell my maid next time that I do not need her help and send her away. So, I could be that gift for you," Laurentia giggles.

"But tonight, I can still eat you alive." He picked her up and carried her to the bed. Jasper put Laurentia on her feet first, then bent down and pulled her nightgown off. "Did I tell you before my favorite color is blue?"

Laurentia nodded. "I shall wear it just for you."

Jasper picked her up and lay her on the bed with her long blonde hair fanning out over the pillows. "So beautiful you are, Laurentia, you are in my dreams, looking as you are right now." He took his cravat off, then his coat, his waistcoat, and his shirt.

"Let me help you with that," Laurentia said, sitting up. She got off the bed, then pushed him to sit on the edge of the bed. She pulled his boots off first, stockings too, and unfastened his sword belt, taking it and laying it on a chair nearby, then his breeches. Jasper's erection did not surprise Laurentia when she pulls them off. Instead, she stared down at it and wet her lips, stepping between his legs.

"You said earlier today we could explore each other bodies later. Did you not, my Jasper? I do believe it is later." She looked down into those pools of blue eyes. Jasper rested his hands on her waist, then pulled her over to him as he lay.

"Oh, yes, it is much later, you may touch away, my sweet."

Laurentia lay on top of him; she first ran her hand along his muscular abs, then with her fingertips, she ran them over his chest. She smiled at the freedom to touch him finally. Laurentia bent down, laying little kisses across his chest.

Jasper didn't know if this was torture or pleasure, letting Laurentia have free rain touching him. He could see in her eyes that she enjoyed touching him freely, but he must take control.

Jasper said through gritted teeth, "As much as you are enjoying this, my sweet, you are undoing me. I do not know how long I can take this."

Lifting her head, she looked him in the eyes, "I

do like touching you. Doesn't this feel good, my touch?" Laurentia ran the tip of her finger across his chest.

"Oh, it feels good, too good. That's the problem."

She looks at him, confused. "I do not understand."

Jasper sigh. "Male bodies work a lot different than a female. When I touch you, I can control my desires, but when you touch me, as you are now, my desires explode through my veins, pumping hard. I can only take so much, and then I must have you fast. I do so much want you to enjoy the pleasure of making love slow and easy pleasurable. You, see?"

Laurentia pouted. "That's not fair."

Jasper decided they'd had enough of talking and flipped her under him as her head hit the pillows. "With me on top, we may touch together."

He took her lips, all demanding, his tongue skimming the inside of her mouth, and she did the same to him. Jasper kissed along her cheek, then down her neck. He lifted his head to look at her breast he was holding in his hands, and that wicked smile appeared.

"You are perfect, my sweet, oh so perfect, everywhere."

With that said, he bent his head, then put his lips around her left nipple to taste her. He took his tongue, flicking her nipple around, circling his tongue around the nipple, and put it back in his mouth to suck. Then he did the same to other breasts. Laurentia moaned on the second one and ran her fingers through Jasper's hair. When she does that, he lightly nipped one nipple with his teeth. He had to have her now. He kissed her wildly as he spread her legs apart, thrusting all the way in. He lifted his head to look Laurentia in the eyes. "We are going to do this nice and slow."

He started moving in and out in a slow, smooth rhythm. "Look at me, my sweet look into my eyes. I want to see the pleasure we are doing together and see you orgasm with mine. That is it, feel that with me." Jasper moved a little faster, and Laurentia met his movement and rhythm, pushing her hips up to his. "You feel so good, so tight around me, my sweet."

Laurentia wished he would go a little faster. Still looking into his eyes, she started to feel the pleasure build below, quivers building. "Oh, Jasper, that feels so good."

He started moving faster, and he felt her body beginning to pulse.

"Come with me, let fly. Can you feel it, my sweet? We shall soar together. Keep looking into my eyes, Laurentia."

Laurentia yelled, "Oh, yes, Jasper!"

Then she went over the edge, shivering and shaking. Jasper now pumped harder, then goes over the edge with her in an eruption that made him breathless. Lying on top of her panting, Jasper tried to collect his thoughts, and Laurentia tried to catch her breath. He rolled over to his back and pulled her into his arms. "I have waited so long to find you. You are mine, Laurentia." Then he kissed her tenderly.

That moved Laurentia. 'Oh, I love him, can this be true.'

Laurentia lay her head on Jasper's shoulder. He had his arms around her, and she snuggled into his side.

Jasper said, "I do think your maid is aware of us, with the pleasure yells we just shared. . I shall talk with her at first light, that she is not to share with my parents' or servants what we are sharing here. Servants do like to talk of their masters and mistress, indiscretions. I shall not have your honor soiled before we are wed."

Laurentia reacts to what Jasper said. She turns over and looks him in the eyes.

"Yesterday morning after you took my maiden the night before, the blood left on my sheets. I had my maid rid them from the household, and I have already told her not to talk of it to anyone. Sandra has been my personal maid since I was thirteen. We have been through a lot together, ups and downs. She is loyal to me."

"That is good to hear; she is loyal to you."

"I did turn you down today earlier when you asked me to marry you. What makes you think that's changed?"

"My sweet we, you and I have made love three times already. You could be with the child. We would need to wed right away, so no question is asked of its conception, my heir. It's as simple as that. My mother and aunts shall help you with all the wedding planning you need to do."

Laurentia sat up. "I did not say yes to your proposal," she thundered and crossed her arms.

Jasper sat up too and did not like being shouted at. He breathed in and out to keep control, then said calmly," Laurentia, I know you have feelings for me, as I do for you. We have the genuine passion we share when we are making love. You are the one I want to share my life with, and I cannot live without you in it."

Laurentia was frustrated. *He has not said he loves me; he is doing the honorable thing for what we shared in bed. Not enough!*

"You would ruin my plan of being independent and seeing the world, my Lord. Therefore, you shall not manipulate me into marrying you."

Jasper was not too happy with what she was saying, and she was back to calling him lord again in private. He tried to control his temper; he took a deep breath and tried to reason with her.

"Laurentia, I shall not force you to marry me or manipulate you in any way. I want you to be mine freely. I could not stand to see any other man touch you as I have. Do you understand what I am saying to you?"

"Yes, you want to possess me like an object, is that it?"

Jasper shot off the bed and began pacing the floor. *'Lord, help me. I made love to her, held her, kiss her tenderly, told her I want to share my life with her. What am I doing wrong?'* He stopped in the middle of the floor and stared at Laurentia. *'I shall just have to show her more how I feel when she is in my arms.'*

Laurentia watched him pace the floor like a caged animal, then when he stopped and was standing there just staring at her sternly, she asked, "Are you going to be leaving now, my Lord?"

"No, I am not! "Jasper strolled right back to the bed, then pounced on Laurentia, sweeping her into his arm and kissing her with passion. Laurentia melted right back into his strong arm. He kissed down her body in between her legs, kissing the insides of her thighs first to tease her. Laurentia lay on her back, panting, letting Jasper have his way with her. Oh, how she enjoys this truly.

Jasper spread her with his fingers and started licking her sweet little bud, which was swelling with each lick. He pleased her with his masterful ways and wanted her to feel the joy he could give her body. Laurentia grabbed the sheets to steady herself as he played her body like a fine instrument, as he was making her sing out his name in ecstasy. Laurentia moaned with bliss.

A big wave of pleasure shot through her body, like a tidal wave, rolling her eyes back and curling her toes. Wow, that was wonderful. Laurentia had never felt anything like that before and was in sheer bliss. Jasper moved back up her body, kissing her neck, then when he reached her lips, he entered her in one thrust and moving fast and steady. He whispered in her ear, "My sweet, you shall come with me again."

Laurentia moaned, "I don't know if I can so soon, Jasper. That was wonderful, oh, so good."

Jasper was building the momentum more. "You must trust me, and we shall soar together. I shall make your body sing even more," he whispered in her ear. Jasper was gritting his teeth, trying not to come until Laurentia started to come with him.

Laurentia felt another wave building below. Oh, how is he doing this to me? This is undoing my mind completely and is so overwhelming. Laurentia grabbed ahold of Jasper's shoulder to hang on.

Jasper felt her body shivering. Yes, she is coming for me. He took her lips to help her explode with him, and they took that ride to paradise together. They roared with passion together, riding a tidal wave that went on and on and on and on…

That was the best one they'd shared; they both were thinking as they came back to earth together as one.

"Wow," Jasper said. "I never have done that to anyone that powerful. That was indescribably wonderful for both of us. You are the perfect woman for me in and out of bed, Laurentia."

"You made my toes curl both times and even more the second time. That felt wonderful and deliciously good."

"It shall be my life's role always to please you in bed and everything we do together as life partners, Laurentia. I pledge that to you." Jasper kissed her tenderly, then rolled to his back. Laurentia snuggled into his side, and he wrapped his arms around her and held her tight. 'That had to prove how much I care for her, my pledge,' Jasper thought and kissed the top of Laurentia's head. They fell to sleep together, in each other arms, safe and sound, in their world of paradise.

Chapter 17

Never Thought She Fine Love

Laurentia glided down the main stairs, thinking of all that had occurred in the last twenty-four hours. Jasper was all she could think about, in his arms kissing her, making incredible love, his proposal, and his demand that she marries him, plus his pledge. I shall not marry him until he says he loves me, and I shall not bend my decision.

Jasper was most definitely trying to bend that, making love to her so overwhelmingly and tenderly holding her as they slept. He left Laurentia's bed about five-thirty, before the house started to awake. Jasper made mad love to Laurentia one more time before leaving her and after a deep penetrating kiss. The Marquess Bellator is the perfect man, and he wants Lady Laurentia Sinclair as his wife.

"Good morning, Wesley," Laurentia said as she stepped off the staircase. He was talking with two footmen, ordering what work needed to be accomplished this morning. It was eight-thirty as Laurentia slept a few more hours after Jasper left her bed.

"Good morning, my Lady, Her Grace is in the dining room, breaking her fast. She wishes for you to join her there."

"Thank you, Wesley. I am on my way. Are my charges up yet?"

"They just woke and shall be down in a half-hour."

Walking into the dining room, Laurentia curtsied to the duchess, bid her good morning, and took the chair across from her.

The duchess said, "You look well-rested; I was worried that when you were chilled yesterday, you may have caught a cold."

"Staying home last night and resting was what I needed. Lady Aurora and Lady Amara are more than excited for their first ball this evening. It's all they spoke of until we retired last night."

"It's mostly family and close friends, close to one hundred or more guests tonight. It shall be a crush. My sister-in-law Lady Louisa always has extravagant balls and parties. The girls' gowns and yours shall be delivered this morning with a seamstress. You shall try them on to make sure all is perfect; the seamstress shall make any last-minute alterations if needed. Then we shall have luncheon and head to Bond Street for last-minute buys we need."

Laurentia smiled, "That sounds like a nice start for the day. I think to keep the twins on steady, but light activities shall help keep their nervousness at bay."

Duchess said, "That is my precise goal for today. I do not want my daughter a bundle of nerves to-night. I want them to be perfection; they are Raventon's; they need to shine. We both know this is not their come out to the ton. That will be next year, of course. I suppose you could say this is a practice run."

Laurentia clapped her hands together, "I know they shall do well, Your Grace; they have both of us to lead them on."

Duchess said, laughing, "Yes, I have a lot of confidence in them and us."

Amara and Aurora entered the room. "Good morning, Mother," they both said as they kissed her on the cheeks.

"Morning, my loves, have a seat. The wellbake apple tart are delicious. Bridget has achieved magic again."

"Good morning, Lady Sinclair," they greeted their governess.

Aurora said, "It's a good thing our brothers are not here. That means we shall actually be able to eat two if we wish."

Amara told Laurentia, "Jasper and Drake love Bridget's bake goods, they never share any of them. When they see them, the rest are gone in minutes if we turn our backs, and the plate is empty for sure." A footman served tea and the tarts to the twins and Laurentia.

Aurora said, "Mother, I hope the day goes by quickly. I cannot wait until we go to the ball tonight."

Duchess said, "We have a lot to do today; time shall go by fast. You shall see."

Laurentia says, "This tart is really delicious. I can see why the plate empties quickly."

Amara said, "I shall tell Bridget you love them too, and maybe she shall make them more often."

"Make what more often?" Drake strolled in. "I smell Bridget's wellbake apple tarts. It's my lucky day to show up here so early."

The duchess cleared her voice to get Drake's attention. He looks to his mother, a cup of coffee in one hand and a plate with three tarts in the other. "Oh, good morning, ladies. It's a lovely day today." He bit into a tart. "I shall have to tell Jasper what he missed this morning when I see him later."

Duchess asked, "Why are you here so early, Son?"

"I have some paperwork to go over with Father. Is he in his library?" Drake sat at the table beside Laurentia. "And besides, where else can I see England's four most beautiful ladies so early in the morning?" Drake smiled handsomely for them.

Aurora said, "Drake, have you seen Jasper since yesterday's garden party?"

"No, I just came straight from the docks. One of my ships came in yesterday with a new shipment that kept me busy all day yesterday in the warehouse. So what happened at the party?"

Aurora hesitated then said, "There was a little boating accident, and Jasper ended up all wet."

Drake raised an eyebrow. "I bet you and Amara had something to do with that. Is that why you asked?"

Aurora said, "Yes, we did, but did not mean to."

"I see. If I did not have to see Father before he goes off to Parliament, I would ask about the story a little more. I shall have to find out later, little sisters. You said Jasper was all wet? "Drake asked with a smirk, and the twins nodded yes together. Drake stood, took one last sip of coffee, and picked up another tart. "I most definitely shall hear that one later, for sure. Mother, is Father still in his library?"

"Yes, he has not left yet," Duchess said before she sipped her tea.

Drake bowed and bade them a good day. "Tell

Bridget she has not lost her touch on making apple tarts." He turned and walked out to see the duke.

Drake knocks on the door then enters the library; he saw his father at his desk. The Duke looks up. "Good morning, Drake. I did not think I would see you here at this hour, with a shipment that arrived yesterday afternoon. Come have a seat, tell me of what new cargo you brought back this voyage." Drake walked over and took the chair in front of the desk.

"This ship had the usual wines and brandy. The new item, I believe, would be a hit is French-made cheeses. I have brought three different kinds back, Roquefort, Camembert, and Brie. I plan to sell them to a few markets and have King George try them, plus his court. Having the palace try them first shall for sure make them spread through the ton. You and I both know that the ton has to have everything new that was served at the palace. What do you think, Father?"

Duke was silent for a moment. "Someone has to start with the new imports; why not us. Cheese, you say. The English have a bland pellet, but different cheese might work, a new taste, and the palace is a brilliant idea."

Drake smiles to his father's approval. "As we speak, a crate with my three new flavors of cheese are delivered to the palace. Compliments from the Raventon Import Company to the King and Queen as a gift."

The duke was beaming, "My son, I have taught you well."

Drake stood," Yes, Father, you have. Well, I need to get back to the warehouse to make sure my cargo is safe and inventory. Did you look over my ideas on the India imports I have in mind for my newest adventures?"

I had and commissioned a new ship to be built, and we shall give it a go. Your Mother shall love the idea of having dibs on the best silks when they come in, along with your sisters. Plus, the new spices and the rest sound intriguing enough."

"Brilliant Father, on the plans for another ship, and yes, all the Raventon women shall have first dibs on the new silks once Mother has her ways." He winks at his Father.

Duke laughed, then stood, and he comes around the desk. "I must leave for my meeting. I shall walk you out, Son."

After Drake and his father met, the duke found the women in the front parlor.

"What is all this laughter I heard earlier?" he asked with a smirk.

The twins stood and rushed to him for a hug.

Amara said, "It's so good of you to stop and say good morning to us before you leave for the day, Father." They both kissed his cheeks.

"And miss out on my hugs from my beauties? My whole day would be off." He kissed their foreheads. He then stepped over to his duchess, took her hand, kissed, "I shall see you at dinner, my love, and do we not have some ball tonight?"

Aurora and Amara both yelled, "Father, you know there is. We have been talking about it for weeks."

Duke laughed, "Yes, I think I remember now."

The duchess smiled at the duke. "You do love to tease them so, my love. We have a busy day ahead of us, and we are waiting for the gowns to be delivered, then we're off to Bond Street, and so on. See you this evening."

Duke smiled down at her and kissed her tenderly. "Until this evening, my darling." He bowed eloquently then left the room, with Drake in this wake. Laurentia could see where Jasper got his charm and his command of a room.

As they approached the front door, the duke instructed Wesley that he was to put it in his suite when the package from the jeweler arrived. "My Duchess seems to have everything in hand. Make sure she has whatever she needed."

"Yes, Your Grace always." Wesley opened the door, then bowed to the Duke and Lord Drake as they left.

They walked down the front stair together, and the duke gave Drake's horse an appreciative look. "I sometimes miss riding a horse as I please."

"Why do you not?"

"Well, Drake, when you get older, and with family, there are standards one should uphold. That beast you ride there does look like fun to have him between your legs. I hear he scares and abuses your stable hands daily."

Drake laughed, "That is what I'm told, but he's a dream to ride."

Drake mounted and relieved the stallion from the scared groom. Drake waved to his father and was off.

The duke thought as the coach rolls into motion, I shall have to find a beast of a horse for myself by the time we retreat to the country after the London season has ended. Drake is right in one aspect; I can do whatever I please. He laughed out loud.

Chapter 18

Shopping Is Never Dull on Bond Street

Jasper was walking out of Heming Jewelers as his mother's coach passed by. Jasper had decided to have a custom engagement ring made for Laurentia. He ordered the ring to have a diamond that was three carats cut marquise with two round-cut amethysts, one carat each placed on either side of the central diamond to match Laurentia's eyes and two more diamonds outside of each amethyst. The band was of thick gold, with an engraving inside the band that read 'With all my heart Jasper.'

He thought, 'I hope she likes it. I want to propose to her again in my mother's garden, in front of the fountain. That is where we first kissed. I had felt her passion that night and wanted her for my own ever since that night.' Jasper shook his head. He had never had feelings for any woman like this before. When I'm sleeping in my dreams, she is always in my thoughts, and those beautiful violet eyes are branded into my memory. Working in my library on estate business, she is there, riding my horse in Hyde Park, she's there, even when I am eating, I can't get Laurentia off my mind. Lord, help me; I believe I am in love. I hope this ring shall convince Laurentia how much I want her to be my Marchioness and share the rest of our lives together. Well, I just paid a hefty sum to have her ring finished by noon on Sunday. I shall find out what my future has entailed for me then. That was the first time Jasper felt the word love for a woman ever, besides his family members, and that was a whole different kind of love.

Jasper watched where the coach stopped, just a short block from him. He decided to stroll over to the coach, nodding to acquaintances as he walked. About twenty feet from the coach, he stopped and leaned against a tree to watch his family and future wife descend from the coach, and then they went into a millinery shop. Laurentia was the last one out of the coach. She stopped a few steps from the coach, looking around as if to find someone watching her. Laurentia said something to the footman holding the shop door before she entered. Now feeling curious, Jasper walked on to the shop. The groom was waiting outside at the door, and he saw Jasper walking toward him. The groom straightened, then bowed to Jasper

"What did Lady Sinclair say to you before she entered the shop?"

The footman answered, "She is certain someone is watching her when she is out of the home. She has said that the last two days on her outings, my Lord."

Jasper raised an eyebrow, "You mean to tell me she felt this before?"

"Yes, my Lord."

"And have you seen anyone about out of the ordinary?"

"No, my Lord, I have not noticed anyone."

"I see. I do want to hear if this continues and if

someone approaches Lady Sinclair. Do I make my-self clear?" Jasper gave him a menacing look.

"Crystal clear, my Lord."

Jasper entered the shop to see his mother talking to the milliner; his sisters were looking at fans near the shop's back, and Laurentia was looking at hats in the front. Laurentia noticed Jasper right away when he entered, and a slow smile lit her face as she looked up to see him there. The four other ladies who were in the shop were astonished to see his lordship in the millinery shop. They stopped what they were doing and curtsied to him. Jasper nods for them to rise.

Duchess was intrigued to see her son standing in a millinery shop; she excused herself from the milli-ner and walked over to him.

"Ah, your Grace, it's a lovely afternoon. I was strolling past, saw your coach out front, and decided to pop in to see how your outing is fairing," Jasper said with an impassive look.

Duchess raised an eyebrow at her son. "We are picking up a few last-minute items for the ball to-night. It is a nice afternoon to stroll, Lord Bellator." The duchess thought to herself, 'My son has never shown any interest in a women's shop before. Not until the new young, lovely governess was hired. What is he about with his actions? She is an Earl's daughter, and this could be good.'

The twins saw their brother; they burst with de-light and rushed over to him. Amara gave her sister a look of solidarity, then said, "Lord Bellator, we are so sorry about what happened yesterday, the boat, the unexpected plunge into the pond, you were all so wet. Shall you forgive us?" They stood in front of him, looking up to him with pleading faces.

"You need to control your behavior better, in and around the ton. Yes, it was your fault about what happened yesterday. But you are my sometimes too high-spirited little sisters that I do love. Yes, I shall forgive you on this incident this time."

"Oh, we do love you too, big Brother," they squealed together as they just about knocked Jasper over, hugging him fiercely. Jasper kissed the top of their heads and patted their backs.

Laurentia was smiling as she walked closer to the little reunion. She caught Jasper's eye, and the corner of his lips twitched.

Aurora said, "I have almost picked a new fan for tonight. I shall return to my task. I have mastered the technique of using a fan when one is talking." She giggled as she walked away. Amara said, "Yes, you have, and I think I should have a new one too. I'm not as good as you, Aurora. But in time, I shall achieve the skill." The twins walked back to the fan display, and they kept opening and closing the fans, trying to pick the right one.

The duchess said to Jasper, "Thank you for relieving their guilt; they have been distraught that you would not forgive them for the disaster they created yesterday."

"They are my younger sisters. I could not stay angry with them for long. They are reckless at times; this time, no permanent harm was done."

"Yes, they can sometimes be a handful; that is all too true. With a little more work on behavior, your sisters shall be the talk of the ton. After all, we are Raventon's, and one has to remember that." Duchess could see Jasper wanted to talk with Laurentia, and she excused herself to finish her business with the milliner.

Laurentia moved closer to talk with Jasper. "You look very lovely today, Lady Sinclair. It is a nice afternoon, not a cloud in the sky, is it not?"

Laurentia tried not to smile. "Thank you for your kind words, my Lord. I would not mind some fresh air, as it is a lovely day. I have finished with what I wanted here."

"It would be an honor to escort you outside for some air, my Lady," Jasper said, as he put his arm out so she could take it.

"I shall just put my items over there and credit them to my account and have them wrapped."

When Laurentia returned Jasper took the wrapped packages and put his arm out to escort her outside. She assured the duchess they would be just outside waiting.

"No need to hurry; I am in good company, your Grace," Laurentia called.

As the two walked out, duchess thought, 'There is most something going on between the two.'

Jasper handed the package to one of his mother's grooms to be put inside the coach and free his hands. Then he saw a bench about ten feet from the coach. He gestured toward the bench to go over and have a seat together.

Jasper said as they sat down. "If eyes were not on us right now, you would be in my arms this minute and my lips on yours."

Laurentia looked up into Jasper's blue eyes. "That is what I desire too, but as you said, too many eyes are on us." She smiled, looking downward.

"When I was walking toward the coach, I saw that you stopped and looked around. What was that about, my sweet?"

Laurentia turned toward Jasper. "It could be nothing. But when I leave your parent's residence, I feel as if someone is following and watching me. It's a strange feeling, I never felt before."

"You only just started to sense that? How long ago did this start?"

"The last two days."

"I shall talk with His Grace, that he needs to increase the number of servants that are out with you, Mother, and the twins. I want you safe and to feel safe."

Jasper picked up Laurentia's hand and kissed it, looking into her eyes. "I haven't asked if you are going to the ball tonight, my sweet."

"Yes, I am looking forward to it. I do enjoy dancing, and I have heard this ball shall be an extravagant event. Do you dance, my Lord?"

"Yes, on occasion, I do. I want your first waltz. No, make it all your waltzes. I do not like the idea of another man holding you that close."

Laurentia looked at Jasper, appalled. "I shall dance with whomever I wish. Don't you dare start telling me otherwise, what I can do and not do. I shall write your name down for the first waltz, my Lord."

Jasper raised an eyebrow at Laurentia's boldness, "You are a challenge, my sweet. We shall see what happens later." Jasper thought, 'No one shall hold Laurentia that close. I shall personally see to that myself.' Looking impassive and changing the subject. "I shall be more than happy to introduce you around the ball this evening; I do know everyone of importance and not important as well."

Laurentia knew that was his way to monitor her.

"That is generous of you to do so, my Lord. I would not want to monopolize your time."

"No, it is not any trouble at all, and I do enjoy your company. So that is settled, my Lady." He leaned his head over to Laurentia's ear and whispered, "I would love to run my lips and tongue down your neck and to your beautiful breasts right now."

That made Laurentia blush and shiver, as she knew the feeling of Jasper's lips and tongue on her body. Still blushing, she pressed her legs together, remembering all they shared last night in her bedchamber. Jasper could see the reaction of what that whisper did to Laurentia; he kissed her ear lightly.

"Jasper, stop that, please! You know what it does to me, and we are on a busy street with people walking by." Laurentia said his first name forgetting, they were not alone.

Jasper straightened, nodded to a few people as they walked by them. "My sweet, I do know. I want you in my bed every night for the rest of our lives."

Laurentia turned her head with eyes big as marbles. "You are very bold, sir. What if someone hears us talking like this."

Jasper said nonchalantly, "It is of no matter."

Laurentia sighed, "Please stop it for my sake, Lord Bellator."

Jasper looked down at Laurentia. "Alright, for now, my sweet. Have you started reading the books I gave you?"

"I have started reading Sense and Sensibility. I enjoy Jane Austen's style of writing."

"I shall have to introduce you to Miss Jane sometime soon. As I told you, she is a friend of Lady Louisa. She was more than likely at the garden party yesterday, a shame we had to leave so soon. Unfortunately, Miss Jane has not been feeling well these days, and I doubt she would be at the ball this evening."

"It would be lovely to meet her. I hope it's nothing serious that is making her feel ill."

"The doctor does not know what it is, I'm told. Miss Jane has some good days and some bad days, one never knows."

The twins came out of the shop, and when they saw them sitting on the bench, they walked over. Amara smiled, "We have finished with that shop. I found a lovely fan to match my gown."

Aurora said, "So have I. We are going to have lunch now. Shall you join us, Lord Bellator?"

"As tempting as that sounds, I have a few more errands to run." Jasper stood offered his hand for Laurentia to take, and when she stood, he escorted the ladies back to the coach. Duchess exited the shop just as they reached the coach, and Jasper helped them in. Before closing the door, he said.

"I shall see everyone at the ball. I know you ladies shall outshine all the other women tonight. But, until then, I bid you farewell."

Laurentia's heart leaped as she watched Jasper stroll away. 'He is so handsome; how can I refuse him anything. I do know the man desires me, but does Jasper love me? Oh, I do hope so, and that he shall say it soon, Laurentia thought as she stared out the window of the coach.

The duchess watched her son and Lady Sinclair, and she wondered if Jasper was courting her right under her nose. She also wondered why no one told her the news or if Jasper was just dallying with her.

She was an earl's sister; he'd better not ruin her. When Conrad arrived home, the duchess would have questions to be answered.

The four had their lunch and stopped at two more shops before they arrived back home. When they arrived back at Berkeley Square, the twins were tired, so the duchess told them it would be a good idea to rest before the ball. They retired to their rooms for a rest. Laurentia asked if she were not needed, she would like to relax before the ball as well. The duchess said she may go and would do the same.

When the duke arrived home that evening, he went directly to see his wife. "Good evening, my love. I heard you requested my presence when I arrived home." He walked over and kissed her softly on the lips. Duchess was resting on the chaise with her feet up in her private parlor. "What has you upset, love?" He could always tell when something had her upset or angry.

"It is Jasper and his actions lately. I do not like being left in the dark on matters."

"Do tell, what matters have you upset."

Duchess sat up, and Duke lowered himself to sit beside her, taking her hands.

"I want to know, has Jasper told you what his intent is with our new governess? He has been doing a lot of things that are out of character for him. Does he really think I would not notice these things, Conrad?"

Duke tried to sound as if he had no idea as to what was going on. "What are these things you speak of that I am not aware, my love." He takes her hand, raises it to his lips, kissing it tenderly.

"Come, Conrad, the recital. Jasper never stays to

listen to the music; he makes his appearance and then stays in the card room until he leaves. And the garden party. You and I both know he does not do activities such as a row a boat. At home on our estate in private, yes. But with a party full of spectators watching every move? No, he would not! And then today, I, the twins and Lady Laurentia, were on Bond Street in a millinery shop, and in walks Jasper, out of the blue. He would have never done that. It is out of character, I tell you. I know it's all because of Lady Laurentia."

"I see your point, my dear. Lady Laurentia could be the one for him."

Duchess asked, "Has Jasper said anything to you about Laurentia and his interest in her?"

"No, but we did talked about him picking a bride this season, to settle down and have an heir. Jasper asked me not to tell you about his plan. He does not want you throwing eligible girls in his path of finding the perfect bride or mothers among the ton doing the same. Jasper said that he would marry by the end of the season, but it would be on his own terms."

"You are telling me he will marry this year?" She looked quite pleased.

"Yes, but there is to be no meddling from you or anyone. Please, I gave my word you would not."

"I do like Lady Laurentia, and she is an Earl's daughter. She is from a good family; she is very lovely, perfect for him. I will not let on that I know of your discussion of him settling down. I am just happy he will give us grandchildren soon. I cannot wait. He better be only courting Lady Laurentia and not dishonoring her. I have heard the stories throughout the years. He is no angel, quite a rake with women."

"Most young unmarried men are, Vivianna. I was before I met you. Look at us now, my love." Duke pulled her into his arms, kissing demandingly. She wrapped her arms around this neck, kissing him with pleasure. Duke stood then scooped her up into his arms, carried her to the bedchamber shutting the door behind him. Conrad took Vivianna to the bed, laid her down, then climbed on the bed.

Leaning over her, he looked into her beautiful green eyes. "You are more beautiful than the day I met you. I do love you. I do believe we have plenty of time to make love before dinner."

Duchess said with a bright smile, "Stop talking and show me how much you love me."

The duke's eyes lit up, and his lips turned up to that wicked smile she adores.

"Nice, slow, and pleasurable, my lovely wife." Their clothes flew off, and the slow and pleasurable love began.

Chapter 19

The First Ball of The Season

As the duke was waiting in the front parlor for the women to come down, he sipped a brandy. The duchess glided in like a summer breeze; her gown was emerald green to match her eyes with a low-cut neckline. The silk shimmered when she walked, and her beautiful emerald and diamond necklace sparkled. She stopped in front of the duke and spun in a circle smiling.

"Do you like my new gown, darling?"

Duke grabbed his wife, kissed her passionately, and holding his duchess tight, looking down into her eyes. "You look beautiful and taste just as good." Conrad kissed Vivianna again.

"Darling, if you keep kissing me like that, we shall miss the ball and go upstairs for more love." The duchess glowed, looking up into Duke's eyes.

"I would prefer that to any ball, say the word, my love."

Duchess, still smiling at her husband, "I know for sure we would have two very disappointed daughters and most likely Lady Laurentia too."

"I suppose you are right, my love." He reached into his coat pocket and pulled out a box. "I have something for you." He set the box in her hands.

The duchess lit up as she opened the box lid. "Oh, Conrad, they are lovely earrings, and they match my necklace. I love them, and I love you. Thank you." Beaming, she kissed him long and deep. When the twins walked in, the duchess broke the kiss. "Look at the gift your father just gave me."

Amara said, "Father, it is not Mother's birthday. What's the occasion?"

Aurora said, "It does not need to be an occasion, silly. A man can give jewelry anytime. They are lovely, Mother, and they match the necklace you are wearing perfectly."

Amara wore a beautiful pastel yellow silk gown with a modest neckline with delicate lace. The hemline had the same lace as the neckline. Aurora was dressed in a stunning lilac silk gown, with a V-shaped neckline and crystals sewn at the hemline. As the duchess was putting on her new earrings, Laurentia walked in.

"Lady Sinclair, you look lovely. Jasper is going to love your gown, being that it is his favorite color." Amara smiled and winked from mentioning the color before to her.

Aurora said, "He is going to love everything. You look like a beautiful princess!"

Laurentia's gown was sky blue silk with an off-the-shoulder neckline and pearls and crystals sewn in the hemline. Her hair was up, with ringlets cascading down her back. The duke and duchess told her she looked beautiful also.

"Thank you, I miss being able to dress up for a ball. I might have overdone it, and blue happens to be one of my favorite colors also."

Amara said, "Jasper will still appreciate you wearing it."

The duchess cut in to take the attention off Laurentia. "You are an Earl's sister. You should enjoy this ball just as much as us."

Laurentia said, "I am the girls' governess; I shall be there for them as support tonight."

Amara said, "We shall be fine, but it's nice to know you are there for us. Please have fun too, we insist."

Laurentia smiled, then took one of each of their hands. "Alright, I shall."

The duke was standing by the fireplace, and he turned to pick up two jewelry boxes sitting on the mantel and turning toward his daughters.

"This is your first real ball with family and close friends. Even if it is not your coming-out ball, I thought my two living jewels needed a real gem for their necks." He handed the twins a box each, and they opened them together.

"Oh, Father, it is lovely," they said in unison together.

"Mother, look, it's our birthstone, a sapphire necklace," Amara said.

Duchess beamed. "Yes, how lovely. Let's put it on. Lady Sinclair, I shall put Amara's on. Could you help with Aurora's?"

Once they were on, the duke said, "Now let me see. Ah, perfect, that is exactly the finishing touch you needed. You both look so grown up and very beautiful." The necklaces were a perfect cut single sapphire, two carats, centered on a gold chain. The girls hugged their father and thanked him and their mother.

Duchess said, "This is all your father's doing; he

gets full credit for your gift, my darlings."

Aurora said, "That makes it more special. I shall treasure mine forever, Father."

Amara said, "As shall I. Let us go look in a looking glass to see how we appear." They walked to the other side of the room to see their reflection.

Amara said, "We do look grown-up." Aurora agreed and hugged her sister with joy.

The duke said, "We better head out for the ball. Is everyone ready?"

"Yes," all the ladies replied together with big beautiful smiles.

"I know I said this last time we all went out together, but I am one lucky man to have four beautiful women to escort tonight. Shall we go?"

After they waited in a small cue outside the Hanover Square mansion, the group departed their coach.

Duchess said, "Heads up, girls, remember we are Raventon's." They paraded up the stairs together, all spectator's heads craning to watch. Laurentia giggled to herself, thinking one could definitely get used to this, and she kept smiling as she walked with them.

They were inside, at the top landing looking down to all. Reginald the butler, first bowed to the Duke and Duchess, then announced:

"The Duke and Duchess of Devonshire, with daughters Lady Amara, Lady Aurora." All heads turned to see them at the top of the stairs. They walk down a staircase to greet Lord and Lady Charlton.

When Laurentia was announced, she paused at the top of the stairs. Everyone stopped what they were doing to look up to see who she was, for they had not heard the surname Sinclair at a gathering in many years. The ton started whispering all around the large foyer and in the ballroom, wondering who she was and noting how stunning she was. Jasper was at the entrance to the ballroom. He had been waiting there for Laurentia to make her appearance, as he chatted with a few friends. Jasper smiled his grandest smile from where he was standing when he saw his love sparkling at the top of the stairs. Laurentia made eye contact with him and smiled back, knowing Jasper was here and looking like he was waiting for her. The crowd broke a pathway as Jasper walked straight through the crowded room to the bottom of the staircase. He stopped to watch Laurentia walk down to him. Laurentia descended the staircase slowly; everyone was still watching her. Jasper held out his hand to Laurentia as she stepped off the last step. She put her hand in his, and he bowed to her and kissed her hand. Laurentia curtsied low to him perfectly at the same time as he bowed.

When he rose, looking into her violet eyes, "You are breathtakingly beautiful tonight, Lady Laurentia Sinclair. I have waited so long to find you." Jasper's eyes sparkled as he said each word clearly and loudly to Laurentia, so all could hear.

Jasper had just made his claim on Laurentia before his family, friends, and most of the ton. Everyone watched them and heard the words he spoke clear as a bell, from Marquess Bellator, the future Duke of Devonshire. Laurentia was speechless and was in shock at what Jasper said out loud in front of all to hear. He kissed her hand again, then turned to the host and hostess.

"Lady Laurentia, this is my uncle, Lord Charlton, and aunt, Lady Louisa."

Still in shock, she smiled and curtsied. "It is a pleasure to meet you both."

Louisa took her hand, "Yes, I am glad to make your acquaintance; I hope you enjoy the evening, my dear."

Lord Charlton smiled. "Welcome to our home." He winked at Jasper with approval and continued, "You look lovely this evening, my Lady."

"Thank you, and you are most kind, my Lord."

Jasper tucked her hand in the crook of his arm."Come, we shall take a stroll, Lady Sinclair?" As if nothing had just happened, but oh, it most certainly had.

Laurentia looked up at Jasper, blinked a couple of times before saying, "Yes, that's a lovely idea, Lord Bellator."

They walked through the crowd as if nothing had just happened. The ton was whispering, asking one another, "Has anyone seen Lady Laurentia before, how long has she been in London, what is her status in the ton? How long had Lord Bellator known her?"

All was buzzing, and tongues were wagging as soon as they walked by. Jasper knew what he was doing. He thought, 'Lady Laurentia is mine, step back any male pursuers or deal with my wrath.'

Laurentia was falling out of shock. She saw a small alcove in the ballroom and led Jasper into the small space. Laurentia turned around to face Jasper, still feeling rattled. "That was a little unsettling, Lord Bellator, what you just did in front of all. Everyone is talking now. Did you mean what you just said to me? And do not toy with my heart."

"Yes, I do want you, as I have told you all along. I am courting you, Laurentia, as of now." He looked very pleased with himself.

Laurentia heard the instruments starting to tune-up. "I believe the first dance is a waltz; I would enjoy that dance with you and about this courting business. I shall permit you to do so, now that everyone is expecting it," Laurentia said, still feeling some shock this was happening to her.

Jasper smiled, feeling pleased with himself that his plan had worked. "Yes, now the ton is aware of my intentions, of you and myself. I am glad we are agreeable on that subject at last. Shall we dance, my sweet?" He held his arm out for her to take, and they strolled out onto the dance floor, waiting for the first bar of music to play. Jasper took Laurentia's hand, then placed his other hand on her waist and pulling her close to his chest. Laurentia took a deep breath, put her other hand on Jasper's shoulder.

Laurentia whispered to Jasper, "Did it have to be a waltz the first dance? It is bad enough that everyone is whispering about us already and watching us too."

"I asked my aunt to make the first dance a waltz. I long to hold you, and you do smell wonderful." The music started, and they glided across the dance floor.

She looked into his eyes. "Do you always get what you want all the time, and does everyone do as you wish, my Lord?"

The corner of Jasper's lips twitched as he answered, "Yes, of course, and why wouldn't they. Your gown is blue. Did you wear blue to please me?"

Laurentia smiled. "Yes, I also think the color blue flatters my hair color and complexion." Jasper nodded in agreement, then twirled Laurentia as they glided across the dance floor.

Laurentia caught her breath, "My Lord, you do

dance wonderfully. I have missed this.

Jasper smiled down at Laurentia, "Well, my sweet, we shall have to rectify that. You shall attend many balls before and after, as you become my marchioness. Tonight, is the start for everyone to see and meet you. So let us indulge in some fun! By the way, all the Raventon men dance well, as we had the best instructors."

Laurentia looked around to the other Raventon gentlemen dancing around them on the dancefloor, and you could tell who they were. They had similar features, stance, and grace as Jasper.

"I see there are quite a few of you here tonight. You do have a large family, my Lord."

"I do, and this is just my father's side. My mother has a large one, also." Jasper liked seeing Laurentia light up with joy; it pleased him. After their dance set, Jasper held his arm out, "Let me introduce you to my family and friends tonight, my Lady."

Laurentia took his offered arm, smiled, and said, "Lead on, my Lord."

They walked off the dance floor to a group that was talking and laughing. They made room as they saw Jasper entering the circle.

Leopold said, "Cousin and Lady Laurentia, I have to say, you two looked good together on the dance floor. Lady Laurentia, if your dance card is not full already, you shall have to honor me with a turn-about the dance floor."

"I would like that. The next one is free, sir." Laurentia said with a smile.

Leopold nods, "You may write my name in that space, my Lady."

Jasper said before the next one started talking,

"Let me introduce you to the circle here. To your left, this is my cousin Kelsey; he is Leopold's younger brother. Next is my cousin Sterling; he's Victor's elder brother, whom you have met already, and you know my brother, Lord Drake." They all bowed to her as they were introduced.

Drake, of course, took her hand when he bowed and kissed her hand. "You look lovely this evening, my Lady. If your dance card is not filled, it will be an honor to have the next dance after my cousin Leopold," Drake said with a wink.

Laurentia curtsied to them all then said, "It is nice to meet you." Then to Drake, she said, "Thank you, and yes, you may have the next dance after Leopold, my Lord."

Next, Jasper introduced the two women in the group. "Lady Laurentia Sinclair, I like you to meet also Lady Rebecca Neville and Lady Sylvia Talbot." The three curtsied and made their acquaintance.

The music started again, and Leopold said,

"I believe, Lady Laurentia, this is our dance." He put out his arm for her to take.

"Yes, it is." She took Leopold's arm with a smile. Leopold escorted Laurentia to her place on the dance floor as a quadrille started. Laurentia looked about as all the partners took their places; the floor was filling fast. Jasper partner up with his cousin Lady Gabrielle; Laurentia recalled having met her at a tea party. She saw Amara and Aurora on the floor also with two nice-looking gentlemen. She would have to meet them later. Finally, the music started, the dance took off, with hands touching to steps, turns, skips, and so on. Laurentia had so missed this; she was laughing and smiling, feeling light on her feet.

Leopold said to Laurentia, "My Lady, you are a pleasure to dance with; I wish all the ladies of the ton so openly enjoyed themselves as you do."

"I do enjoy balls and dancing. I do hope I'm not making a spectacle of myself."

"Not at all, and you look as one should when having fun. I wish others would follow your example. Look around, and you may see what I mean, my Lady," Leopold smiled.

Laurentia glances about the dance floor. "Both gentlemen and ladies, they look so serious. Made you wonder if they care to dance or if they fine dancing as a chore and not for enjoyment."

"Exactly, I believe we should show them how to loosen up and have fun. Your smile is most contagious, my Lady." Leopold and Laurentia laughed and gave the ton a good show of how dancing should be done.

The set ended, and Drake was next to dance with Laurentia. He was right there to collect her at the edge of the dance floor. They twirled, stepped, skipped in this dance also, the Schottische. Laurentia had forgotten steps to this dance, but with Drake as her partner, he perfectly led the way, and it all came back to her. Jasper was right; the Raventon men did dance well.

Laurentia said to Drake, "Did you notice I had forgotten the steps at first? But I have it now, my Lord."

Drake smiled, "No, you dance with true grace, and if you have your gown covered any mistakes. Come, let us twirl." Laurentia laughed as Drake twirled her twice in a row.

Jasper was not dancing this one, as it was not his

favorite dance. Instead, he watched his brother dance with Laurentia; she looked beautiful, flying around the floor and laughing. Jasper could see the glow Laurentia shown as she enjoyed herself. He smiled inside.

From behind, Jasper heard Jesse say, "Ah, watching your future marchioness, and the word is spreading after your statement on the staircase when Lady Laurentia entered the ball tonight, Lord Bellator."

Jasper turned around to face Jesse and said with a growl. "Yes, she shall be my marchioness, so you need to be careful about how you address her in the future, Kingsley."

Jesse stiffened. "I did not realize you had a claim on Lady Laurentia. She is a new beautiful face in the ton. Sorry if you thought I overstepped myself at the garden party."

Jasper changed his expression to an impassive look, then said, "Yes, we've been friends a long time; I should have told you as I had Leopold that I found myself taken with Lady Laurentia. She is perfect, and she's the one. I shall tell you this when you meet the right woman, you most definitely know, my friend. She is always in my thoughts."

"I'm not ready to take any steps in that circle, my friend. But I'm happy for you. Has she agreed to marry you, then?"

Jasper motioned his head and walked away from the dance floor area with Jesse, following him into the next salon that was not crowded. Jasper stopped on the far side of the room, away from ears that would spread the news.

"I had asked her once, but she turned me down, the night before the garden party. She shared that she shall receive her trust fund and plans to live independently when she turns twenty-five next year. Taking this governess work is to live as she pleases, to not be under her brother's thumb or anyone else's, for that matter."

"Trust fund? Have her parent passed away? What about this brother of hers. Is he something to worry about?"

Jasper looking severe, "I had my secretary look into her family, and what he found was she has a sizeable trust fund that shall come to her when she turns twenty-five. But we both know I do not need that money. Lady Laurentia may do as she wishes with that money once we are married. Her parents drowned in a shipwreck traveling to France to visit her brother when she was seventeen. Her bother is a recluse that prefers country life. I found nothing wrong with what she shared with me so far and what my secretary found out."

"I am glad to hear you have checked on her, for she is new to the ton. Before she came to your parents' service, she must have kept low-key, out of the ton's eye."

"That seems so. I have not given up; Lady Laurentia is challenging and feisty. Along with her beauty and her form, she is perfection. She shall be mine, you shall see, and I do enjoy a good challenge, as you know."

"You always get what you want when you set your mind on to it, old friend. It's only a matter of time. She shall say yes to you, and I shall put my money on you if one would make a wager."

Drake walked up to them, and Jasper immediately asked, "Who is dancing with Lady Laurentia now?"

Drake raised an eyebrow, "Brother, she's fine. Sterling is turning the floor with her. She loves to dance and is a pure joy to dance with, and I can see your attraction to her. Besides her beauty, she is fun and intelligent. If I wanted to marry any time soon, she'd be the one. I do hope I find someone like Lady Laurentia someday."

Jasper said, "I am not worried about you, or I would never have left the room. Lady Laurentia is quite wonderful and mine. But I do want to introduce her to more of our family. Lady Laurentia does not have much family, from what I found out. She has one brother and one aunt from her mother's side. I would like her to be embraced by our family. Shall we go back to the ballroom?"

Drake smiled, "Her Grace is looking for you." He laughed. "I'm glad it's not me she has her sights set on right now, dear Brother." Drake laughed again.

"I can imagine that Her Grace is not too happy with this happening right under her nose. Lady Laurentia and I have developed feelings for each other. We had better go back into the ballroom to see what's happening."

Laurentia saw Jasper walking around the edge of the floor with Drake and Lord Kingsley. She smiled at him, and he nodded and waited as she finished her dance. Sterling was laughing at something Laurentia said before they reach the side of the dance floor where Jasper was standing.

She looked up at Jasper, and he said, "My Lady, I think with all the dancing you have done, maybe you would care for something to drink."

"That would be lovely, my Lord. Between your cousins and brother, they are wonderful to dance with, but a little rest and a beverage would be helpful right now."

When they reached the refreshment salon, Jasper asked. "Would you like champagne or punch, my sweet?" When they stopped in front of the beverage table.

"My Lord, you should not call me your sweet in public," Laurentia whispered.

"I believe everyone knows my feelings for you, and I love to see your eyes light up when I call you the endearment."

Laurentia tilted her head and smiled, thinking, He used the word 'love,' he's getting closer to what my heart needs to hear. So now to listen to the words I love you, soon, I hope.

"My Lord, you are right, and I do adore it. I would like some champagne, please."

Jasper nodded to a footman and picked up two glasses from a tray, handing one to Laurentia.

"Shall we find somewhere to take a seat, perhaps?" He leaned into her ear and whispered, "So I can taste your lips, my sweet, that would be better than this drink in my hand." Laurentia smirked and giggled when he straightened up.

Jasper jokingly said, "Lady Laurentia, are you smirking at me in front of everyone here tonight?"

She giggled again, "It must be the champagne, my Lord, for I to make such a bold move." Laurentia giggled more.

Jasper smiled. "Well, if I can hear your delightful giggling more often, I shall have to serve you champagne daily."

Laurentia whispered, "My Lord, there are other things you could do to me that would make me giggle, trust me."

That made Jasper's wicked smile appear, and he put his arm out. "The terrace is this way. I think we both need some fresh air and an escape from the ballroom."

They took two steps toward the terrace doors when they heard a loud, clear voice say, "Lord Bellator, where are you running off to with a lovely young lady on your arm? I would like to meet her."

Jasper turned around, recognizing the voice immediately. The Dowager Duchess, his grandmother. Damn, I so much wanted and needed a little private time with Laurentia. "Grandmother, it has been a while since I've seen you. How long have you been in residence?"

Laurentia turned around to see an attractive gray-haired woman with pale blue eyes and another forty-year-old woman standing by her side. Jasper walked forward, leading Laurentia with him. He kissed the older woman on the cheek.

She said to him, "You very well know how long I have been in London, as you also knew I would be here tonight. I heard that you had made a claim on a young lady tonight. Would this be her?" Grandmother gestured toward Laurentia.

Jasper smiled his grandest smile, trying to soften his overbearing grandmother's mood, "Grandmother, I'd like you to meet Lady Laurentia Sinclair. Lady Laurentia, I would like you to meet my grandmother, Her Grace, Dowager Duchess Devonshire, and this is her companion, Miss Evans.

Laurentia curtsied to his grandmother perfectly. "I am pleased to make your acquaintance, Your Grace."

The duchess eyed her over. "Not as pleased as I

am to meet you, my dear. You are a lovely young woman, yes. Bellator, you may leave us for a while. We are going to go over there and talk for a bit. I want to get to know Lady Laurentia better. Miss Evans, fetch me a glass of champagne if you would and not that dreadful punch they are serving."

Miss Evan bobbed a curtsy, "Yes, Your Grace."

Jasper felt unsure of leaving Laurentia with his grandmother. "Yes, Your Grace, I shall return shortly." He bowed and strolled away but not too far, feeling not too pleased with being sent out like a child. He hoped this would not scare Laurentia away. For his grandmother did not beat around the bush, she would read you and give her opinion of you, whether you liked it or not. Dowager Duchess Devonshire was the Matriarch of this family.

"Well, Lady Laurentia, shall we have a seat and get better acquainted?"

Laurentia smiled. "By all means, yes, your Grace." They walked a short distance to a chaise.

Miss Evans returned with a glass of champagne, delivered to the duchess, who waved her away.

Grandmother took a sip of champagne, then said to Laurentia. "Sinclair, that name sounds familiar, let me think. Ah yes, Thomas Sinclair, an earl, I believe. Your mother was Esme, a lovely woman; they died in a shipwreck, as I remember. Sorry, my dear girl."

"It has been many years. To hear of it does not bother me as much as it used too. I still have a brother, Lucas, and he holds the title now, your Grace.

"Yes, that's right. I do remember they had an heir. My grandson seems to believe you have what it takes to be his future marchioness. He must be in love with you."

Laurentia looked her in the eyes and said, "He has not said the words to me yet. What makes you think he does?"

"Bellator is just like his father and grandfather. They were proud men, well respected, and hold high standards for themselves. Hence, the things he has been doing; the last few days prove that, my dear girl. Should I name a few?"

Laurentia nodded her head, yes.

"From what I hear, Bellator sat in a recital beside you. He has never done that. He would prefer the card room. Rowing in a boat at a garden party with you and his sisters, he would look down his nose at the idea of it."

"That little adventure did not work out so well."

"You were all wet to the bone, quite an embarrassment for him. Yet, he is still pursuing you. Do you think Bellator would have stepped into a millinery shop if you were not there?"

Laurentia thought a moment smiled. "Yes, I see what you are saying, but he has not said he loves me yet. I need to hear the words. I want love in my marriage, as my parents had. I shall not say yes to any proposal until he says he loves me."

The dowager turned toward Laurentia then took both her hands. "Smart girl, he is trying to show you, it might take him a while to say the word, but he shall, that I can predict. Do you love my grandson, child?"

"Yes, with all my heart. Lord Bellator is wonderful, and he makes me truly happy."

The dowager squeezed her hand as she liked Laurentia's answer. "Raventon men are loyal, they love hard, and family is essential to them. He shall say he loves you; give him time, dear child, that's a big word for him to say to you. I would wager he has never said the word love to a woman before, just family members."

"Thank you for talking with me tonight. Unfortunately, I do not have someone to confide in. You have given me hope, thank you, Your Grace." A tear came down Laurentia's cheek at the joy of what she learned just now, and she dabbed it away.

The dowager smiled. "You are exactly what my grandson needs. You may feel free to call upon me anytime you wish, I hope often. One word to the wise, do not let Bellator bully you ever; stand your ground, and you can mold him as you please. Sometimes!" she said with a laugh.

They were laughing together now as Jasper walked back toward them. He stopped in front of them and saw his grandmother holding Laurentia's hand as they talked away to one another. He thought it was a good sign.

"That's what I like to see, my two favorite women, enjoying one another's company." Jasper kept an impassive face.

The dowager said, "You may keep this one. I do like her." She gave her grandson a wink.

"I am glad to hear it, Your Grace, and that you have not scared Lady Laurentia away."

"On the contrary, and you have my blessing, Bellator."

His grandmother stood. Jasper hugged, kissed her cheek, and held her at arm's length. "Thank you, Your Grace, that means a lot to me to hear you say that."

"Well, you two young ones, this old lady needs to stretch her legs. Where has Miss Evans gone off too?"

Miss Evans came from around the corner, saying, "Here I am, Your Grace, who would you like to go visit next?"

"Lady Troy is over that way. She has the best gossip to hear."

Dowager looked back to Jasper and Laurentia before walking away. "Weren't you two going out to the terrace before I came across you? The moonlight is beautiful tonight, so get going!"

Laurentia stood then said to Jasper, "I do like your grandmother. We are going to become good friends."

Jasper felt relieved. "I am glad to hear that, my sweet, she is still very much head of this family, and she has a warm spot in my heart."

Laurentia smiled, "So does she for you as well, I can tell."

Jasper waved his hand toward the terrace. "We had the order to see the moonlight, shall we, my sweet?" He laughed, and so did Laurentia as they walked through the terrace doors together.

The outside was quiet. The ball was in full swing. Only one other couple was outside, and they walked back in when they saw Marquess Bellator enter the terrace.

Laurentia said, "How convenient for them to leave."

"I see it as perfect for us." He looked around to see if anyone was watching. "Come, there is a private bench near a rose arbor over there." He led Laurentia down a few steps and around the corner of the house to the rose arbor.

Laurentia looked around as they walked to the secluded spot, wondering how many other women he had brought here in the past. Laurentia boldly said. "How many other ladies have you brought here, Lord Bellator?"

Jasper raised an eyebrow, "Why would you ask that?"

"Because you know the way so well."

"For your information, my sweet, I do know the garden quite well, for when I was a child, I played here often. Do you know the game hide and seek?"

"Yes, I played that too."

"My cousins and I played here in this garden many summer nights in our youth. The answer to your first question is one, you. I never made it a habit to sneak off from a ball with a lady; that would only bring trouble upon myself. I have not wanted to marry until I met you."

Laurentia felt silly for asking that "I'm sorry for asking."

On that note, Jasper took her in his arms, kissed her hard and demandingly. Laurentia leaned into him, putting her arms around his neck, then falling into the paradise of his hold. They collapsed onto the bench for support. Jasper kissed down Laurentia's neck to her bare shoulders.

"I have wanted to kiss you all evening, ever since I l saw you descend the staircase." He went back to her lips to take all she had to offer.

Laurentia pulled back to catch her breath. "Be careful not to mess me up too much, Jasper. We still have to go back into the ball."

"Can I come to you tonight and have all of you, then?"

Laurentia smiled, "I do wish it was now, and your answer is yes."

She kissed him, and Jasper pulled back with his wicked smile. "Ah, my sweet, are you enjoying the lovemaking we have been experiencing together?"

"You are quite good at that. I have been enjoying it, yes." Laurentia blushed.

Jasper took her hand, and looking into her eyes, he started with her pinky finger, kissing the tip, then the index finger before moving to the middle one, and still looking in her eyes, he took the next finger entirely in his mouth and sucked. That gave Laurentia shivers, and she sighed. Japer, still holding her hand, kissed her palm.

"We shall have to try something new tonight. We should get back before we are missed. Come." He stood and pulled Laurentia to her feet

As they walked back to the terrace, Laurentia thought, what he just did to my hand was so seductive. How is it so easy for him to turn it off and stop in a flash? What shall he do new tonight? Oh my, I wish we were in my room now.

Jasper stopped short of the terrace to see if anyone was about, and seeing they were quite along, he and Laurentia hurried back up the steps to the terrace. Then he turned to check Laurentia's appearance; she looked perfect, with only slightly kiss-swollen lips. He put his arm out for her to take, and they walked back into the ball as if nothing happened.

When they walked back into the manor, the duchess saw them and walked over to meet them, saying. "There you are, taking a little fresh air, did you?" She noticed Laurentia's well-kissed lips.

Jasper said, "Yes, with half of the ton in these

rooms, one does get warm, your Grace."

Duchess nodded to her son, then said. "I suppose you do. Shall we go over here to the side, out of the middle of the doorway? I have some things I need to say to you both."

They walked to the side where not many ears were within hearing distance. The duchess smiled then said low, "I am happy and pleased that you two have found each other, but Jasper, you need to court Lady Laurentia properly. She is in my household, an earl's sister, so please obey the correct rules. Do you understand me?"

Jasper almost laughed, then caught himself. "Yes, Your Grace, of course."

"Good, let's go back into the ballroom, shall we?" Duchess said and led the way.

They entered the ballroom, and the twins came over to them.

"I knew you two had sparks. See Aurora? I was right." Amara said.

"Yes, you were. I did not think our brother was in the market for a bride, that's all."

Laurentia said, "I believe you are all being a bit presumptuous. I have not said yes to a proposal yet. Lord Bellator and I have only started courting tonight."

Duchess said, "Yes, my girls, they are courting, but we can hope for more is all. Come now, let them be so that Lord Bellator can introduce Lady Laurentia to more of our family and friends."

Jasper gave the nod to that and led Laurentia around the ballroom to meet more people. Victor came over to them, "Ah, Bellator and my Lady, there you are. I will be enchanted, Lady Laurentia, if you honor me the next dance." Victor bowed to Laurentia.

She curtsied then said, "How could I say no when you ask so gallantly. I am honored to accept."

With a brilliant smile, Victor put his arm out to Laurentia for her to take. "Shall we, my Lady?" Victor winked at Jasper. Laurentia then let go of Jasper's arm and took Victor's arm as they walked onto the dance floor to take their spot as the next dance was a mazurka. Everyone bowed to their partners as the music started. Laurentia smiled as the dance had her skipping, twirling, stepping again, how she did enjoy this. Jasper watched his love glide across the floor, and he thought, to watch her dance gives me as much pleasure as dancing with her himself. But, maybe not; the waltz is a very intimate dance for the couple to be pressed together that close. I do enjoy that one more.

His uncle Jonathan and aunt Fantina had just joined the group Jasper was standing with. "It is good to see you, sorry I had missed you at the garden party the other day. I had an unfortunate incident with a rowboat, you see."

Jonathan said, "I did not see that happen, but it was the talk of the party afterward."

"I could only imagine," Jasper shook his head.

Fantina said in her thick French accent. "By the evening soiree, Her Grace had all of that event erased. She is fantastic at making things go away."

Jasper said, "Yes, Her Grace is good at that, shutting down talk or rumors of our family."

The group discussed the upcoming parties, and though Jasper listened, his eyes were on Laurentia. She was all he thought about these days. How can one person change my life in a blink of an eye? He caught her eye; she smiled just for him. I do not know, and I shall not change it for the world. She is mine and perfect.' The dance ended, and the supper gong rang.

Laurentia came back with Victor, joining Jasper again. He introduced his uncle—his father's youngest brother, and his aunt to Laurentia.

Laurentia curtsied and said, "It is lovely to meet you both."

As the guests made their way to the supper-room, Jasper put his arm out for Laurentia to take. They went in shortly after his parents as rank in the ton demands proper order to be followed. Laurentia thought, this is lovely, and I am not feeling so out of place on Jasper's arm this evening. She recalled the recital a few nights prior to when she did feel so uncomfortable. He would not let her take her hand away as they walked together; it felt more natural tonight. Perhaps it was publicly acknowledging her and the respect he demanded from the ton. She smiled inwardly. He wants me as his future marchioness

Jasper interrupted her thoughts. "Are you alright, my lady? You seem to be somewhere else at the moment."

Laurentia came back down to earth, "Yes, my Lord, I am fine, as long as I am with you."

Jasper, looking down into her eyes as they walked, "My evening was just made more perfect hearing, you say that." He tilted his head and whispered, "I wish I could kiss you right now."

Laurentia whispered, "I wish the same, my Lord.".

They ate some and gathered around a large table, talking and joking back and forth. This family liked to tease one another in good fun; it warmed Laurentia's heart. They made her feel like a part of the family. The word 'family,' she could see that meant a lot to the Raventon's. They were a tight-knit group. I never thought I'd have that again.

Jasper asked once more, "Are you alright, my sweet? You have not eaten much."

"I'm not that hungry, is all. I am fine, truly, my Lord." Laurentia gave Jasper a reassuring smile.

"The waltz is the next set. Shall we dance that one, my Lady?"

Laurentia purred softly, "Yes, I desire to be in your arms, my Jasper."

Japer's pupils dilated, along with his groin that had grown into a complete, hard erection. Jasper held his breath to control the undoing Laurentia just set on him. Lord, this woman has bewitched me with a spell. No one has done this to me before, and we are at a ball.

Laurentia asked, "Is something wrong? You look distressed."

Jasper wondered if there was time to sneak away to quench the fire Laurentia just set on him. Jasper whispered to Laurentia,

"My sweet, you have just set my groin on fire. So, I think we need to release the flames that are burning."

Laurentia was intrigued. She whispered, "Where shall we go?"

"I shall excuse myself and go out that terrace door over there, and in five minutes after I leave, you shall excuse yourself that you are going to the woman's parlor to freshen up. I shall be there." Laurentia nodded and was a little excited about this new game.

Jasper got up to do as he said. Laurentia looked around to see everyone in the conversation. Laurentia stood up casually, then excused herself to go to the parlor so she could freshen up. She almost reached the salon when a door opened, and Jasper pulled her into the room quickly, shutting the door and locking it. One candle burned on a small table; the place looked to be a study, Laurentia thought as she quickly looked around. Jasper pinned Laurentia up against the wall and kissed her hard and full of need.

Laurentia placed her arms around Jasper's neck, kissing him demandingly. Jasper broke free then whispered in her ear.

"This shall be something new, we have to be quiet, but my sweet, when you whispered seductively to me a few minutes ago plus my name, you unleashed the desire I have for you that flows through my veins. I have to have you now."

Laurentia said, "I want you now, as much as you need me, my Jasper, please."

She could feel his hard groin pushing against her legs as he spread them. Jasper pulled her dress up to her hips, and whatever garment that was in his way, he moved so her womanhood was freed, and Jasper could enter her freely.

"My sweet, I am going to raise you so that I can enter into you, and then you shall wrap your lovely legs around me," Laurentia nodded.

Jasper raised Laurentia, and with one push, he was inside her. Laurentia's back was against the wall for support, and her legs wrapped around Jasper's waist. Oh, he feels so good, Laurentia thought as he moved hard and fast.

"My sweet, you have bewitched me. We both needed this now, so we shall have to come together and strong."

Laurentia could not talk; she nodded on his shoulder; this was too intense to speak. Jasper pumped her hard and wild. He gritted his teeth, for he knew Laurentia was not there yet. Jasper stroked and stroked, then felt her shiver as she tightened around him. He kissed her, scream down, and came with her hard with a few more strong pumps. Then they collapsed to the floor, panting.

Laurentia lay her head on Jasper's shoulder, sitting in his lap. Jasper was still inside her, and he tried to catch his breath. When he did, he said. "That, my sweet, was wonderful. You undo me."

Laurentia lifted her head. "That was divine, my Jasper." She smiled brightly.

"I do like when you say my Jasper, for I know now you are mine. As much as I like being inside you, let us get up and put ourselves back together. I purposely did not touch your hair or over kiss you, so we do not look like we just made wild passionate love." He kissed her nose.

Laurentia looked down at her dress that was in a pile between them.

"I hope when I stand up. My gown is not too wrinkled."

"Ready to stand?" Jasper took ahold of her hips to steady her. Jasper stood and fixed his breeches right, then stepped back to look at Laurentia.

"Your gown looks fine. Well, we look good. I know I feel excellent." Jasper smiled.

"That was fun, very naughty, and I also feel so

good." Laurentia reached up and kissed Jasper softly.

Jasper unlocked the door, peeked out. "Go into the lady's parlor and check yourself, then go back to the ballroom. I shall come back through the terrace door, looking as nothing happened." Laurentia giggled then went out the door first, and all went well as planned. They both ended up in the ballroom as if nothing happened.

Jasper walked over to the group Laurentia was talking with; he nodded to everyone and joined into the conversation. They heard the music was about to start, and Jasper gallantly bowed to Laurentia then asked.

"Shall you honor me with this dance, Lady Laurentia?"

When he rose, she put her hand out, then said, "It shall be an honor to, Lord Bellator."

Jasper took her hand, placed it on his arm, and then walked onto the dance floor, waiting for the music to start. Jasper and Laurentia glided across the dance floor.

Laurentia sighed, "I have to admit stealing away secretly to make passionate love was very naughty and wild for us. The not getting caught part was more fun."

Jasper laughed. "You are a little vixen, my sweet. Yes, that was fun and pleasurable."

Then he kissed her hand and twirled her in two complete circles. Laurentia giggled with joy on the second spin. The rest of the night, they danced with different family members. Jasper even danced a set with each of his sisters, who were on their best behavior that evening.

It was almost one when the duke and duchess arrived back to Berkley Square; everyone was tired. They all said their goodnights as they walked up the main staircase together. Amara and Aurora were still chatting away about all the different dance partners they'd had tonight.

The duke teased them, "I better not have to beat suitors away the next couple of days."

The girls giggled then turned down their wing toward their bedchamber.

Amara said, "Lady Sinclair, you and Jasper look so perfect waltzing together tonight." Aurora said, "Is Jasper really going to start courting you?"

Laurentia said with a smile, "His Lordship did ask, and I permitted him too. So yes, he is."

They reached the twin's door and said their goodnights. Laurentia continued to her room.

Sandra came from her dressing room and asked. "Did you have a fine time tonight, my Lady?" As she is walking over to help Laurentia undress.

"Sandra, it was wonderful; the ton accepted me as one of their own. The Raventon family were especially lovely to me. I met the Dukes' Mother. At first, she was a little unnerving, stern, and then she became almost like my grandmother, caring. I like her a lot."

"It sounds like you made a new friend this evening. If I am not too bold, my Lady, it does not hurt being on the arm of the future Duke." Sandra finished unbuttoning Laurentia's gown to help her out of it.

"Well, Lord Bellator, let everyone know, after I was announced, and I came down the stairs. He was standing at the bottom, waiting for me. Lord Bellator kissed my hand, then said, I have waited so long to find you. Right there, with everyone listening and watching. He made his claim to me tonight. I have to admit, and it was significantly over the top. I was in shock at first.

"I'm not surprised a bit, the house staff here says, Lord Bellator is a take-charge kind of gentleman, they also said he is a fair man and is loyal to his family. You could have found no one better than Lord Bellator, my Lady."

Laurentia smiled, "I believe you're right.

Laurentia now slipped into her nightgown. "I danced the waltz twice with Lord Bellator, and then between Lord Drake and all of the Raventon gentlemen, I danced almost every set. It was like a dream that I longed for, and I enjoyed myself immensely.

Laurentia was sitting at her dressing table while Sandra helped to take the pins out of her hair.

"The twins loved what you did with my hair this evening. They asked if you would do their hair for the next occasion? I told them, maybe you could give their maids some pointers. I do not want to share you with anyone. You are too dear to me."

"Thank you, my Lady. I feel the same for you. I could show them a few things, I guess." All the pins were out of Laurentia's hair. She picked up a brush and started to run it through her hair.

"Thank you, and you may retire for the night, Sandra." Her maid exited the room.

Laurentia felt tired, so she decided to slip into bed and wait for Jasper there. Unfortunately, she fell asleep before Jasper arrived.

Jasper looked down at Laurentia as she slept, standing beside the bed. Her hair was spread across the pillows, and the cover only rose to her waist. She looked like an angel, too beautiful to touch. She is my angel and touching her is the best feeling ever. He walked over to a chair and undressed, putting his clothes neatly on the chair. Walking back to the bed, Jasper slipped in under the covers and pulled Laurentia into his arms. She stirred then blinked her eyes open, smiling when she realized she was in Jasper's arms, the place she loved the best.

"I must have fallen to sleep; I thought I would just wait for you in bed."

Jasper kissed her nose, "You looked so beautiful sleeping like an angel. I look forward to seeing you in my bed that way, waiting for me, soon, I hope, instead of sneaking into my parents' home."

Jasper kissed Laurentia deeply, not giving her time to answer. They made love slower this time, just as wonderfully passionate as at the ball. Jasper slept there, holding Laurentia tight in his arms. He woke just before dawn and before the house became awake.

Jasper kissed Laurentia goodbye for now, then said. "I shall see you this afternoon, my sweet."

Laurentia looked up at him with a warm smile, "Till then, my Jasper," then closing her eyes and fell back to sleep.

Chapter 20

There's Love in the Air

In the dining room, the duke and duchess were breaking their fast. Laurentia strolled in and bade them a good morning as she poured some tea from the sideboard, took a tart, and joined them at the table.

Duchess asked, "Did you enjoy the ball last night?"

Laurentia smiled brightly, "Yes, immensely, I enjoyed dancing, and your family made me feel so welcome."

Duchess said, "We are very fond of you, especially Lord Bellator, it seems."

Duke said, "I am glad our eldest son has chosen you for his future bride. We did notice he was showing a lot of interest in you a late."

Laurentia felt a little shy talking about this, especially if considering what happened in her bedchamber nightly. "I have agreed that he may court me. Lord Bellator did surprise me when he made his claim for me in front of everyone. I had no idea he was going to do that at the time."

Duke said, "My son, he has always been a highflyer, runs in the Raventon blood." Duchess nodded in agreement.

The twin entered the room, still chatting about the ball. "Good morning," they called to everyone.

Duchess said, "Have something to eat, and then we have some calls to make."

They walked to the sideboard, and once their plates were filled, they took a place at the table.

Amara said to her mother, "Do we have to go with you today while you make your calls? Can we not stay here with Lady Sinclair?"

Aurora said, "We know it is your day off. We will not be any bother. Maybe we could go for a carriage ride in Hyde Park? Please, Lady Sinclair."

Duchess said, "I am fine with you, not going with me today. But it's up to you, Lady Sinclair. If you want to go out with the girls for a carriage ride or they can wait until later in the afternoon when I return."

Laurentia said, "I do have a new hat that should be shown off. A carriage ride sounds like a splendid idea for the occasion." The girls clapped their hands together with joy.

Duchess said, "That is settled then. Wesley, have the open white carriage brought around in one hour, for the young ladies."

The duke said, "I want two grooms plus the driver to go out with them today."

Wesley bowed, saying, "Right away, Your Grace, I shall see it done," exiting the room.

Jasper walked through the dining room door, pushing past Wesley and yelling that his family knows who he is and does not need to be announced.

"Good morning, all. I trust everyone slept well after our full night at the ball." He was carrying a large bouquet of roses. He walked to Laurentia then said,

"My sweet, these are for you. They are not as beautiful as you, but I believe ladies do enjoy receiving them." He handed her two dozen red roses.

Laurentia took them, breathed in the delicate scent, and said, "Thank you, my Lord, they smell very nice, and they are lovely."

"You are welcome." Jasper saw fruit tarts on the sideboard, walked over, and helped himself with two on a plate and some black coffee. When he was done, he came back to the table, taking a seat by Laurentia. The duchess looked at him with bright eyes.

"Mother, do not look at me that way. At the ball last evening, your words were that I was to court Lady Laurentia properly. Well, here I am, with flowers, and requesting a few moments with her. Plus, this evening, I understand you shall be attending the theater. I'll be here tonight to escort Lady Laurentia with all of you."

Duchess smiled, "You should come for dinner before we leave."

Jasper nodded as he took a bite of a tart, then said, "Bridget has not lost her touch on making these tarts." He popped another piece in his mouth and took a sip of coffee.

Amara said, "You and Drake always eat all the bake goods up, so please leave some for the rest of us."

Duke laughed at his daughter's boldness toward her brother. "Your sisters and Lady Laurentia are going for a carriage ride in Hyde Park within an hour. So, take Lady Laurentia to the front parlor for a short visit and then come to my library. Edmond and I shall wait for you to go over the estate manners."

"Yes, Father, I shall do that. Mother, are you not going for a carriage ride?"

"No, not this time. I have some calls to make, being the start of the season and all."

Jasper stood and motioned for Jenell to take Laurentia's roses. Laurentia told her, "Please put them in a vase and put them in my room."

Jasper put out his hand to help Laurentia up; he kissed her palm and smiled when she stood. They walked to the parlor hand in hand.

Duchess said after they left the room, "It's nice to see Jasper in love."

Aurora asked, "Is Jasper really going to marry Lady Sinclair? They both look as the love bug has bitten them."

Amara said, "Of course, silly, or Jasper would not be here like this."

Duchess said, "Your brother will be getting married soon. Very soon."

Jasper closed the parlor door behind them, pulling Laurentia into his arms and kissing her tenderly. He pulled away, "Do you have a new hat to show off in Hyde Park, my sweet?"

"Yes, a lovely one, I have just purchased."

"You should have all your new purchases billed to me. I am more than happy to take care of that for you."

Laurentia's expression changed to anger. "I have and make my own money. I do not need you to pay for the things I buy."

"My sweet, I have no problem settling your bills. Just tell the shopkeeper to send the bill to my secretary; he shall take care of it all."

Laurentia tried to free herself from Jasper's hold. The man had arms of steel. She gave up, then said, "We are not yet betrothed or married. I shall not have you pay for the things I want. It would make me feel like your mistress, which I am not."

Jasper saw she meant it, so he tried to ease her mind. "My sweet, I do not think of you as my mistress ever, but you are mine. I want to take care of you, end of subject."

"No, and that is final."

"It's not an issue to pay for the things you buy. I am very wealthy, my sweet." He changed the subject as he was not getting anywhere in that manner and later addressed the topic with his secretary on his own. "The play tonight is a comedy. I have not seen it yet. But I have heard good reviews."

Laurentia saw his tactic of changing the subject. He better leave my personal things alone. She smiled and said, "Yes, I also read the review. I think the play shall be quite entertaining."

Jasper unwrapped his arms from around Laurentia. Now that they agreed on a new subject. "Shall we have a seat, my sweet?" They walked over to the chaise to sit together, Jasper still holding Laurentia's hands.

"Courting you in my parents' home feels odd, for these are the walls I grew up in. I cannot wait to take you to our country estate. Black Crest Castle has been in our family for more than three hundred years, and it's in Devonshire on the coast. We have a large staff of servants maintaining it year-round. I have a whole wing to myself when I'm in residence. Drake and my sister share a wing, Father and Mother have a wing to themselves, and there is another wing for guests or family visiting. I believe there are twenty-eight bedchambers, plus servant's quarters. We have a village outside the castle walls, offering shops, a butcher, blacksmith, stables, inn's, a bakery, café's, fresh markets, dressmakers, and more. Everything you need, just like London."

'My, he is serious about marrying me, if he is sharing all of this with me.' Laurentia smiled, "It sounds charming. Do you own other estates too?"

"Yes, I own a townhouse on Grosvenor Square London, and estates in Bath, Yorkshire, Ayrshire, and Kent, all with plenty of room for family and guests." Jasper said all of that as if it were not impressive.

"Do you go to all those estates yearly, and do you have tenants on all your properties?"

Jasper nodded. "But I've never taken any females to any of them out of London, not even a mistress. I want you to decorate each home to your delight as you see fit. I want children with you, our heir, maybe three or four. I need you in my life, I…" The door opened. Jasper stopped; the twins walked in.

"Lady Laurentia, you need to go change, for the carriage is ready for us," Aurora said.

Laurentia looked to the girls in their carriage attire, standing in the doorway. Darn, she thought to herself. It almost sounded as if Jasper was ready to say the words I longed to hear. She put on a fake smile for them. "Yes, I should get ready, it seems."

Jasper rose from the chaise, not too happy at being interrupted by his sisters. With an impassive look, he held this handout for Laurentia to take as she stood.

"We shall have to finish this conversation later, my sweet." He kissed her hand.

Laurentia sighed, "Yes, I think so, my Jasper

Aurora gleamed then said, "I am happy it's you,

some of the other women that buzz around Jasper; we did not care for too much. Noses in the air, unintelligent, you know the kind."

Amara said, "They would not be a good choice of a sister if we had a word in it. We adore you!"

Jasper almost laughed and said with a hint of sarcasm. "I'm glad my sisters approve. I would not want to displease you or any of the other family members." Laurentia laughed, and so did the girls.

Jasper said as he and Laurentia walked toward the door. "I'm most definitely outnumbered by ladies' opinions here, so I shall make my exit." He kissed Laurentia's hand, forgoing a more intimate gesture, for the girls were watching. "I shall see you at dinner tonight, my sweet." Jasper walked down the corridor to his fathers' library, and Laurentia went upstairs to change for a ride in the park as the twins waited impatiently for Laurentia to return to the front parlor.

When Laurentia returned from changing her attire, she said, "Let's go show off our new hats and hear what gossip is circulating today."

Amara said, "We are ready; this is going to be fun." On the way, the twins talked away animatedly about last night's ball. Laurentia listened to them and laughed.

They turned into Hyde Park's gates; the lanes had a steady flow of traffic moving through the park's carriage roads. They nodded and waved to people they knew passing by.

Laurentia said, "It is a beautiful day out. I'm glad you suggested the carriage ride."

Aurora said, "Maybe we can have our driver go down that lane over there, I see less traffic, and we can have more of a breeze if he goes faster."

Amara said, "Yes, shall we tell the driver?"

Laurentia turned around and told the driver to take the next lane and to go a little faster for a light breeze. He nodded and turned the carriage down the less busy route, and the carriage picked up more speed.

Amara said, "The fresh air is wonderful, oh feel it." Aurora and Laurentia laughed as they felt the wind blow through their hair.

All of a sudden, they heard a loud crack. The ladies looked at each other, wondering what it was. Before they could ask the question, the carriage flipped over to its side, and all passengers went flying through the air. The horses broke free from the carriage, and they raced down the lane, frightened of what had happened.

Leopold and Victor happened to be riding on horseback on the same lane, enjoying the spring day. They had recognized the Devonshire carriage before the whole thing happened in a flash. They looked at each other in fright, then set their horses into a fast gallop to get to the scene, where they could hear their cousins crying. They both jumped off their horses, ran over to the twins, who had landed in a big soft patch of overgrown grass. Amara held her arm in pain, sitting up, and Aurora was standing up crying, also in shock at what happened. Victor went to Amara first and saw her holding her left arm. He looked her over, telling her it could be broken, and tried to keep it still. Leopold grabbed ahold of Aurora and hugged her. She was crying hysterically, and he wanted to calm her down, holding her, saying,

"I am here, little one; all shall be okay, I promise you. Let me check to see if you're hurt, Aurora." Lightly sobbing, Aurora nodded yes.

Leopold asked, "Do you hurt anywhere, little cousin?"

"The side I landed on hurts a lot, Leopold."

"You should sit down and show me where it hurts," Leopold said with concern in his eyes. Aurora told him her left side hurt and took a seat by Amara. Leopold checked the area and looked up.

"I believe you may have bruised your ribs. We shall have to have the doctor check you when we get you back to Berkeley Square. Was there not someone else in the carriage with you? I remember seeing three figures."

Amara said, "Yes, Lady Sinclair." They all looked around, for they did not hear a sound from her. Victor saw her about ten feet from them. He ran to her with Leopold on his tail.

"She is not moving, and her head is bleeding from hitting a large rock," Victor said. Panic set in as they looked at each other, confused as to what they should do.

Leopold said, "This is not good! She is bleeding and unconscious. Look at the size of the rock she hit."

Victor said, "I saw two grooms and a driver. Where are they?" The two looked around quickly. One groom was walking over to where they were standing, and the other was sitting on the ground, holding his leg in pain. They saw the driver stand up with a look of confusion.

Leopold said to the groom, walking toward them. "Are you alright, there?"

Groom answered, "Yes, I feel fine, just had the wind knock out of me, but I'm good now."

A few carriages stopped when they saw the accident and asked how they could aid. Victor said as he crouched down over Laurentia. "Lady Sinclair needs a doctor right away. She is bleeding from her head and is knocked out cold. Not good at all, and my cousins need a doctor also. They may have some broken bones themselves."

Earl Hainsworth said, "We can use my carriage to take them to Berkeley Square."

Leopold said, "Yes, thank you. We need the carriage to come over here as close as possible, so we do not move Lady Sinclair too far. My cousin Lord Bellator is going to be most unhappy, and we need to send word to him at once."

The groom said, "When we left Berkeley Square, I know his lordship was there. His horse was in the stable."

Amara yelled, "He was with His Grace, having a meeting in the library when we left."

Leopold said, "Let's hope Bellator is still there as well."

The carriage came over; Leopold and Victor pick up Laurentia together, one on each side, making sure her head was elevated, hoping their best that she would be alright, for her and Jasper both.

Countess Hainsworth was in the carriage, and she directed them. "Put her head on my lap so I can hold her most still when we move. Bring the Raventon girls over in a hurry. We must get Lady Sinclair a doctor right away."

Leopold said to Victor, "You follow the carriage. I'm going to fetch the doctor, and I shall ride as fast as possible. The doctor and I shall meet you at Berkeley Square. Have that groom that is alright, stay with the broken carriage until it is moved to my company warehouse. I smell sabotage, not an accident, cousin."

Victor's eyes went big as marbles when Leopold said there was no accident here. Leopold mounted his horse and raced off for the doctor; he was scared for Jasper's sake. Jasper loved Lady Laurentia, and then he felt sorry for the person or persons when Jasper took revenge on their poor soul.

A large crowd had gathered around, and Victor gave the groom the order to stay with the broken carriage, and the driver also volunteered to stay.

Victor said, "You do that, but when you get back to Berkeley Square, the duchess will demand you see the doctor." He knew his aunt, and so did the driver.

Next, Victor mounted his horse and caught up with the carriage already in motion. The groom with the broken leg sat on the back platform of the carriage. Sitting, he gave Victor a thumbs up that all was well. Victor nodded and hoped so, not just for the groom but for the ladies as well.

Chapter 21

The Hainsworth carriage pulled up the drive; Victor rode in front of them. He jumped off his horse quickly, and then he ran up to the front door. Wesley opened the front door, and Victor told him what he needed and ran back to the carriage to help. Duke and Jasper came out of the library to see what all the commotion was. Wesley informed them the Devonshire carriage overturned in the park, and the ladies were hurt. When Jasper heard the carriage overturned, he was out the front door before Wesley finished his explanation. The duke saw his son run, and he was right behind him. Jasper saw his sisters sitting up in the carriage and not Laurentia. His heart felt as if it stopped beating, and everything was in slow motion. He rushed to the carriage yelling at Victor,

"Where Is Lady Laurentia? Why Do I Not See Her? Victor, Tell Me At Once!"

Victor stood by the carriage and hesitated before saying, "She is lying on Countess Hainsworth's lap."

More panic went through Jasper's face. He threw open the carriage door, jumped up into the carriage, and stood over his love and the countess.

Countess said, "She has not come to yet. You must be careful; she has a head injury and is still bleeding, my Lord."

Pure terror entered Jasper's eyes, as he dropped to his knees, saying in a controlled voice, he had been trained to perform for many years. "I shall have her now and shall be careful."

Jasper gently scooped up Laurentia, with her head resting on his chest. Looking down to where Laurentia's head had been resting, he saw a lot of blood in the countess's lap. The countess handed him a small blanket she had been pressing to Laurentia's head to slow the bleeding. He took the blood-soaked blanket, thanking the countess before turning and stepping down from the carriage.

Victor asked, "Do you need help, Bellator?"

Jasper said instill a calm voice, "You can help my sisters to the house. I have Lady Laurentia."

Victor said, "Leopold was riding with me when this happened. He has gone to fetch the doctor, and he should be here soon."

Jasper looked up at Victor as he was passing him. "You must give me an account of what happened this afternoon, later after everyone has been attended to."

"Yes, we shall talk later, Bellator." Victor put on a brave face for his cousin's sake.

Jasper walked by the duke, who was watching his daughters stepping out of the carriage cautiously, Victor helping them.

Duke said to Victor, "Did I hear right, that Leopold has gone already to bring the doctor here?"

"Yes, he is on horseback and should be here soon.

Your daughters may have a broken bone, but Lady Sinclair has a head injury. She has not woken up yet, Your Grace.

"I'm glad you two were there to help. Let's get my daughters inside. Amara, you're holding your arm, my dear."

Amara sniffed. "That is where it hurts. I landed on it when we were thrown from the carriage, Father."

Aurora said, "My side hurts a lot, Father." She had tears in her eyes. Duke put this arm out for them to come to him. They embraced, then they told their father that they were never so scared and were terribly worried for, Lady Sinclair."

"Come, my darlings, let's get you inside." Duke saw the earl and countess watching his actions, "Please come inside. I am grateful you were there to assist my family in a time of crisis."

Earl Hainsworth said, "One of your grooms has a broken leg. My two grooms could help him to his quarters."

Duke said, "That would be helpful; I shall have Wesley send ice to help the swelling until the doctor can see you."

The groom said, "Thank you, I shall be fine. Make sure the ladies are looked after first, Your Grace." Duke nodded, then walked his daughters into the house.

The twin's maids took the girls up to their bedchamber. Duke told the maids to keep them comfortable while they wait for the doctor's arrival.

Duke ordered Wesley, "Send for Her Grace at once. See to it that the Earl and Countess Hainsworth are able to clean up and bring them some refreshment."

Wesley informed the duke that Jasper had taken Lady Sinclair to her room. The duke was about to climb the stairs when the front door opened, and Leopold and the doctor came in.

"I know my nephew has told you already of what has taken place at Hyde Park. However, Lady Sinclair needs your attention first, as she is still unconscious. This way, Doctor," Duke waved his hand toward the staircase.

All the Raventon men went up the stairs to Laurentia's bedchamber. Entering the room, they saw that Sandra was cleaning Laurentia's head wound as Jasper held her. Jasper was relieved to see the doctor entering the room.

"Her wound has stopped bleeding; she still has not woken up yet, doctor," Jasper said, informing the doctor of Laurentia's well-being.

The doctor said, "I shall examine the young lady now, so all you men can go out for now."

Jasper said, "Let me know as soon as you are finished examining Lady Sinclair. I want to know what is wrong with her and why she has not regained consciousness yet."

"Yes, my Lord, I shall do so, now let me examine her."

Duke, Victor, and Leopold walked out, but Jasper was hesitant to leave.

Duke said, "Come, son, she is in good hands now." Jasper walked out with the duke, not happy leaving Laurentia's side when he felt she needed him most.

The men were walking down the stairs when the duchess enter through the front door. Duchess ran to the duke's side, "Conrad, our girls, are they alright and Lady Sinclair?"

"The doctor just arrived. He is seeing Lady Sinclair first. She has a head jury and has been unconscious since the accident. For our daughters, Amara may have a broken arm, and Aurora's side is in pain. They are both still in shock from the whole ordeal. Their maids are with them now but, they need you, my love."

"I shall go to them at once."

The men went into the front parlor; the earl was waiting for his countess to return from cleaning up from holding Laurentia's injured head.

"I do not know about the rest of you, but in this situation, I need a drink." Duke poured a brandy for him and the others.

Drake walked in, looking frightened from the news he'd heard. "What happened?"

Jasper looked at Leopold and Victor and saw some of Laurentia's blood on their coats. He demanded, "I want to know what happened in Hyde Park, now."

Leopold started recounting the tragic incident, "We were riding on the east side of the park, on one of the not so busy carriage lanes. We noticed the Devonshire carriage coming toward us."

Jasper asked, "How fast was the carriage going as you approached?"

Victor cut in, "The carriage did not seem to been going that fast. The accident happened so quickly, and we were about ten yards from them."

Leopold said, "The carriage's axel seemed to snap, and it flipped to its side, throwing all passengers in the air. I have told Victor already that the accident was no accident at all. It would not have happened unless someone tampered with the carriage, I am sure." Jasper and the duke's expression turned to rage.

The duke barked out first, "Are you sure, Leopold?"

Jasper said, "Where is the carriage? I want that checked. There shall be hell to pay if you're right."

Leopold said, "The carriage is being moved as we speak to my company warehouse. I left orders when it arrives to have them inspected the carriage from top to bottom. But I know my carriages. The spot where it had broken should not have happened. Yes, I am sure."

Duke drank down his brandy in one swallow and slammed down his glass on the table he was standing by.

"Someone is trying to kill my family. I have made a lot of enemies in the past but to go after my women is wrong in so many ways. Whoever has done this shall wish they were never born once I get my hands on them."

Jasper said, "You mean we, Father, I shall help you. We shall turn London upside down until we find who is responsible for this act against our family. Mark my words."

Leopold said, "You can count me in on that. I shall help you. This is a family matter. As soon as my men tell me the result of the carriage inspection, I am 99 percent sure of what I had shared with you earlier on the carriage."

Victor said, "I'm with you too! We Raventon's stand together."

Drake nodded his head in agreement, saying, "London, is our home, and we won't stand for this attack against our family."

The countess entered the room and asked, "How are the ladies faring, Your Grace?" She walked over to where her husband was standing.

Then Wesley walked in and announced, "The doctor has finished with Lady Sinclair, and he is with your daughters, Your Grace."

Jasper walked out of the parlor with no words spoken and took two steps at a time, climbing the stairs. He entered Laurentia's room, and as he came close to the bed, he could see Laurentia in a night-gown, her eyes still closed. He asked Sandra, who was standing by the bed.

"Has she opened her eyes yet or spoken?"

"No, my Lord, the doctor says she should soon. He thinks she shall be alright, just a bad blow to the head, no brain bleeding that he can tell as of now. He checked the rest of her and found no broken bones, just a lot of bruising on her left side, my Lord."

"I shall sit with Lady Laurentia. You may go." Sandra bobbed and exited the room.

Jasper pulled a chair closer to the bed to sit and hold her hand. Jasper kissed Laurentia's hand tenderly.

"Come back to me, my love. I need you. Please wake up so I can see your beautiful violet eyes and hear your lovely voice, plus your fantastic giggle I adore. I would even enjoy hearing your feisty voice when you are cross with me. I do admire that you stand your ground with me."

The duchess came in to check on Laurentia's progress, and she walked over to the bed.

Jasper looked up and spoke, "You should be with the twins; they need you."

"The doctor is setting Amara's broken arm. He

already wrapped Aurora's ribs; they are bruised, not broken. They were lucky it was not worse than they received. You need me too, my Son." Duchess took his free hand and held it. "How is Lady Sinclair faring? Has she opened her eyes yet?"

Jasper looked back to Laurentia, "She has not opened her eyes yet. I shall stay here until she does. The doctor is sure she shall soon."

Duchess now put her hand on Jasper's shoulder and squeezed lightly. "Stay with her so she can see your face first when she awakes. She shall adore that. Do you love her, Jasper?"

Jasper looked back at his mother. "Yes, I do love Laurentia. I want to spend the rest of my life with her. I cannot imagine losing her now or ever."

"I am happy to hear you say that. I want all my children to find love. Just like your father and I have. It's important to have love and to share that with someone special."

"Thank you, Mother. She is the air I breathe and the sun that shines on my face."

"I should go back to the girls. I got queasy seeing Amara's arm being set, and I had to leave. Call for me when Lady Laurentia wakes up, my darling." She bent down, kissed Jasper's cheek, then walked out of the room.

A while later, the doctor came back in and asked, "How is my patient doing?"

"The same," Jasper told him.

The doctor checked the head wound, then her eyes. "She has stitches; it looks fine with little swelling. She will wake up soon, and when she does, call on me to come back. I want to recheck, Lady Sinclair then."

Jasper said, "I shall do that. Thank you for your service."

The doctor nodded and left.

At dinner time, Sandra brought in a tray of food for both of them. She was hoping Laurentia would smell the food and wake up. She did not.

As Jasper ate, he said to Laurentia, "The ham is good and the yams. Cook has done a great job. Wake up and join me, my love." When Sandra came back in, Jasper told her to take the tray away.

"When, my Lady wakes up, we will have something fresh brought up," Sandra said before she left the room.

Next, the twins came in. Amara asked, "Has she open her eyes at all?"

Jasper answered, "No, should you not be resting yourselves?"

Aurora said, "We are worried about, Lady Sinclair."

Amara said, "My arm hurts but not as bad as it had earlier. Jasper, we are sorry this happened. We truly are. It was our idea to take the carriage ride." Aurora nodded too.

Jasper said, "Do not blame yourselves. Leopold came back later with the report of the carriage. The carriage axel was sawed three-fourths of the way through. With the right bump or hole in the road, the axel was waiting to bust. It's not your fault; someone wanted to hurt this family. Father and I shall find out soon. They shall be sorry to have messed with the Raventon family."

The girls hugged Jasper and went back to their room to rest. Later that evening, the duke and duchess came in to bade goodnight and check on Laurentia's recovery

Jasper said, "She is the same. I plan to stay here

until she wakes. I hope you are alright with that?"

Duke answered, "It does not surprise us, my Son. We are exhausted with all this worry; I hope tomorrow is a better day, and we shall start our investigation then to find out who is responsible." Duchess kissed Jasper's cheek and bade him good night.

It was about midnight when Laurentia opened her eyes. She blinked a few times, wondering how she got here. The carriage was what she remembered last. "Ouch." Her head hurt as she moved some to look around. A single candle lit the room. Then she noticed Jasper asleep in the chair beside the bed, holding her hand. She smiled; it was nice seeing him here beside her bed. My bed and everyone knows, oh no.

Jasper felt the movement from Laurentia stirring; he looked straight to Laurentia's opened eyes. He sat up fast and grabbing both her hands, kissing them and then her lips softly.

"You are awake, my love. How long?"

Laurentia smiled when he called her his love. "Just now, what time is it? You should not be in my room like this, especially in the daytime. What if the duke and duchess see you in here?"

"Darling girl, do you not remember what happened in Hyde Park today?"

Laurentia thought, "Yes, I went for a ride in the park with your sisters in the carriage. Oh my, we were thrown through the air. That is all I remember."

Jasper sat on the bed, still holding her hands, and she sat up looking into Jasper's eyes.

"My love, when you were thrown from the carriage, you came down on a large rock, and you hit your head."

Laurentia touched the back of her head, "Ouch," she said out loud this time. "That figures; I have been sleeping all day. Is that what you are telling me, Jasper?"

"Yes, you have. I stayed here all day by your side in that chair, holding your hand, wishing you to open your eyes for me."

"All day there?" Laurentia pointed to the chair.

"Yes, not the most comfortable chair, I shall tell you that. But, I have been worrying, and I would not leave your side. I love you too much."

Tears started rolling down Laurentia's face. Jasper had a confused look on his face.

"My love, do not cry. What is wrong? Shall I call for the doctor? Do you hurt in other places? Tell me, please," Jasper pleaded.

"I do not hurt anywhere, only the back of my head if you touch it. These are tears of joy, Jasper. You just said you love me, and you keep calling me your love. Oh, Jasper, how I longed to hear you say those words to me. The first night we made love, I fell in love with you, and I so much wanted to say yes to your proposal the second night. But I would not marry you until you said you love me; I want love in my marriage as my parents had shared. Oh, Jasper, you have made me so happy. I love you too." They embraced, kissing so profoundly and yet so tenderly.

Jasper pulled back, looking into Laurentia's eyes. "The day when you walked into my parents' parlor when I looked into your beautiful violet eyes the first time, you had captured my heart, Laurentia. You hold the key, my love, and my heart has been doing time. Laurentia, I love you."

"Oh, Jasper, I love you." She threw herself into

Jasper's arms, and they kissed passionately.

"Jasper, please make love to me now!" Laurentia broke their kiss and pled.

Jasper pulled away and said, "Laurentia, you have a head jury, and you have not told me if you hurt anywhere else."

"I do not feel pain anywhere. My head does hurt a little. I shall not lie about that. I feel fine, really. Please, Jasper, make love to me. I need you, and I love you."

Jasper had his wicked smile on his face. "Yes, my love, you read my mind. I need you badly. I have this passion for unleashing from sitting here all day looking over you, worried sick, you must realize. Now we both said the words of love. Nothing could stop me now. You are mine Lady Laurentia Sinclair, all mines."

He leaped off the bed to lock both doors, and then his clothes went flying off. Jasper crawled onto the bed like a black panther, ready to seduce his prey. His black hair shone, and every muscle rippled as he moved to her. Laurentia wet her lips, and every nerve in her body came alive, seeing that wicked smile on Jasper as he crawled over her and took her lips.

Jasper kissed down her neck, saying between a kiss. "I am going to make deep passionate love to you, Laurentia. Every inch of your body is going to scream more, and I promise you that." He took her nightgown off and threw it to the floor. "You are so perfect, my love." He kissed her lips again, then licked and kissed his way down her neck, shoulder to shoulder to her breasts.

Laurentia was panting to the seductive pleasure

he was unleashing on her. He took one nipple in his mouth, sucked it, then swirled his tongue around the sensitive bud, and then sucked the nipple again. He kissed his way to the other nipple and did the same. Laurentia arched her back off the bed and grabbed the sheet in her fist to hang on.

"Oh, my Jasper, you are driving me crazy," she panted out.

"Good, my love, that is what I want to hear from your lips." Jasper kissed and licked his way down to her stomach, side to side, every inch he hit. At her navel, he swirled his tongue round and round, then sucked with his whole mouth over it.

Laurentia was in ecstasy. She cried out, "Please, Jasper, take me now."

Jasper lifted his head and said, "Oh, no, my love, to give you pleasure gives me even more pleasure."

He kissed and licked down her left leg, all the way to her foot. She giggled, for Jasper's tongue hit her ticklish spots on her foot. He smiled, loving the sound of her giggle, and did it some more. Jasper moved to her other leg and did the same. He came up the inside of one thigh, licking and kissing as he went. Jasper saw Laurentia grabbing the sheet again and realized he had her where he wanted her. Took two fingers to spread her folds open to her womanhood, and Jasper licked her slow and easy, making Laurentia pant again. He picked up the pace so that she would come hard for him. He licked and licked, playing with her bud, and hit the right spot that took Laurentia over the edge. She shivered and shook and screamed. "OOOhh, Jasper."

That was what Jasper wanted to hear, his name off her beautiful lips. He came up her lovely body and kissed her lips feverishly and said seductively.

"When I hear you say my name, that makes my blood pump harder through my veins, my desire for you burns hot like lava from a volcano, and all the heat that is pumping hard through my veins make me thirstier for you. That I have to have you, my love."

Jasper spread her legs, and in one thrust, he was inside her. Laurentia wrapped her legs around him as Jasper moved slowly at; first, a steady rhythm. She felt so good around his manhood.

Jasper moved faster and whispered in Laurentia's ear. "Come with me again, my love. I can hold back until you're ready."

Jasper took her lips and kissed her passionately as Laurentia put her arms around his neck, kissing just as wildly. Laurentia felt like she was in paradise. 'Jasper is so good at bringing the passion and love out of me, 'she thought, as her mind raced.

Then it happened; Laurentia felt the quivers building inside her. "Oh Jasper, I love you so," her orgasm was over the top.

Jasper let go of his seed, looking into Laurentia's eyes as he pumped hard. "I love you too, Laurentia,"

He lay on top of her, trying to catch his breath, not putting all his weight on her.

Jasper asked, panting, "My love, are you alright?"

"I would say that was our best one yet, and yes, I feel perfect."

Jasper rolled off Laurentia to his back, lying beside her. "Yes, I would say that was our best one. I think we shall have to keep trying to outdo our last one each time. If you do not kill me first." He laughed, and then she laughed too. Jasper pulled

Laurentia close into his arms to cuddle.

"Is your head, alright?" I mean, does it hurt, my love, from being injured much earlier today?"

"No, I do not hurt. I feel really relaxed right now. I'm kind of hungry."

"We would have to get dressed. I could ring for something to eat right now, for you."

"Let's wait for a while. This feels nice being in your warm arms. I did not ask, are your sisters alright? Did they get hurt too?"

"Amara has a broken arm, and Aurora has bruised ribs, and one groom has a broken leg. You all were fortunate; Leopold and Victor were about ten yards away on horseback. They came to your rescue, along with the Earl and Countess Hainsworth. They brought you back here in their carriage."

"I shall have to thank them in person. The girls shall be fine, I hope."

Jasper snorted a laugh, "I bet they shall take advantage of their injuries to get out of doing the things they dislike. I know Aurora and Amara too well."

"You are probably right. What else happened today that I missed?"

"You had a lot of visitors. All the Raventon's came to see if you and my sisters are alright."

"In my bedchamber, when I was unconscious?"

"Yes, my love, they had to see you, give you well wishes, even if you were not conscious to hear them. We are a tight-knit family; we all care deeply. You shall see in time. They shall love you as I do. Well, perhaps not as much as I love you, but close."

"It's genuinely nice to feel loved and for them to care. I shall have to thank your family also for dropping by, even if I did not see them."

"I almost forgot your brother Berwickshire came here today. He stayed only a short time, looked in on you, talked a few minutes, and said he would come back tomorrow. He hoped you would be awake then."

"That's strange in his last letter he did not mention he was coming to London. He would have said so, and I would have made certain our family home on Portman Square was opened up correctly for him."

"He was here; I say around three. The doctor was still here, and he reassured your brother, you should recover."

She rolled from her back to her front to look into Jasper's eyes as they talked. "I would have liked a better way for you to meet my brother for the first time. We are remarkably close. He and I only have each other now."

Jasper kissed her forehead "My love, do not worry. Your brother and I share a common interest. We both love you, dearly. We shall more than likely get along. I did tell him that I am courting you and plan to marry you soon."

Laurentia smiled, "What did Lucas say?"

He smiled back, "His words were, 'A future Duke, huh, my little sister has always done well. Not bad, not bad at all.'"

Laurentia laughed out loud. "That sounds like my brother. I am not surprised, very bold of him, but not surprised." She laughed some more.

Jasper said, looking not amused, "If he were not your brother, I would've put him in his place, believe me."

Laurentia stopped laughing, "He is not used to

being around others who outrank him. He seldom comes to London. I shall talk to him about proper etiquette if that makes you happy."

"Yes, that would be wise, my sweet."

"Some cheese, bread, and fruit would be nice. My stomach is growling now." Laurentia smiled with big eyes.

Jasper laughed, "I felt that we needed to get you something to eat, my love. I shall dress."

Jasper kissed her and rolled Laurentia off him as he got up to get dressed. He threw Laurentia her nightgown from the floor. She put it back on and nodded when she was ready. Jasper unlocked the doors, then pulled the rope for the maid.

Sandra arrived shortly and smiled when she saw Laurentia was conscious. "My Lady, you are awake. Oh, what joy. You had given everybody a fright, you did."

"Yes, I have probably scared everyone, not by choice."

"No, my Lady, definitely not. Is there something I could bring you?"

Jasper cut in, "Lady Laurentia seems to be hungry. She would like cheese, bread, and fruit," looking at Laurentia.

Laurentia nodded in agreement that would be nice.

"Have Wesley inform my parents that her ladyship is awake now."

Sandra curtsied, "Yes, my Lord, right away. I'm delighted you're awake, my Lady." And she ran from the room to spread the news and to get her mistress something to eat.

Jasper walked back to the bed, bent down to kiss Laurentia, took her hand, and sat on the edge of the bed.

Laurentia asked, "Did you have to awaken your parents? It has to be passed one in the morning."

Jasper kissed her nose, "You are almost a member of this family. We are courting, are we not? Plus, they were apprehensive about you. Mother said she wanted to be notified immediately when you woke, my love."

Laurentia sighed, "When Sandra brings the tray of food, I was hoping you could join me back in bed. To hold me and more whatnots."

Jasper laughed at her cuteness. "May I ask, what you are referring to, by these whatnots?"

Laurentia smiled, looking innocent. "You can make my pain go away with some more of your divine lovemaking skills."

Jasper raised a brow, "I think you should have more rest, and for my lovemaking skills, you are incorrigible, you know."

"I know, my Jasper," Laurentia purred.

"Laurentia, stop that! You are the one who wanted food, and my parents shall be along any time now." Jasper stood to get some distance; she is learning too well how to stir him into seduction.

A knock sounded on the door, and Jasper said, "Enter," quickly. Thank god. She is crafting to seduce me. I like it, but the wrong timing.

Sandra brought a tray of food over to the bed. Laurentia sat up, placing the tray on her lap. "Thank you, Sandra. I hope it was not much trouble in the kitchen."

"No, my Lady, Bridget, was happy to hear you were awake and Mr. Wesley too. Mr. Wesley is notifying the duke and duchess you are awake. Is there anything else I could do for you, my Lady?"

"No, this shall do. You may retire for the night." Sandra curtsied and exited.

"This looks good." Laurentia picked up a piece of sliced apple and ate. She also had cheese, bread, a slice of pound cake, and tea.

Jasper came back over to the bed; this time, he sat in the chair and watched Laurentia eat.

"Bridget is a treasure. She has a very caring heart and is a wonderful cook and baker." Laurentia nodded, for her mouth was full of food.

"You are hungry; that is a good sign you shall be alright."

A knock sounded on the door; the duke and duchess walked in, lighting up when they saw Laurentia sitting up and eating.

Duchess said, "My dear girl, you're awake, thank heaven, and you are eating. That is wonderful. Jasper, how long has she been awake?"

"About an hour, my Lady, was hungry as you can see and is very responsive, as you can also see." Jasper looked at Laurentia with a twinkle in his eye.

Duke said, "We are thrilled to see you awake. You gave us quite a scare, my dear."

Duchess said, "It is rather late, Jasper. I think you should stay the night. In your bedchamber, that is."

"I prefer my own bed at my townhouse. But, thank you, Mother, for the offer. I shall sit and watch my love eat her little spread of food. Then tuck her in and go home."

"Son, I want you here early tomorrow. We have a lot to discuss. Come, my duchess, it's late, and good-night Lady Laurentia." Duchess said good night too, and they went back to bed.

Laurentia asked, "What was your father referring to, to discuss what?"

Jasper sighed, "The accident today was no accident. Someone tampered with our carriage, and they shall pay." He had not wanted to tell Laurentia about that to refrain from frightening her.

Laurentia's eyes went as large as marbles. "Someone tried to kill us today? Oh, Jasper, who, why?"

"We do not know yet. But we will find out. Father, I, Drake, and the rest of the Raventon men are going to find out. If it means tearing London apart, so be it. We do not take lightly to someone trying to kill one of us."

"Jasper, this does frighten me so. They almost succeeded today with the carriage. Thank heaven the horses were not in full gallop."

"I know, starting today, you, Mother, and my sisters are not to leave this home without one of the men or a footman. Do I make myself clear?"

Laurentia looked at Jasper mutely, blinked a couple of times, started to say something, and then stopped. "Jasper, I'm at a loss. This does scare me. Whoever did this today could have killed us."

"My love, someone will pay for this, do not worry. We do not take this lightly. So please do not go anywhere out of the mansion without one of us men. Promise me. You are important to me, Laurentia."

She sighed, "Yes, I promise."

"You look like you're done eating. Let me take your tray."

Jasper took the tray and placed it on the small table in front of the fireplace out of the way before returning.

"I told my parents I was going home, and I always keep my word. You shall shortly find out that is always true. I shall be here early in the morning. I shall see you then, my love."

Laurentia put on a pouty face, "If you must."

"If we were married, you would be in my bed, not here. So, I suggest we do that soon. Then I would not be leaving you as I am and seeing that beautiful face pouting as it is now." Jasper kissed Laurentia long and demandingly. Then, he pulled away with reluctance.

"Good night. I love you." He kissed her forehead and turned and strolled out the room. Laurentia could hear Jasper walking down the corridor whistling happily.

Chapter 22

The Aftermath from the Carriage Incident

Early the next morning, the Raventon men and the duke's secretary, Mr. Edmond, gathered around a large table in one of the back parlors. They were drinking coffee and having a bite to eat. Duchess had a sideboard set up with eggs, sausage, biscuits, and pastries. Duke was at the head of the table, and they were all talking about the reason they were there.

His Grace cleared his throat to have everyone's attention. "I'm pleased that you have come here this morning, as you all have been discussing already that someone has committed a violent act against our family, and that is something I shall not tolerate."

Charlton spoke first, "Do you have any idea who?"

Duke answered, "I have had a lot of enemies throughout the years. As you know, I am a head figure at parliament, but, no, right now, I cannot think of anyone in particular."

Jasper said, "Mr. Edmond, have you made that list. His Grace asked you to make of the people that might act out upon us."

Mr. Edmond shuffled through his papers. "Yes, Lord Bellator, here you are."

Jasper took the list and looked over it, seeing no name that stood out as a threat. He handed it to his father, who looked it over before speaking.

"I have put one of my men to follow each of those named on this list. They shall be watching every move they have made as of yesterday afternoon."

Leopold said, "Is there anything to go on yet, Uncle?"

Duke said, "Lord Beaumont has been seen down on the docks, watching Drake's three ships. Also, Earl Merionreth, I have been told that he has been asking a lot of questions about the Raventon affairs at Whites in the last few weeks."

Johnathan spoke, "Merionreth, he is not so squeaky clean that one."

Jasper said, "He is not someone I would call a friend, but I know the man. He drinks and plays cards a lot at Whites and a few other gambling halls.

Victor said, "Yes, I have seen him around too. He likes to be flashy with money, talks a lot, and is a poor loser in cards."

Drake said, "Merionreth and I have played cards a few times. You're right; he is a sore loser. I took a couple of good hands with him at the table last week at Whites."

Duke said, "We have one more to watch closely, the Marquess of Wiltshire. We had words the last two sessions at parliament. He is not happy with some new changes that went through."

Victor asked, "How are the twins and Lady Sinclair doing today? That ordeal most definitely gave me some gray hair yesterday."

Duke answered, "The twins were up this morning already; they were breaking their fast with the duchess in her private parlor upstairs. They are still not themselves this morning. I would say the whole event still has them scared. Lady Sinclair had a tray delivered to her room and is taking it easy also."

When Laurentia's name was mentioned, Jasper smiled to himself, recalling last night's lovemaking and proclamations of love. However, he kept an impassive look on his face as he listened.

Kelsey said, "Uncle, give me a copy of that list of suspects. Then, I shall have a look at what finances or any last bank deposits they made in the previous six months." Kelsey has an office set up; he deals in investments and the stock exchange.

Duke looked at Mr. Edmond and directed him to make a list.

Kelsey said, "I shall leave here and go to my office to work on that list."

Charlton said, "Being it's Sunday, I can come with you to help out. I know your staff is off today, Son."

Kelsey said, "That would be helpful. We should go then." Edmond handed them a copy of the list, and they stood and bade goodbye.

Charlton said, "We shall let you know what we come up with later." Charlton and Kelsey headed out to work on the list that was given to them.

Leopold said, "Victor, Sterling, Drake, and I could go to Whites, act like nothing happen to our family yesterday, have lunch. We could ask close friends a few questions to determine if they saw or know anything about the carriage incident."

Duke said, "Good idea; let me know what you hear and be discreet."

Jasper said, "I shall look in on Lady Laurentia, then mother and the twins. Then join you at Whites afterward."

Drake said, "Jasper, I hate to say this, but when you are around, people do not talk freely. You intimidate most people."

Jasper said nonchalantly, "You say that as if it were a bad thing. I always get what I want out of people my way."

Victor said, "Yes, the scare tactic, Cousin." Then he laughed.

Duke cut in, "Jasper, I want you to come with me. I am going down to the docks to see what I can come up with."

Jasper looked at Drake as he spoke, "Fresh air sounds good. I shall go with you, Father."

Duke said, "Johnathan, you should come with us for more men's power." Jonathan nodded, yes. They all stood and went on their ways.

Jasper said to his father as they climbed the staircase, "I shall not be long checking on Lady Laurentia, then I shall come to mother's parlor."

Duke said, "Take your time; it is still early. Come along, Johnathan, let us check in on my duchess and daughters."

Johnathan said, "I'm right behind you. I shall send a message to Fantina and Gabrielle to come over and keep company with your ladies today. We do not know who's after our family or if they have any other plans in trying to harm us before we put an end to the criminals." Duke agrees; it's the right decision to have all the Raventon women under one roof for protection.

Jasper went to Laurentia's room, knocked, and entered when he heard Laurentia call. He found her sitting in the chair by the fireplace, sipping tea. Her face lit up when she saw him. He walked over to her and kissed her tenderly.

"Good morning, my love. You look very refreshed and beautiful as ever."

"Thank you. Is your meeting over?"

Jasper nodded then kissed Laurentia again. "You taste excellent like raspberries." He took a chair across from hers.

Laurentia smiled, "Bridget put the berries in my tea, and it's delicious. She is a gem."

Jasper studied Laurentia, then said, "I know, I wish she would come and join my household, but she is loyal to my parents. Although I had asked Bridget if she would, she turned me down. I even offered to double her salary."

"You are awful, trying to steal your parent's cook from them."

Jasper almost smiled then said casually, "Are you surprised? Most of the time, I do get what I want."

"Lord Bellator, you live a charmed life."

Jasper tilted his head, staring into Laurentia's eyes. "Its' almost perfect since I met you."

Laurentia casually asked, "Why almost?"

"When you marry me, when you share my bed, then it shall be perfect. What was that word you have used? Charmed? Especially moments like this, when all I want to do right now, this minute is to make love to you."

Laurentia licked her lips and crossed her legs. "How can you sit there and say things like that to me. You do not even look affected by your words, as they do affect me."

Jasper looked impassive, but the corner of his lip twitched. I like where this is going. "From the age of a young boy, I was taught to control feelings, expressions, patience, to have stronger willpower, and more. That is how a duke works. Ninety-nine percent of the time, I get what I want. It is a pretty damn good life, Lady Laurentia."

Laurentia was so turned on by Jasper, and he knew it too, looking so smug. Two can play this game. She was uncrossing her legs.

"I missed our dawn love making this morning before you left my bed. I'm so relaxed and feeling ever so wonderful. I usually sleep peacefully for a couple more hours." Laurentia sighed.

Jasper saw her game. She's trying to make me break my control and seduce me. I do like it. I knew once I unleash Laurentia's passion, she would be a fun challenge and very playful in bed.

"What do you like the best that I do to you, my love? Suckling your breasts, licking and kissing your body, the inside of your thigh when I lick and kiss there, licking the fold in between your legs, finding that little bud of yours or when I am inside of you, Laurentia?" Jasper still had his cool look on his face, and his eyes seemed to be sparkling bluer.

Laurentia said, "All and you know it!" She sprung off her chair, and in two steps, she was in Jasper's lap, kissing him madly.

Jasper won that game and was receiving what he wanted. As he kissed Laurentia, he unfastened the front of his breeches then helped Laurentia to her knees, pushing away all her undergarments in the way so she could ride and straddle him in the chair. Jasper broke the kiss before penetrating her.

"This shall be new. Put your hands on my shoulders, my love, and use them to help yourself ride me and move. I shall put my hand on your waist to help, and you are in control this time."

Laurentia smiled, liked the idea she was in control and nodded yes. Jasper lifted her a little higher over his erection; Laurentia sunk all the way down as he filled her. Their lips met, and they moaned with pleasure. Jasper guided Laurentia to move up to the tip of his penis and back down. He helped her twice then let go of her waist; she went slow at first to enjoy the entire feeling of their togetherness as one. Laurentia was starting a nice rhythm, going a little faster and smoother. Laurentia wanted this, it felt so good, and Jasper was letting her take complete control.

Jasper held back, waiting for Laurentia to come with him. He felt a quiver starting in her, so he kissed her harder so she would not scream out, to stifle her as she orgasmed. Laurentia was shaking as her orgasm overcame her. Jasper retook Laurentia's waist to keep her moving, and he came inside of her, filling her with his seed and groaning in the pleasure of true bliss. Jasper wrapped his arms around her, holding her tight as they both came down.

Catching her breaths, Laurentia giggled on Jasper's shoulder. "That was quite naughty of us," and she laughed some more.

Jasper looked into Laurentia's eyes, "I love you and your delightful giggle."

Laurentia kissed him. "I love you, too, but I better get off your lap like this before someone sees us."

Jasper helped Laurentia to stand. She fixed her garments as he pulled up the front of his breeches. They laughed a moment, and she then walked to her dressing table to look at herself in looking glass, to see if she seemed fine or not.

"You look more beautiful right now with a glow from our making love."

Laurentia turned around quickly. "Sssh, someone might hear you."

Jasper stood and walked over to Laurentia. "Good, then we can marry tomorrow with a special license." He kissed her on the nose.

Laurentia looked up at Jasper, "You have yet to propose to me again, and I would like a church wedding."

Jasper looked amused. "Is that so? Later today, that may happen." He shrugged and walked to the door. He turned back and looked over his shoulder. "I have to go now. Father and I have a quest to find out who tried to wrong the family yesterday. I shall be back later today, my love." And out the door, Jasper left. She heard his whistle again as he walked down the corridor.

Laurentia stomped her foot in frustration and said out loud.

He is so full of himself, and I want a proposal now. Then again, he is so wonderful, and I do love him." Laurentia shook her head and sighed.

When Jasper reached his mother's parlor, the duchess said, "Jasper, good morning, how is Lady Laurentia faring this morning?"

"She is feeling much better. I'm happy to report. And how are my two lovely sisters this morning?" Jasper put his arms out to hug the twins. They stood and ran into his arms for a much-needed hug. Jasper was careful not to hurt their injuries further as he kissed their foreheads.

Amara said, "Uncle Johnathan has asked Aunt Fantina and Gabriella to come and spend the day with us."

Aurora said, "Aunt Louisa is coming too. It's going to be a lady's day of fun." The twins both beamed with joy as they let go of their brother's embrace, taking a seat again

Duchess said, "We are still carrying on with the dinner party tonight. Your father wants us to look as normal as possible, as nothing had happened."

Jasper looked to his father, "Makes sense. He may be watching us. Then we should put our men out there to spot him watching us."

Duke said, "That is correct. The women coming here today shall give us peace of mind when we are all out today. I have ordered six men to stand guard at all perimeters of the mansion and six more men to watch from different angles from across the streets for anyone looking suspicious."

Jasper and Johnathan both nodded in agreement.

Jasper said, "We should head out; we have a lot of ground to cover."

"Yes, we should. We shall be back in plenty of time before the dinner party this evening, not to worry, my darling," duke bent down to kiss his duchess.

"That is not what I am worried about; it is this whole tragedy hanging over our heads, Conrad."

"I know, my love, and I am sorry this has you upset. However, we, Raventon men, are determined to have this over within no time. Mark my word."

"In the meantime, I hope nobody else gets hurt or killed," Duchess said, then sipped her tea.

Jasper said, "That's why we should act fast and hit hard."

Johnathan said, "Then let's go, men!" They all bade goodbye and were on their way.

Duchess said to the girls, "We should go down to the front parlor to await our company to arrive." On her way out, she told her personal maid Myra to let Lady Laurentia know the plan for the day, and she should come down soon to join them.

In the parlor, the duchess looked over the dinner party's seating chart that night, and the twins were doing embroidery when Laurentia walked in. Laurentia bade good morning to all, then asked the twins how they were faring.

Twins echoed together, "Much better, thank you."

Duchess asked, "Are you well, my dear? How is your head? I should have the doctor summoned to take a look at you."

"I am feeling fine, Your Grace. The doctor is not necessary."

"He did want to check you when you gained consciousness. I think it is for the best." Duchess rang for Wesley.

Wesley entered and bowed, saying, "Yes, your Grace."

"Wesley, have the Doctor come. My two sisters-in-law are coming soon, and my niece. When they arrive, have tea and cakes brought in, please."

"As you wish, your Grace," Wesley, excited to do her bidding.

A half-hour later, Lady Fantina and Lady Gabrielle arrived. The twins lit up to see their cousin meeting her halfway in the parlor.

Gabrielle asked, "Are you well, my dear Cousins? When I heard what happened, I was so scared for you both and Lady Laurentia."

Amara said, "I have a broken arm, as you see, but the rest of me is fine."

Aurora said, "My ribs and left side are bruised. The doctor has wrapped me, so I do not hurt as bad."

Fantina walked up to the twins, hugged the girls softly, not to hurt them.

"Oh, my lovely nieces, that was so awful to happen to you." Fantina stepped over to Lady Laurentia and took her hand. "You, my dear girl, were knocked out cold, I have heard. Are you all alright? Lord Bellator must have been so worried for you. We were all worried too, you see," she exclaimed in her French accent.

Laurentia smiled at the memory of Jasper sitting by her bedside and telling her he loved her for the first time. "I truly feel fine; the duchess just sent for the doctor to check on me."

Fantina said, "It is a good idea; one must be checked with a head injury."

Duchess said, "Come have a seat. Louisa should be along soon; we shall have tea." She waved her hand to the empty chairs.

When the doctor arrived, the duchess invited him into the parlor so he could examine Lady Laurentia.

"Ah, our patient is conscious, I see." He walked over to Laurentia, set his bag down, and took her wrist to check pulse first. "Very good. How do you feel? Is your vision blurry? Does your head hurt?"

"My vision is fine. My head hurts a little, like a headache."

"Let me look at your wound."

The doctor looked to the duchess if it's alright to do so in the company. Duchess nodded yes, and he took the bandage off.

"I see no infection or swelling; it looks good." He

felt around the wound. "I shall put a smaller bandage on" The doctor wrapped a smaller bandage to the back of Laurentia's head, and he covered it with her hair.

"If you feel more pain, have a blackout or blurry vision, I am to be called upon immediately. Now let me check my younger patients." The doctor turned to the twins, checking Amara's arm for swelling and Aurora's ribs to see if her swelling had gone down. He nodded his head in approval that all was well.

"Your daughters are on the mend, Your Grace. Please call on me if anything changes with my three patients."

Duchess said, "Thank you, doctor. Wesley shall see you out."

When he was gone, the duchess said, "I'm glad to hear all my girls are healing well."

Laurentia looked over to the duchess, and a tear came down from the corner of her eye; she wiped it away.

Duchess saw the tear then said, "Yes, Lady Laurentia, you are one of my girls. I hope you do marry my son soon with my blessing."

Laurentia felt a little overwhelmed; she started to feel like a part of the family even more than before. More tears came down her cheeks. The twins jumped up and went to Laurentia, giving her a hug.

Amara said, "Do not cry; we already think of you as our big sister. You are family, Lady Sinclair."

Laurentia said, "I am crying for I long to have a family again, and all of you are so wonderful to me. Thank you. I think it's time you may start calling me Lady Laurentia. I had felt when I was hired as your governess, it was proper at the time to address me as Lady Sinclair. But as we all know, things have changed suddenly."

Amara said, "Mother, did you hear she said we might call her by her first name."

Duchess said, "Yes, I am pleased."

Amara asked, "Did Jasper ask you to marry him, and you said yes?"

"Yes and no. Jasper did ask me before the ball, and I had said no. But at the ball, I agreed he might court me. As you know, and I am finding out, your brother does not give up on what he wants. So, Jasper has not asked me yet again. But, I believe he shall when the time is right."

Amara looked at her sister then said with a smug smile, "I have won this bet too, Sister."

Duchess asked, "Tell me, my girls, what did you bet this time?"

Aurora said, "We were betting whether Jasper shall or shall not marry this season."

Amara cut in, "I said that he would and marry Lady Laurentia."

Aurora said, "I bet he was not ready to marry anyone this season."

Amara was all smiles. "I won!"

Duchess told Laurentia, "My daughters like to make bets, of all nature. They have been doing this since they were four years old. I believe it's a twin thing. Sometimes they're funny, and sometimes you're shocked at what they bet on." She shrugged and then laughed. They all chuckled together.

When Louisa came in, she said, "I heard laughing from the corridor. What did I miss, dear family?" Amara told her aunt what they were talking about, and of course, Aurora cut in to say her part of it. They were all laughing now.

The group was interrupted by Wesley entering and announcing, "Lady Laurentia, you have a guest. The Earl of Berwickshire has requested a visit."

Laurentia said, "Do have him come in, Mr. Wesley. He is my brother."

Brother and sister met each other warmly in the middle of the parlor, hugging tightly and kissing one another's cheeks, smiling brightly.

Stepping back from their embrace, Laurentia spoke, "It has been so long; I have missed you terribly, Lucas."

"Yes, sister, it has been too long," his sky-blue eyes warm with emotion.

Laurentia turned back to the room. "I would like you to meet my brother Earl of Berwickshire. First, I would like you to meet the Duchess of Devonshire."

He bowed. "Your Grace, it's an honor to meet you. You have a lovely home here in London."

"It's a pleasure to meet you. Shall you be staying in London long?"

"I may stay for a few weeks, Your Grace."

Laurentia continued, "Her daughters Lady Amara, Lady Aurora, the twins I wrote to you about."

Aurora cut in, "I hope she wrote all good things."

Earl bowed, and the girls stood and curtsied.

"Most of it was good," Lucas laughed and winked at the girls with a bright smile, making the twins giggle.

"This is Lady Louisa, the duchess's sister-in-law."

He bowed then said, "I am pleased to meet you, my Lady."

She stood to curtsy, then said, "Thank you, my

Lord, I can see the family resemblance."

Laurentia then introduced Lady Fantina and her daughter Lady Gabrielle.

He bowed to Fantina first. "Fantina, est une nom française?" (Fantina, is a French name?)

Fantina stood to curtsy then said,"Oui, et vous parlez français couramment" (Yes, you speak French fluently?)

Lucas answered, "Oui, j'ai appris français dans ma jeunesse. J'ai etudie et a vécu la pour trois ans avant la mort de mes parents (Yes, I learned French in my youth. I studied and lived there for three years before my parents died)."

Fantina said, "Je suis désolé d'entendre parler de vos parents. Votre français est tres bon" (I'm sorry to hear about your parents, your French is excellent).

Lucas smiled, "Merci beaucoup" (Thank you very much).

Lucas turned to Gabrielle, and he bowed then said. "I am enchanted to meet you, Lady Gabrielle. You are lovely," he smiled.

Gabrielle blushed as she curtsied; she raised. "Thank you, and I am pleased to meet you, my Lord," still blushing.

Laurentia cleared her voice to have her brother's attention again, and he looked back to Laurentia. "Come have a seat, tea is about to be served soon, we can visit, and you can tell me what brought you to London unannounced. You did not write to me that you were coming, dear Brother."

Lucas took the seat in a plush chair beside Laurentia. He looked her over then said, "What is this business with a carriage accident?"

"I was riding in Hyde Park with the twins, and

the carriage axel broke. According to the duchess's nephew, the axel on the carriage was cut. Someone is trying to hurt the Raventon's or worse. That is the reason all the Raventon ladies are here now. For the Raventon, men are out combing London to find out who could be behind yesterday's tragic event."

Duchess said, "His Grace is a well-respected man in London, as is the rest of my family members. They shall find who did this. It is just a matter of time."

Lucas asked, "Are you alright? I understand the two young ladies were with you?"

Laurentia said, "I hit my head on a rock when I was thrown from the carriage. The doctor just left before you arrived. He said I am doing fine, but I do have a slight headache. Amara has a broken arm, and Aurora has bruised ribs. They are recovering, and it could have been worse."

Lucas, looking impassive, said, "I am glad all of you are alright. When I arrived yesterday and found you unconscious, it did scare me. You are my only living family."

Laurentia reached out and patted his hand, telling him, "All is well now, do not worry, dear Brother."

Lucas said with concern in his eyes, "I hope not."

Jennell came in with the tea cart.

Duchess said, "Lady Amara and Lady Aurora, you may serve the tea for our guests."

They walked to the tea cart, worked together, poured tea, and served everyone with a plate of small cakes and a cup of tea. They looked to the duchess for approval after they finished. She smiled and nodded to them and mouthed, "Flawlessly executed, my darlings."

Louisa asked, "Is the dinner party still planned for this evening, Your Grace?"

"Yes, we shall not be frightened. We shall continue our plans as normal. Lord Berwickshire, would you care to join us this evening? I am having a dinner party tonight with family and some close friends. There shall be music and dancing after we dine."

Lucas looked at his sister; she nodded to him.

"It shall be an honor to join you this evening, Your Grace."

Lucas thought to himself, 'With the Raventon men on a search to find who did this and stop it, all shall be well. I remembered all the Raventon men yesterday, and I do not think I should tamper in this yet.' Lucas drank his tea and finished the cakes on his plate. When Jennell came over to offer more tea, he said no and took his cup and plate. Lucas watched his sister as she chatted back and forth with the other ladies. He noticed how she fit in and how they made her feel at home. He smiled, for he was happy for her. Lord Bellator cares for Laurentia deeply, staying by her bedside. Yes, she shall be fine.

Lucas stood, saying, "Thank you for the tea, Your Grace. I now have to go and run errands, being I just arrived in London and all."

Laurentia stood, "I shall walk you out."

Lucas bowed then said, "I shall see all you beautiful women this evening." He gave his grandest smile. The ladies smiled at Lucas, bade goodbye, and went back to talking amongst each other.

Laurentia walked her brother to the front door. First, they hugged, then Lucas said.

"You look like you fit in well with this family. I watched it as we had tea. Is this what you want as your future, dear sister?"

Laurentia smiled up at Lucas. "Yes, I do love

Lord Bellator, and he loves me too. Plus, his family in this short time have made me feel as I belong. I am delighted you are coming to the dinner party tonight!"

"What time shall I return this evening?"

"Six is when the guests are arriving. I am greatly pleased you have come to London for some of the season, Lucas."

Lucas bent down, kissed her forehead, then said. "I shall see you this evening. Maybe some London entertainment should suit me well for a change."

Laurentia nodded, "I agree, till then, Lucas." She opened the door, watched her brother walk down the stairs, and waved to him as he stepped into his coach.

As she walked back to the parlor, she thought, 'I have noticed all the extra men out front on guard today. The Raventon's do not stand down in the sight of danger. Jasper was right, and he did say that his family would love me as he does. I am delighted! But when is he going to ask me to marry him again? Is he making me wait because I said no the first time?' She giggled, 'remembering about all the pleasurable acts they had shared in private together.' Laurentia was still smiling as she entered the salon and took her seat to continue her afternoon with her new family that had been embracing her with love.

Chapter 23

The Raventon Men Are Out Combing London for Answers

Leopold, Drake, Sterling, and Victor walked into Whites. It was not that busy for a Sunday morning. They walked into the library; a few gentlemen were reading the paper and drinking coffee. The four sat in wingback chairs in a corner, and a waiter immediately came over to serve them.

After giving their order, Leopold said, "We should break up; I think talking one on one to different gentlemen would be easier to get the information we need out of them."

Victor said, "We should drink some coffee first, chat, then break up. Try not to look as if we are up to something." They all nodded in agreement as the waiter came back with the coffee and sweet rolls.

Leopold said, "I shall go into the next salon, Drake, Victor, you two hit the cardroom, and Sterling, you stay in this room."

Drake said, "Do not be direct in questioning them. Instead, talk around what you want to know, and then push in a few questions."

Sterling said, "At one-thirty, we shall meet in the dining room for lunch. We can discuss what we have learned at that time." They drank the coffee and ate the sweet rolls that were served as they chatted back and forth.

Drake said, "Well, gentlemen, we should get onto our reason for coming here now. See you at one-thirty in the dining room." They stood up and departed the directions they agreed upon to complete their interrogations in the different rooms of the club.

The duke and Jasper, along with Johnathan, decided to take Johnathan's coach because the duke's coach was too flashy, and they wanted the least attention on them as possible.

Jasper said, "I need to stop on Bond Street to pick up something I had made at the jeweler. It is not to be ready until noon, but I had paid extra to have it done at an earlier time."

Duke said, "I take it that it's something for Lady Laurentia?"

"Yes, I had a ring made for her."

Johnathan tapped the small door on the ceiling, and his driver opened it.

"We need to stop on Bond Street," Johnathan said, then looked to Jasper for where.

"Heming Jeweler Shop," Johnathan repeated that to the driver

After retrieving the ring, the coach moved on; Jasper said, "If someone had asked me a week ago that I would be asking a lady to marry tonight, I would have laughed in their face."

Duke said, "When you find the right woman, you know, and the rest of your life is blessed, my Son."

Johnathan said, "That is the truth of it all, and your bed is never cold after your wedding vows." They all laughed together at the last words spoken.

They rode down to the docks and pulled up to a tavern called the Rusty Anchor, one of the watering holes that sailors and ruffians frequented.

Duke said, "This place was known for hanging low, hired men that had nothing to lose come here. Let us start here first."

When the three well-dressed gentlemen walked in, everyone stopped what they were doing to stare. As they walked to the bar, the crowd went back to their business.

"What can I get ya, Gov?" asked the barkeep.

Looking formidable, Duke said, "Three ales to start with."

The barkeep poured three ales, slapped them on the bar in front of them, not too friendly-like, and asked.

"Is there anything else ya need, Gov?"

Extremely irritated, the duke glared into the man's eyes, "You can tell me which one of these men here would be hired to cut an axel on a carriage."

The barkeep said, "Ya have to pay for that information, Gov." He smirked at them.

Duke reached into his pocket, threw a few gold coins on the bar. "That is for the drinks." Then he threw twice as much down, then said, "That is for the information if I like it."

Barkeep went to grab all the coins from the bar, but the duke slammed his fist on top of the barkeep's hand that was covering the coins on the bar.

"Information first." Duke's voice was cold and uncompromising. Jasper and Johnathan grabbed the grips of their swords.

The barkeep looked up to the duke and the two men beside him, and he swallowed. "I don't want any trouble here, Gov."

"There shall not be any if you answer the questions, I just asked," Duke growled.

The barkeep looked around, then back to them. "The man in the back left corner sitting alone with his back to the wall, that's the man you seek."

Duke stared into the barkeep's eyes as if he would rip his head off any moment. "He better be the right man."

The barkeep said, "Yeah, I'm sure he is." He looked down at his hand, and Duke let go.

"Stay here at the bar. I am going to have a conversation with the man in the corner."

Jasper said, "We shall watch your back."

Duke walked over to the man and looked down at him with a deadly glance in his eyes. The man was colossal and well-dressed for this establishment. He nodded for the duke to take a seat. Duke pulled the chair out, never losing eye contact with the man.

The man said, "This isn't your part of town, Your Grace."

The duke said, "You know who I am, I take it."

The man almost laughed, then said, "Yeah, you're Devonshire. What brings you to my neck of the woods?"

"Since you know my name, it's only polite to tell yours. I'm told you're the one to talk to."

"You can call me Mr. Smith. Tell me, what information do you seek, and what makes you think I know the answer?" He leaned back in his chair.

Duke lost his patience. "Enough with these games. Yesterday someone crossed the line endangering my family by cutting the axel to one of my carriages. I need to know who did this." He leaned back in his chair, looking menacing.

"Yes, I can see your problem. I can tell you this; it was not one of my hires. But I could ask around to find some answers. For a price, of course."

Duke looking impassive, said, "You do that, and if you give me answers I wish to hear, I shall pay heavily. Send me word that you found who is responsible, and I shall set another meeting with you."

Smith nodded, and the duke rose and returned to the bar where Jasper and his brother waited.

Duke said, "It's time to take our leave."

They walked out, watching over their shoulders. When they reach the outside, the three walked down the street to their next destination.

Duke said, "That man knows something, but he is not talking yet. I shall send one of my men to follow him."

Jasper said, "We shall wait a couple of days. Then, if he does not give us answers, I shall come back here and beat the answers out of him myself."

Duke looked at his son and knew he meant what he had just said. They walked two blocks to another tavern. As Johnathan had ordered his driver to do, the coach followed them down the road and parked across the street.

Before walking in, Jasper said, "I shall take this one, Father."

The duke nodded to his son, and they walked into the tavern, gaining the same reaction as the last establishment as the crowd watched the well-dressed aristocrats enter. This place was called Devil Edge, a place sailors, cutthroats, and thieves frequented. When they walked to the bar, the barkeep said with a smirk on his face, "I think you're in the wrong place, gentlemen."

Looking formidable, Jasper said, "I believe we are in the right place."

The barkeep looked around the room, then said, "What will you have?"

Jasper answered, "Three whiskeys in clean glasses, to start." He glared into the barkeep's eyes.

The barkeep swallowed, reached under the bar, pulled out glasses that seemed clean, dropped them on the bar, and poured whiskey. "I do not want any trouble here today."

Jasper picked up one of the glasses, sniffed its contents then drank the whole thing down before slamming the glass back on the bar.

Looking menacing, Jasper said, "There shall not be any trouble unless I do not hear what I came for."

"What makes you think I know what you seek to hear?"

Jasper reached into his coat pocket and threw down five gold coins, then eight more before he said, "Every man has a price."

The barkeep went to grab the coins, but Jasper quickly pulled out a large dagger, its handle encrusted with rubies, from his inside coat pocket and stabbed the bar in between the barkeep's fingers. The barkeep froze and looked up to Jasper's face making a gulping noise.

"I missed your fingers on purpose. The next time, I shall not. Do you know who I am?"

"Yes, you are Marquess Bellator. Most men know and fear you."

"Good, now tell me who tampered with my family's carriage, and the coins are yours."

"If I do that, I would be a dead man."

Jasper growled, "Where I am standing now, I see

a dead man already if I do not get my answers, and my patience are wearing thin." He glared down at him.

The barkeep looked around, but nobody seemed to want to help him. He said, his voice shaking, "I heard two men talking yesterday that the job they did with a carriage did not kill the passengers."

"Who were the men?"

"They have never been in here before, new faces. I swear." Barkeep trembled.

"Are they here now?"

The barkeep looked around, then shook his head no.

Jasper said through gritted teeth, "If they come back in here again, I want your word that you shall send for me. If they leave before I arrive, you have them followed. Do I make myself clear?"

"Yes, my Lord, I will send for you at once."

Jasper pulled his dagger out of the bar and put it back into the inside of his coat pocket. He nodded to the barkeep and took a step back. "Tell me what these men look like?"

"One is about my height with brown hair, dark eyes, and has a scar on his chin. The other is skinny, tall in height, with curly blond hair. He has a tattoo of a bird on his left lower arm."

Jasper threw down two more gold coins and said, "You may take them now. I shall want to hear from you soon."

The duke and Johnathan picked up their glass, drank down their whisky, slammed their glasses down on the bar, and walked out with Jasper.

Out on the street, they walked across the road to Johnathan's coach.

Once inside, the duke said, "Good touch with your grandfather's dagger in there. He would've been proud to see you have it and used it."

Jaspers said casually, "It has become one of my favorite daily accessories. I always carry it. One never knows when you may need a sharp blade."

Duke said, "Precise, Son. From that tavern, we may have a description of the men who sabotaged my carriage. I feel we are getting closer to finding them."

Jasper said, "We shall take care of him ourselves when we find them, one by one. The Raventon way!"

Johnathan said, "I am with you on this." They all nodded in agreement.

Duke said, "Let's stop at one more tavern before home. Do you want the lead on this one, Jonathan?"

"I'm here for support, plus it's enjoyable to watch you two in action." They all laughed together. They stopped at one more tavern to make sure all knew that the Raventon's were searching to find the ones responsible for the event in Hyde Park.

Duke said, "God, help their soul when we find them. They shall pay dearly and be sent to hell." Jasper smiled menacingly, and Johnathan nodded.

Back in the White's dining room, Drake started their meeting by asking Leopold what he'd learned.

"The carriage incident is the top talk of conversation today." They all nodded in agreement. Leopold continued, "I learned that Merionreth has been asking many questions that were mentioned this morning in the meeting before we came here. He was asking about the Berkeley Square mansion and the manpower that is there."

Sterling said, "I found the same answers. Also, Lord Wiltshire has been bad-mouthing His Grace a lot about supporting the new laws passed." The waiter came back with their drinks, and they stopped talking until he left.

Victor said, "Word out, a new phony investment company Vander Star or something like that, has been circulating, and Merionreth has something to do with it."

Drake said, "Yes, I heard the same on Merionreth; no one has seen him today either. After we eat, I'm going over to let Father know what we discovered so far."

Leopold said, "A lot is pointing toward Merionreth, not good as I see it. Bellator, Kingsley, and I found him beneath one's quality to let him hang with us in our days at Eton and feel the same in present time." They all agreed. "That said, we need to find him and interrogate him to get the answers we seek." Leopold continued. Finishing their lunch, they parted ways and said, "We shall see each other tonight at the dinner party."

When Drake returned to Berkeley Square, he looked for the duke and Jasper. It was three-thirty, and they had not yet returned.

Wesley said, "The duchess and the other ladies have been busy with this evening's arrangement for the dinner party. The young mistresses are in one of the back salons arranging flowers. Her Grace and the others are in the dining room and ballroom."

"Thank you, let me know when His Grace has returned." Drake decided to see his sisters and Laurentia when he walked into the room.

Aurora said, "Drake, come and see our flower arrangements."

Drake walked over to the table, "Your arrangements look lovely."

Amara said, "Brother, do you think so?"

"Yes, you could work in a flower shop. My sister has mastered the art in flower arrangements," Drake said dramatically, and they all laughed together.

Aurora said, "That would never happen, working in a flower shop, that is. Mother would have us both married off to the first Marquess or Earl that come along. He could be old, fat, or ugly. Mother would not care if that meant to stop us from ever working in a flower shop or any sort of labor."

Drake said, "Yes, I could see that happening, our mother taking swift actions to stop something she would not approve of."

Amara said, "I want a handsome husband; he has to be wealthy too. Mother would want him to have a title, and I do know that."

Laurentia said, "In a few years, you shall find the perfect husband, both of you."

Aurora said, "I am in no hurry to marry. I want to experience a lot of things in life first."

Amara said with a big smile, "I do too."

Drake said, "I'm glad to hear that you both have plenty of time ahead of you. Gabrielle, I almost did not see you from behind that large vase. Hello Cousin, it is good to see you."

Gabrielle peeked around the arrangement, "Do you think I went overboard on my flower arrangement? Hello Drake."

Laurentia said, "That one can go on the table in the front entrance; it is lovely."

Amara said, "Yes, that would be perfect, Gabrielle; the colors are grand. Mother will love it." The arrangement was 's in a vast crystal vase filled with white and red roses, purple iris, various colors of carnations, and some gerbera.

Jasper strolled in and went straight to Laurentia, for they no longer had to hide their affection for each other. Jasper took her hand, and looking into her eyes, he turned her hand over, then kissed her palm tenderly.

"You are more beautiful now than this morning, my love." He wore that wicked smile she knew too well.

Laurentia smiled with a twinkle in her eyes, "Thank you, my Lord."

Aurora broke their bubble, cutting in. "Jasper, Lady Laurentia permitted us today that we may address her by her first name."

Jasper raised an eyebrow, still looking into Laurentia's eyes. "That's a nice little sister. I am glad to hear it."

Laurentia smiled, "We are almost betrothed. Are we not?" She tilted her head, waiting for his answer.

Jasper looked to everyone watching them, then said, "Yes, I believe that is right." Jasper noticed Drake standing there watching him. "Was White's helpful in providing information?"

Drake said, "Yes, I've been waiting on your return to share what we learned and to hear what you found as well."

"Come, let us go to the library; that is where Father is now. If you would excuse us, ladies." Jasper bowed then left the room with Drake on his trail.

Laurentia thought, 'I could watch him all day.

When he moves around, he is so graceful and perfect, my Jasper.'

In the library, Duke, Johnathan, Jasper, Drake, and Mr. Edmond were sitting around the large desk discussing the new information they'd found today.

Drake started first on the matters of Earl Merionreth. "This Vander Star company I learned about today is a phony investment scheme, and Merionreth has something to do with it. All four of us heard the rumors on that from several people. He also asked questions about our Berkeley Square residents, including our staff and how many servants we have. As for Wiltshire, he is just badmouthing you, Father, because he's not happy with parliament business, is all. I do not believe he would try to hurt the family.

Duke agreed with Drake's opinion on Wiltshire but still wanted to keep a watch on him.

Jasper asked, "Was Merionreth at the club today?"

Drake answered, "No, he has not been seen today."

Jasper said, "It is odd for him to be asking about the servants here. Father, call Wesley in here. We need to question the staff." Duke was thinking the same thing and rang for Wesley.

When Wesley arrived, Duke said, "Wesley, it's come to my attention that outsiders have been inquiring about my staff and what goes on in this residence. What do you have to say on that subject?"

Wesley looks shocked at first, "Your Grace, I am not aware of this, but shall get to the bottom of it right away."

Jasper said, "This might have something to do

with the carriage incident; we need the answers now."

Wesley said, "Yes, my Lord, I'll being inquiries immediately."

Duke said, "Go and be prompt about it. You know what to do with insubordination."

When Wesley had gone, Duke said, "He shall find out what is going on in my home. Then maybe we can put the pieces of this puzzle together quickly."

Drake asked, "What did you find out at the docks today?"

Duke said, "We visited a few taverns put the word out that we Raventon's shall not look kindly on someone trying to harm the family. One man knew of what hiring goes on for money, hits, and whatnots. He said it was not him who did the hiring but shall investigate it for a price. A barkeep said he overheard two men talking of the event at Hyde Park. That he never saw the two before but shall let us know if they come in, again for a price, of course."

Jasper said, "I do not care for this waiting around, Father. Find out if your man is still following Meri-onreth and what he is doing."

Duke said, "Edmond, do we have any reports on him?"

Edmond shook his head. "No, Your Grace, it seems he is staying at his home today. I just received that report."

Jasper said, "Anyone going in and out of his home?"

"Just his valet. He went to the tailor to pick up what looked like a couple of new suits."

Duke asked, "Which tailor does he use?"

Edmond said, "On Bond Street, Fletcher's and Son."

Drake cut in, "They have been around for quite a few years. Never used them but knew a few who have."

Johnathan said, "I have used them a time or two; they seem respectable."

Duke said, "Edmond, put a man outside that establishment. I want a list of everyone who steps in and out that door."

"Yes, Your Grace." Once Edmond had departed to complete his task, Duke stood then said, "As you said, Bellator, it is a waiting game to find out our next move to get our man." He did not look happy.

Jasper and Drake excused themselves to go home before the party tonight. Duke came around his desk to his brother.

"Should we find our ladies to see what they have been up to?"

Johnathan smiled, "Maybe we could have a snack before dinner. We did skip lunch today."

The two brothers walked toward the noise in the dining room; they knew their wives would be in there supervising for tonight's event. They stood in the doorway, watching them order the staff around.

Duke looked at his brother and said, "They have been busy in here. The room looks as if an enchantment happened in here."

Duchess looked up from what she was doing, then rushed over to her husband. "Conrad, what do you think of the room?"

"My Duchess, you have amazed me. I just said to Johnathan here that the room looks like an enchantment happened has occurred." Duke took her hand and kissed it, smiling.

Duchess beamed from the compliment. "That is

the reaction I am looking for, thank you. I know if you said it, everyone else shall too." The room shined with crystal stemware that lined the grand table. The silver gleamed next to beautiful china plates trimmed with gold. Fresh linen tablecloths and napkins were a lovely cream color with delicate red roses embroidered on the edges. Family crested antique candelabras all lined down the table every three feet. The table looked as if it were set for the King and Queen. There were vases of springtime flowers throughout the room, smelling as lovely as the duchess's garden.

Duchess said, "I did have my two sister-in-law's helps today. It made everything go much faster to achieve all this. Wait until you see the ballroom."

"My brother and I missed lunch today. Maybe you could have Bridget fix us a snack before the dinner party." Duke smiled.

Duchess took pity on them. "Go out to the terrace, and I shall have Jennell bring you something out there. I do not want you messing these rooms up or any other."

Duke kissed her on the lips tenderly. "We shall be out of your way, my love." He cut through the dining room to the terrace door, walking eloquently as a Duke should, with his brother by his side. Duchess watched her husband stroll through the room, thinking, 'He has not changed in all these years. He still makes my heart flutter, just watching him walk. I am a lucky lady to have him.' She sighed. She first summoned Jennell to see that the duke had something light to eat and brought it out to him and his brother on the terrace. Then she went into the ballroom for some final touches before going upstairs to change and check in on her girls' progress to ensure all was well with them. Duchess smiled at her sister-in-law when she returned to help with the finishing touches in the room. She thought all would be well; Conrad would not allow anything more to happen to their family.

Chapter 24

At the Earl Berwickshire's resident on Portman Square, Carlson knocked on the front parlor door. "A letter just arrived for you, my Lord." Lucas looked up from the book he was reading and motioned he would take it here. Grasping the envelope, he did not recognize the writing addressed to him. Lucas nodded to Carlson to leave so that he might read the letter in private. Lucas broke the seal finding that Mr. Hughes knew he was in London. Damn this man. Lucas felt outraged in reading the letter.

Hughes wrote: Was the carriage incident enough to show you I am serious about my demand for the money that is written in the contract, that is to be paid immediately. Lucas looked up from the letter, outraged with the acknowledgment that this man Hughes was still demanding money, knew his whereabouts, and almost killed his beloved sister. Damn again, what should I do? I will not be manipulated to paying something I never signed, and now he tries to blackmail me into paying by using my sister as leverage to get to me. This whole account is truly madness. I believe Laurentia is in a safe place, and the Raventon's should be able to protect her, as long as she does not venture out from their home alone. The duke has a lot of men watching and guarding the Berkeley Square mansion. I shall tell her to stay in; it's best for her, for the Raventon's think that someone is after them. My secretary is trying to find out what this company is about, get out from underneath this, and stop this fraud. Laurentia shall be okay, and I need to buy my time. I do not need to cross or get on the wrong side with the Duke of Devonshire, his sons, any the Raventon's as far as that goes. Lucas folded the letter back up and placed it in the inside pocket of his coat. Perhaps I will hear at the party this evening that they have caught who is behind all of this and be done with it.' All shall be well, I am sure. He picked up his book and sipped his tea.

Inside the back room at Fletcher's and Son tailor shop, Hughes sat at a desk waiting for the Earl of Merionreth to arrive. His valet had been here earlier to pick up the money already collected and paperwork that went along with it. Plus, a letter that Hughes needed to speak to him, and that he would be awaiting his arrival. Merionreth told Hughes that under no circumstance was he to visit his home or being seen anywhere in public together. So, they rented a space in the tailor shop to do business, if needed. The earl always came after hours, so no employees were around to identify him, to associate Merionreth with Hughes' dealings. The shop was closed, and if Merionreth were not coming, he would have sent word to meet somewhere else.

Hughes heard horse hoofs and a coach in the back alley. Hughes went to the back door and looked out. He saw a man with a black hooded cape step down from an unmarked coach, holding his head down so no one could recognize him. He walked up to the door, and Hughes stepped aside to enter and shut the door behind him. When the door was closed, the hood came down, revealing Earl Merionreth.

Merionreth barked, "There had better be a good reason for you to ask for this meeting." He stepped further into the room, then looked around to ensure that they were the only ones there.

Hughes said, "Yes, of course, there is, or I would not have asked. Come, have a seat so we can talk. Everyone is gone, as you can see." He waved his hand to the small area in the corner with a desk and two chairs. Merionreth walked past him, taking the seat behind the desk to feel more in charge, and Hughes sat in front of the desk.

Hughes cleared his throat before speaking, "I have collected the money from our easy prey that have signed up to invest in the Vander Star schemes we have going. But only one has refused to pay, the Earl of Berwickshire. I plotted a carriage accident to hurt his sister to intimidate the repayment of his debt, and the bloke still won't pay."

"Yes, I and all of London heard of the tragic accident. Today I stayed home until now, so nothing of this incident pointed toward me. Did you write Berwickshire another letter that we mean business here?"

"I did, and he did not reply! That is why I called this meeting so I may obtain the approval from you to proceed on the next move we previously discussed."

Merionreth pondered a moment, "Berwickshire's sister is employed at the Duke of Devonshire as their governess, I'm told. You had your man nose around watching her routines. I bet the duke does not even suspect that it is the governess we are after, Mister all high and mighty and that son of his too Lord Bellator. I tried to befriend Bellator at Eton, and all he did was look down the nose at me. Yes, go with the next step. I am sure we shall get what we want then."

Hughes smiled, "A few more days, and we shall be done with this portion of our scheme. Then I can start a new phase and move more north to find new pigeons, or should we say suckers to prey on." Both men laughed.

"You know what to do. I shall meet you in Kent in a couple of days. I am leaving tonight." Merionreth stood and walked around the desk.

Hughes also stood, then said, "I have a few details to work out in London, and I shall see you in Kent, my Lord." Merionreth nodded, pulled his hood back up, and departed quickly. Hughes walked to the door too. First, he had to go down to the docks and locate the two men he'd hired for the last plot. The money Hughes paid the last time; he bet the two were using it for drinking and having a loose woman in the taverns. It should not be hard to find them. Hughes thought as he walked outside and climbed up into his carriage to head to the Devil Edge Tavern.

Hughes parked on the side street from the tavern he was heading for, felt like someone was watching him. He decided to keep going and ride around the docks to shake the tail that was following him. Hughes shook the reins, and his horse started down the road again. He was driving a two-seater carriage with a roof. He rode down two blocks, made a right turn, went another block, and turned left before taking the next right. He looked over his shoulder to see if anyone was following him. Not seeing anyone, he believed he had lost them. To be safe, Hughes parked his carriage a block away and decided to walk and cut through alleys to find the men he needed for this job.

Hughes saw a young lad and said to him, "You watch my horse and carriage here. I shall give you a coin now and one when I return."

The lad said, "Sure thing, mister, I have nothing else to do." He held his hand out for the first coin.

Hughes tossed one to the boy, "I shall be back soon, and this gold coin shall be yours when I return." Showing the boy, the gold coin. The lad nodded and took a seat by the horse. Hughes went down a couple of alleys but decided to check the Red Dragon Tavern first. He remembered Davis said he frequented that one. He walked in and looked around before going to the bar.

The barkeep came over to ask, "What'll you have?"

"An ale would do." The barkeep poured the ale and placed it before him.

"Is there anything else you'd like? Food or a warm bed with a woman?"

"I am looking for two friends of mine, one called Davis and the other Simon. Davis has a scar on his chin, brown hair, and eyes. Simon is tall, thin, with curly blond hair. Have you seen them?" He threw three coins down.

"Yeah, they should be down soon. The two went upstairs with two of my girls, about an hour now. Throw me a few more coins, and you can join them with Sarah here." A redhead stood beside him.

Hughes looks at the woman. "Maybe later with your Sarah. I shall wait for them to come down and drink my ale."

"Suit yourself and let me know when you are ready for my girl here." Hughes nodded and picked up his ale and drank some down as he waited.

Twenty minutes later, the two men came down the stairs laughing and having a good time with the two women on their side. They walked over to a table, and all four sat down, still laughing. Hughes saw them and walked over to the table.

Davis looked up and seeing him standing there, "Hey, look, it's me, old friend Mr. H here."

Hughes looked around the table, then said. "I have another job for you if you're interested?"

Simon said, "I worked up a thirst, me girl, go get us an ale if you would and give us a few minutes to talk to our friend here." Both girls gave a pouty face but got up.

Davis said, "Ye can come back after we talk here, alright?"

The blonde one kissed Davis, then said, "If you must, we shall bring back some ales when he leaves." She motioned toward Hughes.

Davis slapped her ass then said, "That's me, girl." The girls giggled as they walked away.

Hughes asked, "May I have a seat?"

Simon said, "By all means, take a seat, can't have you lurking over top of me."

Hughes took a seat at the table. "Do you want the new job I am offering, or should I find someone else?"

Simon said, "You have not said what it is yet if I remember right, mate."

Hughes said, "It is the same girl we were after before. Remember what we talked about if the carriage act did not work in my favor?

Davis said, "That job will cost a lot more to do."

Hughes nodded. "Yes, I do realize that. I shall double what I paid you last time. I do not want the girl to be hurt or touched. Do you get my meaning?"

Simon smiled, showing his yellow teeth. "We won't touch her in any unnecessary ways."

"Good, we agree then. Let us hope the lady does her usual routine tomorrow morning, and you two will be a little richer." Hughes smiled.

Davis said, "Sounds good to me. What you think, Simon?"

"Yeah, you can count on me in this job too."

"I shall be at the place we talked about tomorrow. Till then." Hughes stood up, left the tavern, then went back to where he left his carriage and horse. The boy stood up when he saw the owner come back to his carriage.

"I stayed here and watched over your horse here and carriage, mister. I let no one harm them." Hughes reached into his pocket, pulling out the gold coin and flipping it to him.

"Thank you, mister," then he was off down an alley.

Hughes stepped up into his carriage to head to his hideout for the rest of the evening. He thought to himself as he rode along, 'In the tavern, the reason he did not say out loud what the job entailed was that there were too many ears listing. They had made plans for this act when they did the first job. If the first one did not get the point across to pay, the backup plan showed he meant business. So yes, this next incident shall work for sure; Earl Berkwickshire shall pay now.' He smiled, clicked his reins to make his horse go faster. He needed to get a good night's sleep for tomorrow's event.

Chapter 25

Devonshire Dinner Party

Wesley was in his glory, having fifty guests arrive for his duchess's dinner party.

An hour before the guests should arrive, Laurentia heard a knock on her door. She was sitting at her dress table, having Sandra put her hair up. "See who it is."

A footman held out a letter for Laurentia. Sandra delivered it to her mistress.

"Thank you, and I wonder who it's from."

Laurentia broke the seal then read: My love, I would like you to meet me in the garden at five-thirty, at the fountain—your Jasper.

Laurentia beamed a smile and holding the letter to her chest. "It is from Lord Bellator. You have to finish my hair quickly as he asked me to meet him at five-thirty in the garden."

"I shall finish in a jiffy, my Lady. We cannot keep your future husband waiting, can we?" Sandra smiled at her mistress.

"No, we cannot. Thank you for understanding. This could be it; my love might propose again."

Laurentia hurried down the front staircase shortly before five-thirty, and seeing no one around, made her way to the terrace door that led to the garden. She was so excited to go out there as it was the place Jasper first kissed her. Could this be it; was he going to ask me to marry him. Oh, how romantic, she thought, going as fast as her little feet could go without running. Finally, she came around the bend, and seeing Jasper sitting on the fountain, looking comfortable and elegant, Laurentia slowed down to a casual walk.

Jasper looked up, seeing Laurentia walking toward him. He had butterflies in this stomach, for she did say no the first time he'd asked her to marry him. Jasper smiled when she approached him and stood. Laurentia in front of him, waiting to hear why he summoned her to the garden. He looked into her beautiful violet eyes, taking a deep breath, and telling himself to relax, remembering she loves you, as you love her. Laurentia was wearing a butter yellow gown with a low-cut neckline that glimmered with sequins. It had a tight-fitting waist and a bell skirt that fell to the ground. Her hair was piled in cascades of curls on top of her head, with a few ringlets in the back hanging down.

Jasper said, "You take my breath away, my love. You are so beautiful and perfect in every way."

"Thank you, my Jasper. You look very dashingly handsome yourself this evening." Jasper wore a black evening coat with tails; his black waistcoat surprisingly had a pattern of gold-threaded paisley design and gold buttons.

"I like the gold design in your waistcoat. A little color is nice." Laurentia smiled, feeling nervous.

Jasper looked down at his waistcoat, "Sometimes, I put a touch of color in my clothes." He shrugged.

"We shall have to work on that more in our future." Laurentia reached up on her tiptoes and kissed him softly.

Jasper broke the kiss and said, "I summoned you out here for a reason, my love, so stop distracting me."

Laurentia went back to flat feet. "Sorry, I could not help myself. I love you."

Jasper cleared his throat, "I love you too." He went down on one knee holding her hands, looking into her eyes, and spoke clearly.

"The first time I saw you in my parents' parlor, you had my heart. I fell in love with you that first moment when I looked into your violet eyes. Remember, I said you're beautiful. I then realized you were the one that I had been waiting for all my life. Laurentia, please do me the honor and be my wife and my marchioness. I love you, and I cannot live without you."

Tears rolled down Laurentia's cheeks. She nodded her head, yes, saying, "You have just made me the happiest girl in the world. Yes, Jasper, I shall marry you and spend the rest of my life by your side."

Jasper came off his knee, grabbed her off the ground, kissing her with full passion before putting her back down. He reached into his coat pocket and pulled out a box, and handed it to her.

Laurentia beamed up at Jasper, then looked down and opened the box. "Oh, Jasper, it is beautiful and so exquisite." She took the ring out of the box and held it in her fingers.

"Read what I had engraved in the inside band, my love." Jasper smiled.

She looked inside the band then read, "With All

My Heart Jasper." Tears rolled down her cheeks.

"My love, I do not believe you are to be crying now," Jasper said, wondering if he had done something wrong.

"They are tears of joy." She handed the ring to him. "Please put my ring on to seal our love."

Jasper said as he pushed the ring onto Laurentia's finger. "I had your ring specially made for you. The two amethyst stones are to match your eyes that I love so much. Do you like the ring, my love?"

Laurentia looked down at the ring on her hand. "It is perfect. I do love my ring, and it means so much to me because you had it made special for me. That warms my heart for you even more." She smiled up at him. Jasper wrapped his arms around Laurentia, pulling her close to his chest. Laurentia leaned into Jasper, putting her arms up around his neck. They kissed to seal their pledge for each other to marry.

Jasper kissed down her throat, then into her ear, he whispered. "Too bad, we have this dinner party. I'd rather take you to bed and make love to you all night long."

Laurentia said pertly, "We cannot do that yet; we are not married."

Jasper lifted his head and looked into her eyes. "We shall not have a long engagement. I want you in my home, my bed, and in my life by my side." He pulled out a paper from his coat inside pocket, and not letting go of her. "I have already purchased a special marriage license, as you can see. We can marry tomorrow if you like or even tonight." He smiled eagerly.

Laurentia looked at the paper he was holding, "I

told you already; I want a wedding in a church."

"My love, if that is what you wish, and if that shall make you happy, then how can I say no? Plan away, and Mother shall be more than happy to help you as well as my aunts. Tomorrow morning, I shall have my sectary send the announcement of our engagement to the London Chronicle, The Morning Herald, and Gazette. Being today is Sunday, a week should be long enough to plan our wedding, especially with the Raventon women to assist you. Next Sunday, we shall wed, and you shall be all mine."

Laurentia smiled up at Jasper. "It seems you had figured this all out, have you?"

"My love, I am a patient man to a point. But not being able to touch you, kiss you, and make love to you whenever I desire to, a week is all I can stand." He kissed her tenderly.

Laurentia broke their kiss, "I see your point. Yes, next Sunday we shall marry. Jasper, we should go in and share our news with everyone."

"I'd rather kiss you a little longer here, but you are right; it is most likely six o'clock, and the guests are probably arriving." They kissed one last time, then Jasper let go of Laurentia, put his arm out, and said. "Shall we go spread the good news, my betroth?"

Laurentia took his arm. "Lead the way, my future husband." They walked back to the house, where the party was starting; the coaches and carriages were lining up to the front entrance that very moment.

Duke and Duchess were at the front of the receiving line, welcoming their guests to their home, and his sisters were there smiling as they greeted the guests. Duchess saw her son escorting Laurentia from the terrace and wondered what mischief they had been up to. However, she kept smiling, greeting her guests for the evening. Since Jasper and Laurentia lived here more or less, they blended in with the crowd of people who had already arrived. Leopold and Victor were chatting with Victor's father and mother as they joined them.

Gabrielle also walked over to join them; she noticed the large diamond ring on Laurentia's left hand. "Lady Laurentia, that is a lovely ring you are wearing on your left hand. Is there some news you would like to share with us?"

Laurentia looked up at Jasper standing beside her, and he nodded for her to go ahead.

"Lord Bellator has just asked me minutes ago to marry him. Of course, I said yes."

Fantina stepped forward, taking Laurentia's hand to see the ring closer. "Nephew, that is a lovely ring you chose for your bride." She hugged Laurentia then said, "Welcome to the family."

Leopold slapped Jasper on the back and hugged him. "Congratulations, Bellator, you're the first to marry in our pack." The others offered their congratulations as well.

With all the noise and hearing congratulations, the duke and duchess left the receiving line to come over and see for themselves what was going on.

Jasper saw them coming forward and said. "Yes, I have asked Lady Laurentia for her hand in marriage, and she accepted."

On that note, the duke said, "Can I have everyone's attention, please." All the talking in the room stopped. Duke continued proudly. "My son Lord Bellator, my heir, has just informed me that he and

Lady Laurentia Sinclair are betrothed to be married. My Duchess and I are announcing this to all of you now and saying congratulations to them both. Wesley, we are in need of champagne now to toast the groom and bride to be. At once."

In minutes, trays of champagne were being served, five footmen holding trays were going around the room to make sure everyone had a glass. All the guests had arrived and were standing in the ballroom, so there was enough room for everyone to see and hear the toast. Duke raised his glass then said.

"To my son, Lord Bellator, and Lady Laurentia. My Duchess and I welcome Lady Laurentia to our family. We are pleased with this union, so raise your glasses up and toast to the happy couple. To Lord Bellator and Lady Laurentia Congratulations." Everyone raised their glass and repeated congratulations to them. The room's noise was deafening as everyone came over to wish the new couple well wishes and congratulations.

Jasper bent his head to Laurentia's ear and whispered, "I believe all of London shall know of our engagement by morning. The word does spread fast through the ton."

Laurentia looked up into Jasper's eyes and smiled. "This is so wonderful, and I am so happy, Lord Bellator." A tear rolled down her cheek.

Jasper bent and kissed her tear from her cheek. That was the first show of affection in front of everyone, spurring applause.

Lucas made his way over to the new couple; finally, he kissed Laurentia's cheeks then said, "Congratulations to you and Lord Bellator. Mother and Father would have been proud of you snagging a future duke and all."

Laurentia slapped his arm. "Lucas, stop being so forward; we are in the ton's presence. Besides what you just said, I do love Lord Bellator with all my heart."

"Being a governess, these few years has taken all the fun out of you. You know I am only teasing you, Sister."

Laurentia smirked at Lucas, "Just behave yourself is all, and no, I have not lost my fun."

Lucas smiled back, "Good to hear." He looked to Jasper, then said, "She is my only family, so do take care of her. My parents left her a large dowry for when she marries. We need to sit down in the next two days to go over paperwork and so forth.

Jasper answered, "Tomorrow morning at my residence on Grosvenor Square. Nine o'clock shall work for myself. Bring all the necessary forms, and my secretary shall be present as a witness. You should bring yours as well.

"I shall be there at eight-thirty. Breaking our fast together would be a good start for the meeting."

Jasper was trying to remember this was Laurentia's brother, and he held back his annoyance for the boldness shown toward him. He shifted his stance to control his temper.

"I shall have my cook make up a sideboard of morning food before we start our meeting."

"Excellent, till then, my Lord. I think I shall make a round of the room. I see some interesting faces I would not mind meeting." Lucas strolled away like he owned the place.

Jasper glared down at Laurentia, and she said. "I know I have not talked to him yet. He needs a brush-up on the ton's etiquette. I think only you and your father outrank him tonight, plus maybe a couple more. I shall talk with him tomorrow." She smiled up to Jasper, trying to smooth his feathers.

"This one time, I shall let slide, but I do suggest you go talk with him now. There is my father to worry about in the first place, and there are five marquesses here this evening. Plus, he needs to be introduced to all single lady's; you know that."

"You are right; I shall go pull him to the side and talk to him now. Sorry, he is not used to being among the ton. He stays in the country too much. I shall be back." Laurentia walked away to find her brother, and she led him out to the corridor.

Lucas stopped outside of the ballroom. "Laurentia, what is so urgent to bring me out here so fast?"

Laurentia pulled him to the far side of the hallway. "Lucas, I'm telling you this because you are my brother, and I love you." She took a deep breath, then continued. "You need to brush up on your proper etiquette among the ton when you are in London."

Lucas raised an eyebrow then said, "What are you talking about? I am charming, am I not?"

"It is not the problem; you have to watch your ranking, your station in the ton. For instance, Jasper is a marquess; you can talk pleasantries with him and jest lightly. But you do not tell him to have food set out before a meeting in his home. If he wanted it or suggest it, that is fine. Do you understand? I am used to your boldness and understand your ways. But in London, you must realize your rank in the ton. And you cannot talk to a female unless you are introduced to her by someone else who knows her. Okay?"

Lucas rolled his eyes. "Am I that bad, Laurentia?"

She nodded. "I hope you're not angry with me. I do not want you to offend, for the ton would cut you in a snap. Jasper loves me; that is why he did not put you in your place just now. He shall next time, he is highly respected in the ton, and because we are in a small crowd tonight, he did not."

Lucas said, "I'm sorry. I have been out in the country too long, is all."

Laurentia smiled, "I do realize that no harm, no foul. Shall we go back in and enjoy the evening?"

Lucas put his arm out, then said, "I thought you would never ask." He grinned, and she laughed as they walked back into the ballroom.

Upon re-entry to the ballroom, Lucas noticed Gabrielle. "I met Lady Gabrielle this afternoon at the tea. I shall talk with her if you excuse me." Lucas bowed and walked away.

Laurentia kissed him on the cheek before he walked away. She looked around for Jasper but did not see him. That was because he came up from behind her.

He leaned forward and whispered in her ear. "You smell divine, my love. I wish we could be alone right now."

Laurentia turned around slowly, "I would like that too."

The dinner gong rang, and that broke their thoughts of disappearing for a while. Jasper thought, 'Food is not what I am currently hungry for, damn it.' He shut down his irritation and disappointment for not fulfilling his desires with Laurentia. He smiled briefly, then put his arm out for Laurentia to take, and they strolled into the dining room. Jasper entered after his father, as it is protocol in the ranking of the ton.

Jasper whispered to Laurentia. "I'm hungry for you, not food."

She looked to see the corner of his lip twitching as they walked through the door to the dining room. Laurentia whispered, "Maybe we could sneak away after dinner before the music starts for dancing."

Jasper whispered back, "My little vixen, you are thinking my same thoughts. We shall have to do that." They reached their seats at the table, and Jasper pulled out Laurentia's chair as gentlemen always do and helped push her chair in, taking his place beside her. On the right side of the table by his father.

Everyone took their seats at the long table. Laurentia took in the table's beauty, with the crystal wine glasses, lovely china, the lighting that was flickering from the candelabras made the table glow. She hoped her wedding tables would be like this, as attractive.

Jasper took her hand, then asked. "Is something amiss, my love? You are noticeably quiet at the moment."

"I'm enjoying your mother's beautiful work before us, the table, and the room, and I am hoping our wedding tables will be as lovely."

Jasper raised her hand to his lips and kissed it gently, then said, "They shall be. You shall have my mother's help in the planning, not to worry, my sweet."

Laurentia smiled. "It is a week away. We shall have to start tomorrow with the planning."

Jasper stood up at the table, and everyone stopped talking to take notice that Lord Bellator had something to say. "Family and friends, my engagement was announced minutes ago. I and my lovely bride to be, thank you for all the congratulations and well wishes. We have decided not to have a long engagement, for we want to start our life together soon. To do that, we have chosen next Sunday to wed, and all of you are invited plus many more."

The dowager duchess spoke first. "Which church shall the wedding be held, and the wedding breakfast is to be where, Grandson?"

Jasper looked down at Laurentia, and he held his hand out for her to stand and join him. She took his hand to stood beside him. Jasper asked, "Where would you like to marry, my Lady?"

Laurentia announced, "St Paul's Cathedral is where we would like to wed. My parents married there, and it would mean a lot to me to have my wedding in the same church."

The duchess stood then said, "That is a lovely church. I would like to assist you in any way you would need a mother's guidance. You have become very dear to me, Lady Laurentia, and I would love to help and be there for you."

Jasper gave a little squeeze on Laurentia's hand, and she looked up to him as Jasper mouthed, 'told you so.'

Laurentia looked down at the table where the duchess was still standing. "Thank you, Your Grace, that truly would make me happy to have your help, and I am blessed to have you as my new mother-in-law."

Duchess nodded and sat back down. "This dinner party has been changed this evening into my eldest son's engagement party. We have much to celebrate. Wesley, please start the first course." Wesley signaled the footmen to start serving, and Jasper and Laurentia sat back down. The table of fifty guests was back to the night's festivities, with different conversations carrying on all around.

The duke looked over to Jasper, then said to him, "Well done, Bellator, you made both our women happy just now."

Jasper nodded, "I am learning, Father. Seeing to Laurentia's needs makes me happy, to see that special spark in her eyes and smile that is just for me alone."

The duke leaned a little closer then said, "That, my Son, is love."

Jasper raised his glass to his father's. "I shall drink to that." They toasted, and both laughed together.

Laurentia asked, "What was your toast about?"

Jasper answered, "Men, stuff!" and left it at that.

The footmen started serving the first course, a soup of crab bisque, followed by an appetizer plate of fine cheese, baguettes from France with a variety of sliced apples. Next, the entrée was served, which included roast duckling, ham, and trout, with various vegetables, including parsnips, asparagus, and carrots. Finally, they ended the meal with a custard tart and fruit fool.

'I feel like a stuffed goose,' Laurentia thought, not remembering when she ate so much in one sitting. But with the room's great festive atmosphere, it was so easy to indulge in good wine and food. Thank goodness there would be dancing later.

Duke said to Laurentia, "I am putting in a request now to have a dance with my future daughter-in-law before my sons and nephews monopolize them all."

Jasper said, "The first dance shall be a waltz. That one is mine. After that, my love, you may dance with whomever you wish."

"Your Grace, I shall put you on my card for the second dance, Your Grace," Laurentia said with a smile.

Duke nodded, "That shall be grand, my dear."

Leopold, from across the table, said, "Lady Laurentia, put me down as your third partner if you please." Then one by one, the other gentlemen requested their dances.

Jasper said, "My love, the Raventon men, and your brother may have all your traditional dances, but I request all the waltzes."

"My Lord, you are written down on my card in those spots as you have requested once before," Laurentia said with a twinkle in her eyes.

Jasper raised her hand to his lips, said, "Thank you, that pleases me." He kissed her hand, looking into her eyes with that wicked smile she knew so well, and that still made her shiver. Jasper felt her shiver, and that raised his desire for her even more.

The duke stood up then said, "Gentlemen, I have an excellent brandy, port, and cigars, if you follow me into the next room. Our ladies can freshen up if they wish before the music part of our evening starts."

Before Jasper could tell Laurentia where they could meet for their rendezvous, the duchess quickly came behind Laurentia.

"Lady Laurentia, I want you to meet my mother and dearest friends of mine. Jasper, do not give me that look; you have the whole night to talk, so run along with the men."

Jasper stood; his mother was the only person he stood down to, so he walked with Leopold and Drake into the other room, not feeling pleased.

Laurentia followed the Duchess to the other end of the dinner table, where everyone talked in little circles. Duchess came to a group where the twins were talking to a lady; she had blonde hair with a bit of gray blended in the front, green eyes, and facial features resembling the duchess.

The woman smiled when they enter the circle. Duchess said.

"Lady Laurentia, I would like you to meet my mother, Marchioness of Cheshire. Mother, this is Lady Laurentia Sinclair."

Laurentia curtsied. "It is a pleasure to meet you, my Lady."

The marchioness took Laurentia's hand. "I can see why my grandson is taken with you so, you are exceptionally lovely. I am to understand you are the late Earl of Berwickshire's daughter."

"Yes, that is correct. My father and mother passed away many years ago in a shipwreck traveling to France."

Marchioness said, "I am sorry to hear that. You have a brother here this evening, and he was most charming. I met him before we sat down for dinner."

Laurentia smiled, "Yes, he is my only sibling. I do have an aunt on my mother's side still alive, Countess Angus. My aunt and uncle live north of Berwickshire. My father had no siblings."

Duchess said, "We shall have to make sure they are on the guestlist for your wedding. I do suggest we start tomorrow incredibly early for your wedding plans. We have a lot to do; invitations need to go out tomorrow, we must have your wedding gown made, we must set up your bow to Queen Charlotte."

Laurentia said, "Oh dear, is a week enough time

to do all that needs to be accomplished before next Sunday?"

Duchess smiled. "My dear girl, with myself helping plus my two sisters-in-law, we can achieve anything, you just ask."

Louisa and Fantina came over to the circle.

Louisa said, "We Raventon women can move a mountain together, with no problem."

Amara said, "Aurora and I shall help; also, we are so excited to have you as our sister."

Gabrielle entered the circle, "Count me in too. I'd love to help."

The dowager duchess came over and said, "This old lady shall help too. After all, one day, you shall be the Duchess of Devonshire, my dear. We, duchesses, have to stick together, you know," she winked at Laurentia.

Laurentia looked around at all the women so eager to help her with her wedding plans. "With the bottom of my heart, I thank you all."

Duchess said, "You shall see that the Raventon's are a family unit. We always go the extra mile for each other. We are a strong family with a lot of love, and we always have each other's back. My son has picked you for his wife. I can see he loves you, and you love him. I have not said this yet for all to hear; I welcome you to our family, Lady Laurentia." Duchess held her arms out for Laurentia. She embraced the duchess, and then the whole circle hugged her one at a time, welcoming Laurentia to the family.

However, when it came time for the dowager duchess to hug Laurentia, she stopped then said, "Let me see the ring my grandson bought you first."

Laurentia held out her left hand. The dowager duchess took her hand, lifted it close to her eyes to see. "That is a beautiful ring, dear girl, with our Jasper that doesn't surprise me. He does have good taste, especially nice indeed. Welcome to the family." Then she gave Laurentia a bear hug, a kiss on the cheek, and winked at her, saying, "I told you only had to give him time, and you would hear those magical words."

The men came back into the room, and the women talked and made suggestions for the nuptial next Sunday. By this time, they started to go into the ballroom; the small quartet was warming up their instruments.

Jasper made his way to Laurentia. "I believe the first dance is mine, Lady Laurentia."

Laurentia smiled, looking into his blue eyes. "Yes, it is. Shall we dance, Lord Bellator?"

Jasper took Laurentia's hand and led her onto the dance floor; other couples gathered around them. The music started, and Jasper took Laurentia's hand then placed his other hand on the small of her back, pulling her close.

They glided around the floor, adding a few twirls. Jasper looked down into Laurentia's violet eyes then said. "Have I told you that you look beautiful tonight?"

"Yes, a couple of times, thank you."

"Have I told you I love you?"

Laurentia smiled, "Yes, never stop saying those words to me ever."

"I love you, Lady Laurentia Sinclair."

"I love you, Lord Bellator." Jasper kissed Laurentia's hand, then twirled her. She giggled, and he brought her back to him, close to his chest.

Jasper whispered in her ear, "I do like to hear your giggle. I cannot wait until I make you giggle in my arms, making love to you later this evening in your bedchamber."

"Mmm, me too, Jasper," Laurentia said as he held her tight.

Once their dance ended, the duke came over to collect Laurentia for the next dance, a quadrille.

As they were dancing, Duke said. "You dance exceedingly well, Lady Laurentia."

"As do you, Your Grace. I do enjoy dancing."

"Yes, my dear, it shows, you are light on your feet."

Laurentia looked around the dance floor and saw her brother Lucas dancing with Gabrielle. They looked good together. Jasper was dancing with his sister Amara, and Drake was dancing with a light brown-haired woman, about twenty-two, and lovely. The rest of the Raventon family and their guests had also paired up to dance. The night went by quickly with all the dancing, laughing, and having a good time all around. It was 12:45 when the last of the guests departed for the night.

Duke was talking with Wesley in the front hall as the duchess came up behind them.

"Is everything alright, Conrad?"

Duke turned to her, "Yes, I was giving Wesley a few things I want to be done in the morning."

"Shall you belong, my love? Or should I go up with the girls?"

Duke looked at his duchess, "You look exhausted. Go with the girls, and I shall come to you when I am done down here."

Duchess nodded then went to the main staircase. Laurentia was already halfway up, and the twins were waiting on the bottom.

"Let's go, my darlings; it is very late. Your father shall come up when he finishes down here."

Aurora said with a yawn, "My feet hurt. I am so tired, Mother."

Amara said, "Not I; I could dance a few more hours easily. Tonight, was so much fun. Laurentia, your brother, is so funny and a good dancer as well."

Laurentia stood at the top landing. "I am glad you like him; he is very dear to me. He has always made me laugh since childhood. As for his dancing skills, we had the same instructor, plus we danced a lot together for practice and fun.

Aurora said, "I found the Earl very charming too."

"He can be a charmer. mother always said the apple does not fall too far from the tree. My father was a charmer, too; that's where he gets it from. mother also would say all the ladies in the village would flock around my father. Then father would say, they did until I met you, my love. Then no other woman could compare to your beauty, and you stole my heart. It seems like yesterday that I can still remember hearing my parents tease each other. They are excellent memories."

Duchess said, "That is a lovely memory, Laurentia, and your brother seemed to enjoy himself tonight. We shall invite him to join us more often."

Laurentia said, "That's kind of you. Thank you."

Duchess plainly said, "That is what family does. Girls, your maids will be in your room waiting for you to help you get ready for bed. No dawdling, go to bed; we have a busy day tomorrow helping Laurentia with her wedding planning."

Laurentia and the twins walked to their bed chambers. The twin's door came first, Laurentia said. "Good night," and the twins bade good night too.

Laurentia continued to her room, opened the door, and walked in. Sandra came from the dressing room to help her get ready for bed. Sandra helped her out of her gown, then into her nightgown. She sat down at the dressing table; they both took the pins out of her hair. Laurentia picked up her hairbrush then said. "You may go to bed, Sandra. I can finish brushing my hair out, and it is late." Sandra bobbed and bade good night and left the room.

Laurentia was brushing her hair when she sensed Jasper was waiting to come in, and less than a minute later, the secret door opened. She was still brushing her hair when Jasper walked over to her and ran his fingers in her long beautiful hair, making eye contact in the looking glass with her.

"You are so lovely. All night I have been waiting for this time to be alone with you, my love. Just breathing in your scent right now is undoing me."

Laurentia set down the brush, not losing eye contact with Jasper through the looking glass, "Tell me what you want to do to me, my Jasper. Tell me about your desires."

He smiled that all too familiar wicked smile of his. "I want to taste you, make you come hard with my tongue, and then I shall make you come again when I enter you and have you. Is that what you wanted to hear, my Sweet Laurentia?"

Laurentia felt hot and wanting him at that moment, plus she loved this game they were playing. So, she said two words to him: "Take me."

Jasper scooped Laurentia up, carried her to the bed, placed her down, and pulled her nightgown over her head, dropping it on the floor. He stood in front of her and removed every piece of clothing. Laurentia watched him and licked her lips when the last part of clothing hit the floor.

Jasper moved over top of her. "You are mine. I wish our wedding day were now. We would stay in bed for days, and I would never grow tired of you ever, my love." He kissed her hard and wild, licking his tongue around the inside of her mouth, tasting her, and Laurentia did the same to him. He lifted his head, then kissed his way down her body to her womanhood.

Laurentia started panting, anticipating what he would do. He licked in between her folds and found her little bud. Laurentia grabbed the coverlet, lifted, and arched her back off the bed, and came back down with a moan. Jasper continued arousing her, licking and licking with that magic tongue of his. Laurentia moaned and shook, crying, "Oh Jasper, yes, that feels so good." She melted into a pool of heavenly delight.

Jasper sat up and said, "I want you hard, Laurentia. I needed this. Get on your knees for me, and we shall try something new." She went on her knees and waited.

"Now hang on to the headboard, hold on tight, I shall make this good for the both of us, I promise." He kissed her bottom.

Laurentia said, "I trust you, Jasper. You have

never disappointed me."

Jasper took hold of her hips and thrust in hard and smooth. He was on his knees, pumping a fast rhythm behind her. "Oh, love, you feel so tight and perfect around me, heavenly," he said as he rode her hard and fast, pumping and pumping.

Laurentia held on, feeling him and feeling very aroused. She started to feel a flutter building inside, then the quivers and the orgasm. "Oh, Jasper," she yelled.

On that, Jasper stopped holding back; he let it all go, filling her with his seed pumping a few more times hard. When he pulled out of her, he then looked at Laurentia, still gripping the headboard.

Jasper panicked and grabbed Laurentia, saying, "Darling, you can let go now." He fell back with her in his lap, holding her in his arms. "My love, did I hurt you? I'm so sorry, forgive me, please. I did not mean to be so rough. You are a lady, and I should not have done that with you."

Laurentia looked up at him and kissed his lips tenderly, then said with a slow smile, "Jasper, you did not hurt me. I am fine."

Jasper tilted his head, trying to read her, "Are you certain? You did not look like you were the way you had hold of the headboard."

"I have to admit lovemaking that way was very arousing. I did not let go of the headboard yet, for I was still coming down too."

Jasper was hugging Laurentia tighter. "Now, I know you are the perfect woman for me. Laurentia, you amaze me; I love you so much." He kissed her long and passionately.

Laurentia broke the kiss and smiled, "I do love

you. I would like to cuddle now; it is my second fa-vorite part after we have made love." Jasper un-wrapped his arms from around her, then they laid down together, cuddling, and talking.

Laurentia said, "Your mother welcomed me to the family tonight when you were having your brandy with the men. As a matter of fact, all the Raventon women welcomed me to the family. It was truly lovely."

"I did not doubt that they would. I told you my family would love you as I do."

"Yes, you did say that. I am delighted to have a family around me again, as it has been a long time."

"We have been very active in the part of making our own family. You know?"

She sighed. "Yes, we have, and it is gratifying, I must say."

"You could be carrying my heir now, and that is one reason why we need to marry promptly. I do not want your honor ruined, my love. It would be my fault if it happens. After all, I did seduce you, and I wanted you."

"Jasper, I also wanted you to make love to me. I was just as willing and desired you just as much."

"That may have been, but it would still be my fault. No one has seen me yet come and go. I have been meticulous." He kissed the top of her head and nuzzled her some more. "How many children would you like to have, my love?"

Laurentia hesitated a moment, then said, "Two or three, it would depend on the second child. I want a boy and a girl."

Jasper liked her answer then said, "As you know, to have a son is an important responsibility to my ti-tle. I would like two sons, for the sake, if something happened to our first. I also would like to have a little girl that looks just like you. I would spoil her as I want to do with you."

Laurentia rolled over to her front side and laid on top of Jasper so that she could look into his eyes. She kissed him softly, "We have to be fair with all our children and give them equal love. But let's talk about the spoiling me part you mentioned." She smiled, and her eyes sparkled.

Jasper laughed, "That, my love, definitely sparked your attention."

"Why, yes, it has. Please enlighten me on what spoiling me involves."

"I remember our first night together. You mentioned that you would travel the world when you received your trust fund. Well, we do not have to wait for that. I shall take you everywhere your heart desires to go and more. I also want to buy you the latest fashions we see in each country. I want my marchioness turning heads everywhere we go, making everyone envious. You are breathtakingly beautiful as you are. I want you to look unsurpassed, and you shall have only the best of everything, my love. That is how I shall spoil you."

Laurentia smiled, "Can we start that on our honeymoon traveling, please?"

Jasper nodded, "Yes, where would you like to go first, my sweet?" He raised his hand up to play with a ringlet of her hair hanging by her cheek.

Laurentia was excited. "Rome first perhaps, I would like to see the Colosseum where the gladiators fought and to see the Sistine Chapel. Maybe we could meet the pope and shop as you mention. Then we could go to Egypt to see the pyramids and then to Africa to see real lions, gorillas, giraffes, and zebras. I want to see all the things I read about; that would make me truly happy, my love."

"I shall take you to all those places and more. It shall bring me true joy to see you happy."

Laurentia glowed from hearing what Jasper said, and she squealed with exhilaration, then kissed him with such passion that it sparked another round of lovemaking.

Jasper left at dawn before the house awoke, and he left the bed without waking Laurentia. He dressed, watching her sleep. 'She is so beautiful like an angel.' he thought as he stood by the bedside. Damn it. I hate leaving her; this is true torment. One more week and she shall be all mine, he said to himself as he walked over to the secret door that he went through every night to be with her. I must keep my control and patience. It shall be worth the wait. He left, feeling the pain of their separation.

Chapter 26

Early Morning Walk

Laurentia woke up at 7:00 a.m., too restless to sleep. She kept thinking about Jasper and of all the promises he'd made to take her to the wonderful places she'd dreamed of traveling to someday and the love-making they'd shared. So, she decided to dress and take a walk, for the rest of the house was still asleep.

Sandra helped her dress, then while sitting at her dress table having her hair pinned up, Laurentia said. "It shall be good to have some fresh morning air. A lot happened yesterday. This morning walk shall clear my head, for all the planning of my wedding we shall start today."

Sandra asked, "Should I accompany you, my Lady?"

"It's quite early; I shall slip out and be back in no time before anyone rises." After her hair was finished, Laurentia walked downstairs to discover that nobody was around, so she walked out the front door.

There was a footman at his post just as she stepped out the door. He bowed then said, "Good morning, my Lady."

"It is a good morning, nice for a walk. I shall not be long."

"My orders are not to let anyone go out alone from this residence, especially a lady. The duke orders," Footman stepped in front of Laurentia taking his duties and orders quite seriously

"No one is up yet. It shall be alright if I go and come back in no time."

The footman shook his head no. "I shall have another footman take my post, and I must accompany you, or the duke shall have my head, my Lady."

"We cannot have that happen, can we?" Laurentia smiled at her jest.

"No, I like my head where it is. Just give me a minute, I shall have someone take my post, and we are off." Laurentia nodded, yes. Gus walked to the side of the mansion and came back with a replacement for his position.

As was customary, the footman walked four feet back from Laurentia. When they were a block away from the Devonshire Mansion, a man came up behind Gus, knocked him on the head, putting him out cold, while another man jumped out from behind a tree and grabbed Laurentia. She tried to scream, but his hand went over her mouth like a vice. She kicked and fought but could not break free. She saw Gus lying unconscious on the ground; he was no help for her now. The other assailant was waiting near a black coach just four feet away, holding the door open, waiting for Laurentia and the man holding her.

"Come on, get her in here fast, so we're not seen already," the brown-haired man said. The curly blond-haired man said, "I'm trying to. She is like a wildcat, this one." He was trying to make his way over to the coach, but Laurentia was kicking, scratching, and biting his hand so she could scream, but his other hand moved too fast to cover her mouth before she could let out a sound.

The man holding Laurentia said. "Damn it, man, get over here and help me! She's biting me." He shook his hand in pain. The other man ran over, grabbed Laurentia's legs to hurry her to the coach. The one holding her legs stepped in first, then the other entered, yelling to the driver to go as he closed the door.

They sat her on the seat, tied her hands together, and put a gag in her mouth to stop the screaming they knew she would attempt. The brown-haired man looked her in the eyes as she sat there, scared.

He said to her, "Look here, miss, we ain't here to hurt you, so stop with this fighting us, and this shall go by much better for everyone. We got you for a reason, and hopefully, it be over soon, and you be able to go home." Laurentia looked all around her. The inside of the coach they were in was old, with dark curtains so no one could see in or out the windows.

The blond haired man said, "Sit back, and we shall be there soon."

Laurentia was worried. Where are they taking me? What is this all about? What shall come of me? Shall I see Jasper, his lovely family, and my brother ever again? A tear rolled down her cheek.

The brown haired-man saw the tear, "Miss, you don't have to cry. We are not going to hurt you; that's our orders, you see."

The other man said, "We are almost to our drop point by now. I don't care for this kind of work." He looked at his partner.

The other nodded. "Yeah, the payout is better, is all."

For the rest of the ride, they kept quiet. Then, about ten minutes more, the coach came to an abrupt stop. Laurentia guessed they rode for half an hour or more. She wondered if the footman who was with her had gained consciousness and returned to tell everyone she had been abducted.

The door opened, revealing a tall, well-dressed man of medium build. "It is about time. I was beginning to wonder if you did the job or not. I see you have, come, my Lady, let me help you down from the coach." He put his hand out for Laurentia to take, then noticed her hands were tied together, and a gag was over her mouth. He then looked at the two he hired to bring her here. "I told you two fools not to harm her in any way. So why is she tied and gagged?" He barked, not looking happy at all.

The blond-haired man said, "First of all, she bit my hand. I had my hand over her mouth to stop her from screaming, and she also would not sit well with all the fighting she did when I grabbed her. So, we tied her hands and gagged her to stop the carrying-on she was doing. We had no choice."

The man standing out of the coach yelled, "Untie her hands at once, so she does not bruise her wrists or get rope burns, you idiots."

The brown-haired man untied her hands quickly. The man standing out of the coach put his hand out again to help Laurentia down, "My Lady, let me help you now from the coach so we can go inside."

Laurentia hesitated at first, not knowing where she was going next but then took his hand as she stepped out of the coach. He ushered her into a large building that looked like a warehouse once she descended from the coach. She smelled the salt air that told her they were at the docks, near the waterfront. Once inside the building, he walked her through the warehouse full of crates stacked all around. They walked to the back of the building, and he opened a door and took her inside, shutting the door behind them. She noticed four men in the warehouse area standing about when they walked through. The room they entered was an office with a desk in one corner, a chaise on one wall, and two wingback chairs.

The two kidnappers came in a few minutes later. Laurentia sat on the chaise, with her hands in her lap, looking all around. The blonde-haired man said.

"We delivered her as you hired us for, so, as I see it, we are done with this job. So pay us, and we be on our way if you don't mind, Mr. H."

Hughes walked over to the desk, opened a drawer, and pulled out two bags of coins.

"Here, you did as I requested," he held out the dough. The blond-haired man walked over and took the bags, then counted their contents.

Satisfied, he said, "We shall be off now, and if there are more jobs you need taken care of, you know where to find us."

Hughes said, "I suggest you two disappear for a while, stay out of sight for a few days. The lady you kidnaped here is from a very resourceful family. Once they know she is missing, they shall be looking for you two, no doubt."

The brown-haired man said, "Yeah, I figured she did, coming from that rich fancy mansion with a footman in tow. We decided to leave London for a couple of weeks, have some kin north of here."

Hughes said, "Good idea."

The two kidnappers left the room, leaving Laurentia and Hughes alone.

He walked away from the desk over to her. "I shall take your gag off now; no one shall hear you if you decide to start yelling. Shall you behave if I take it off you?" Laurentia nodded, and he untied the gag from her mouth.

"Why are you doing this to me? I do not know you, nor have I ever seen you before."

"I have my reasons. Your rich brother signed some papers to invest in my company and refuses to pay what he owes. I warned him that we would come after you, and he thought I was bluffing but, I was not as you can see."

"It was you who caused the carriage accident in Hyde Park. You are not after the Duke of Devonshire's family. It was me all along."

Hughes nodded, "Smart, Lady! Your brother came to London knowing all of this and did not even warn you, it seems."

Laurentia was in shock that Lucas knew of this. He did not try to stop this or tell the Raventon's what was happening. Lucas could have asked for help from Jasper or the duke, and he did not.

"What shall happen next?" Laurentia asked with concern in her eyes.

Hughes walked over to a comfortable chair not far from her and took a seat. "I have sent another letter saying I have you and that the young earl needs to pay by this evening or harm may come to you. Simple, you see."

"You shall hurt me if he does not pay, is that right?"

Hughes smiled. "I shall not be the one hurting you. I would sell you to a whorehouse for a hefty price. There are a lot of them in London. The owner shall get his money back with you, as one of his new whores. You are quite a beauty, I could sell you to the first house we go to, and I definitely shall try you out first before I sell." He laughed.

Laurentia was not amused one bit. "My brother shall pay once he knows I'm taken. I know he shall."

"He did not pay before the carriage accident. Or after. Does he care? It makes you wonder, does it not?"

Laurentia said firmly, "He shall pay, and if he does not, Lord Bellator is my betrothed. He shall come after me once he knows I am missing."

"That is interesting to hear, my Lady." He looked at Laurentia's' left hand and saw the massive ring on her finger. Standing, he walked over to her, grabbed her hand, and looked at the ring. "What an extremely nice ring you have here." He pulled the ring off her finger quickly and moved away.

Laurentia was outraged. She jumped to her feet to follow him, then as he turned to sit down, she slapped him across his face. "Give me my ring back this instant, you horrible man."

Hughes laughed in her face, then grabbed her wrists so she could not hit him again. Still holding her wrists, he stood, looking down at her menacingly.

"Little one, you have a bad temper, don't you? I suggest you do not hit me again or I shall return the same fate to you. Do you get my meaning, Lady Laurentia?" Still holding her wrist, he hauled her back to the chaise and spoke. "Now, you made me angry. Do not get up off this chaise until I tell you otherwise."

He pushed her roughly to her seat.

Hughes walked across the room to a looking glass hanging on the wall to see a red spot where Laurentia slapped him. He turned around, not looking too pleased with the slap mark on his face.

"I shall keep this ring for now, as a security deposit." Hughes put Laurentia's ring in his inside coat pocket and smirking at her.

Laurentia was furious, and she knew Jasper would not take lightly that this man had her ring and forcefully took it off her finger.

Laurentia asked, "What do we do now?"

"Wait, see if your brother pays to get you back. Have you had anything to eat yet today, my Lady?"

Laurentia snapped, "No, I was having a morning walk before I broke my fast. Your men abducted me before I returned home, as you can see."

"I have not eaten yet either. I shall have one of my men go out and bring in something for us both." He walked out of the room, leaving Laurentia alone for just a few minutes. When he returned, he seemed calmer.

"We shall have something brought in to eat soon. There is a bakery not far from here; one of my men is making the trip."

Laurentia decided to go along with him on his change of mood and be pleasant to him. Maybe he shall leave me alone a lot longer, and I could escape. She put on a fake smile, then said.

"That would be lovely. I hope your man brings back some tea too."

"Yes, of course, there shall be tea, my lady. I also enjoy a good cup myself every morning." He smiled.

Laurentia could only sit and wait for her break or

someone to come to rescue her. She hoped Jasper would come soon. He shall; she knew that in her heart.

Chapter 27

Lady Laurentia Is Discovered to Been Kidnapped

As the footman escorting Lady Laurentia on her walk came to, he sat up, rubbing the backside of his head where he was struck. Then he remembered he was out walking and protecting Lady Laurentia and two men ambushed him. He did not see the one who hit him from behind but saw the one grabbing Lady Laurentia before he was completely knocked out. He got to his feet, not knowing how long he had been unconscious for and ran back to Devonshire Mansion.

Wesley was the first person he saw when he arrived. Gulping for air, he blurted out, "Lady Laurentia missing; she went for a morning walk little after seven. I was escorting her. They hit me on the head from behind, and she was grabbed; they took her away. We need to tell the duke at once, Mr. Wesley." Gus was in a panic. Wesley was now in fear, knowing the lady had been missing for forty minutes, at least. They hurried to the dining room where Wesley known both the duke and duchess were eating. Wesley rushed in with the footman on his heel to tell them the terrible news.

"I am sorry, Your Grace, to rush in like this, but

something horrible has happened that cannot wait."

Startled, the duchess asked, "Is it my daughters, Wesley? What is wrong, my sons?"

"Lady Laurentia went out this morning for a walk. The footman, Gus, was escorting her. He was hit on the head from behind, and they took Lady Laurentia away."

Duke yelled, "Who took her, Gus?"

Gus answered, "Before I was knocked out completely, Your Grace, I saw a tall man with curly blond hair grab her. He jumped out from behind a tree."

The duchess asked, "When Gus? How long ago?"

"I believe a bit after seven, Your Grace. I'm so sorry." He hung his head in shame.

Duke said, "Lady Laurentia should have never gone out. Wesley, send for Lord Bellator immediately. Go now. We do not have time to waste."

Wesley rushed out of the room and had their fastest messenger ride to Lord Bellator's townhouse on Grosvenor Square to tell him that he needed to come at once, for Lady Laurentia had been abducted.

The duke said to his duchess, "I need to change into my riding clothes. Tell Wesley to have Drake, Leopold, Kelsey, Sterling, Victor, and both my brothers summoned to help with the search."

Duchess rushed out of the dining room on the duke's tail to give the order as he went upstairs to change from his formal wear to riding wear.

Jasper arrived at his townhouse with Lord Kingsley and Drake when he quickly saw one of his father's messengers coming down the street on horseback.

The messenger reined in as he reached them and blurted out in panic. "Lord Bellator, the duke, needs you to come at once. Lady Laurentia has been abducted."

Upon hearing those terrible words, Jasper yelled to his butler, who was standing at his front door,

"Earl of Berwickshire is due here in ten minutes. Tell him his sister was abducted. He must come to my parents' residence at once."

Mr. Everett said, "Yes, my Lord, as soon as he arrives."

Jasper reared his horse around, and he flew down the street like a flash of lightning, calling to his brother to follow him.

Drake said, "I'm right behind you, Bellator."

Jesse said, "I am with you, too; the more men to help, the better." The three raced down the street together, destination Berkeley Square.

When Jasper arrived, he raced by Wesley and burst into the library to find his father in riding clothes.

With fire in his eyes, Jasper said, "When and how, Father?"

Duke told Jasper, Drake, and Jesse what he knew and assured them that the rest of the Raventon men would arrive soon to conduct an extensive search party.

Jasper was as angry as hell. "We shall comb all the streets of London to find her, and whoever took her shall be sorry they were ever born. If one hair on Laurentia's head is out of place or they have touched her in any way, I shall kill them, mark my word." Jasper paced the floor like a caged animal, waiting to pounce once the door opened.

Duke said, "Son, we shall find Lady Laurentia. We shall knock on every door in London till we do."

Jasper stopped pacing, then said, "This is like a bad dream. I finally meet the woman I am to marry, spend the rest of my life with, and she is ripped out of my hands. I can only imagine how frightened Laurentia must be at this point. That alone pains me more for her welfare." He continued pacing.

The duchess entered the room. She heard what Jasper said and saw the pain in Jasper's face. Duchess went to him and tried to calm and comfort him.

"Jasper, we shall find her. Laurentia is a strong woman, and you know that, my darling." Duchess stepped in front of Jasper, so he stopped pacing and looked at her.

Jasper stopped looked into his mother's eyes. "I cannot live without Laurentia, Mother. She is everything to me. I can only imagine the horror Laurentia is going through as we speak."

The duchess embraced him, and Jasper hugged her back.

"Laurentia shall come back to you. I know it, your father shall ride by your side until she is found, and the rest of the Raventon men shall be there to help."

Jasper let go of his mother. "Thank you, Mother, for your words of wisdom. I feel more in control now." He let out a deep breath.

Duchess said, "I am here for all my children, no matter how old or independent they get. Remember that, Jasper," she smiled up to him, putting her hand on his cheek, and Jasper nodded.

When all the Raventon men had arrived, the duke said. "Now that we are all here, there has been an abduction this morning. Lady Laurentia has been taken, and we do not know why."

Earl Berwickshire walked in, then said, "I know why, and I have a letter from the kidnapper here." He held the letter he received that morning in his hand.

Jasper walked over to Lucas and grabbed the letter to read it. He snapped his head up after reading the entire content of the letter and looked straight into Lucas' eyes.

"It says here that you know how much to pay to get her back. Berwick, how would you know how much to pay? Unless the kidnapper demanded the money before today?" Rage was brewing in Jasper's eyes. He grabbed Lucas with both hands and lifted Lucas onto his toes. Jasper said through gritted teeth.

"You knew this was going to happen. Did you not? The carriage incident, you knew of that too."

Lucas was not in a good place. "Yes, I knew. I did not think this would occur the kidnapping."

Not letting Lucas finish talking, Jasper punched him square in the face and shook him like a rag doll, yelling, "The carriage incident, they all could have been killed. Laurentia, my sisters, and my mother had she gone that day. You, miserable bastard." Drake caught Jasper's fist before it made contact with Lucas' face again.

Drake, Leopold, Kelsey, and Jesse tried to release Jasper's hold on Lucas before Jasper choked him to death. Victor had joined in, and it took all five men to restrain Jasper. He was not a force to be reckoned with when provoked his anger. Jasper tried to shake off his family to get back to Lucas to finish what he had started, but they held him back.

Leopold had been with Jasper in their younger days in school when a fight broke out. He remembered well how good a fighter he was.

"Cousin, stop. Before you kill him, we need to get information out of him to find Lady Laurentia." Leopold said as he stood between the two men.

Jasper stopped, took a deep breath to shut down his anger for the moment, to regain his control. He looked into Leopold's eyes.

"Yes, you are right. I am fine now. You may let go of me, all of you." They released Jasper but kept close just in case.

Duke walked to where Lucas was standing, looking intimidating. "I am not pleased with you, Berwick. My family is the most important reason I get up in the morning. You endangered them, and they could have died in that carriage accident. My son is in love with Laurentia and shall marry her soon. That makes her a part of this family; we all care for her welfare. You had better come clean now, or I shall let Jasper have a go at you again."

Lucas' mouth was bleeding from Jasper's punch. He took out his handkerchief and wiped the blood. He then told them about the man he'd met in Lincolnshire at the Inn and the subsequent visit from Hughes and finished with, "I did not tell you, for I thought my sister was safe with your family under your protection. My secretary has been working hard to clear up this matter but, we keep coming up empty."

After he was finished, it was silent for a minute. Finally, the duke said, "This man, Hughes, what does he look like?"

Lucas described him and the other man who came to his place.

Leopold said, "My friend Lord Cowell told me recently about this gentleman. He sounds like your Hughes. Tried to talk him into investing with him.

Of course, Cowell turned him down."

Duke said, "Sounds like Hughes is making his rounds with the wealthy. Leopold, go visit Lord Cowell, see if he can tell you anything else, maybe where Hughes stays or places, he likes to haunt."

Leopold said, "I shall go to his home now to talk. Sterling, come with me, and if Cowell does not know where to find him, then we shall go to Whites to ask around if anyone else has had an encounter with Hughes."

Duke said, "Yes, we need to find out as much information as possible. Go now." The two left, then the duke summoned Smith, the duke's head man of his security.

Smith bowed then said to the duke when he entered. "I have checked with every post around the mansion, as you ordered, Your Grace. The two men across the street remember seeing Lady Laurentia and Gus walking. They also saw a black coach, an old model with two gray mares, parked a block away around that time. But they did not see the abduction, only Gus running back toward the residence without Lady Laurentia."

Jasper said abruptly, "Nobody saw anything, is that what you are saying?"

Smith nodded, "My apologies, my Lord, that is all I have."

Charlton cut in, "It sounds to me that the kidnappers have been watching this residence, making a note of Lady Laurentia's activities and routines."

Duchess said, "She went for a walk every morning before breaking her fast. Plus, we always go for an afternoon carriage ride in Hyde Park." Duke dismissed Smith and told him to keep watch on the mansion.

Duke then said, "This man Hughes is no amateur in his dealings, it seems. He is desperate to receive this money. That only tells me there is someone higher than him in this scam. He is answering to someone else, a boss."

Jasper said, "I agree on that, Father. Hughes is working for someone." He turned to Lucas. "In your demand letter, there is a time and place for the money to be exchanged, and they indicated after the money is received, you would get your sister back in a different location. We shall set up a trap to follow the men with the money and reveal all involved. We want to get Laurentia and the money back and put an end to this scam."

Lucas said, "You shall do this to help my sister and me?"

Jasper said, "Your sister is my betrothed. That shall not change. You, I am still not too happy with; I know if I end this investment matter that is hanging over your head, that would please Laurentia. But, believe me, I would not do it otherwise. You are a fool to have let this go on so long. You should have told us about this when you first stepped foot in London. My family has a lot of resources."

Duke said, "Let me see that letter so that we can plan this trap."

Lucas handed the letter to the duke to read. After he was finished, everyone else in the room read it so that they would all know what they were dealing with.

Jasper said, "The day I went into the milliner shop, and we sat on a bench out in front of the shop, Laurentia shared with me she felt as if she was being watched when she was out. That is when I told you, father, to have more security with the ladies. I should have paid more attention to Laurentia's words and stayed with her as a guard myself; this might not have happened. If Hughes's men are still watching us, we must have some of us leave to act as a decoy. Then we can form our plan and execute what needs to be done."

Drake said, "Bellator, we did not believe Lady Laurentia was the target when the carriage overturned. The family thought it was someone not happy with father since it was father's carriage. Do not be so hard on yourself. We get shall Lady Laurentia back." He patted his brother's shoulder.

Duke said, "Let us get to work on our plans to get Laurentia back. You are right, and they could still be watching us. A decoy is a good idea to start. Charlton, Drake, and Kelsey, you go down along the docks, check around the taverns, warehouses, and look for the coach Smith described. Let me know if you find out anything. Johnathan, Victor, and Jesse, you shall comb the streets in this district. Maybe you can find someone who saw the coach and what direction it went. Let me know what you find in two hours."

After the men left, the duke walked over to the duchess. "Darling, I think it's better if you go check on our girls and keep them close. I shall tell you later of the plans." He took her hand and kissed it.

The duchess wanted to stay to be a part of helping, but she realized the duke was right; she should be with their daughters.

"Yes, I shall go. We shall be in my private parlor. Do let me know of any news." Duchess reached up to kiss Conrad's lips softly before seeking out the twins.

The duke sat at his desk. "Come, let's plan this trap we need to execute."

Jasper and Lucas took a seat in front of the desk. The three worked together to put a plan together. Jasper was still worried about Laurentia's whereabouts, and he wanted vengeance on the person who had her. God protect their soul when he found them.

Chapter 28

Time to Spring the Trap

The duke and Jasper had worked out a foolproof plan to end the extortion and get Laurentia back safe. They listened to all the family's feedback when they returned, then plotted their final stages. It said in the letter from the kidnapper that Lucas was to have the money prepared for the exchange at four o'clock at St. James Park's far east corner near Duck Island. There was a cluster of fig trees where the kidnappers planned to wait. Jasper and the Duke planned to watch from a pump house at the edge of Duck Island bridge and wait for their time to execute their plan. The men were broken up into partners and would remain at various places in the park surrounding the exchange spot. They would be able to see whoever entered and left the entire area. Jasper was eager to get his love back. Rage kept building inside of him, and he was at wit's end of keeping his emotions in check.

They decided not to inform the law to help them; this was Raventon justice.

Lucas stood at the designated spot the kidnapper said to be at with the money at the appointed time. Duke told Lucas to make this exchange look as authentic as possible, which meant he needed to have the money with him. Of course, Lucas was not happy with that but, it was his sister's life they were dealing with, so Lucas held an envelope of cash in his inside coat pocket, waiting impatiently.

Back at the warehouse where Laurentia was being held, Hughes had made sure Lady Laurentia was comfortable, and he had seen to all her needs. Hughes said to her. "Just because we are in this dilemma was no reason not to be a good host to a lady."

They had excellent fresh-baked cinnamon rolls with tea to break their fast. A picnic basket was brought in at lunch with a bottle of fine wine, delicate finger sandwiches, and a potato salad. Then at two, tea was served with little cakes. Laurentia thanked him every time he served her, though she thought to herself, 'It's better to be gracious than to be bitter. He'd already shown his angry side to her earlier, and that was not a welcome experience at all.' Laurentia felt more relaxed with him at tea, so she asked a few questions instead of idle chit-chat.

They were chatting about inconsequential topics like the weather, things they enjoy most. Laurentia commented that she enjoyed reading and taking walks in the lovely garden.

Hughes smiled at her answers and was finding Laurentia was a true lady. He hated the thought of having to hurt her if his plot did not work out.

Laurentia asked, "What small pleasures do you enjoy, sir?"

Hughes thought for a moment then said, "A good cigar and a nice brandy by a fire. Plus, chocolate cake."

Laurentia laughed, then said, "Yes, I have noticed you ate all three on the plate and had not one vanilla."

"Oh, dear, that was rude of me, my Lady. Did you want one?"

Laurentia shook her head. "No, I have to watch my waistline, but thank you anyway."

"I hope that Lord Bellator knows how lucky he is to have you as his future bride."

"We are both lucky to have found each other."

Hughes thought, 'Lord Bellator does not deserve her; he already has the life of privilege and was born with a silver spoon in his mouth.' So, he smiled, then said, "Yes, a fortunate man."

"What time is the exchange for me and the money to take place?"

"Four o'clock this afternoon."

Laurentia fished a little more and asked, "Am I going to that exchange at four?"

Hughes shook his head, "No, you are not."

She felt bold, then asked, "Is that not how it works, you get the money, and I am set free?"

"I do not trust your brother, for this is the third time I asked for the money, and he denied me twice. Therefore, you shall be let go after I am satisfied and not until then. Simple as that, my Lady."

Laurentia realized it may get tricky to have her freedom and be back in Jasper's arms. She noticed he did not mention the Raventon's being involved in this. She knew that Jasper and the rest of the family must be involved as well, for when Jasper claimed something as his, one did not touch or harm it—especially when it came to his love. She decided to change the subject when one of his men came in.

Hughes rose from his chair and said, "If you would excuse me, I have some details to work out with my men. Do finish your tea. I shall be back shortly." As Hughes left, Laurentia heard the door locked behind him.

Laurentia's mind was going a hundred miles an hour. Should she try to escape or sit and wait? If her brother did not come to rescue her, Jasper surely would. She stood, then paced the floor a couple of times before stopping. I cannot just wait here. It's not in my nature to do that. She looked around the office and saw no windows and only one door that was just locked by Hughes. She noticed a couple of air vents in the far wall from the door. I could crawl through there. I bet they lead to the outside wall then out. Yes, that might work; Laurentia strolled over to one of the vents and looked to see what was needed to open it. Then she searched for something with a flat edge to get between the vent and wall to pry it open. Laurentia walked over to the desk finding the side drawer locked, but the top drawer was opened. Fishing around inside, she found a letter opener, just what she needed. It was heavily built and sturdy. Laurentia took the letter open, then grabbed a chair from in front of the desk, which looked more stable to stand on. She dragged the chair over to the vent and set the chair against the wall before climbing up to work on the vent. With the sharp tip like a knife, she pried it in between the wall and vent. Working all around the edge, prying it off, it broke free, and she was able to pull it from the wall and put it in on the floor. Laurentia decided to keep the letter opener, slipping it into her dress pocket, just in case she needed it later. Grabbing hold of the opening in the wall, she pulled herself up from the chair. It was a tight squeeze, just big enough for Laurentia to crawl through. After crawling about four feet, she came to a tee. She looked to the left and then to the right, and then she heard something moving from the right tunnel coming toward her. She wanted to scream but could not; they would certainly hear her. She saw a rat walking toward her, and she bit her bottom lip rather than scream. She pulled out the letter opener from her pocket, apologized to the rat, and killed it with one hard stab. Yuck, Laurentia thought as she pushed the rat to the side. She looked again down each tunnel. Laurentia felt a breeze coming from the right, and she figured the direction of the air was coming from the way out, so she went in that direction on her hands and knees. Laurentia quickly discovered that crawling with a dress on was not an easy task, but she continued. When she reached the end, about fourteen feet, she could see outside and feel the cold air on her face. Laurentia pushed the vent out, and it fell to the ground with a light thump. She turned herself around to go out feet first to land on the ground. Hanging on, she lowered herself down and dropped, landing on her feet.

As soon as she stood up straight, two large hands grabbed her from behind on her shoulders, asking, "Was that a fun exercise, Lady Laurentia?" Mr. Hughes asked. "I hope so because now I have to tie you up. That means no more exercise for you. I cannot have you taking off on me again. Come, we shall be going back in for a while yet, and I shall not let you out of my sight."

Laurentia was escorted back to the front of the warehouse to the front door. He did not take her back into the office but instead walked her to a wooden chair and proceeded to tie her up as promised. She was not happy with this situation, but she'd brought it upon herself, as Hughes explained. 'Damn, it probably would have worked if he did not come back so soon and found me missing.'

Laurentia sat in the chair watching two men and Hughes go over a map, discussing the direction they would go when they left London. They better go fast when they leave, for they would no doubt be pursued once she was released. I guess there is nothing to do; I shall have just to sit here and wait.

Hughes said to his help, "Lets' load up and go. We cannot waste time."

One of the men said, "Everything is loaded for this trip, sir."

Hughes said, "Good, lets' go." He turned to Laurentia and said, "Lady Laurentia, it is time to go on a trip." He walked over, untied her from the chair. When he finished untying her, he put his hand out for her to take. She stared at his hand, not saying anything.

Hughes finally said, "I don't bite. You can take my hand, my Lady."

Laurentia looked up at his face, then said, "I am not leaving London with you or anybody else for that matter."

Hughes knew a lady of wealth could be difficult at times but now was not a time to test his patience. "You are going. You can walk on your own or I shall carry you. What shall it be, my Lady?"

Laurentia was not amused at all at his smug expression, and she turned her head as if ignoring him. Hughes scooped Laurentia off the chair, then tossed her over his shoulder and walked out the door to his coach.

Laurentia screamed in protest, "Put me down at once. You are an animal! How dare you, this is highly inappropriate for a lady."

Hughes kept walking, "I did give you a choice, my Lady. As I see it, your choice was this to be carried." He opened the coach door, put her on a seat, then stepped in to sit across from her. "Sorry, I had to do that, but it is time to go."

Laurentia glared at him then asked, "Where are we going?"

Hughes tapped the roof to let his driver know he could go, then said, "On a trip to Kent for now. If your brother paid my men, your stay would be short, and you may go home."

"It seems I do not have a say in this, do I?"

Hughes shook his head no and leaned back in his seat to get comfortable. "Let's hope your brother was smart this time, and this shall be over soon. We should be at our destination in twenty-four hours. We shall be riding through the night. If you'd like a blanket, just let me know. They are under the seats in the storage box." They rode through the night as Hughes said, and Laurentia prayed for Jasper to come for her, to end this nightmare.

Back at St James Park, just before four, Jasper and the Duke saw two men riding horseback toward Lucas.

One dismounted and started talking to Lucas. "Mr. Hughes sent us here for the payment you owe on your contract."

Lucas got a little tick at the terms of 'contract and

payment owed.' "You mean ransom to pay for my sister's return."

The two men looked at each other. The one on the ground said, "Yeah, Hughes does have your sister, so it is smart to pay now."

"I do not see my sister with you. If I pay you now, how and when do I get my sister back?"

The one on the horse said, "Hughes sees it this way, you pay us now, and we set up a place for you to receive your sister back at a later time. He said because this is the third time requesting payment, she is your collateral see. So that is how this shall work." Lucas wanted her back, so he agreed to their conditions pulling the money envelope out from his inside coat pocket.

The man on the ground took the envelope, looked inside, making sure it was the money, and then mounted his horse quickly.

"When this money is in Mr. Hughes's hand, we shall contact you with arrangements to receive Lady Laurentia back."

Jasper and the Duke heard the whole conversation transpire. They rushed out of the hut to ambush the men on horseback. They both drew their swords to stop them. Jasper ran to the one who took the money, who also drew his sword when he saw Jasper running toward him with his blade in the air. The two swords collided hard with a crash, and Jasper knocked his opponent to the ground. The man was lying on his back, jumped to his feet swiftly, and circled one another, waiting for one another to make the next move. Jasper thought, 'I do not want to kill him yet. I need to know where Laurentia is first.'

Jasper lunged forward, hitting his opponent's

sword with a crash of metal, then struck, again and again, knocking his sword out of his hand. This time, Jasper lunged forward, raising the tip of his blade to the man's throat, smiling with his declared victory.

"You shall tell me where Lady Laurentia is being held hostage or die."

The man gulped, "Hughes shall kill me if I tell you."

"As I see it right now, I shall kill you if you do not. Plus, I also want to know if it was you and your partner that did the kidnapping and dared to put your hands on my future wife," he said with a glare in his eyes that said he had no choice but to answer.

The man looked for his partner, who was riding away, finding no help. He looked back at Jasper. "She is at this moment being transported to Kent. It was not us that did the kidnapping part. Hughes hired two men from the London docks for that job, I swear."

Jasper saw his brother Drake and Leopold riding up on horseback, and they stopped where Jasper was holding a sword to the man's throat.

Drake asked, "Has he said where Lady Laurentia is yet?"

Jasper nodded, "Yes, it seems Laurentia is on her way to Kent."

Lucas walked over to join them, "Are you sure? That seems to be a distance away, as I see it."

"If you want to live, you better be right. My men here shall escort you to a place where you shall stay until I retrieve Lady Laurentia. If you put me on a wild goose chase, I shall kill you when I return. Do not test me." Jasper said the last part looking menacing

The man gulped, then said, "That is where they

are going. I swear on my mother's grave."

Victor and Jesse rode over with Jasper's horse and horses for the Duke and Lucas. Kelsey and Sterling rode over next.

Jasper lowered his sword, "Kelsey, Sterling, take this man as a prisoner to my townhouse, tie him up and watch over him until we return."

Kelsey said, "Sterling, it looks as if we are on watchman's duties." He pulled out his sword to took charge of the prisoner, "Come along, mister, get on your horse, and we shall go.

Sterling pulled out a revolver and pointed it at the man, saying, "No funny stuff, I never miss my target." Then the man got back on his horse and knew he better do as he was told.

Jasper asked one more question: "Where in Kent are they taking, Lady Laurentia?"

He answered, "Just outside of Maidstone on Buckland Road, there is an old farmhouse made of brick. That is where she shall be."

Jasper mounted Lucifer then said, "Let's ride; the daylight shall not last long."

Duke, Jasper, Leopold, Victor, Lucas, Jesse rode in a mighty pack to claim Lady Laurentia back and end this scam on her brother Earl Berwickshire.

Chapter 29

On The Road to Kent

The Raventon men, along with Lucas and Jesse, rode hard in their saddles; the horses were bred champions and could take the long ride through the night. The horses came from Sterling's stables, and he always made sure his family had the best and nothing less. The duke rode in the front between his two sons, and he was proud of them both. He looked over to Jasper's impassive expression, but he could tell his son was holding back his anger and hurt, for it was he who spent hours in training him to perform as a future duke as his father had done for him. Someday soon, Jasper would do the same for his son, which made Conrad's heart fill with pride and love. He loved Drake just as much, and he knows both his sons shall make their mark on the world one day.

Duke said to Jasper, "Son, we shall get her back; I believe Laurentia is a strong woman. She has to be to marry a future duke. She shall be fine through all this."

Jasper answered, "Yes, Laurentia is strong, but I should have been there to protect her and not put my guard down so easily. That keeps racing through my head. I shall put a hurt on this Hughes when we catch up with them."

"She was in my household, Jasper; some of the blame should go on myself."

Jasper looked over his shoulder to see Lucas in deep conversation with Victor behind them. He rode closer to his father's horse before saying.

"The room Laurentia is staying in, Father. I have been spending the last few nights with her. I always leave at dawn before the house awakes. I have been going through the secret passageways behind the wall. This morning I did not wake her before I left. I should have told her again not to go out. That is why I feel wholehearted to blame. She looked so beautiful sleeping; I did not want to wake her."

"Son, I figure that is why you put her in that room when she was hired. I could tell the way you two looked at each other that there was something more between you. Let us both be partial at fault, and that shall make us more determined to find her."

Jasper nodded, "I am going to find her; she is my future marchioness. I shall move boulders to have her by my side always."

Duke said, "Yes, my son, that is how I always felt and feel for your mother, and that feeling never stops."

Drake felt left out of the conversation, so he said, "I take it you two agree on who to blame now?"

Duke answered, "Yes, we hashed that out."

"I am here for you, Brother, plus I like the idea of having Laurentia as a sister. That makes her a Raventon in my book, and I always have your back."

"Thank you, Drake. That means a lot to me, and you know I am always there for you as well."

Duke said, "The night is falling fast; I say we are about three miles out of London now. We shall ride most of the night, for it is cooler on our horses. About four, we shall stop so the horses can rest and catch some sleep ourselves. We do not know what is in store for us when we arrive in Kent, and we need to be alert."

Jasper said, "I believe the kidnappers are at least three hours ahead of us. They are riding in a coach, and they are more than likely changing horses in a few Inn stables."

Leopold rode up beside Jasper and said, "There is a shortcut up ahead. Horses can only travel that road because it is narrow and rocky. But we can cut an hour or more off our time if we choose to take that route."

Jasper said, "Sounds good to me."

Drake said, "I know that way. I have used it a time or two, and it is up around the bend. Leopold is right; it shall take much-needed time off our journey."

Duke said, "The full moon is exceptionally bright tonight, giving us enough light. We should be fine using the old road." They rode around the bend, then turned off the main road and took the shortcut as suggested. They kept a steady pace on this road, one so narrow, they could only ride two of them side by side for a short time and then back to single riders.

It was about half-past eight, and Laurentia was curled up in the corner seat on her side of the coach. Hughes sat comfortably on his side, and he looked up from a bit of nap to see Lady Laurentia shivering in the corner seat across from him. He stood up, then turned toward his place and lifted the cushion to pull out two blankets. He handed one to Laurentia, but she shook her head and looked away.

"My lady, you are cold. Take the blanket to cover up with and keep warm. It would not be good for you to catch a chill and become ill on this little trip we are taking."

Laurentia turned her head back to look into his eyes, "I am cold. Thank you." She took the blanket and draped it over her. "If you truly want to make me happy. Take me back to London, to the Devonshire home on Berkley Square. That would please me, sir."

Hughes did not say anything at first, seeming to think of a response. "You see, my dear Lady, I cannot do that. We all have someone to answer to, for I even have a boss, and your brother's money he has not paid yet is an important part of the plans we had made. I want to start phase two but cannot until phase one is finished. I said before you shall be freed when I receive the money and not before that, sorry, my Lady."

Laurentia did not think he was sorry one bit, and he seemed to be enjoying this game of power over her. Most men did like being in authority over others; she learned that at an early age when her parents died. She had helped Lucas at first when the estate was left to him. That was when she saw and watched the power plays. Lucas was incredibly young when he stepped into his title, and it took a while for him to earn the respect that went with the title.

The horses were slowing, and she suspected they were pulling into an Inn, their first stop since leaving London. Laurentia looked out to the courtyard as they stopped. Perhaps she could make her escape. The coach came to a rocking halt, then the door opened, and the step was put down.

"We are here for a half an hour to change the horses and have a quick late supper. You shall act as my wife, and I shall have no funny business from you. I do not want to hurt you, but if you force my hand, I shall. Do I make myself clear, Lady Laurentia?"

"Yes, I understand." She did not like it, but understood.

"Good, we agree. Shall we go have something to eat? I am a bit on the hungry side."

Hughes stepped out first then turned around to assist Laurentia out of the coach. He put his hand out for her to take, and Laurentia stepped down, looking around at the surroundings. Hughes put his arm out for Laurentia to take with a smile, and he led her to the front door. This Inn did not look familiar to her; the name she read above the door, Burton Inn. It seemed to be a lively place; she noticed as they walked inside. The tavern was busy for a Monday night.

The innkeeper greeted them as they walked in. "Would you like a room this evening?"

Hughes answered, "No, we need a change of horses for my coach and a quick supper if possible."

The innkeeper clapped his hands together, then said, "Of course." He looked to a young man to his right and told him to have a team of horses exchanged on the coach. He turned back to them and said, "My son sees to the horses, come with me, and I shall have my wife bring you out some venison stew with warm bread and cheese. If that shall suit you this evening?" They followed the innkeeper to a table.

Hughes said, "Yes, that shall do. I would like an

ale and my wife a glass of your finest white wine."

Innkeeper clapped his hands together, "yes, I shall see to that," then hurried away. Minutes later, a woman with light brown hair looking to be in her early thirties brought out a food tray from the kitchen. She greeted them, setting their drinks down first, then a bowl of stew in front of them and bread plus cheese in between them.

She said, "If there is anything else I could get you, let me know."

Laurentia said, "No, this smells excellent. Thank you."

Hughes said, "The stew does look and smell good." He broke a piece of bread off the loaf, dabbed it in his bowl, and started eating.

Laurentia took a bite and a sip of wine. Both were good. "The cook did nice work in making this stew. The bourbon sauce has taken the game taste out of the venison."

Hughes smiled, "I have stopped here a few times before. The food is always good."

They both ate their dinner and shared some small talk. When they finished eating, Hughes said, "I need to settle up with the innkeeper for the meal and horses."

Laurentia said, "I need to freshen up before we leave."

Hughes said to Laurentia, "I shall be out front in the courtyard waiting for you, with my men.

"I shall be out shortly." She turned then, after discretely asking the innkeeper's wife about a place to freshen up, she followed her up the stairs to one of the rooms. Laurentia hoped to write a note to Jasper and then give it to the innkeeper's wife. She briefly considered telling the innkeeper what was happening but feared Hughes's cutthroats would harm the couple. When Laurentia was alone in the room, she looked for paper and a pen, finding what she needed on the dressing table. She wrote Jasper a letter and sealed it. Laurentia decided to freshen up with the water in the washbowl and use the chamber pot also. When she was finished, she searched for the innkeeper's wife, finding her in the tavern.

Laurentia hurried over to her, then said quickly. "I have written a letter for Marquess Bellator. He shall be traveling through here not long after we leave. Give him this letter, and he shall reward you when he knows it is from myself. He has black hair, blue eyes, and he always wears black and is quite handsome. He shall be with a few more men who resemble him. I beg for you to give him this letter, please?" The innkeeper's wife agreed, and Laurentia thanked her and rushed outside so Hughes would not come looking for her and find the letter.

Outside, Hughes talked with his men who were escorting them, and he stopped when he saw Laurentia walking toward them.

Hughes said, "Let us get back on the road, shall we."

Once they were underway, Hughes said, "We are fed, have been freshened up, and now we shall not stop for a long time.

Laurentia nodded, "I shall get some sleep now and hope morning comes soon."

Hughes asked, "Why do you hope for the morning to come soon?"

"So tomorrow comes, and this can be over, and I go home." Laurentia sounded unamused.

"Is my company that bad, my Lady?"

"No, your company is fine; if it were under different circumstances, I would say pleasant," Laurentia said with a fake smile.

Hughes smiled, "I can live with that. Thank you."

Laurentia closed her eyes; she covered up with the blanket given to her earlier and dreamed of her black-haired, blue-eyed betrothed whom she missed so and loved.

The shortcut Leopold suggested took an hour or more off their time crossing that area. They were back on the main road when the duke said, "There is an Inn a mile more on this road. We shall stop briefly to rest the horses, have something to eat, and check to see if a coach has passed through there."

Jasper agreed but wished to keep going on instead. When they reached the Inn, most of them were glad for the break, for it was the first time they stopped since leaving London.

Jesse said, "I have stopped here a few times before. The food is always good."

Victor and Lucas offered to take the horses to the stable. The horses needed food and water.

Victor said, "Order me an ale. It shall not take long to take the horses to the stable and see to their needs."

Lucas said, "Make those two ales." The rest dismounted, and they walked to the Inn's front door.

Drake read the sign, "Burton Inn, I have been here a time or two. A pleasant couple runs the place."

They walked in, looked around, and the innkeeper recognized the duke. He bowed then said,

"Welcome to my inn, your Grace. Would you like a room or some food and drink? My wife is an excellent cook."

"We need food and drink for seven." The innkeeper was so pleased that the Duke of Devonshire had come into his Inn.

The innkeeper asked, "Would you prefer a private dining room or my best table in the tavern, your Grace?"

"The tavern shall do. We have been in the saddle for over four hours and have many more miles to ride tonight. We need a quick supper if your kitchen is still open."

The innkeeper clapped his hands together. "This way, your Grace, my wife, shall be overjoyed to serve you and your party." They followed him into the tavern, and they were seated at a banquet size table.

The innkeeper's wife came over to the table, and when she saw how excited her husband was acting, she said, "Dear me, I can see now why my husband is so filled with joy." She curtsied to the duke and down the line to all the rest as her husband introduced her to the table.

She turned back to Marquess Bellator, reached into her apron pocket, and pulled out the letter that was left for him. "A blonde lady was here earlier this evening, and she gave me a letter to give you, Lord Bellator. She was sure you would pass through here tonight." She handed the letter to him.

Jasper took the note, but before he opened it, he asked, "Did the lady have violet eyes, madam?"

"Yes, my Lord, she did, and she was lovely too. She described you and your family to me. She did not exaggerate, saying how handsome you are too."

Jasper's eyes lit up now, knowing the letter was from Laurentia. "Thank you for delivering the letter. It means the world to me to receive this." He reached into his coat pocket, pulled out five gold coins, and handed them to the woman, thanking her again. She curtsied to Jasper as she looked at the gold coins in her hand. She had never received so much money at one time from anyone.

As she rose, she said, "Thank you, my Lord. The Lady did say you would reward me, but this more than I expected." She said to the duke, "I heard you say a quick supper is what you wish. I will have food out to you in a jiffy, your Grace." She curtsied then hurried to the kitchen.

Jasper sat back in his chair and broke the wax seal on the letter, and read.

My dearest Jasper, my love,

I know your heart is filled with worry for me. I am fine under these circumstances, and the kidnappers have not hurt me badly yet. In my heart, I know you are on your way to finding me; please hurry; I feel pain in my heart being away from you too long. My kidnapper's name is Hughes, and he is taking me to Kent. That is all I know to help you on this quest.

I love you, Laurentia.

Jasper looked up from the letter, blinking to hold back his anger. He hurt being away from Laurentia. His thoughts raced, 'I shall kill this man named Hughes, who took my woman away from me, and he will feel the pain he is putting me through.'

Jasper stood and pushed away from the table, rage pumping through his veins.

Duke looked up at Jasper, "Son, what is it? Is Laurentia hurt?"

Jasper spat out, "I cannot sit here and break bread with you when Laurentia has been ripped away from me. I must go now!"

Duke stood, walked over to Jasper, and put a hand on his shoulder.

"Son, it is good to let the horses stop for half an hour to feed and drink. The letter you are holding does it state Laurentia is in danger?"

Jasper looked down at the letter, and then he looked up to meet his father's eyes.

"She wrote that she is fine under the circumstance, and he has not hurt her badly yet. Yet, it is the word 'yet' that is stuck in my mind. I am going to kill this Hughes if it is the last thing I do, your Grace."

"Bellator, we are with you on this. Take a deep breath, and calm yourself down. You need a clear head when you encounter this man."

Jasper listened to his father, took a deep breath, and closed his eyes, trying to bring down the demons inside him that we're fighting to be released. Finally, Jasper opened his eyes, released the breath he held, and came down.

"Sorry for almost losing control. I have it now, your Grace."

"Son, you are a human with feelings. We shall get to Laurentia in time before anything bad happens to her, I promise you that. Let us have a quick bite, and the horses should be good to go by then."

Jasper let out another breath he was holding, said between gritted teeth. "Yes, I shall wait and leave with you."

Duke said, "Good, let's have a seat."

As he sat, Jasper put his letter from Laurentia in

the inside pocket of his waistcoat close to his heart. Then, with help from two young women, the inn-keeper's wife laid out a spread of food over the table. There was cold meat for sandwiches, cheese, bread, and steaming bowls of soup in front of each. They all dug in and ate, as did Jasper too.

Duke looked down the table at the men. When they caught up to the kidnapper, he knew it would probably take all of them to hold Jasper at bay, and his son would more than likely kill this man named Hughes. That is where I shall come in, he thought to himself, to cover up the mess, if any, that nothing comes out to harm his family name at the end. Duke's father and grandfather always made sure the Raventon family secret stayed secret, and so shall he. After they had their fill of good food, they walked to the small stable to retrieve their horses in order to mount them and ride into the night after the assail-ant. The moon was still high in the night sky, giving them the right light to ride all night long if needed.

Chapter 30

Arriving in Maidstone

In the coach, traveling all night long, Hughes had two men taking turns driving, so they would not have to stop for the night. They pulled into the second Inn at 4:30 am to change horses once again, to carry them on the rest of their journey to Maidstone. It was seven-thirty when Laurentia opened her eyes to see across from her the look of desire in the eyes of a man she's grown to hate more and more as time goes on. She looked to the window to see it was morning and sat up straight in her seat from her sleeping position, taking her blanket off, folding it, and setting it beside her.

Hughes broke the silence between them. "Good morning, Lady Laurentia. I trust you slept well."

Laurentia had to bite her tongue, not to say her honest thoughts. Instead, she said, "Well enough, for riding in a coach all night. Where are we now?"

Hughes said casually, "We are in Kent, almost to Maidstone. I say we shall be at our destination less than six hours."

Time was going too slow for Laurentia. She wondered if Jasper received the letter she left in Burton Inn and how far behind they were. She dreamt of him through the night, holding her tight in his strong arms; it helped her keep her sanity. To be kidnapped was not something Laurentia ever imagined would happen to her. She tried to think of something pleasant to say. "The sun is shining, that is good making, for a pleasant day."

"Yes, I do think today shall be good once we reach Maidstone soon. My two men who retrieved the money from your brother shall arrive not long after our arrival. Then you may go home. Simple, you see."

"I do hope it is that simple. I have been away too long as it is."

Hughes looked out the window and changed the subject. He asked, "Are you hungry? There is a small village coming up, if I remember right, I believe a bakery is there. We could have something to break our fast there."

Hughes was correct; there was a bakery, and the coach stopped out front. The door to the coach opened, and Hughes asked, "Would you like to stretch your legs?"

"Yes, that would be nice."

Hughes stepped out of the coach first, then turned around and helped Laurentia out of the coach. She took his hand to step down from the coach, letting go when her feet hit the ground.

Laurentia said, "Thank you, what a lovely little village. I have never been here before. What is the village's name?"

"Yes, it is a nice place. The name of the village is Aylesford. Come, they always have fresh apple fritters this time of day. They're the best you could ever have." He put his arm out to escort Laurentia into the shop. She took his arm not to cause any problems. When they walked into the shop, a little bell rang that sit at the top of the door.

A red-haired woman with bright green eyes standing behind the counter recognized Hughes. "Mr. Hughes, 'tis nice to see ye again. Let me guess dat's be two apple fritters to go," she said with a wink.

"Make it three, Annie. I have told my friend here they are the best."

"A pretty young lass ye have on your arm dere, and her name be?"

Hughes smiled, "I'd like you to meet Lady Laurentia. Lady Laurentia, this is Annie, the best baker in the kingdom."

Annie curtsied to Lady Laurentia, "He is a true bragger this one. It's a pleasure to make your acquaintance, me Lady."

Laurentia nodded, "Your baked goods smell wonderful. Your accent is Irish, Annie?"

Annie smiles then said in a rich Irish brogue, "Ye stand correct; I'll marry a handsome Englesh lad, here I be baking my eart away farhr England now instead of me homeland."

Hughes says, "I always stop here when I am passing through. Once you bite into Annie's baked goods, you shall see why."

"I cannot wait to try some; I do enjoy apple fritters. I shall try one," Laurentia said with a smile.

Annie pulled out two for Hughes and two for Laurentia, then said, "I poeht an extra one in dere, me Lady, ye might snack it later."

Hughes paid Annie then said with a warm smile, "See you next time I'm passing through."

Annie nodded, "I be here waiting for ye."

Once they returned to the coach, Hughes said, "My drivers and men shall go in now, and then we shall be on our way." Hughes unwrapped the apple fritters and handed one to Laurentia. When Laurentia took a bite, her eyes lit up in delight. "Always worth the stop, is it not?" Hughes commend, seeing the delight in Laurentia's eyes.

"I am glad Annie gave me two." Minutes later, the coach was moving again as they continue to travel on to Maidstone

Jasper and the rest of the party rode until three before camping by a stream so the horses could drink and rest. Jasper woke at five-thirty, too restless to sleep; the dawn was quiet and peaceful. He was over by the stream, collecting his thoughts, when he heard someone walk behind him. Jaspers' hand went to his sword's grip.

Jesse saw Jasper's stance quickly change. "Bellator, I hope I won't lose my head this early in the morning. I kind of like where it lays."

Jasper turned to greet Jesse; he recognized his voice and let go of his sword. "Sorry, I was deep in thought when you came up behind me. It was just my natural reaction to take guard. I did not think anyone was awake yet."

"Aye, lucky for me, you realized who I was in this dusk light." Jesse stood beside Jasper as they spoke. They turned to the stream, and Jesse said, "We been through a lot together, dear friend. I have never seen this much anger building inside you in the last twenty-four hours. I know from childhood you excel in everything you do, always on top of your game. I guess what I'm saying is, I hope this change in you does not consume you."

Jasper thought for a moment about how to answer his friend's concern. "I had never felt true love for a woman before until I met Laurentia. She has become the most important thing in my life, besides my family and my duties. You are like a brother to me also, you know that." Jesse nodded. Then Jasper continued, "Laurentia is my destiny, she has made her stamp on my heart, and when someone is trying to take away what is mine, they shall suffer my wrath. I'm fighting with the feeling I never had before. I do feel a lot of rage and anger that needs to be unleashed. But, not to worry, I can come down from this once I have Laurentia back in my arms."

"I'm still worried about you. I guess I've never seen you in love before. I am truly happy for you. I am definitely glad it is not me at the end of your wrath, dear friend."

Jasper laughs at his last remark, "Thanks, and I'm glad you have come with us to get Laurentia back. It's nice to know you have my back as I always have yours."

Jesse smiled, "Always!"

Leopold came walking up behind them. "The sun coming up. Let me stretch a bit, and I am ready to ride again." He patted Jasper's shoulder.

Jasper said, "Let's wake the rest, then get on our way."

They walked back to the camp to find the duke sitting up. He stood when he saw Jasper walking over from the stream with Leopold and Jesse. Duke knew the three of them to have a strong bond since childhood, and it pleased him to see them still so tightly together.

"Let's saddle up and be on our way, Father." The

words Jasper spoke were like thunder that woke the rest of the men in the camp. They all saddled their horses in a matter of minutes, and we're back on the road to arrive at their final destination mid-day. The noise of hoofs on the road sounded like a troop of warriors heading for battle on their warhorses. They were riding with the real passion for defeating anyone who got in their way. Known throughout England, the Raventon Family are well respected.

When they had been back on the road for almost six hours, Victor yelled, "What is the name of the village we are seeking?"

Jasper answered, "Maidstone, I say we should be there less than three hours."

Drake, who was riding in the second row by Victor, said, "Berwick, is Maidstone the village you met this man Hughes for the first time?"

Lucas rode on Victor's other side. "No, I was much farther north in Lincolnshire. I have never been to Maidstone" They rode on thinking of what lay ahead of them when they reached the brick farmhouse on Buckland Road.

The coach pulled off Buckland Road onto a drive to a large farmhouse that sat far back from the main road. Laurentia looked out the window as she felt the horses' slowing and the different sound the wheels made on the gravel drive to the farmhouse. She saw another coach in the driveway, a much newer coach with refineries that stated the person had wealth, not like the older and worn one she was sitting in.

Laurentia looked back at Hughes, sitting across from her in the coach. "May I ask who lives here?"

"This is my home." The coach stopped with a

rocking motion. "Come; we shall go in." He opened the door, stepped out, then turned around to help Laurentia down. Once she had disembarked, Laurentia looked at the outside of the farmhouse. It was large, with two barns to the house's right and a stable with a fenced corral.

Hughes watched her as she took stock of her surroundings. "Let's go in, my Lady. It has been a long drive to get here." Hughes held his arm to escort Laurentia in, but she shook her head no.

"There is no one around to watch if I take your arm or not. So, I prefer not to, sir."

Hughes' eyes narrowed at the decline of his good manners. He sniffed, then said, "As you wish." He walked on to the front door, saying over his shoulder, "Do come along, or I shall have one of my men drag you along."

Laurentia looked at the four men standing guard, two at the door and two that traveled on horseback with them. She decided to walk in on her own and not being carried or dragged by others. She still remembered being carried over Hughes' shoulder yesterday. When Laurentia walked into the house, she was surprised to see that the inside was decorated lavishly.

Laurentia asked, "Do you have a wife?"

Hughes laughed at her, then said, "What makes you think that?" As he led her to a front parlor.

"Your home is beautifully decorated."

"Your answer is no. I enjoy having the best money can buy, as you may see. So have a seat, and I shall ring for tea and refreshments."

Before Hughes could pull the cord to summon a servant, a well-dressed gentleman walked in saying,

"I see you brought company with you."

"Yes, I had to. That twit of an earl her brother Berwickshire, I do not trust him to pay. So, I brought her here as collateral."

The gentleman walked into the room then sat in a wingback chair as if he owned the place. "Allow me to introduce myself, Lady Laurentia; I am the Earl of Merionreth." He smiled as if she should know who he was.

Laurentia sat on a plush velvet chaise across from him. "I do not believe we ever met before. I am not one bit amused being brought here today against my will, something I believe you already know, my Lord."

Merionreth said, "Yes, I can see you are not happy, my Lady. But sometimes, things happen you cannot control. If your brother paid my man here long ago, you would not be here now." He put on a look of compassion.

Laurentia said, "This whole matter you have with my brother should have never involved me. Gentlemen should be able to sit down and discuss things of importance without this kind of extreme action you have taken, my Lord."

Merionreth smiled, "I can see why the Raventon's hired you for their governess, for their two lovely daughters. You are knowledgeable and beautiful. I just read in the paper that Lord Bellator and you are betrothed to be married. So, you shall be a marchioness soon. How nice."

Hughes then said, "Yes, that's right. I have here in my pocket a token of affection from Lord Bellator. I took it off her finger yesterday." He pulled out Laurentia's diamond ring.

Merionreth said, "Now that had to cost a pretty penny." He stood up and walked over to Hughes to take the ring to see it closer. Laurentia grew angry as she watched both of them handling the ring that she wanted back so desperately. She bit her tongue, knowing Jasper would be here soon. Laurentia had felt Jasper's presence grown stronger by the minute, just as she had felt in London. She kept telling herself, 'Don't let them push me. All shall be well soon; my love is near.'

Merionreth said, "This is genuinely nice. The man has good taste in jewelry and woman, I see." He pocketed the ring and continued, "Lord Bellator, he thinks he is better than all around him. I recall my years at Eton, with him always outdoing everyone. Mister, all high and mighty. Perhaps I should taste what he thinks is his."

He started going toward Laurentia when Hughes grabbed his arm to stop him. "No, do not touch her. I rode in a coach with her for a whole day. That was enough to drive one insane with her beauty. If anyone has her, it shall be me first. But we must come to our senses. She is here for the money; I say we wait, and my men should be here within the hour or so."

Merionreth shook his arm free from Hughes. "On this, you're right; we shall wait. Put her upstairs in one of those back bedrooms for now. Who knows? We might have a treat later to share," he said with a laugh.

Hughes walked over to Laurentia, "Come, my Lady, it's time to go upstairs." He ushered her out of the room, then walked her up the stairs to the back of the house. He opened a door, and she walked in when he motioned her to do so. The room held a bed, a dressing table, plus a pitcher of water with a washbowl and towel. "You can get fresh up if you wish. I shall have someone bring you up something to eat." With that, Hughes left, locking the door behind him.

Laurentia heard the key turn in the door; she walked to the window to look out; she could see only the stable from this view. She walked over to the washstand, poured some water in the bowl, then took a washcloth and washed her face. The cold water felt refreshing to her hot skin and soothed her temper. Those two men talking to me like that, they both needed a quick thrashing. She knew if she spoke out at them, they would retaliate, and she did not want that to happen. She laughed a little to herself; she learned to control her emotions, just like Jasper does. Maybe being a marchioness isn't going to be so hard, after all.

After drying her face, Laurentia put the towel down, walked to the dressing table, and sat down. She saw a hairbrush and comb lying on the table in front of her. Laurentia sighed and decided to brush out her hair and re-pin it.

She heard the key in the door, then it opened, revealing a young woman of twenty or so. "My Lady, Mr. Hughes, told me to bring you this tray of tea and a sandwich here. I shall place the tray on the stand over here for you."

Laurentia looked over to the maid and asked, "What is your name, miss?"

"Emma, my Lady. Is there anything else I could bring you? You should like the sandwich the cook made you; it's ham, nice and fresh."

"Thank you, Emma. I shall eat after I finish my hair."

"You have lovely hair; if you don't mind me saying, I am to leave you now." Emma curtsied and left, locking the door behind her.

Downstairs, Hughes and Merionreth were discussing the next phase of their plan. Emma entered, and Hughes asked, "Did you take a tray up to Lady Laurentia as I ordered?"

Emma stepped farther into the room. She did not care for Merionreth when he was here. Keeping her head down, she answered, "Yes, sir, I have. She is a fine lady."

Hughes asked, "What was she doing when you brought in the tray?"

"She was sitting at the dressing table, brushing her hair, sir."

Hughes saw Emma had another tray for him. "You may put that tray over here. I shall serve myself, and you may go back to the kitchen now." Hughes took a bite of his sandwich and then drank his tea as they continued talking about what needed to be completed before they traveled north.

Another knock on the door revealed Taylor. Hughes looked alarmed and said, "Where is Lincoln? Why is he not with you?"

Taylor said, "Sir, we went to St James Park as you instructed us; the earl was waiting there. He asked the whereabouts of his sister and why wasn't she there for the exchange."

Hughes then said, "Did you tell him how we would do the exchange as I told you?"

"Yes, he seemed to agree on it. He handed the money envelope to Lincoln. That was when it happened."

Merionreth said, losing his patience, "What happened, you fool?"

Taylor gulped, then said, "Two men rushed us with swords in the air, and the older one came after me. I was still on my horse and was able to get out of there with my life. The younger gentlemen had a look in his eye as if a demon had possessed him. Lincoln was on his horse; he pulled his sword out to fight, but that demon of a man knocked Lincoln off his horse in one hard blow of his sword. Lincoln jumped to his feet fast when he hit the ground, but he was no match to that demon. The last I saw was the demon had his sword to Lincoln's throat, and I escaped."

Merionreth said, "The demon you are referring to was Marquess Bellator, and the other man sounds like the Duke of Devonshire, his father. Demon indeed!"

Taylor said, "I swear he looked possessed, my Lord."

Hughes asked, "I fear Lincoln must have talked and told them where we were headed. How much of a lead do you think you have on them? They shall be coming after us soon."

Taylor shrugged, "More than likely. I rode all night, and my horse did slow the last few hours. I say less than an hour behind me."

Hughes said, "Good lord, I thought Berwickshire would pay to have his sister back and keep this entirely quiet."

Merionreth stood, clearly upset how this had played out. "This is the last thing I need to happen to myself, to be here and seen by the Duke of Devonshire."

Hughes jumped to his feet, "Lady Laurentia has seen you and me. We are in this together now."

"How many men do we have here at this farm?" Merionreth said the word 'farm' as if it were a bad taste in his mouth. This land had been Hughes' family home where he was raised.

Hughes was not going to let Merionreth's superior attitude irritate him now, he answered, "Six men and us. Taylor, alert the men in the stable and out front that we shall have company soon and be ready. I need to go upstairs and change my clothes to ready myself for what lays ahead of us."

When the two men had gone, Merionreth started pacing the floor, rambling, "I could not leave now. I would end up passing the Raventon party on the one road leading to here. What should I do?"

Merionreth stopped pacing when he heard loud noises out in front of the house. The front door burst open, revealing Lord Bellator, followed by three others. Merionreth froze, looking at them, and saw Lord Bellator had so much rage on his face as he neared him and now understood why Taylor said he looked like a demon. Jasper, sword in hand, saw Merionreth standing in the middle of the floor looking at him.

Merionreth demand, "What is the meaning of this bursting in here. You have no right's here, Lord Bellator."

Jasper took a look around, stepping closer, "You have someone here who belongs to me. If you are a wise man, you shall drop your weapon now."

Merionreth laughed at him and pulled out his sword to challenge Jasper. "I have waited so long for this. This fight is between you and me. Tell your cronies to back off."

"I never back down to a challenge. Do not worry; they know not to interfere; believe me." Jasper circled Merionreth with rage in his eyes.

Leopold, Drake, and Jesse stood back to watch the match. Leopold said, "This won't last long."

Jesse said, "Two minutes top."

Drake said, "You want to put a coin on that? I say three minutes."

Leopold said, "I shall go with four minutes. How much are we betting gent's?"

Jesse said, "Let's all bet five gold coins. Winner takes all."

"Let's start now with the timing," Drake said as he pulled out his pocket watch.

They turned back to watch and nodded in agreement.

Merionreth says, "In Eton, you always had to outdo everyone, be the best, untouchable. You had the group you hung with, not letting anyone join with you." He pointed his sword at the gentlemen watching them.

"That is true; I have a group who are loyal to me and me to them. I have been raised to be and do my best at everything. The respect I received from the ton is something you earn, not buy."

Merionreth lunged forward with his sword, and Jasper took a simple step to the left to avoid his sword.

Jasper circled and asked, "Where is Lady Laurentia? You had better not have harmed her in any way. She shall be my future marchioness, and no one takes something I hold dear to me."

"She is here, upstairs." He reached into his pocket and pulled out Laurentia's ring, holding it up so Jasper could see it. "I believe this is your future bride's ring." He laughed.

"That was one stupid move, and he is done for," Leopold whispered from the sideline; Drake and Jesse nodded in agreement.

Seeing the ring he'd given Laurentia in the other man's hand was like lighting the fuse of a bomb. Jasper lunged forward, striking Merionreth's sword out of his hand in one mighty blow. Jasper's sword tip was at Merionreth's throat. Jasper gritted his teeth demandingly, held out his other hand. "Give me that ring before I kill you."

Merionreth did not put the ring in Jasper's hand, as told. Instead, he instantly pulled a small revolver out of his inside pocket from his coat, intending to shoot him. Jasper saw the weapon and was quick with his sword, pushing it forward and slicing Merionreth's throat wide open. Merionreth dropped to his knee, the revolver tumbling to the floor. Blood ran down his throat and out of his mouth.

Merionreth looked up at Jasper and his last words, "I always hated you."

"Scum like you, I'm somehow not surprised." Jasper then pulled the sword out of Merionreth's throat, and he drops to the floor, dead. In his hand, he still held Laurentia's ring. Jasper pulled out a handkerchief that was in Merionreth's inside pocket. "I do not think you shall be using this anymore." He bent over again, took the ring out of his hand, cleaned the ring of any blood, then dropped the soiled handkerchief on the body before walking away. Jasper tucked the ring in his riding coat inside pocket for safekeeping.

Jasper walked over to other men and said, "One down, one to go."

Drake held out his hand to collect his winnings, looking at Jesse and Leopold with a smile. "That was three minutes, you two." They both pulled out the coins, dropping them in Drake's hands.

Leopold said, "After we are finished here, the first round of ale is on you."

Drake laughed, saying, "Yeah, at the first tavern we come to, you're on."

Jasper looked around the room once more, "I do not know whose place this is, but it looks like they have done well for themselves."

Jesse said, "Nice taste for riff-raff in here."

Leopold picked up a vase and said, "Some pricey stuff here," then set it back down.

"Let's go upstairs. That is where Merionreth said Laurentia is." Jasper said as he walked out of the front parlor to the staircase that led upstairs. "Leopold and Drake, you two go through the kitchen, then go up the servants' stairs to make sure we do not run into any surprises. Jesse and I shall go this way." Jasper instructed as he used his sword, pointing the directions to go.

Drake said, "Good idea; I shall see you up there."

Leopold and Drake walked down a hallway with their swords out if they needed them if ambushed. Jasper still had his sword out as he headed up the stairs with Jesse right behind him, sword out and ready for action. When Jasper and Jesse reached the top landing, they looked from left to right. Jasper motioned to go left to the back of the house, and when they stepped down the hallway, they saw five doors. Jasper stepped in front of the first door and turned the doorknob, finding it unlocked. He looked at Jesse and whispered, "On three." Jasper counted, and on three, he busted the door open, and both charged into finding the room empty. They did the same at the second door.

Laurentia heard Jasper's voice in the hallway; she yelled out, "Jasper, I am down here in the last room. Jasper, I'm here, my love."

Jasper heard Laurentia yell for him, and he charged to the end of the hallway only to find the door locked. "Laurentia, I am going to kick the door down, stand back."

Laurentia stepped back a few feet and waited. Jasper did just that in one swift kick, and the door flew open. He saw Laurentia standing there with eyes only for him. Jasper stepped into the room, and Laurentia ran into his arms.

"Oh, Jasper, I knew you would come for me. I felt it in my heart, and I am truly overjoyed to be in your arms again."

"You are my life, Laurentia. I would climb the tallest mountain if that meant to find you and bring you back to me, where you belong, my love." They kissed with passion.

Jesse was checking the other doors to see if anyone was in the rooms. Finally, the last door before the room Laurentia was in, Jesse was just about to turn the door handle when the door flew opened, and a man with a loaded revolver hit Jesse in the head with the butt end of the gun. Jesse went down, hitting the floor, unconscious. Hughes stepped over Jesse, then walked into the room Jasper and Laurentia were standing in. Jasper turned toward the door with Laurentia still in his arms; he heard the sound in the hallway. He saw Jesse lying on the floor and saw a stranger standing in the doorway with a revolver in his hand.

Laurentia panicked, "It is Hughes; he is the one who had me kidnapped, took me from London and from you."

On hearing that name, Jasper jumped to action, knowing Hughes was the whole reason for this trip, taking what was his. Jasper let go of Laurentia, telling her to stay back out of the way. With his sword in hand, Jasper charged Hughes, looking like the demon Taylor described. Hughes did not know what to make of this man, charging him with the look of death on his face. Hughes shot just as Jasper rammed him. The gunshot went into the ceiling with the force of impact, and the revolver went flying out of Hughes' hand to the floor.

Laurentia screamed, her hand going to her mouth, seeing Jasper charge Hughes with a loaded gun. Hughes then pulled his sword out, and the metal of the two swords colliding showered sparks in the air. Jasper struck again hard, and Hughes stepped back from the attack. However, Hughes kept up with the hard blows of Jasper's sword, trying to hit as hard, blocking, and keeping his defense up.

Jasper looked and sounded evil. "It seems that you had some training in sword combat. Not bad defensive move, Hughes. That is your name?" He demanded.

Hughes danced in a circle with Jasper, trying to find that specific move to win the fight. "Yes, I'm Hughes. With you looking such friendly minutes ago with Lady Laurentia, you must be Marquess Bellator. I have heard about."

"In the flesh, sir." He bowed elegantly while not losing a step in this game.

"I have trained in sword fighting with the best,

my Lord, but watching you do a bow like that and still be on top of your game. Therefore, I say you are an overachiever."

"How kind of you to say, I do have a tendency of winning in everything I do. But enough with the talk, you took something that I consider mine. I do not take too kindly to that. Especially Lady Laurentia shall be my future marchioness."

Hughes shrugged, "It was all business, I assure you."

Jasper lunged forward, striking twice with Hughes' sword, then he struck again and sliced his shoulder. Hughes felt the pain from the deep cut on his shoulder. It was his sword arm that was hit, an excellent move to weaken your opponent. Hughes lunged at Jasper, missing him. Jasper dodged, then spun around, striking Hughes' same shoulder again, only inches away from the last wound. Hughes's sword arm went down in pain from the second blow with blood pouring down his arm, and he nearly drops his sword.

Jasper circled Hughes, tiring him out. He knew he was winning this fight. Hughes wrapped both hands around the sword to swing it at Jasper, and he missed him again. Jasper had not a scratch, but Hughes' two deep cuts on his shoulder were bleeding badly.

Laurentia watched the swordfight and almost felt sorry for Hughes until she recalled what he'd said to her. That she would be sold to a whore house, Merionreth and Hughes would rape her, take turns with her. But, no, Laurentia did not feel sorry for Hughes; she did want this over with and to go home.

Jasper looked over to Laurentia; he could see the pain she had been through, and it hurt him that someone purposely harmed her, his true love. More rage and anger pumped through Jasper's veins as he thought about it more. Jasper looked back to the man in front of him, still trying to lift his sword with both hands. Finish this, he heard in his head, and on that last thought, he lunged forward again, pushed his sword hard into Hughes' chest, and slicing downward before pulling it out. Hughes dropped his sword, fell to his knees, and then fell backward dead.

Drake and Leopold stood in the doorway, watching the last of the fight. Drake said, "I take it that was Hughes?"

Before he answered, he saw Laurentia running to him, and he embraced her. "Yes, it was, stands correct."

Drake said, "We found no one else coming up the back stairs. In the kitchen, I saw a cook and one young maid. Father, Victor, and Berwick have all the rest outside detained. I say we are done here."

"Yes, it looks that way," Jasper hugged Laurentia and kissed the top of her head before releasing her.

Drake turned around to see Jesse sitting up, rubbing his head.

Leopold bent down beside Jesse on one knee to take a look at his head, "That's a nasty bump on your head, dear friend. Do you feel well enough to stand?" Leopold stood and gave a hand to Jesse to help him up.

"I shall be fine once I am on my feet. That cad hit me before I realized what happened." Jesse, now standing, looked in the room behind his friends and saw the man who hit him dead on the floor. "That was Hughes, and Jasper took care of him?"

Leopold answered, "Was, is correct. You are

most likely going to have a headache with that bump on your head.

Jesse rubbing his head, "There is an ale calling my name at the nearest tavern. That should fix it. Shall we go?"

Leopold nodded his head yes, "By all means, that sounds like a hell of a plan to me and a good meal too."

Drake looked over to Laurentia then asked, "Laurentia are you, all right?"

She smiled at him, "I am now that you are all here, thank you."

Jasper said, "Let us get you out of here and outside."

Laurentia said, "That is music to my ears."

Jasper took her hand, and they walked past the body on the floor, down the hallway to the stairs. Laurentia stopped before walking down the stairs. She looked up at Jasper then said, "Did I hear, right? My brother came with you?"

Jasper raised her hand, kissed her fingers before saying, "Yes, he came with us. He finally confessed after you were kidnaped. This whole ordeal was because of him. I shall admit, I almost took his head off when he did. Unfortunately, Drake caught my second punch before I hit him again, and a few of my family members had to get me off your brother before I killed him."

"I understand your reason for hitting my brother. I am not upset, Jasper."

Jasper bent down, kissed her softly, then said, "I do love you."

"I never had a doubt, and I love you." She kissed him softly back, and they stared into each other's eyes.

He kissed her nose, "Shall we continue out of here, my sweet?"

Laurentia giggled softly, hearing Jasper calling her my sweet again, "Yes, by all means."

"I love your giggle, but what was it for just now?" Jasper had a confused look on his face.

"You called me, your sweet. That was the first endearment you called me when we met. It made me giggle because it makes me happy to hear you say it again. I was so scared that we would never be together again, and hearing you say those words just now made me feel I am home in your arms again, where I belong. I love you so much."

Jasper embraced her again, "I shall never let you go. You are mine. I love you, Laurentia."

They kissed again, long and passionate—the rest of the men long gone downstairs ahead of Jasper and Laurentia.

Jasper said, "As much as we are enjoying our reunion, we should go down now. All shall wonder where we are." Holding hands, they walked down the stairs together and out the front door.

The duke was out front of the house in the small courtyard with Victor and Lucas, and they had what was left of Hughes men tied up sitting on the ground.

Lucas saw his sister coming out of the house, and he went to her, taking both her hands. "Shall you ever forgive me, Laurentia? I am so sorry this happened. I did not believe this would have gone this far. I honestly thought with you being under the Raventon's protection, nothing would have happened to you, and I am in their debt for helping you and me." Laurentia loved her brother; she put her arms out to embrace him.

As they hugged, a few tears came from Lucas's eyes. "I love you, Laurentia. I was so scared for you. I would be lost in this world without you, dear Sister."

"I forgive you, and I love you, dear Brother. You are the only blood family I have. We've been through a lot together, and we shall get through this too. Just promise me in the future, if something like this ever happens again, you shall share with me before things go too far." Laurentia holds Lucas at arm's length, looking into Lucas's eyes.

Lucas smiles, "You can count on it. No more secrets." She kissed his cheek, and they hugged again.

Jasper left Laurentia's side so she may have her reunion with her brother. He was talking to his father, and when he finished, he came back over to Laurentia. She let go of Lucas and turned to face Jasper taking his hand.

Jasper looked down at Laurentia's hand and raised it, saying, "You are missing something, my love." He reached into the pocket of his coat and pulled out her ring.

"Hughes took that from me before we left London; my heart was in pain when he had. And when we arrived here, that nasty earl had it, he grabbed it from Hughes, and that is when I saw my ring last." Again, Jasper put the ring back on Laurentia's finger, where it belongs, and this time was looking in her eyes as he kissed the palm of her hand.

"Jasper—" He stops her words by kissing her lips passionately.

When they broke the kiss, Jasper said. "It's all over, my love. We do not need to talk about this anymore, understood?"

Laurentia nodded. "What is next?"

"I shall take you into the village, to an inn. Drake shall ride in with us to find the local magistrate and bring him back here to clean this all up. Then father and our family here shall come to the village afterward. We shall all take a room at the inn, clean up from this journey, and enjoy a meal together. Tomorrow morning, we shall all leave together to go back to London after a good night's sleep and rest."

Laurentia asked, "You are not coming back here to help?"

"No, I shall stay with you. Any argument on that?" Jasper raised an eyebrow, for he'd be damned if he'd let Laurentia out of his sight.

Laurentia smiled up at him, got on tip-toes, and kissed him lightly. "Never, my love."

"Good, we shall ride in on Lucifer."

They walked over to the duke before leaving. "My dear girl, I am glad we have you back. My son would have traveled to the end of the earth to find you." Duke hugged her, kissed her cheek just like he did to his daughters.

Laurentia smiled up at him, "Thank you for being here with all this, your Grace."

Duke answered with a wink, "That is what family do for one and another."

When Jasper returned with Lucifer, he asked, "Are you ready to go, my love?"

"Yes, take me away from this place. I do not want to see it ever again."

Jasper picked up Laurentia by her waist to put her in the saddle first and then mounted behind her. He kicked Lucifer, and they were off riding down the driveway with Drake by their side. Away from this nightmare. Jasper had his arms around Laurentia as she leaned back against his muscular chest, home in his arms, and she sighed in relief.

Chapter 31

Jasper and Laurentia Reunited

Jasper, Laurentia, and Drake were riding on Buckland Road, heading toward the village of Maidstone. Their first stop when they arrived was to the magistrate's office to inform him of what transpired at the farmhouse. They had a half an hour ride, with Laurentia sitting in front of Jasper in the saddle on Lucifer and Drake riding on his horse, Zeus. Both stallions were fast and a beautiful sight to look upon, with their shiny coats and muscles. They had the stance of pride and superiority above all around them.

Jasper was starting to come down from the rage he'd felt that build up inside him. Breathing in Laurentia's scent, plus the feel of her pressing against his chest, was soothing to him and brought down his tension throughout his body.

Laurentia turned her head to look up to Jasper's eyes, "Are you alright, my love?".

Jasper looked down into her beautiful violet eyes, "Yes, I'm fine, especially now with you so near. Why do you ask?"

"I can feel your body shaking as if you are coming down with something." She had a look of concern on her face and touched his cheek.

Jasper thought, intelligent girl, to realize what he is doing. He sighed, "When you went missing, my whole life stopped." How can I say this? He thought, then continued. "You are my life now, my everything. When the kidnapper took you from me, it filled me with great rage and hatred. What you feel in my body right now are my demons shaking back into my control, all my tension soothing back down to the right. I shall be fine. Now I have you back, not to worry, my Love."

Laurentia smiled up at him, "You are my everything, too. I love you."

Jasper kissed her tenderly.

Drake yelled out, "Your brother is here; remember."

They both stopped kissing and looked at Drake guiltily. Jasper wrapped both arms around Laurentia's middle section to hold her close as he held the reins of his horse in one hand.

Laurentia said to Drake, "Thank you for coming with Jasper to rescue me."

Drake smiled, "He is my big brother, and you shall be my sister soon, and we have one's back always."

Jasper said, "All of us Raventon's stick together."

Laurentia said, "I see that now, and I am proud to become one soon."

Jasper changed the subject to what they need to do when they enter the village, "After we go to the magistrate office, tell our story of events that happen. We shall go to the Inn, check-in, and reserved rooms for everyone."

Laurentia said, "I want a hot bath, is what I wish for when we arrive at the Inn."

Drake said, "I shall return to the farmhouse and help finish up there. When I return to the Inn, I wish for an ice-cold ale, and then maybe a bath would be nice to get the road dust off."

Jasper said, "I shall buy you that ale when you return, Brother, and one for the rest of the family also."

Drake said, "I shall tell them on my return; you said that."

They are nearing the village now, and they slow the horses down as they enter the village limits. The horses walk through the town; they saw people walking from shop to shop, going about their daily routines. It is an average size village with the usual faculties, general store, bakery, seamstress, florist, blacksmith, stables, and more. They pull in front of the magistrate's office; Drake dismounted first, then Jasper, and he lifted Laurentia down from the saddle. Jasper put his arm out for Laurentia to hold as they walk together. Laurentia felt total relief when she realizes it was Jaspers' arm she is taking again, not Mr. Hughes.

The three walked into the office, they see two desks and one holding cell. At one desk sat a large man; he was writing in what looks like some paperwork.

Jasper clears his throat, for the man in front of them did not hear them enter as he wrote. He looks up, "What bring you in today, gentlemen and my Lady?"

Jasper said, "I am Marquess Bellator, my brother Lord Raventon, and my betrothed Lady Sinclair.

The big man stood and bowed. "Yes, your father is the Duke of Devonshire. If I'm correct, I have met his Grace a few years back."

Jasper said, "You stand correct, sir."

The man said, "I am the law in these parts; my name is Evans Daniel. How can I assist you today, my Lords?"

Jasper and Drake told the story of their event that brought them to Maidstone.

Evans said, after the tell he just heard. "His Grace is out at that farmhouse now, as we speak? Jasper nods, yes.

Evans said, "We cannot let the Duke of Devonshire wait around like that. We need to go back there right away." He walks over to a hook on the wall to pick up his hat and put it on his head. "Let us go, and time is a wasting,"

Drake said, "I am going back with you. My brother here and Lady Sinclair are staying in town."

Jasper said, "My betrothed had experience enough of this bad tale. We shall stay at an Inn and wait for the rest of my family to return."

Evans said, "I understand completely. We have two Inns here in town; I suggest the Hasting Inn. It's nicer than the Lionsgate Inn and a better crowd there, my Lord."

Jasper said, "I shall take your word on that. Which end of the village is the Inn located?

Evans said, "You shall go right out of here, and they have a stable for your horses too. Tell the Innkeeper that I sent you, and he shall give you the best room they have." Then he thought for a moment. "Shoot, all you have to say's who you are, and they shall give you the best room anyway. The Innkeeper's misses is a hell of a good cook, and you shall eat well there tonight, my Lords and my Lady."

"Shall we venture to the Hasting Inn, my lady?"

Jasper put his arm out for Laurentia to take, and they all walked out together. Drake mounted Zeus, and Evans horse is tied there also.

Drake said before he rode away. "I'm looking forward to that cold ale when I return, Bellator."

Jasper answered, "I shall join you all when you return." Drake kicks Zeus, and he was off out of town with Evans by his side.

Laurentia looked up to Jasper, "Evans said to go to the right, shall we? I am looking forward to a bath."

Jasper tilted his head toward Laurentia, close to her ear, and whispered. "I'm looking forward to some time to ourselves, before father and the rest return." They turned right and strolled together.

Laurentia looked into Jasper's eyes, "That time shall be well received, my Lord."

Jasper thought as they continue walking, 'I truly know how to make Laurentia giggle behind closed doors. Music to my ears, and I long to hear. I can pay the Innkeeper enough to not talk of my private time with my betrothed. Now that is an excellent plan in the making.' Jasper walked with Laurentia looking impassive as always, but really, he was wearing his wicked smile that she knew all too well underneath. Laurentia saw the modiste shop and immediately stopped.

Jasper asked, "Is there something wrong, my love?"

"After I have my lovely bath at the Inn, I have no clean clothes to put on. Perhaps this shop has something already made I could purchase. Jasper, please, can we go in?"

"If this shall make you happy, by all means, my love, let us go in."

Laurentia is almost giddy with excitement as Jasper tied Lucifer to a pole. They walked into the shop, and an attractive blonde woman of middle age greeted them.

"Good afternoon, is there something special I can help you with?"

Jasper chimed in fast, cutting Laurentia off. "Why, yes, I am Marquess Bellator, and this beautiful woman is Lady Laurentia Sinclair, my betrothed. She needs a lovely new gown, preferably now. What do you have for her? I shall pay handsomely." Jasper quickly gained the woman's attention.

"Come with me, my Lady; I can show you a couple of things I finished not minutes ago and have not delivered yet."

Laurentia looked over to Jasper, then whispered, "Thank you." She followed the modiste, who showed Laurentia four different gowns she could have, and they were all lovely.

Laurentia turned to Jasper, "This could take a bit of time, trying the gowns on and whatnot. Would it be alright, my Lord?"

"Yes, my dear, it shall be fine. I shall go down to the Inn, put Lucifer in the stable for the night, and check into the Inn for the rest of our party and us. Then I shall come back here for you. And by the way, all four of those gowns would look lovely on you."

The modiste said, "If they make the lady happy, you may purchase them all."

"I shall try them all on then." Laurentia lit up with happiness, and Jasper was pleased to see joy once again on Laurentia's face.

On that note, Jasper turned and strolled out of

the shop. He untied his horse then said to him, "To think, Lucifer, how a little thing like a new gown could make my Laurentia so happy is beyond me. I guess I'm learning about the things that make her happy. If Laurentia is happy, then I shall be rewarded. I shall find out later, shall I not?"

Jasper continued down the road to the Hasting Inn, four doors down from where he left Laurentia. He walked into the courtyard to the stables, and a stable lad came up to him. Jasper told him what Lucifer needed and that there would be six more horses coming in soon. Jasper tossed a few coins to him and strolled back through the courtyard to the Inn's front door. As he enters, looking around at his surroundings, Jasper was pleased with the lobby's looks, well-kept with a few nice touches of art on the walls. At the counter was a gray-haired man who straightened when he saw Jasper enter.

"Good afternoon, my Lord. Are you interested in a room for the evening?"

Jasper was impressed the man recognized his status. "I am Marquess Bellator, and I need eight rooms tonight. Two of the rooms need a connecting door that is discrete.

The Innkeeper said, "My Lord, is your father, the Duke of Devonshire?"

Jasper answered, "Yes, he is, and I am his heir."

The Innkeeper bowed to Jasper now, a little late in Jasper's thoughts. "Lord Bellator, I apologize for not knowing your status."

"All is forgotten. I do not travel to this part of England. Let's get back to the rooms, shall we? My betrothed Lady Sinclair is traveling with my party and I. Our rooms are to have the connecting door, and I shall pay you more for your discretion. Are we clear on that subject?"

Innkeeper smiles, "Yes, my Lord, crystal clear."

"Good, we have an understanding. The other rooms shall be for my father, my brother Lord Drake, two of my cousins. Then we have Earl Kingsley and Earl Berwickshire."

"I am thrilled to have all of you staying here tonight. I have twenty rooms here, and the best ones shall be for your party."

Jasper was relieved to hear that. It has been a stressful trip, and a room with a good bed would be a pleasure for the night.

The Innkeeper asked, "Shall you and your party be with us for dinner this evening, my Lord? I have a few private dining rooms."

"Yes, when the gentlemen arrive, they shall go to your tavern first to relax, then we shall all have dinner together. One of your private dining rooms sounds right for the occasion."

"I shall have the misses cook a special feast for you all. Only the best for you and your family. I am so thrilled the Duke of Devonshire shall be staying in my Inn tonight and, of course, the rest of you nobility such an honor, my Lord."

"Outstanding then. Lady Sinclair shall be arriving first. I have to go back four doors down to retrieve her at the modiste. She is requesting a hot bath when she comes in; I want the hot water brought up to her immediately upon her arrival."

"If there is anything else you or your party needs for your comfort, let me know, and I shall see it done personally, my Lord."

"We shall let you know. You may count on that."

The Innkeeper turned around to a wall of keys; he picked off two sets of keys and handed them over, saying, "Room seven and eight for you. It has the door as you requested, it is at the end of the hall. Eight is a fancier room; your betrothed shall appreciate that room more."

"Excellent, you may give the others in my party their keys when they arrive."

"As you wish, my Lord."

Jasper nodded and went out the front door to bring Laurentia back to the Inn. She should be finished with her new gown or gowns if she wished. Jasper wanted to bring some happiness to her after this awful event. If she liked all four of the gowns, they would be hers. They could ship home the ones she did not wear tomorrow.

Laurentia was having a lovely time at the modiste shop. When Jasper walked in, he saw Laurentia standing on a pedestal talking with three women who were working around her. She looked up with a smile as he came near and had a twinkle in her eyes. "My Lord, is it not beautiful?" Laurentia spun around on the pedestal.

'You take my breath away is what Jasper would have said if they were in private.' Instead, he replied, "Not nearly as beautiful as you are, my Lady, but it does look lovely on you."

"Thank you for the compliment. How you flatter me, my Lord. This gown is the last one that needed fitting out of the four gowns. Two of them are completed already. I shall take them with us now."

One of Jasper's eyebrows rose as he said, "I only speak of the truth of your beauty. How long till you are finished here, my Lady?"

Laurentia looked down to where the two women

were working on the hemline of the gown. "I believe they have the right length now; I just need to slip out of this, and we are on our way."

One of the ladies said, "Yes, we have it. You may step down, my Lady." Jasper stepped closer, putting out his hand to assist Laurentia down.

"Thank you, and I shall not belong to change, my Lord." She walked to the back of the shop and went behind a vast curtain.

Japer saw the first woman they talked to when they first walked in earlier. He addressed her, "Madam, I shall settle up with you now."

She walked over to where Jasper was standing. "Lady Laurentia decided to take all four gowns, a few new undergarments, and accessories, my Lord."

Jasper reached into his pocket and pulled out a card. "You may send your bill here, and you may add an extra 40 % to the cost on pleasing my betrothed today."

"Thank you, my Lord, of course. I did not have a chance to introduce myself to you. I am the owner of this small shop, Miss Claudia," she curtsied.

Jasper nodded, "You have made Lady Laurentia happy today, and her happiness is essential to me. I am forever in your debt, Miss Claudia."

Laurentia came back from changing and overheard their conversation. She smiled to herself at the last part Jasper said, that her happiness is essential to him. To think this elegant, very handsome gentleman loves me, and it does not hurt that he is a future Duke too.

Jasper turned to Laurentia when she stopped beside him. "I am ready to leave now, Lord Bellator," Laurentia said with a smile.

Jasper then said, "Miss, have the two gowns that are completed delivered to Hasting Inn, and the other two delivers to the address in London." Claudia thanked him again and curtsied to both of them as they left.

As Jasper and Laurentia walked the short distance to the Inn, he told her he'd ordered a bath for her. However, he did not share that their rooms were connected, for he decided it would be a sweet surprise for both of them.

In front of the Inn, Laurentia said, "How charming this place looks."

"Yes, of what I had seen so far only entering the lobby area, it seems to be quite charming, my love."

They walked through the courtyard, then entered through the front door. Laurentia hesitated to look around the lobby when they entered. The Innkeeper rushed around his desk to greet them. He bowed to them, then said, "I am enchanted by your beauty, my Lady, and welcome to my Inn."

Jasper said, "This is Lady Laurentia Sinclair, my betrothed."

Laurentia said, "Your Inn is lovely and well-kept from what I have seen already."

The Innkeeper said, "How nice of you to say, my Lady, thank you. I do hope you enjoy your stay with us. Please let me know if you need anything at all."

Jasper wanted to go upstairs now more than anything, to be alone with Laurentia before the rest came into town. So, he said, "My Lady, shall we go upstairs?"

"Yes, I am looking forward to a bath. Excuse us if you will."

As they headed for the staircase, the Innkeeper

called out, "I shall have your water brought up to you immediately."

Jasper escorted Laurentia upstairs, and they went down the hall to the last rooms at the end of the building. At room eight, he unlocked the door, then ushered her in. Laurentia walked in and looked around, turning as she did. Jasper came in behind her. "This looks suitable, my Sweet. You should be comfortable here this evening."

Laurentia turned to face him. "Yes, I do like the room, but we have not yet married. Therefore, it is not proper for us to share this room, Jasper."

Jasper smiled down at her. "My love, I have a room next door. This is your room, as you see, all is well." Jasper wrapped his arms around Laurentia's waist, pulling her close and kissing her passionately. Laurentia wrapped her arms around Jasper's neck, falling into him and surrendering to him. Not even a full minute passed when a knock on the door interrupted their sweet desire for each other.

Laurentia said, "It must be my water, I see the tub in the corner over there."

Jasper sighed and let go of Laurentia. The last thing he wanted now was an interruption. He much preferred her naked and in bed with him. Jasper walked over to the door and opened it to find a maid holding two large boxes.

"These were just delivered. My father told me to bring them up for the lady." Jasper stepped back, waved his hand to enter. The maid bobbed a curtsy then walked in.

"My new gowns are here already; how fabulous. Please bring them over here to the bed; you can lay them down.

The maid put the two boxes on the bed, then said, "My two brothers are on their way up with your water for your bath, my Lady. Would you like me to stay and help you undress and assist you?"

Jasper was just about to say no when Laurentia said, "Yes, that would be lovely, for I am traveling without a maid today."

The young girl walked over to the bathtub to ready it for the water. She opened a cupboard door by the tub, pulling out towels, washcloths, bath oil, and finely milled soap. Jasper stood watching her; then, two young lads appeared in the doorway, each holding two buckets of water. They looked up at Jasper for instructions.

"The tub is over there, as you know." Jasper waved his hand to the tub. And behind them came the innkeeper with two more buckets. They all poured the steaming water into the bathtub and went back out of the room. Laurentia's eyes lit up with the delight of the bath, ready for her. The maid poured in some bath oil that smelled like roses.

Laurentia walked over to the tub. "That smell lovely rose oil."

The maid nodded and looked at Laurentia as if asking if she was ready. Laurentia turned to the door where Jasper was still standing.

"You should go for now. I shall have my bath and ready myself when the others come. I shall come down later for dinner, my Lord."

Not happy at all, Jasper said, "Yes, my sweet, it seems you have the help you need. I shall see you in a while downstairs." He bowed his most elegant way and exit. Jasper looked at Laurentia's door from the hallway, feeling irritated, and walked down the hall to the tavern. As he was walking, he said to himself, "I do not care what it takes. We are marrying this Sunday as planned. I shall be dammed if I am excused from my wife's room then.

Laurentia could not wait to get into that tub, but she was thinking, 'besides riding on Lucifer with Jasper the short time it had taken to come to the village, we have not had any time alone since Jasper rescued me. I could tell by the look on his face when the maid came in first and then the others with my hot water that he was not happy to leave me, but he knew the water was coming. I suppose it was the real first time we were alone together. I shall have to make it up to him later.'

Laurentia looked at her bath, then said to the maid, "Let get me out of these clothes so that I may enjoy my bath."

"Right away, my Lady, we shall have you in that tub in a heartbeat."

As Laurentia stepped into the tub, her whole body cried in thanks. "Let's wash my hair first, and then I like to soak for a while." Laurentia smiled up at the maid.

When Jasper reached the tavern downstairs, he walked directly to the bar. The barkeep came over and asked, "What can I get you, my Lord?"

"A cold ale." When Jasper got the ale, he picked up his glass and drank down half the glass before sitting it back down on the bar.

Drake, Leopold, Victor, Jesse, and Lucas came walking in. Seeing Jasper at the bar, they joined him. Drake was loud as always. "Barkeep brings us all an ale, and this round is on my brother here, Lord Bellator."

Jesse and Leopold stood by Jasper, and Leopold

slapped Jasper's shoulder. "Glad this ordeal is over with, and it all turned out alright."

Jasper replied, "So am I; where is father now?"

Drake said, "He is writing mother a letter, telling her all is well, and we have Lady Laurentia back safe and sound. He shall send a messenger to run it to London."

Lucas asked, "How is my sister faring after this mess, Lord Bellator?"

"She seems to be doing well. On the way to the Inn, we came across a modiste. Lady Laurentia asked if she could see if they had any gowns pre-made. She wanted something clean to wear. I ended up buying four new gowns today. Now Lady Laurentia is upstairs in her room having a hot bath." They all laughed at him.

Lucas said, "My sister has an eye for fashion, plus she never walks out of a shop empty-handed. I say she never leaves a shop with less than four items."

Jasper shrugged. "It put a smile on her face again to have something new; it was worth it to buy her a few new things."

Jesse said, "That definitely makes the lady happy, clothes or jewelry. With my mistress, I buy her one thing, and it's a sweet delight for me that night." They all laughed again.

Leopold was noticing a new softer side to his cousin, and he didn't know if it was alarming to him or not. There was no way a woman was going to put a shackle on his leg any time soon. The gentlemen drank their ale; they joked and laugh with each other, trying to unwind from their full day. The duke strolled in, and everyone in the tavern took notice of him. The barkeep almost tripped over his own feet, rushing to the duke to serve him.

The barkeep asked, stumbling over his words, "Your Grace, what can I get you? I mean, what would you like?"

Duke looked to see what his boys were having, and he noted their glasses of ale were almost finished. "It looks like my family could use another round here, I shall have the same, and the round is on me."

Leopold cut in and said, "No Uncle, this round is on Drake, for he won the wager we had earlier today and said he would buy the first round when we came to a tavern."

Duke asked, "May I inquire about the source of your bet?"

Leopold answered, "When we went into the farmhouse, Jasper's first sword fight was with Earl Merionreth. We went to Eton with him, so we all knew he was not any real challenge for Bellator. We bet how many minutes Bellator would finish him or win. Drake won and opted to buy the first round."

Jasper asked, "How many minutes were bet?"

Drake said, "Kingsley went with two minutes, I said three, and Leopold went with four. You did it in three minutes, Bellator."

Jasper burst out laughing at them and the bet, and they all laughed together now. Jasper was trying to catch his breath and said, "He could never fight his way out of a wet paper bag if his life depended on it. I was not going to kill him at first, just knock his sword from him, but he gave me no choice when he pulled out that revolver and cocked the hammer back, pointing it at me."

Jesse said, "We all saw what happened, Bellator. It was him or you would die at that moment. He had that revolver pointing at your head, and you were much fast with the sword, dear friend."

Jasper looked at them; all nodded in agreement. "Yes, you are right. I had no choice but to kill a man, no matter the reasons, is still regretful."

Leopold said, "It is what happened. I shall vouch on it if needed."

Duke said, "No one shall need to do that; the magistrate took my word on what happened there, plus all the evidence that was found in that house and the fake paperwork. They have been at it for a while, cheating wealthy gentlemen out of their money on phony investment scams. No more now."

After they all had their drinks, Lucas said, "I insist the next round is on me. My sister and I thank you from the bottom of our hearts for helping us both in a time of crisis. Thank you."

Jasper looked at Lucas then said, "I shall marry your sister soon, so you are considered family now. We protect our own."

Lucas nodded and raised his glass, "To a family, I am honored to be a part of now."

Duke said, "My Duchess has been telling me that my lovely daughters have this thing of making wagers and bets. They make a bet on events that happen with the family or in the ton. I would say they are copying my sons and nephews' games." He raised an eyebrow and continued, "Would anyone like to enlighten me on this matter?"

Drake said, "It must be harmless fun they are doing, Father."

Duke answered, "They had bet on my two sons when Lady Laurentia was first hired. To whom would show up first to dinner the first night. I was informed it was Bellator."

Leopold asked, "Do they bet money?"

Duke said, "Yes, they do. My Duchess tells me."

Victor said, "My little cousins are clever, are they not?"

Jasper said, "I am not surprised that they have been doing this betting. Do not underestimate them, and they are the most clever girls."

It had been past an hour since Jasper came down to the tavern, from leaving Laurentia's room so that she could bathe. When Laurentia stood in the door, the tavern people stopped talking and turned their heads to look at the beautiful woman standing there. Jasper was one of those staring at her, and he almost felt speechless, so he stood up and walked over to her. Laurentia was smiling at him when he stopped in front of her.

Jasper took her hand, kissing her fingers tenderly and looking into her eyes. "My love, you take my breath away, you look beautiful tonight."

"Thank you, Lord Bellator, I am overdressed for the Inn and tavern, but my new gowns are lovely, as you may see."

Jasper's gaze swept her body. "It's too bad that I am not taking you to a ball this evening. You would turn everyone's head to see how beautiful you are, as you have done here this evening. I do like the gown you are wearing, and I like your hair down like that, my love."

Laurentia's gown was the color of a summer sky with gold thread dancing a feathery pattern throughout, with a low scalloped neckline showed a hint of her cleavage, and she had her hair down in ringlets. Jasper took her hand and led her to where his family was standing at the bar.

Laurentia curtsied to the duke, then he said, "You look lovely tonight, my dear."

"Thank you, your Grace. A nice bath can make everything better."

Jesse said, "Missing lunch today, I feel famished. May I suggest we have dinner now." Everyone agreed it was time to eat.

Jasper said, "I had requested a private dining room for this evening meal. Barkeep, be a good man, and let them know the Raventon party are ready to be seated for dinner." Barkeep left to do Jasper's bidding.

As they took their seats in a private dining room, Drake said, "I could eat a whole chicken right now, with missing lunch today."

Victor said, "A nice two-inch-thick steak would satisfy me right now."

The dining room door opened, and in walked a middle-aged woman pushing a serving cart that looked to have a large pot of steaming soup on it and soup bowls. She stopped behind the duke first, and as she scooped soup from the pot.

"I'm the Innkeeper's wife, Zelda. I have fixed you a special meal this evening in honor of having you stay with us this evening. We shall start with Lorraine soup." She set the bowl down in front of the duke, then continued serving the rest. Another maid poured wine into everyone's glass on the table. Another young maid came in with hot loaves of bread cut and ready to eat with the soup.

Sitting by Jasper and her brother, Laurentia tried the soup, "This soup is delicious."

Lucas said, "Delicious is an understatement; it is excellent, and the bread also."

Jasper said, "Bridget has always been my favorite cook, but whoever made this soup is taking the number two spot beside her."

Drake said, "Yes, I agree on that, Bellator."

The door opened again, and platters of ham, roast duck, and venison were brought next, and roasted potatoes and vegetables too. It was a feast fit for a king but, in this case, a duke and this family.

After everyone was served, Zelda said, "Enjoy your meal, and I made fresh apple pie for dessert." Then, she bowed her head and exited the room.

There were not many conversations at the table; everyone was enjoying the excellent meal. Jasper raised his glass and made a toast. "I want to thank everyone here tonight for standing by my side, helping me finding Laurentia, and bringing her home to be my future wife. Thank you all!" Everyone toasted to it.

Then the Duke said, "Tomorrow, we Shall go home and put this whole ordeal behind us and move on, and we have a wedding to attend in a few days." Everyone raised their glass to that too. They finished the meal and even had the apple pie. They sat and talked for another hour after the pie and then retiring to their rooms. They agreed to get an early start in the morning, to go back to London.

Laurentia had dismissed the Inn's maid, who helped her to undress for the evening. She sat at her dressing table with only her chemise on, brushing her hair, when the door opened connected to Jasper's room to her own. Jasper stood in the doorway with no clothes on, watching the brush go through Laurentia's hair, not saying a word to her.

Laurentia looked over her shoulder and said with

a purr, "I have been waiting for you to come to me, my Jasper."

Jasper still did not move or say a word. He just leaned against the door frame with his arms crossed, watching Laurentia brush her long silky hair. Laurentia set the brush down, knowing he was playing a game of wills with her. She took her hair that was hanging down her back and moved it over her shoulder to the front, then picked up the brush again so she could brush it out some more. She swung it back over her shoulder, so her hair cascaded down her back. The hair was shiny, wavy, long, and silky.

Jasper longed to put his fingers through her beautiful hair. He finally broke the silence. "Watching you makes my heart flutter. I am anticipating the feel of your skin against mine, Sweet Laurentia."

Laurentia still did not move from her chair; she turned in her chair to look at her handsome man. She wet her lips with the tip of her tongue, just watching him. 'His body was so muscular and tight, with the broad shoulders and a narrow waist. He is perfection,' she thought to herself.

"Why don't you come in and join me then, my Jasper," she purred.

Jasper smiled to himself, liking Laurentia was learning well how to play the game with him. He stepped into the room but did not go to her, but instead decided to go to bed. He sat at the end, watching Laurentia still, with a wicked smile on his face and eyes that glowed.

"I long to taste your lips; I think you should come over here to me, my sweet."

Laurentia could not believe he walked naked around the room so comfortably, like a Roman god.

Laurentia stood and took two steps toward him, and stopped. He sat there watching her, and he was so gorgeous. Laurentia was still trying to play this game of wills with him. She looked into his eyes, trying to look seductive, standing five feet away from him. They both were still, and it was a standoff of control and will. Who would break first?

'His eyes, they call to me,' Laurentia thought. 'Damn it, he wins.' Laurentia could not resist his allure anymore. "You have won, Jasper, and I want you!" She ran across the room, plunging into his lap, wrapping her arms around his neck, and kissing him madly.

Jasper laughing to himself. 'I won this time, but she is getting better at the game, much better. I wanted her; I almost was going to get up and grabbed her up myself,' Jasper thought as he kissed her back.

Jasper sat with Laurentia in his lap, her legs wrapped around his middle section. He stopped kissing her, lifted his head, and looked into her violet eyes he adored.

"You have too many clothes on for my taste." He scooped up the bottom of her chemise and pulled it up and over her head, tossing it to the floor. He smiled, "That, my love, is much better."

His hands went to her breasts, and as he held her perfect flesh, he flicked over her nipples and watched as they hardened. Laurentia sighed, feeling of his hands on her, making her body sing to his touch, and she was anticipating what was coming next.

Jasper's voice was low when he said, "I have ached all day for you, wanting you to touch you and to taste you." He lowered his head to her left nipple and licked and sucked, playing his tongue around the nipple.

Laurentia breathed in, then released a soft moan. He did the same to the right breast, holding them in his hands. Not letting them go, he kissed his way up her neck to her lips demandingly, and Laurentia kissed him just as madly with wanting. He let go of her breast to wrap his arms around her waist, traveling up the bed to where the pillows were, and he rolled her to her back, so she was underneath him. They kissed and tasted each other's nectar, the love they felt overpowering.

Laurentia broke the kiss panting, "Please, Jasper, I need you inside of me. I need to feel our love connecting us as one."

Jasper looked into the pools of desire in Laurentia's eyes. "I shall stay here in your arms all night long, making love to you. I, too, feel the urgency to be connected to you as one." He moved over top of her, looking in her violet eyes. In one smooth thrust, Jasper was inside of her, watching her face when they joined. Laurentia makes a sound of pleasure as his rock-hard staff stretched her, and she tightened around him. Jasper did not move for a moment; he was feeling the pure joy of their connection. He smiled down at her, taking her lips as he started slowly moving, a pleasing slow rhythm.

As Laurentia kissed him, she let out little moans of pleasure as he brought her to paradise with his masterful lovemaking skills. The sweet cries Jasper heard from Laurentia fired his desire to make this last as long as possible for both of them. Laurentia was starting to feel little flutters as he moved faster to bring her over the edge with him. He was pumping and pumping, and they both were ready to let go.

Jasper whispered in her ear, "Come with me, my

love." On that last word, Laurentia orgasmed hard, making her yell out, "Jasper!" He pumped hard a few more times and filled her with his seed, and as he found his release, he yelled out with the passion they shared. He was panting on top of her, feeling the afterglow of coming back down together from paradise. He pulled out of her and rolled to his back to take his weight off her. He pulled her into his arms and held her tight, so they remained joined.

Laurentia was cooing like a dove in his arms as they lay there together. "That was wonderful. I did feel like I was in paradise with you. Lets' do that again." She kissed him tenderly.

Jasper broke their kiss then laughed a little. "My sweet love, we shall do that in about half an hour. I need a short time in between."

Laurentia had a confused look in her eyes. "Why, do you not find me desirable?"

"Yes, you are the most desirable woman I have ever met; that's not the problem. My body needs time to recover is all; it is how one works the male body."

"Oh, is that so? Can I help the recovery come faster with my kisses?" She moved on top of him and started kissing his chest, going across in small, delightful movement, then up to his neck.

Jasper's groin twitched and came back to life instantly; he was being bewitched by his beloved. By the time she reached his lips, he was ready for her. Jasper wrapped his arms around her and flipped her to her back in one motion.

He broke the kiss then said, "My clever girl, you shall be the death of me yet, and now I am ready for you."

Laurentia giggled in happiness, feeling his hard penis pressing at her womanhood opening. "I'm so ready, my Jasper, take me. I am yours."

He kissed her passionately, then entered her opening and started moving in his perfect rhythm of making love. They rose to paradise together.

Afterward, they fell asleep in each other's arms, content. They woke up a couple more times during the night to climb that delightful edge of glory together and always felt that happy bliss as one.

Chapter 32

Going Home to London

Duke, Victor, and Drake were already in the private dining room, breaking their fast. Zelda set up a morning sideboard with eggs, sausage, bacon, fried potatoes, fresh fruit, coffee, and tea for the lady. Jasper and Laurentia walked in, holding hands talking as they entered. They bade everyone a good morning. Jasper pulled out Laurentia's chair for her when she took a seat, and he sat down beside her. A server brought them what they desired from the sideboard. Lucas came in sat across from Laurentia; he had some of everything from the sideboard and coffee. Jesse and Leopold came in together, laughing as they entered the room and decided to help themselves to the food and take a seat.

Once they all finished eating, they walked out to the courtyard. Jasper bought a horse for Laurentia to ride. She refused to ride in a carriage or coach.

Laurentia sternly said, "I shall not be the one slowing everyone down on the return to London." She told Jasper that she was just as good of a rider as they were, meaning all the men in the riding party, and had been riding horses from the age of five. Lucas reassured them it was correct when they were eating this morning, especially Jasper, who was worried that it was too long of a journey for her to ride. Jasper would had preferred to have a horse from Sterling stables, he could handpick himself for her, and only the best would do in his book when it came to Laurentia's safety. They'd had a heated debate when they woke that morning on the subject, and Laurentia won this time; she was riding with them all.

The mare was four years old, chestnut color with a white star between her eyes. All the horses were in the courtyard waiting to be mounted. When Jasper walked down the Inn's steps, still not happy about Laurentia's stubbornness of riding a horse and not being in a carriage as she should be. With his best impassive look, not showing his real feelings on the matter, he walked to the mare, rechecking her legs and feeling the body for she would do was what he hoped.

Laurentia walked over happily. "Lord Bellator, she is lovely; I am truly excited to ride her." She walked to the horse head, reached up, and rubbed behind her ears, cooing at the mare. Laurentia asked, "My, Lord, what is her name?"

Jasper came around where Laurentia was standing, "Her name is Lily, and she is four years old. Come, let me help you mount." Laurentia walked over to the left side; Jasper put his hands on her waist, lifted her into the side saddle, and handed the reins to her.

Before Jasper mounted Lucifer, he asked Laurentia, "Are you good with that saddle? Does it feel right?"

Laurentia sighed, "Yes, my love, I feel perfect.

You can mount Lucifer now." Everyone was on their horse, waiting for Jasper to mount. He looked at Laurentia one last time, then went to his horse and mounted.

The duke asked, "Are we ready to go?"

Jasper said, waving his hand forward, "Yes, Father, we are ready. You may proceed."

Drake, Duke, Victor led the group, then Jasper, Laurentia, Lucas, Leopold, and Jesse brought up the rear to start the ride back to London. Laurentia rode between Jasper and Lucas; she was remembering the wonderful time in bed with Jasper last night and waking up in his strong arms that morning. She looked over to him and sighed, then says to herself, 'can life get any better than this?'

Jasper looked at Laurentia, "My love, you do look beautiful with the light breeze blowing through your hair. I am sorry if I upset you with my overbearing ways. I just do not want any harm to come to you, is all."

"I know you only worry about my safety. I shall be fine, riding beside you, as you shall see." Laurentia smiled.

Jasper reached for her hand, leaning a little toward her, raised it to his lips, and kissed her hand before letting it go.

Laurentia said, "I love you."

Jasper answered, "And I you."

Lucas cuts in, saying, "I think I shall stay in London for a few weeks, Laurentia. It is time I should start socializing and stop being a hermit in the country as I have been doing for the last few years."

"I would like to see you more. Yes, you have been a recluse in the country too long, dear Brother."

"You do look exceptionally fetching in your saddle, dear Sister."

Laurentia smiles, "Thank you, Lucas, it is a grand day, not a cloud in the sky."

They rode on till stopping for lunch by a stream. Zelda had packed lunch for their journey. They stopped by a brook so that the horses could drink. Jesse and Leopold stayed close to the horses. Laurentia saw to the food, and Jasper stayed by her side and helped her. She handed him a blanket to lay out for their picnic. Jasper spread the blanket out under a tree for shade, while Laurentia put the packed sandwiches and two jugs of drink out, ale, and lemonade. Victor, Drake, and Lucas came over, sat down, and helped themselves to a lunch and drink. Laurentia handed Jasper a sandwich, and they both started to eat. After finishing his sandwich, Jasper excused himself, saying he would return shortly. Jasper walked over to the horses where Leopold, Jesse, and now the duke was talking.

As Jasper reached them, he sensed something was not right. "Is there something wrong I should know about?"

Leopold said, "About a mile back, we picked up a couple of followers on horseback. They are staying back half a click from us, and I do not know their purpose yet."

Duke said, "They just share this dilemma with me too. They might be highwaymen."

Jasper looked in the direction they'd come from and saw no movement.

Duke said, "We need to put an end to this before we are back on the road."

They all nodded. "Come," Jasper said, "We

should act as normal as possible. Let us take lunch, and I shall send Drake to backtrack and put an end to this."

Leopold says, "I shall stay with the horses, just in case they feel brave and make a move on them."

With Jesse, they walked over to where the rest were having lunch. Laurentia handed a sandwich to the duke and Jesse when they came over to the blanket area; they both took the sandwich.

Jasper made eye contact with Drake; he stood and walked over to his brother, who stood on the edge from the rest, watching.

Drake said low, "What is amiss, Bellator?"

"Leopold and Jesse told Father and I that two men on horseback are following us; they are staying a half a click back. I need you to circle back and take care of this."

Drake smiled, then said, "Sounds like fun; they shall not know what hit them."

"I trust you to be careful too."

"Yes, I shall be back in no time."

Drake walked away as if he was going over to the horses but cut off through the wood to backtrack. Jasper looked over to his father, nodding that Drake was at work and would be back shortly. Ever since Drake was ten years, he learned to track and scout like a bloodhound through the woods. Drake could circle back without being seen, and it was almost like a game to him.

Victor noticed the body language and nodded between his family members. "I shall take a sandwich to Leopold and help tend the horses." Victor went over to find out what was going on and bring Leopold something to eat.

Jasper moved closer to Laurentia just in case danger started so he could protect her. Laurentia was sitting on the blanket, chatting with Lucas and Jesse. She smiled up at Jasper when he neared, not knowing what was happening around them. Jasper had his usual unreadable expression. He listened to what was said in front of him and listened to what was in the distance. Sometime had gone by, and everyone had finished eating. Laurentia started packing up the leftovers and noticed that no one seemed to be in any hurry to start traveling again. Laurentia put her hand out for Jasper to help her up from sitting. He took her hand, pulling her up, and talked about unimportant matters as he tried to stall time for Drake to return. Relieved, Drake appeared walking down the road from the direction they'd come from earlier. He strolled toward them as if he hadn't a care in the world.

When Drake reached them, he said, "All is well. I have taken care of the problem."

Jasper raised an eyebrow at his brother.

Looking at Jasper for an answer, Laurentia asked, "Is something wrong?".

Jasper said, "Not to worry, my love, let me take what you have there, and we shall be off." He walked Laurentia over to the horse and helped put the blanket and whatnots back in a saddlebag, so they may leave and get back to riding.

Lucas and Victor came over to where Laurentia and Jasper were standing by the horses. Jasper said, "I shall be a minute, my sweet; I need to have a word with Father and Drake."

Jasper walked away. Laurentia said to Lucas, "You men must think I'm daft if you believe I did not notice that something is going on here."

Lucas looked at Victor to help him in this situation. He did not want Jasper angry at him for saying what was happening, for Jasper had not told Laurentia anything or she would not be asking him for answers. He would ordinarily answer his sister, but he had already learned the hard way with his future brother-in-law, you do not cross him, especially when it came to Laurentia's well-being. Victor shook his head no, to not say anything.

So, Lucas sighed. "Lord Bellator shall have to be the one to tell you of anything, Laurentia."

Laurentia did not like his answer. "Lucas, I insist you tell me at once."

Lucas looked over to where Jasper was talking to the Duke and Drake. He then changed the subject, trying to step away from the questions she was asking. Lucas started talking about artwork, knowing Victor could help him with this subject, keeping Laurentia from asking more.

Jasper said, "Tell me, Drake, what happened."

Duke asked, "How many men were there?"

Drake replied, "I cut through the woods and found the two young lads; I'd say they were eighteen or nineteen at the most. I came up behind them. They did not even know I was there until I tapped my sword blade on the bigger one's shoulder. I had my revolver in my other hand when they turned around to see me. Their eyes were as large as a saucer, blinking at me, not knowing what to do with themselves."

Jasper asked, "What did you do with them?"

"I asked first what business they were doing following us and was there more coming after them.

The two lads said they are in a gang of ten men, high-waymen, that they were the scouts who were supposed to be tracking us and were planning on robbing us. The rest of the gang shall be coming soon, for they would not be returning with news of their find. I tied them to a big tree with their own rope from their saddlebags. They are just boys who I could not see hurting."

Duke said, "Yes, that is what I would have done."

Jasper said, "We better get a move on it before the rest come after us. I do not like having Laurentia in danger. You said the two you already tied up were boys? Who's to say the rest are the same? A scout is usually more seasoned than eighteen."

Drake said, "You have a good point there, and those two I can say were not too bright."

Duke said, "I agree, we should go, just to be on the safe side." They walked back over to where the horses were.

When Jasper came over to Laurentia, he said, "We are ready to ride now. Let me help you mount your horse so that we may go."

Laurentia put her hands out in front of her to stop Jasper. "No, not until you tell me what is going on here. I can plainly see there is concern about something."

Jasper gazed down at Laurentia with a look that said he did not have time for this.

"I'm not moving until you tell me. Am I not a part of this family now?" Laurentia glared up at Jasper, not budging.

Jasper thought for a moment, frustrated. "Laurentia, I need to have you on your horse so that we may go. When we are on our way, then I shall tell you what you want to hear." He put his hand out for her to take. Laurentia lowered her hands and accepted Jasper's offered one, allowing him to assist her into her saddle.

Before Jasper let go of Laurentia's waist, he said. "We shall be riding hard now. If you feel it is too much for you, let me know, and I shall put you on my horse with me. Alright?" Laurentia agreed, and Jasper walked to Lucifer and mounted him quickly. He looked to his father that he was ready, and they all rode out in a tight pack. They rode at first in a light gallop, staying uniform in their rows.

Jasper looked over to Laurentia, "We are more than likely being pursued by highwaymen. We need to keep ahead of them. When we stopped for lunch, Leopold and Jesse informed father and I we were being followed. Drake scouted through the woods and overtook the two young men following us. He got the information out of them that they are in a gang of ten. He tied the two up. The others shall be following soon, so we need to put some distance between them and us."

"Thank you for telling me. In the future, do not think for one minute that you should hide important matters from me that shall not work for us as life partners. Now let us put that distance between the highwaymen and us."

Jasper smiled; still looking at Laurentia, he said to all, "You heard, my Lady, let us ride" they all kicked their horses and rode with the wind.

They rode three-fourths the way to London before they stop for the night in the town of Croydon. Jasper dismounted, walked to Laurentia's mare, and lowered her to the ground. The duke dismounted and join them; the others rode the horses to the stables making sure they were cared for with food, water, and rest. The duke entered through the Inn front door, Jasper and Laurentia behind him. At the front desk, they found a middle-aged woman with a pleasant smile. As soon as she recognized the Duke of Devonshire, she came out from behind the desk to curtsy. "Your Grace, welcome to my Inn. Would you be standing the night?"

The duke answered, "Yes, we need a few rooms. This is my eldest son Marquess Bellator and his betrothed, Lady Sinclair."

The Innkeeper curtsied to them, "I'm so happy you have picked my Inn here. I run the place with my sister, and we are both widows. Would it be three rooms you seek, Your Grace?"

"There are several more in my party who have been traveling with myself. I need eight of your best rooms and a late supper to be served. Is that possible?"

The Innkeeper said, "Yes, Your Grace, I can accommodate you; it is a slow night. My rooms are only a quarter filled this evening. My sister takes care of the kitchen, and she shall be more than happy to have something fixed for you and your party. No problem at all, Your Grace, I a sure you."

Jasper said, "After we dine, have a hot bath brought up to Lady Sinclair's room for her."

The Innkeeper said, "Yes, my Lord, I shall order that for you."

The front door opens a young man early twenty's that resembles the Innkeeper features walk-in. The Innkeeper seem to turn nervous when he entered.

She said right away, "Your Grace, Lord, and

Lady, this is my son Henry. Henry, this is the Duke of Devonshire, his son, Marquess Bellator, and Lady Sinclair.

Henry bowed, "I know you have made my mother incredibly happy coming here tonight. I'm pleased to make your acquaintance."

Jasper was looked him over, wondering why his mother went nervously when he entered. Jasper could read people easily, and this he saw was something to keep a watch on.

The Innkeeper, trying to dismiss her son, said, "Are you in for the night? If so, go to the kitchen, tell your aunt to put together a warm supper for eight, and you can have something also in the kitchen."

"Yes, Mother, I'm in for the rest of the night. If you would excuse me, Your Grace, Lord, and Lady, I'm off to the kitchen." As he walked away, he looked over his shoulder at them before entering through the door to the kitchen.

Laurentia noticed Jasper was looking him over and even more as he was leaving. The front door opened, and in walked the rest of their group to join the duke's party.

The Innkeeper smiled, "This must be the rest of your party, such handsome men I see before me."

Jasper was not amused and was feeling fatigued from riding all day, as the rest were too. "Madame, if you would show us to a private dining room, it would please us to be able to relax after a long ride," he said in a clipped tone.

"Yes, my Lord, if you would all follow me this way." She walked down a short hallway that had two doors.

Opening one door, "I have two private dining

rooms. This one is my best one." Taking a paper spill, she lit it in the fireplace then walked around the room, lighting candles before excusing herself.

Laurentia looked around the room, seeing a long sideboard against one wall, a table that seated ten, and a chandelier hanging over the middle of the table. The furniture looked relatively new and the linens too. It was a pleasant room, and she nodded her approval.

Leopold walked over to the table then took a seat before anyone else. "From the outside of this Inn, I would not have expected such finery, Bellator. What is your take on this?" Leopold was looking at Jasper, knowing he was already analyzing their situation.

Jasper walked around to the other side of the table, so he could face the door, escorting Laurentia with him. After they were seated, he answered Leopold.

"I would not be surprised if the Innkeeper's son was one of the highwaymen that were following us today." The rest sat down at the table, their interest piqued.

The duke said, "Son, I know you have this uncanny ability to read a person in a couple of minutes conversing with them. Are you sure of this?"

Jasper arched an eyebrow at his father, then said, "Ninety-five percent sure, Father."

Lucas said, "Should we stay here at this Inn? It could be dangerous for us."

Jasper answered, "It is better to be in the den with the wolfs, than to be out running as his prey."

Jesse said, "You are right on that; I do see your point. I'd rather be in here than out there being picked off."

Duke says, "No one is going too, as you said, pick us off. We have the upper hand in this, for we are aware of the situation."

The door opened and in walked two maids and the Innkeeper carrying trays of food. They served them in a home-style manner with plates and a bowl of hot food set down in front of them. One maid walked to each, filling wine glasses for them. Before the servers left, the Innkeeper said pleasantly, "Let me know if there is anything else I can bring you this evening."

Duke said, "This all looks acceptable for a late supper. Thank you."

"Then we shall leave you to enjoy your meal."

Once they had gone, Victor said, "I am so hungry. This smoked ham in front of me looks delicious." He stabbed his fork in the meat, helped himself first, and then picked it up to hand it to Leopold sitting next to him. They passed the food around the table and chatted about their dilemma and agreed they would be fine here tonight in the Inn, for they knew the highwaymen did not realize they had been identified.

After finishing the late meal, they all opted to go to their rooms to retire for the night, so they could make an early start in the morning to make it to London by late afternoon.

Laurentia was in her room; the maids just finished filling a vast tub with steaming water and exited. She heard a light knock on her door. Laurentia walked over to the door to find Jasper standing there with his wicked smile. She looked up into Jasper's eyes and smiled.

"I was hoping it was you." Laurentia opened the

door wider for him to come in.

Jasper entered the small room, which contained just a bed, one chair, and the tub, closing the door and locking it. He turned to see Laurentia standing by the tub filled with steaming water. Jasper walked over, took Laurentia in his arms, kissed her softly, then said,

"Let me help you undress so you can enjoy your hot bath, my love." He spun her around so that he could unbutton her dress.

Laurentia sighed at the feel of his fingers going down her back as he quickly undid the buttons. He pushed her dress off her shoulders and kissed along her neck to her shoulder.

Laurentia said, "I need to get into the tub before my water goes cold, my love."

Jasper, still nibbling on her shoulder, let out an "Mmm, huh." Her dress fell to the floor, and she stepped out of her dress and away from Jasper. She turned, seeing the desire in his eyes, then bent down to pick up her dress from the floor so it would not get wet and set it on a chair a couple of steps away. Laurentia finished undressing by the chair, placing the rest of her garments there. She walked over to the tub and stepped in, lowering herself into the hot water.

Jasper watched every move Laurentia made, not saying a word till she sat down.

"How is the water, my sweet?"

"Nice and delightfully warm; I think this tub is big enough for two. Would you care to join me?"

That most definitely caught Jasper's attention. His left eyebrow raised. "My lovely vixen, that sounds like a heavenly idea. Yes, I shall join you."

He walked to the chair Laurentia put her dress on, then proceeded to undress, laying his clothes with hers. Laurentia licked her lips, watching him from the bathtub.

When Jasper walked to the tub, he said, "Move forward so I can get in behind you." Laurentia scooted forward, and Jasper stepped in to sit down behind her, putting his legs out on the other side of the tub, so she was between his legs. Jasper took his hands and wrapped them around Laurentia underneath her breasts to pull her back to lay against him.

Jasper said, "A perfect fit we are. I now know why you love a bath; it does feel good after a long ride in the saddle to soothe one's muscles."

"Yes, it does. I love the feel of clean skin too."

He picked up a bar of soap sitting on a small table beside them. "I shall wash you first." He picked up a sponge, lathered it up, then started with her arms washing one and then the other.

Laurentia watched Jasper doing his handy work washing her, then he lathered the sponge again, then started on her chest, taking one of his hands and lifting one breast. He washed lightly around and down with his other hand and did the same to the second breast. She never thought being washed like this could be so seductive; she bit her lower lip, not wanting to moan.

He kissed her neck lightly, then whispered in her ear, "I could feel your body enjoying my touch."

Laurentia said on a sigh, "Yes, very much so, you do that so well.". She could feel his erection pressing against her bottom and lower back.

Jasper whispered, "Put your hands on each side of the tub. I am going to lift you so that I may penetrate you." Laurentia did as said, and he lifted her with his hands holding her bottom, and lowered her down onto his penis that was hard as a rock and waiting for her tightness to go around him. They both felt the bliss of their joining together.

Laurentia moaned, and Jasper said, "You feel so good; let us make this better. Are you ready, my Sweet?"

"Oh, yes, so ready, my Jasper."

"We are going to do this together, and I shall do most of the work lifting you. Keep holding the tub." Jasper started lifting and lowering her down, building a nice, extraordinary pace. Laurentia felt a pleasant building sensation that came extremely fast each time she was lowered down. She moaned, "Oh, Jasper, that feels so divine."

Jasper says through gritted teeth, "Come with me, darling, let me feel us together going over the edge."

She moaned out, then felt a wave of shudders and shakes as she rode out her orgasm. Jasper let go and filled her with his seed when he felt her trembles start and rode the waves with her as one. He let go of her bottom, still inside her. Laurentia leaned against him, feeling the beauty of the afterglow.

Jasper said, "That my love was beyond good. Perhaps being in a tub of water escalates the feelings."

Laurentia sighed, "That felt wonderful." A bath is on my top list of places to make love in the future."

Jasper rested his head on her shoulder. He bit her earlobe then said, "Mmm, mine too. I am going to lift you now and put you in between my legs again. We should finish bathing." With Laurentia between his legs, he found the sponge floating on the surface of the water.

Laurentia took the sponge from him. "Let me wash you as you did me." She then stood and turned to face him before sitting back down and wrapping her legs around him. Now facing each other, they both smiled. Jasper bent forward, taking her lips with his, kissing her gently, then tracing his tongue around the inside of her mouth, tasting her, and kissing her once more before letting go.

Laurentia beamed up at him, "I love you."

Jasper kissed her nose. "I love you too. Are you going to wash me now?" He handed the soap bar to Laurentia, which she took then lathered the sponge. She washed his arms first, then chest, and whatever else she could reach from her position. Jasper liked the tenderness they were sharing; he had never felt this before with anyone. He lay back on the tub, letting Laurentia do as she pleased to him.

Laurentia looked up to him as he watched her, seeing him completely relaxed. "You look relaxed now. The tension you've been holding all day has left your body." She leaned forward and kissed where his heart was.

"Yes, I am relaxed now, but I do worry about your welfare constantly. I could not live with myself if something happened to you. You are my life now, my sweet."

"I shall be fine. I have you and all the rest of our party protecting me."

Jasper sighed. "Let's get out of the tub. Can you stand up first, my love?"

Laurentia nodded, then stood, not stepping out of the tub yet. Jasper stood, got out of the tub first, picked up a towel, and wrapped it around Laurentia. He then lifted her out of the tub and dried her from head to toes. When Jasper was done, he picked Laurentia up, carried her to the bed. Only when she was settled did he walk back to the tub, pick up another towel to dry his body off. Laurentia watched every move Jasper's body made, his muscles flexing and rippling when he moved. Finally, Jasper tossed the towel onto the floor, hoping that it might absorb some of the water that had splashed from the tub.

Once Jasper was in bed beside Laurentia, he whispered, "We should get some sleep. We shall be returning to London tomorrow, my sweet."

Laurentia snuggled into Jasper's arms. "I cannot wait till we are married. I'm getting quite used to sleeping in your warm arms every night. It is truly wonderful, and I feel cherished."

"We shall marry this Sunday as planned, my love. You belong in my bed with me, and I shall not have it any other way. And I am pleased you feel cherished, for I shall cherish you every day of your life, Laurentia." Jasper snuggles Laurentia closer to him, breathing in her heavenly scent.

"But, I have been gone, not making my wedding plans. I do not know if all shall be ready to marry Sunday." She propped up and looking at him sadly.

Jasper said one more time, "We are marrying Sunday, my love, all shall be grand, do not worry."

Laurentia started to say something, then Jasper cuts her off, "Hush, my darling, let's go to sleep. You shall be my wife on Sunday, I shall promise you, and that's the end of the subject." He kissed her forehead, pulled her closer to him, and they both drifted to sleep together.

Chapter 33

London, Is A Half Day Ride Away

Laurentia was walking around her room with her chemise on, brushing her hair, and chatting about what had to be completed before the wedding on Sunday. Jasper lounged on the bed wearing knee breeches, no shirt on, with his hands behind his head propped on pillows, watching, and listening to Laurentia as she paced. She stopped walking and looked at Jasper, noting the silly smile on his face was making her wonder if he was listening to her or not.

"Did you hear what I have just said of our wedding day?"

Jasper blinked a couple of times, trying to remember what she'd been talking about. He was enjoying watching her brush her long blonde silky hair, thinking how beautiful she was and not truly listening.

"My love, I'm sorry, I was not listening, I admit. I became distracted watching you brush your hair. You are the most beautiful standing there." He puts his hand out to her to come to him.

Laurentia sighed, then walked over to him and sat on the bed beside him.

"I am just worried about our wedding day being so close, is all."

Jasper reached up to put his hands on her cheeks, looking into her eyes. "Stop worrying; I'm certain my mother is working on the wedding as we speak and my aunts too." He pulled her down to him and kissed her passionately. Laurentia surrendered to his kiss by putting her arms around his neck and leaning into him. Jasper kissed her neck and whispered softly in her ear.

"You have too many clothes on for my liking, my love." He pulled off her chemise and flipped her to her back. Then he kissed down her neck to her breasts. "You are my angel from heaven," he said, taking her nipple in his mouth to feast.

"We should get dressed and go downstairs with everyone else." Laurentia was panting and trying not to give in to Jasper's seductive pleasures.

He broke free and looked her in the eyes. "Do you want me to stop pleasuring you and get dressed now? Once we are back in London, we shall not have private time like this until our wedding night, my Sweet Love." Jasper said, so seductively with his wicked smile, she knew so well.

"Yes, I mean no, I believe we have time for this. Take me."

"That, my love, is music to my ears." They stayed in bed for another hour or so before joining the others downstairs.

Down in the same private dining room, the Duke, Drake, Leopold, and Victor were breaking their fast.

Leopold said, "Uncle, I took a walk out to the stable this morning before coming in here. I saw to our horses and looked around some. Beside our horses, their stables are empty. I asked the one stable hand out there if they have any other livestock, and he answered no."

Drake said, "The Innkeeper's son had a horse last night. I remember he rode in just after us."

Leopold said, "He must have gone already. Like I said, only our horses are there now."

Lucas and Jesse came in, and they helped themselves to the food laid out on the sideboard. They sat down and started to eat, then Laurentia and Jasper strolled in, holding hands, chatting, and laughing together. They bade everyone good morning, walk to the sideboard, take a plate of food, coffee, tea, and join the rest.

Duke said, "We need to leave as soon as everyone finishes eating. This place is too quiet and unsettling for my taste."

Jasper looked up from his plate. "Has something happened, I do not know of yet?"

Duke answered, "No, just a bad feeling is all."

Victor said, "I have finished here. I shall go start saddling the horses." Leopold and Drake joined Victor so that they could move out faster.

Duke said, "I shall go settle up with the Innkeeper as the rest of you eat, and then we shall be on our way."

Jasper said, "We shall be out to the courtyard in ten minutes or less." He looked to Laurentia's plate, seeing she was almost finished eating too.

In the courtyard, all the horses were saddled, waiting to depart. Jasper and Laurentia walked down the steps. The duke was talking with Leopold and Jesse as they stood by their horses.

Jasper walked over and asked, "Is the innkeeper's son still about?"

Leopold said, "No, I came out to the stable early. He and his horse were gone before six."

Duke said, "We cannot put our guards down, not knowing if they are smart enough to stop their pursuit of us again."

Jasper said, "Does everyone have a gun to use if we come across them again?" They all said yes, then Laurentia looked up at Jasper.

"I know how to shoot. Father taught me when I was twelve. I should have a gun also."

Jasper opened his saddlebag and pulled out a loaded revolver. He handed it to Laurentia but did not let go when she tried to take it.

"I'm giving you this only to use if necessary. I do not want someone shooting back at you. Do I make myself clear?" She nodded, and he let go of the gun.

Duke said, "Let's mount our horses and go home, shall we?" They were all in agreement with that, mounted their horses, and rode out of the Inn's courtyard.

Jasper, Laurentia Duke, and Leopold rode in the first row, followed by Lucas, Victor, Drake, and Jesse as they headed toward London. As they rode, they chatted about the fight at Jackson Boxing saloon on Thursday night.

Drake said, "I have put quite a few bets on that fight, and I'm glad we shall be back to see it tomorrow evening."

Lucas said, "Tell me about this fight and the odds." Drake talked about the event, while Victor and Jesse told their account of the action that would take place at Jackson's. Leopold spoke with the duke on his new line of carriages he would have come out in two months. Jasper reached over, and took Laurentia's hand, raised it to his lips, kissed it, and looking into her eyes, he mouthed, "I love you."

Laurentia smiled and mouthed back, "I love you too."

Duke said, "I think it would be a brilliant idea to teach my girls to shoot. Of course, one never knows when it would be necessary to have that skill."

Jasper was the first to give his opinion on that idea. "I am not too sure about that idea, Father. The two of them get themselves in enough trouble. Remember two years ago at the castle? They had a fascination with fire and almost burned down the small woodcutter's cabin. They had a huge fire going in that small fireplace. It's a good thing we saw the smoke, and we came in time to put it out."

Duke said, "All children like to play with fire. I want my girls to be able to shoot a gun in a time of need."

Laurentia said, "I have learned in my short time teaching the twins that they are most clever and quick to learn. I agree they should learn to shoot."

Jasper said, "Clever is an understatement when it comes to my sisters."

Duke replied, "Yes, they are smart, my two beauties. I shall teach them myself when we go back to the country."

Drake said, "I shall help you, Father, it could be fun shooting targets with my sisters."

Duke said, "I remember when Drake and Jasper did target practice. Jasper used his brother's head as a stand putting fruit or vegetables on it and shooting. You, Drake, let him do it."

Laurentia, looking surprised, looked back over her shoulder at Drake. He shrugged his shoulders like it was no big deal. "I trusted him, plus he gave me five gold coins to do it."

Laurentia said, "You must have trusted Jasper. How old were you both?"

Jasper said, "I was ten and Drake eight."

Leopold said, "He wanted me to do it, but I told him he was crazy, and he did not offer me gold coins to do it at the time."

Laurentia laughs then said, "Would you have done it if he had?"

Leopold thought for a moment, "No, he had only been shooting his new gun for two days. I like my head as it is." They all laughed at that.

Jasper said, "Money always worked with Drake."

Drake laughed again, then said, "He always paid well, and to this day, Jasper has brilliant skills; he is always good at doing the most things he tries."

Laurentia smiled at Jasper and asked, "You trusted him, Drake?"

Drake answered, "Yes, I trust Jasper with my life."

Jasper turned back to look at Drake, "Thank you, Brother. As I do you."

Duke smiled, hearing his boys talk to each other in such a way. Laurentia was still smiling when Jasper turned back around in his saddle; it warmed her heart to see a family so close, who were not ashamed to tell one another they cared. Laurentia was thrilled to become one of them and have all the Raventon's as her new family.

Laurentia said, "Thank you," to Jasper, and he smiled and asked, "May I ask what for?" Laurentia simply said, "For loving me and making me a part of your family."

"You are my soul mate, and you are most welcome, my sweet." Then he squeezed her hand and kissed it again.

After they had been riding two hours at a steady pace, they came to a small town. Many people they passed ran to the road as they rode by, for it was not everyday nobility rode by on horseback. The villagers waved at the duke and his family, and they waved back almost like a parade.

Fifteen minutes after they left the small village, Lucas said, "I hate to say this, but ten men on horseback are following us."

Drake looked over his shoulder, "Father, they are coming up fast."

Noting a large cluster of trees ahead, Jasper yelled, "Let's take cover in those trees ahead."

Leopold yelled, "I was just thinking the same, Cousin, let's go." They all kicked their horses for more speed, raced into the trees, dismounted, pulled out their guns, and took cover. When Jasper hit the ground in a flash, he automatically went to Laurentia's mare and pulled her down out of her saddle, then found a big tree to shield themselves together. The rest did the same, waiting now for the highwaymen to do their worst. The Raventon's looked forward to a good challenge and fight.

The highwaymen kept riding toward them, noting the group they were following had taken cover. Nevertheless, the highwaymen still charged them, shooting their guns, in the apparent hope of hitting someone sticking out from behind a tree.

Duke yelled, "Fire," when their attackers were right in front of them, still on horseback. The highwaymen's horses reared up and danced in a circle in the confusion of gunfire. They took cover to, across from the Raventon's on the other side of the road. Drake hit one in the shoulder with his first shot. Jasper shot hit a horse, but the one riding took cover quickly. The two sides re-loaded their guns.

The Raventon's finished reloading first, for they were experienced marksmen compared to the young men across from them. Victor shot hit another one in the shoulder, making two wounded. He yelled, "That's one for me."

Jasper looked over at his cousin, smiling, then he took aim and shot and hit one man in the chest, dead center. "If we are keeping track of points, that makes one horse and one man for me," Jasper smirked at Victor.

On the other side, the highwaymen had three wounded, with the man hit in the chest, not doing well. One man yelled, "Timmy is hit, and it's bad so much blood. The front of his shirt is all bloody. We need to leave and get him help, or he won't survive."

The leader said, "I have been hit in the shoulder. Josh is hit too. Damn it, this is not going well, and I know they have a lot of money to fill our pockets."

The first man said, "We are down one horse too, I'll put Timmy on my horse with me, and the rest of you follow." They mounted their horses and re-treated down the road, the same way they come.

Lucas yelled, "Look, they are retreating."

Duke said, "No wonder we shot three, and the last one Jasper hit was in the chest. That cannot be good at all." They all came out from behind the trees.

Leopold asked, "Has anyone been wounded or hurt?" They saw that everyone was unharmed, not even a mark on them looking around at each other.

Laurentia said, "That I can say it has never hap-pened to me before. Does this happen often when one is traveling?"

Jasper, standing beside her, said, "It is becoming more common these days, it seems."

Duke said, "Yes, that is true. At a recent parliament meeting, we have been discussing making the punishment harsh if caught as a highwayman."

Jasper said, "Let's get out of here in case some of them decided to come back."

Drake said, "Brilliant idea. I'm with you, Brother. Getting shot is not in my plans today." Lucas chimed in, "Neither in mine, getting shot, that is." They were soon all mounted, and on their way, again.

Leopold rode between Jesse and Laurentia. He said, "I believe the supposed highwaymen that just tried to rob us need to find a better line of work."

Jesse said with a laugh, "Undoubtedly, yes, they did not shoot well at all."

Drake in the front row said over his shoulder, "Or ride. Did you see their horses going in circles and dancing when we shot at them at first?"

The duke said, "That was because they were all young pups and wet behind the ear."

Laurentia riding next to Jasper, said, "Why are they doing that so-called line of work, being boys."

Duke said, "They must have had a taste of the easy money and thought to keep it going till they get killed or caught. Always happens, and the young Henry was among them, I'll take notice."

Laurentia said, "Maybe not having a father like the Innkeeper's son."

Lucas said, "We were orphaned quite young. I find that as no excuse."

Laurentia said, "I suppose you are right."

Lucas said, "Yes, I know I'm right. However, I think we should shake this whole ordeal off and talk of something else, something more cheerful and all."

Duke said, "good idea. I do not think those boys shall be after us anymore, at least not today."

Everyone changed the topic of conversation; they were soon back to laughing and chatting about the upcoming season in London and the fight tomorrow at Jackson's Boxing Saloon.

Mid-afternoon, they finally entered London city limits, feeling relieved they made the rest of the journey with no more problems.

The duke said, "We should all go to my residence. That is more than likely where the rest of the family is at this moment." They rode to Berkeley Square as a unit to show they accomplished what they set out to do, bring Laurentia back home.

They rode into the front-drive and in the courtyard of the Devonshire mansion. Groomsmen came running when they saw the duke had returned. Jasper was helping Laurentia down from her mare when the front door opened. The Duchess came out, the twins behind her, Charlton, Louisa, Johnathan, Fantina, Gabriella, and the Dowager Duchess. The duchess first ran to the duke, and he opened his arms for her embrace.

Duchess said, "You are home, how I worried for you and our children." They kissed and hugged. Letting go of her husband, the duchess rushed to Laurentia next, grabbing hold of her and hugging her tight. "My darling girl, you have returned to us, safe and sound." She kissed each of her cheeks. Then, looking up to Jasper's proud face. "I had no doubt you would find Lady Laurentia and bring her back to us where she belongs." She gave Jasper a fierce hug.

The twins push through everyone to get to Laurentia.

Aurora said, "We are so happy you are back with us, Lady Laurentia." The twins flung their arms around her, crying with joy and hugging her. Jasper stood back some so the family could embrace his bride-to-be, proudly watching.

The dowager duchess made her way to Laurentia after she hugged her son.

"Welcome back home, Lady Laurentia. I told you my grandson was in love with you. Do you believe it now?"

Laurentia turned looks over her shoulder at Jasper standing behind her, and he took her hand and stepped beside her. "Yes, I do believe he does love me. He rode day and night to rescue me from the awful kidnappers. I do feel loved by Bellator and all of this family before me, for they were there by his side to bring me home." Tears ran down her cheeks.

The elderly lady took hold of both Jasper and Laurentia's hands, smiling. "I say we have a wedding on Sunday to attend." She hugged them both. "To find your true love is a precious thing. Embrace it and never let go," she kissed Jasper's cheek and then Laurentia's. Then dowager duchess walked over to her other grandsons who had just arrived home to welcome them back too.

The Duchess cleared her throat to receive everyone's attention, and everyone looked her way. "We should go into the mansion now. I believe we have given our neighbors enough of a show for one day. We shall have a celebration dinner tonight for all the family, and that means Lord Jesse and Earl Berwickshire too."

Laurentia's brother said, "I do believe you all are my family now. It shall be an honor if you call me Lucas."

Laurentia smiled at him, and the Duchess said, "Lord Lucas, please join us."

"Thank you. I do not have any other plans tonight, Your Grace."

Duke said, "Come, everyone, let's go inside as my Duchess suggested moments ago." He turned to walk up the steps with his duchess, and everyone followed. As Jasper walked up the stairs with Laurentia, he asked Johnathan, "Why do I not see Sterling and Kelsey here?"

Johnathan answered, "They are at your townhouse in the stables watching over your prisoner."

"Oh yes, him, I still have that matter to deal with." He took out his pocket watch to see the time. Putting it back in his pocket, Jasper said to Laurentia, "My love, I need to go relieve my cousins of their guard duty. I shall be back no longer than an hour."

"If you must, I shall tell all of your absence. Do not be long."

Jasper raised her hand to his lips, kissed her fingers, looking into her eyes. "Never too long, I promise, now that I have you back."

Jasper looked for Leopold, and Jesse gave them a look to join him; they had, and the next thing you saw was the three of them riding down the road. Laurentia turns back to the stairs after watching Jasper disappear down the road. Everyone has gone inside for light refreshments before dinner, and they were in the front parlor.

Duke walked over to Laurentia, who was talking with Gabrielle and Louisa. He asked, "Where did

Jasper go to, with Leopold and Jesse, my dear girl?"

"To his townhouse. Jasper said he had to relieve Sterling and Kelsey of guard duty and would be back in an hour, Your Grace."

"Ah yes, almost forgot about that, do carry-on, Ladies." He walked over to the duchess to tell her where the missing Raventon men were.

When the three gentlemen arrived at Jasper's townhouse, they walked directly to his stable Sterling saw them entering and said, "As much as I enjoy horses, I'm glad to see you back. Did you find and get Lady Laurentia back?"

Jasper answered, "Yes, we did. She is now at Devonshire mansion, awaiting my return."

Kelsey said, "That is good to hear for this one's fate. He has been quiet as a mouse." The man was tied up sitting on the floor in one of the stalls.

Leopold said to Jasper, "Should we take care of him our way or turn him over to London's magistrate?"

Jasper said as he glared down at the man, "I shall grant that he did tell me the truth to where Lady Laurentia was taken to."

The man piped up, saying, "Yes, my Lord, I had, I mean I did. So you have got your beloved back, that should count in my favor, don't you think?"

Jasper demanded, "What is your name, man?"

"I am Jerry Lincoln, my Lord." He held his head down as if trying to look humble.

Jasper was feeling generous given to the fact that Laurentia had been in his arms for the last two days and nights. Plus, he did get to her before something terrible could happen to her. Merionreth and

Hughes not receiving the ransom money would have put Laurentia in danger. Jasper said, "Lincoln, you know who I am?"

Lincoln, still holding his head down, "I am told you are Marquess Bellator and heir to a Dukedom by my would-be guards here." He peeked up a little at Jasper.

"That is correct; I do feel some gratitude toward you for telling me the truth and reaching my beloved before she was harmed. However, you need to find a different line of work for your future and never cross me again. Could you do that, Lincoln?"

The others watched Jasper putting fear into this man and wondered where he was going with this line of questioning.

Lincoln said, "My lord, I most certainly can do that. Do you have any suggestions?"

"I own many Estates throughout England; perhaps some farming work would interest you? Are you married with a family of your own?"

Now sitting up straight, Lincoln said, "Yes, I have a misses, but no children yet. I could do farming work if given a chance. My Pa farmed before his death. The farm has a new tenant now."

Jasper said, "I shall let you farm five acres of my land. Let's see how you do with your first crop. If you do well with your first year and turn a profit with what you harvest, then I shall let you have three more acres for the next year and farm eight in all. Out of your profit, you shall pay to rent for the land use and living on the land as a tenant. What would you make of that?"

"I would be so grateful to be given a chance for myself and my wife. I shall be so grateful, my Lord!"

"Then it is done, I shall send a letter to my steward at Ayrshire that you are coming. Is that a problem?"

"No, I'll collect my wife from the small flat I've been renting by the docks and be on the way by first light, my Lord. Thank you so much for giving me a new chance in life."

Jasper said coldly, "Untie him and be on your way. Do not disappoint me. I shall not give you a second chance."

Once he was untied and standing, Lincoln bowed to Jasper, still thanking him, with tears in his eyes, and he walked out of the stable as a new man.

Jesse said, "That was most generous of you, my friend. You have developed a heart, I see."

Jasper turned toward the door to walk out, and the rest followed him as he stepped outside. "Yes, finding love has softened me a bit. But we shall not speak of it again. I do have a reputation to uphold," he laughed.

Leopold said earnestly, "If love makes you soft, you may keep it is all I am saying."

Kelsey and Sterling nodded in agreement with that; they needed no shackle of marriage for them.

Jasper said, "You shall feel different when you find the right woman someday. Mother is having a celebration dinner at the Berkeley Square mansion in honor of bringing back Laurentia and that everyone is back in one piece. The whole family is there, and we should all return before we are missed."

Kelsey said, "I'm there if it is Bridget's cooking."

Sterling said, "I shall second that. I am right behind you, plus I'm starving haven't eaten since morning."

Jasper mounted his horse, and the others did the

same and headed back to Berkeley Square, where the rest of the family awaited their return to celebrate the rest of the evening. The duchess never held back on making her parties spectacular, only the best of everything when the family came together for all celebrations.

Chapter 34

The duke and duchess were breaking their fast in the dining room, looking like newlyweds talking when the twins came in. Aurora said as she took a seat at the table.

"Father, it is so good you are home again. Mother is happier when you are here, as I am too." Amara nodded in agreement taking a seat next to Aurora.

Duke smiled. "I do not like to see my ladies unhappy; I shall keep that in mind to not go away too often." He kissed the duchess's hand.

Amara said, "Oh, Father, you tease us so, and we mean that." She had a sad look on her face.

"I know you do, but sometimes I have duties to attend to, and this time your brother needed my support."

Amara said, "Yes, we are delighted that Laurentia is back with us again. Of course, that bad man that kidnapped Laurentia shall not come back here again, shall he?"

Duke answered, "No, he shall not, so not to worry, my darlings."

Duchess reassure the twins, "Jasper made sure, my loves, we shall all be fine."

Aurora says, "It is only a few days, and Laurentia shall be with Jasper, not living with us anymore. That makes me sad not having her under our roof anymore."

Laurentia walked in and heard what Aurora said. "Yes, I'm marrying your brother, but remember that shall make us true sisters. Grosvenor Square is not that far away, and I shall be at Black Crest Castle when the season is over."

She sat down by Amara, who took her hand and said, "I hope my brother knows how lucky he is to have you. For my sister and I were fortunate to have you as our governess, if only for a short time."

"I'm the lucky one. I have all of you, my new family. I do believe Jasper and I are both blessed to have fallen in love."

The footman served them tea, poached eggs, thick slabs of ham, and freshly baked apple muffins.

Aurora said, "Get your fill of apple muffins now. I swear my brothers can smell them a mile away, and they shall eat them all."

Duchess laughed, for Jasper had just walked in with Drake right behind him.

Aurora waved her have toward her brothers entering the room, "See, it is true!"

Drake's eyes lit up for the smell of Bridget's baked goods. "Sweet heaven, Bridget has done her wonderful baking again. I shall have coffee, eggs, ham, and two to start with the muffins." He sat by the duchess and kissed her cheek.

Jasper sat by Laurentia, "I shall have the same." He picked up Laurentia's hand and kissed her wrist, looking into those violet eyes of hers., "Good morning, my love."

Laurentia smiled, "Good morning, Jasper."

Duchess said, "It is nice to have my family together so early. Laurentia and I have a busy day ahead of us, finishing wedding arrangements if you are to marry on Sunday."

Jasper, looking his impassive self, took a sip of coffee, then said, "I would not dream of getting in your way, Mother, but I do request to take my betrothed on a carriage ride in Hyde Park; let say five."

The Duchess did not blink, "Yes, that would fall into my schedule this afternoon."

Since Laurentia had been away when the announcement of their engagement ran in the paper, she needed to be seen by all in Jasper's company. A carriage ride in the busiest park at five would be perfect, and Jasper knew it too.

Laurentia knew what the two of them were doing. "I would like to go to the Royal Theatre this evening." That made them take notice of her in the room. Having two influential people wanting to monopolize her time by playing tug of war with her was slightly disconcerting to Laurentia.

Jasper said, "My sweet, you wish to go to the theater this evening?"

Laurentia smiled, for she knew the big fight was at Jackson's tonight; she had heard them talk of it all the way to London.

"Yes. Is it not of the utmost importance for us to be seen together due to our absence for days from the ton?"

Duchess smiled, approving Laurentia's move, good girl. Jasper looked to Drake and his father for help but saw none against the women.

"If that is your wish, we shall go, by all means. I

have a box there. Mother and Father, would you care to join us and perhaps Drake?"

Duchess smiled and said, "Yes, I think that is a splendid idea, Conrad, do you not think so?"

Duke hesitated, then said, "Yes, that sounds good. We have not been since we came to town." He stood to glare at Jasper then said to all, "I shall see you this evening then. I must be off to my Parliament meetings." He bent down to kiss the duchess good-bye.

Duke kissed his girls on the way out of the dining room and bade a good day to the rest. Jasper looked at Drake for his answer on going to the theater also.

Drake smiled, then said, "I have plans this evening already, but thank you for the invitation, Brother." His smile turned into a smug look.

Duchess said to Laurentia, "Let us eat up; we need to get you to your dress fitting in forty-five minutes, my dear. I am going upstairs to change. Yes, girls, you are coming too. I shall meet you, ladies, in the front parlor in a half an hour."

Laurentia had finish eating and was sipping her tea. She said to Jasper, "I need to go change for my outing. I shall see you at five for our carriage ride." She kissed Jasper's cheek before leaving the room, and the twins followed her.

Drake said, still looking smug, "Too bad you shall miss the fight at Jackson's this evening. It shall be a good one."

"I have no choice in the matter; Laurentia wants to go to the theater. We were away for too many days. I cannot have talk starting on why we were missing, Laurentia being kidnapped and all. Damn it. It is none of their business, the ton, those harpies, and the unnecessary tongues wagging."

"You see, that is one reason I shall not be marrying any time soon, no ball and chain for me. I do enjoy my freedom, dear Brother," Drake said before taking the last bite of his muffin.

Jasper said, "One sometimes has to give up little things to be rewarded later with bigger things."

"You can just keep telling yourself that, Brother, and maybe you can believe it's true. Well, I need to get going. See you later."

Drake stood, grabbed another muffin on his way out, and left Jasper sitting alone at the big dining room table. Jasper picked up his coffee, took a long drink, then thought to himself, 'Laurentia is more important to me than the fight at Jackson's, and that is the truth of the matter.' He stood and walked over to the sideboard to take another muffin for the road.

Laurentia stood in front of a looking glass, seeing herself for the first time in her wedding gown. She spun then said, "Your Grace, it is beautiful; how on earth did you know my size so perfectly?"

"Easy, my dear, I took one of your gowns from your wardrobe, brought it here to use to size your wedding gown. You look lovely. What do you think, girls?"

Amara said, "Jasper will be so pleased when he lays eyes on you on your wedding day."

Aurora smiled and said, "You look like a beautiful princess on her wedding day."

Laurentia spun again in front of the looking glass, then said, "Your Grace, you have exquisite taste. I'm speechless of how pleased I am. I do love my gown, thank you from the bottom of my heart."

The wedding gown was cream white; the color went well with Laurentia's golden blonde hair. The front top of the dress had a low scallop cut neckline, just enough to show a hint of cleavage. The neckline also had delicate pearls sewn along with it; the skirt belled out to the floor and had sequins plus bright jewels stitched in the hemline that sparkled like diamonds when the light shone on them. Her train was fifteen feet long, and the veil had a tiara of genuine diamonds that would sit upon her head.

The Duchess said, "The tiara that you have on I also wore on my wedding day. It is a Devonshire tradition for the future Duchess of Devonshire to wear. You shall be the eighth bride to have worn it."

Laurentia reached up to touch it as it was sitting on her head. "I shall wear it with pride, as you must have on your wedding day, Your Grace."

Duchess said, "Yes, I did. I loved Conrad so and even more, as we grow old together. Jasper has chosen well to make you his future marchioness. I can see when you two look at each other the love you share, and it warms my heart."

Laurentia had a tear coming down her cheek. She caught it with the back of her hand.

"Thank you for everything you have done for me to make my wedding beautiful. I just wish my mother and father could be here for my special day."

Duchess stepped over to Laurentia, took both of her hands in hers, holding them tight.

"They would have been proud of you, Laurentia. You have grown into a beautiful and smart young lady. The Raventon feel honored for you to become one of the family, my dear."

More tears came down Laurentia's cheeks. Amara ran over with a handkerchief and handed it to Laurentia.

"Oh, thank you, Amara," Laurentia dabbed her cheeks.

Amara said, "This is a happy time, not the time for tears to be falling."

"Oh, my tears are both happy and sad. Mostly happy ones. I should get out of my dress before I ruin it with my silly tears."

Duchess said, "Your tears are far from silly. The fit on the gown is good, but I think the hem needs to be a tad shortened." She waved her hand for the modiste to come over to do the work.

As they were walking out of the Bond Street dress shop a bit later, Laurentia asked, "Where to next, Your Grace?"

"Would you like to see the flowers that have been picked out for you? My two sisters-in-law helped with that, plus the cake. In addition, I choose the food for your wedding banquet."

Aurora said, "Mother, Amara, and I help too. Let us not forget."

Duchess smiled at her girls, "Yes, you did help. Your insight on the flower arrangement helped splendidly and made the choices go faster. Four doors down is the flower shop, shall we?" She waved her hand toward the shop.

Laurentia was excited to see all that was done in her absence. "By all means, let's go, and then after that, I would like to go to the bakery and so on."

Duchess smiled then said, "After the flower shop, we are meeting Louisa and Fantina for a luncheon at home. Remember, you have a date with Jasper at five to ride in Hyde Park."

Laurentia said, "I have not forgotten. I wish we could cancel that. But, we did spend a lot of time together on the road back to London. I'd rather see what's been done for the wedding, and I have to practice for my presentation to the Queen tomorrow."

Duchess says, "My dear, everything is going well with the planning; you shall see and not to worry. But you need to go riding in a carriage with my son in Hyde Park. You see, the Raventon men do not go for rides or walks in Hyde Park or any other park with a female unless he is making his claim to marrying the lady. He is showing that today."

Laurentia looks directly at the Duchess then said, "Never?"

"Never, so you see, you have to. You should have done the ride on Monday, the day after the announcement was in the papers, and Jasper knows it."

"I guess we must then, and there is so much to do yet."

Amara said proudly, "Not really; Mother has covered it all, with our help, that is."

Before they walked into the flower shop, Duchess said, "Stop worrying. All is going well with the arrangements. We cannot have our bride in stress, and you must not worry. We do not want the stress lines on your beautiful face on your big day. Do you trust me to make this the most wonderful day for you? After all, you are marrying my son. You do realize this shall be a big event that shall be talked about how grand it was and no less."

Laurentia smiled, "I trust you, yes, I shall try not to worry so."

"Good girl. Let's go see your lovely flowers for

your wedding day." The groom who accompanied them opened the door to the flower shop, and they strolled in happily.

Later that afternoon, Jasper returned to his parents' residence to pick up Laurentia for their first carriage ride in the park. Before he put his hand on the door-knob to go in the front entrance, Wesley opened the door for him.

"Good after, Lord Bellator. Lady Laurentia is in the front parlor waiting for your arrival. I shall announce you. This way, my Lord."

Jasper was in such a good mood; he let Mr. Wesley do his job to announce him at the home he grew up in, a first.

"Do lead on, Wesley. We do not have all day."

Wesley froze for a moment, feeling ecstatic that he did not have to battle with Lord Bellator to do his job this time. "Yes, my Lord, this way." When they reached the parlor, he announced, "Lord Bellator, Your Grace."

She nodded to Wesley to show him in, and Wesley stepped aside so that Jasper could walk in. Jasper strolled into the room, and he surveyed all who occupied the place. He saw Laurentia sitting on the chaise beside his mother, his two sisters, Gabrielle, and his two aunts, Louisa and Fantina, were in wing-back chairs. All eyes were on Jasper as he walked to the chaise where his mother sat with Laurentia. It was proper protocol to acknowledge the hostess of the room first. He bowed to his mother. "Good afternoon, Mother; it is a lovely day to take my be-trothed for a carriage ride, is it not?"

Duchess waved her hand to dismiss Wesley, then

said, "Yes, not a cloud in the sky. You both should have an enjoyable ride." She thought to herself, 'I like this new side of my son, very polite and letting Wesley announce him, a first. He always shows correct etiquette, no doubt, with that. It was nice to see a little softer side to him.'

Jasper turned to Laurentia. She put out her hand out to him, and he bowed over her hand, then said, "My sweet, you look lovely as ever." He then kissed her hand as he looked into her eyes.

Laurentia smiled at him, then said, "Thank you, my Lord."

The Duchess said, "Would you care to join us for tea?"

Jasper was still looking into Laurentia's eyes. "No, I do not care for anything." He then turned to greet the rest of the room.

Aurora said, "I'm so happy for your wedding day on Sunday, and I am delighted you are marrying Lady Laurentia."

Jasper said, "Lady Laurentia is a treasure one finds only once in a lifetime. She has made me a happy man by agreeing to marrying me." He looked over their heads to Laurentia's smiling eyes.

Laurentia said, "We are blessed in finding each other, my Lord."

Louisa said, "You two make a lovely couple and match."

Jasper said, "I tend to agree on that also, Aunt Louisa. Thank you for the compliment."

Once he had greeted everyone, the Duchess said. "Son, an hour ride in the park today shall show to all you made your choice in a bride. Do not keep Lady Laurentia out any longer than that, for this is unchaperoned."

Jasper bit his tongue to not argue with his mother on the matter. If she knew of their nights together, she would have his head on a platter for it.

Instead, Jasper said, "Yes, Mother, an hour in the park shall do. We have the theater tonight also to spend time together."

Duchess says, "I am glad you are taking your engagement seriously. However, we must not compromise Laurentia's reputation. After all, I am aware of your days as a rake."

Jasper raised his eyebrow at his mother's words to him, and he was not amused that she'd said that to him in a room of women, especially with Laurentia in the room. Yes, he'd had his share of womanizing and sowing his oats.

Jasper said calmly to her, "Mother, this is not the time nor place to talk of my past, so I prefer not to speak of it now. Lady Laurentia is my future Marchioness. I would never jeopardize her in any way. I assure you on that." He glared down at his mother as he walked over to the chaise, she shared with Laurentia.

Duchess saw he was not too happy being cornered like this, but Laurentia did not have a mother looking out for her best interests, so she was taking the role to do so. Jasper had a bad temper when pushed, so she changed her tactics.

"Son, I am just looking out for Lady Laurentia's best interests. I apologize if I offended you."

"That is very noble of you, Mother. Lady Laurentia's reputation is the most important factor, yes, and it shall stay clean. Not to worry." Jasper stepped over to Laurentia and offered his hand for her to rise. Laurentia took Jasper's hand, stood, and walked to the door together, but Jasper turned back to the room before leaving.

"I shall have my betrothed back in a reasonable time and fashion. Good day ladies." He bowed then exited the room with Laurentia on his arm.

Once they were settled in the carriage, Laurentia noted the vehicle was relatively new. The bench seat they shared was plush soft, deep burgundy leather, the mahogany wood had a high gloss finish, and the brass fixtures shone. Jasper had a team of two black thoroughbred horses that looked magnificent pulling the carriage. The carriage spoke of wealth, and it was awe-inspiring to be seen riding in it. As they traveled farther away, Laurentia broke the awkward silence between them.

"Jasper, what was all that about in the parlor? Do you think your mother knows of us sharing a bed?"

Jasper kept his team of horses at a steady pace, and he looked down at Laurentia's questing eyes.

"I do not believe no one has seen me going through the passageways or leaving the mansion. Mother is mot clever; things do not pass her too often. So, for her to attack me as she just had, she is fishing to find the truth."

Laurentia lowered her head, feeling the shame of the nights they spent together. Jasper saw the hurt in Laurentia's eyes before she lowered her head and staring downward. He put both reins in one hand, then with his free hand, he put his finger under her chin to raise her head to look at him.

He looked into her eyes, then said, "My love, the first night I share your bed and I took your virginity, I had already decided to marry you. I would not have done it otherwise. You are my destiny and soulmate for life. I love you." He smiled down at her. A tear rolled down Laurentia's cheek, and Jasper caught it on his finger, then leaned in, wishing he could kiss her but knowing to do so in public would ruin her reputation, and then he sat up straight.

"I love you too. I do not regret us sharing our passion for each other. It is an awkward feeling your mother may know. I think we should not share a bed again until our wedding night."

Jasper looked ahead to make sure his team was still going on route to the park. Then, he turned back to Laurentia.

"My love, you can not mean that. I shall go mad not to be able to have you till then. It is Thursday, which means three nights. Remember, I have purchased a special license to wed, and we shall marry now, today," Jasper brought the horses to a halt.

Laurentia could see in Jasper's eyes that he was serious about marrying today. She swallowed, then said, "I do not want to do that, Jasper. I want my church wedding, please." Jasper saw that was what she desired to have; he could not take that from her, being selfish for his own needs.

He sighed, "Very well, we shall stick to Sunday to wed, but we shall have to figure out how to come together for our needs and pleasures. My love, I cannot do without you, once I have tasted your passion and love."

"It is just three days."

"I do not care. You shall miss me tonight in your bed, mark my words."

He clicked the reins, and the horses start walking again. When they reached the entrance to Hyde

Park, the carriage trails were busy. This is something new for Jasper, for he had only ridden horseback in the park, never in a carriage or coach. Women, married couples, and some men courting rode in carriages. Never a Raventon man did unless he intended to marry the female companion who was riding with him. Jasper nodded good afternoon to the ton as he passed by. Laurentia smiled at everyone they passed and nodded also. She noticed almost everyone they passed craned their necks to see and watch them go by, and she giggled.

Jasper looked down at Laurentia then asked, "What is so amusing, my love?"

"It's comical to watch the ton almost break their necks to see you in a carriage seat instead of a horse saddle." Jasper nodded to a few more as they moved on.

"Yes, I can see now what you mean. Some of them are being ridiculous, almost falling out of their carriage. Well, my love, this is telling everyone I made my choice to marry, just like you have."

"I am merely an earl's sister, is all."

Jasper picked up her hand and kissed it tenderly, then said, "You are the most beautiful woman in the whole ton, and you are mine. They are staring or looking at you too, trust me they are, and you shall be the future Duchess of Devonshire, though I do hope it is a long time before I come to my title."

Laurentia sighed, "I shall have big shoes to fill someday. Your mother has an important role among the ton. She is loved and respected by all. So, are you too." She fidgets in her seat.

Jasper laughed at Laurentia, then said, "They shall love and respect you too, just as I do, and my family does." He kissed her hand again.

Laurentia then says, "There are Drake, Leopold, and Jesse riding on horseback. Oh, they saw us and are coming this way."

Jasper thought to himself, 'great, here it goes with the jab and pokes to the status of my bachelorhood life saying goodbye. He loved Laurentia, and nothing else mattered.'

As they rode up, Drake said, "Brother, it's hard to see you in a carriage in Hyde Park and not on horseback like us. You look old!"

Jasper pulled his carriage to the side so others could pass by while they talked.

"I am only two years older than you; that hardly makes me old."

Leopold said, "This has definitely taken you off the market, which means more chits for us. Laurentia, he is a lady's man, or I should say he was." Jasper glared at Leopold to shut up.

Jesse said, "I hear you are not going to Jackson's for the fight tonight, too bad it is going to be a good one to watch. And the bets are going crazy, off the chain as another way of saying."

Jasper knew the chain talk referred to him as having a chain around his ankle, keeping him back. Leopold laughed out loud, and Drake was getting Jesse's joke and laughed too.

Jasper said, "Yes, friend, I get your jest. No, I am not going to the fight at Jackson's. I am taking Laurentia to the theater this evening. Someday you shall see and feel differently when the right woman comes into your life. Mark my words, your life changes for the better." He smiled at Laurentia and squeezed her hand lightly.

Laurentia smiled back, then said, "Since everyone is talking openly today of your past Lord Bellator, how many ladies are we speaking of, may I ask."

"Oh, look over there, I see the Earl of Surrey on horseback. I believe; I shall join him and catch up on the latest news of the ton. Good day, Cousin, Lady Laurentia." Leopold kicked his horse then was off.

Jesse said, "I'm right behind you, Leopold."

Drake shrugged his shoulders, "I should join them and let you two have some privacy, Brother." He nodded his head then followed the other two, riding away.

Jasper looked back to Laurentia, who was staring up at him, waiting for an answer to her question. Jasper tried to shrug it off as no big deal.

"My love, that is all old history. None of those matters now."

"Twice today, Lord Bellator, I have been told that you have had a very, shall we say, entertaining past. I'd like to know how many?" She looked stern as she waited for an answer.

Jasper notices she said 'Lord Bellator' to him, not his first name; he was used to hearing her use his given name, so he knew she was angry that he did not answer her question.

"It's the past, my darling." Laurentia had an angry look in her eyes. Jasper blurted out, "A dozen or two, perhaps."

Laurentia blinked now, then said, "I see, and to you, that is not a big number."

"My love, I never said that. You asked, and I answered you."

Laurentia looked away from him for a moment, then looked back to say. "Yes, I did ask you, you're correct, and no, I do not like the answer you gave me, that is true. But I must accept it, and it is your past, as you have just said."

Jasper did not let go of Laurentia's hand when she tried to pull it away when he finally answered her. Instead, Jasper turned toward Laurentia, taking both of her hands into his now, looking into her eyes and saying sincerely.

"I never felt love for any of those women, ever. It was just bedding sport and companionship. You have captured my heart the first day we met, and I knew then as I know now. I love you, Lady Laurentia Sinclair. You are my life, my forever love." Jasper did not care who saw them; he leans forward and captures Laurentia's lip with his and kiss her so passionately, and it made her toes curve.

Jasper was shocked when he pulled back, "My love, don't cry. I shall do whatever it takes to make you happy. I swear!" Another tear came down her cheek.

"My darling, they are tears of joy to hear you declare your love for me, and that kiss you given me said it all." Laurentia smiled brightly.

They laughed together, and Jasper looked around to see who was watching but not caring. He loved Laurentia and did not care who saw them kiss and now laughing and gazing adoringly at one another.

Laurentia looked around, also knowing that showing such obvious affection was not the thing done out in the middle of the busiest park in London.

She looked up at Jasper, and he smiled that wonderful, wicked smile she knew so well.

"I am the Marquess Bellator, and you are my future Marchioness. We can do and get away with a lot of things most cannot, my love. We should get you back to Berkeley Square so that you may have a small rest before the theater tonight."

"I'm not tired at all, but we do not need the wrath of the duchess for being gone too long."

He turned back toward the horse, giving them a flick with the reins. They took one more lap around the park before headed toward the park's entrance. Laurentia moved a little closer to Jasper on the bench they shared, and she smiled up to him when he noticed her move of boldness.

"It is fun being wicked and improper with you in front of all the ton. I'm sure we shall be reading in tomorrow's Gazette and the Observer about our ride in the carriage in Hyde Park," Laurentia giggled.

Jasper said with a warm smile, "To think we have only started our life together, I do believe we shall read at least once or twice a week of something we have done together in those papers you mention, and I do love to hear your adorable giggle. It is music to my ears, my love."

Chapter 35

Going to Theatre Royal

Duke of Devonshire's coach awaited them outside Berkley Square Mansion. A footman opened the door to the coach when they walked up to enter. The Duke and Jasper sat facing the back, and the Duchess and Laurentia sat opposite, facing forward. They rode through London wearing their most elegant attire.

Laurentia glanced out the window, then said, "It is a lovely evening tonight for early Springtime."

Jasper said, "Yes, the night is fairly warm for this time of the year. Have I told you yet how beautiful you look tonight?" He could tell Laurentia was feeling nervous.

Laurentia said, smiling, "Yes, you told me that when I came into the front parlor before dinner, but I never tire of hearing you telling me again."

Duke said, smiling at his Duchess, "Son, we are lucky men to have the most beautiful ladies of all England as our brides. All the gentlemen in London are envious when we walk by with our lady on one arm."

Jasper said, "That we are, Father."

Duchess cut in, "Laurentia, I'm with you on this;

I never tire of hearing it neither. Conrad tells me so at least four times a day or more."

Duke said, "I only tell the truth, my love." He looked obviously smitten with his wife, and he winked.

Jasper said, "The play tonight is a comedy, one of Shakespeare's, and the critics from the Observer and the Gazette gave it a good review. It is called A Midsummer Night's Dream."

Duchess said, "Yes, a couple of my friends have told me it is delightful and funny. I am looking forward to seeing the play."

Laurentia said, "I've read a few of Shakespeare plays, but I have never seen one performed. It shall be quite a treat."

Duchess asked, "Have you been to the theater before?"

"Once, when I was sixteen, with Mother, Father, and Lucas. We went for my birthday. I shall never forget it."

Duchess said, "It must be a lovely memory for you."

Laurentia smile, then said, "Very much so, with many others."

The coach rocked to a stop when they pulled up to the front entrance to the Theatre Royal. One of the footmen jumped down fast from the coach's platform to put the footstep down and open the door. The duke steps out of the coach first. He eyed the crowd around them and turned back to the coach to help his Duchess down the steps. They waited a couple of feet from the coach, knowing Jasper would come out next and help Laurentia down himself.

Laurentia shook out her gown when her feet hit the

ground. Jasper watched Laurentia, and they made eye contact when she finished making her gown right and took his arm when he put it out for her.

Laurentia whispered, "So many people are watching us."

"When the Devonshire coach arrives with the family crest on the door, it is always like a parade for us. Plus, they all want to see my bride-to-be." Jasper smiled down at Laurentia.

Laurentia took a deep breath, then said, "Yes, they are curious. I do love a parade." She tried her best to walk with her head held high, like Jasper and his parents demonstrate.

They followed the duke and duchess as the walkway cleared a path as they strolled through the crowd. Jasper was surveying the people as he walked to the theater entrance, taking note of the importance of those in attendance. He saw the Marquess of Dorset; he nodded to him as he passed him and his charming wife. Jasper thought to himself, 'that there are quite a few gentlemen here tonight and not at Jacksons' boxing match.'

He then saw his friend Earl of Surrey and the Countess, and as he passed, he bade them a good evening.

As they entered the theater, the duchess said, "It seems to be quite a crush tonight, a big turnout for a Thursday evening."

Duke said, "I wonder, my darling, did you mention around town this afternoon that we were coming here tonight?"

Duchess gave Conrad a brilliant smile, "I may have told a few friends or so."

"I thought as much, for a lot of the gentlemen

here tonight would have been to Jackson's to watch the fight. Their wives had a much different plan when you mention to them the Theatre Royal was the place to be tonight."

Duchess said with a stifled laugh, "Of course it is." They climbed the main staircase to go up to the Devonshire private box.

Jasper took two glasses of champagne from a waiter as he walked by. He handed one to Laurentia, and she sipped it as they mingled through the crowd. They stayed in the lobby so Jasper could introduce her to some of the ton. Everyone seemed eager to meet the future Marchioness.

Laurentia asked, "Where did your parents go, my Lord?"

Jasper replied, "They went up to the family box. Their close friends are more than likely up there also." He lifted her free hand to his lips, kissing it tenderly, looking into her eyes. That sent shivers through Laurentia, and Jasper felt it too, for he looked into her eyes with that wicked smile he did so well for her. Jasper leaned forward to whisper in her ear.

"I would love to taste you in a more intimate place than your hand, making you pant and shiver." His lips brushed her earlobe before he lifted his head.

Laurentia was shocked he would say such a thing to her in a crowd like this. He was so naughty at times, she thought to herself. They stared into each other's eyes, not breaking contact at all. It was like the whole world stopped around them, and they saw only each other. Jasper mouthed, I love you, and Laurentia mouthed back, I love you more.

From behind, Jasper heard a familiar French female voice saying, "Lord Bellator, it has been many weeks since I set my eyes on you." She pushed past Laurentia. "Oh, how I missed you, my Lord." The woman curtsied, giving her hand to Jasper.

Jasper took it as she rose, trying not to look irritated at her. "Yes, I suppose it has been a long time, Countess."

She reached up, and touched his coat lapel, running her finger down it, saying seductively, "Oh, you are such a tease, you know it has."

Laurentia was getting more than annoyed that this over-perfumed woman had the nerve to just push past her like she was not even standing there at all. Jasper looked around her to Laurentia.

"Countess Glamorgan, I would like you to meet my betrothed Lady Laurentia. Lady Laurentia, this is Countess Glamorgan."

The countess turned around quickly to see Laurentia standing there. She looked her over, then said, "My Lord, you are jesting, are you not?"

Laurentia said sternly, "No, he is not." Then she showed the impertinent woman her engagement ring. Jasper stepped in between the women to put space there.

The countess was twenty-six, a widow with auburn hair, green eyes, and a well-endowed figure. Jasper saw this was not going well for his future Marchioness to meet his former mistress. He wished that Léopold or Jesse were there to intercept Angelique away from him and stop this unpleasantness.

Countess said, "I read of the engagement in the Gazette earlier this week, but I could not believe it true, Lord Bellator." She looked up at Jasper, pouting. Uncle Charlton and Aunt Louisa cut into the circle that was developing around Jasper and Laurentia.

Charlton said, "Ah, Lord Bellator, there you are, with your lovely betrothed. His Grace has asked me to find you that your presence is required in the Devonshire box at once. Shall we go? We must not keep his Grace waiting," he winked at Jasper.

Jasper reached out, took Laurentia's hand, then said to all that had gathered around them, "If everyone shall excuse us, I must see to what pressing matter the duke has summoned me for." He bowed eloquently and led Laurentia away to their private box, with Charlton and Louisa in their wake.

They climbed the staircase that led them to the balcony. Jasper glanced down to Laurentia, noting she did not look pleased with what happens below minutes ago. They walked down a corridor to the entrance to their box; Jasper pushed the private curtain to the side so Laurentia then Louisa could enter first, then Charlton.

Jasper grabbed his arm and whispered, "Thank you, Uncle, that was not going well."

"Old or young; we Raventon men must always look out for one another. Your Aunt noticed the crowd that gathered around you first, and then I took action."

"I shall have to thank her later. As I said, it was not going well there."

"Yes, as everyone was watching, we noticed." They stepped into the box together, laughing.

The duke looked over to his son and brother when they walked in, wondering what they were laughing about. Jasper walked to his father.

Duke stood, asking, "What is so funny, Bellator?"

Jasper said, his voice low at first, "Go with me on this. Yes, I shall see to that first thing in the morning as you request, Your Grace." He raised an eyebrow indicating it was his turn.

"Please do and then report to me directly when it is finished." Duke now whispered, "I hope you shall share with me later what this little show is about."

Jasper whispered, "Yes, later." Charlton stood there looking all innocent, putting in a few words here and there.

Laurentia sat with the duchess; a couple of the duchess's friends were visiting before the performance started. Duchess introduced Laurentia to them when she came in. Finally, the bell rang, letting everyone know the play would be starting soon.

The ladies, with their gentlemen, bade everyone goodbye, then left the Devonshire box to go to their seat across the way.

Laurentia asked, "Your Grace, which seat shall I take for the play?" She was already sitting in the second row behind her in the box.

"Conrad and I shall sit the two seats to the left front, and yourself and Jasper can sit to my right front. Charlton and Louisa can sit behind me. Johnathan and Fantina, when they come in, they shall sit to the right second row." Laurentia stood up to take her correct seat.

As she did, Jasper walked over to join her, and they sat down together. Jasper said low to her, "I'm sorry for what happened below, my love. Unfortunately, the Countess has a way of being rude to others."

Laurentia said quietly, "Was she your mistress at one time, Jasper?"

"She is a widow; her husband passed two years ago. Only for a short time, she was, yes." He tilted his head, hoping she was not mad at this.

Laurentia sighed, then said, "You share with me you had many before me. As long as it's your past and not present, I shall have to deal with this."

Jasper took her hand and kissed it, not losing eye contact. "I only desire you and no other, my love." He kissed her hand again and lowered it to her lap, not letting go of her.

Laurentia said, smiling, "That is all I have to hear, then enough said on that. I shall not let it ruin my first night at the theater with you. I hope we shall come here often in the future."

"If the theater brings you joy, we shall come often, and I shall take you to more theaters all over Europe when we travel, my love."

"I shall like that, my Jasper." He kissed her hand again; it pleased him to hear his name spoken from her lips.

Jasper said, "Let us enjoy our first play together." Then the curtain opened, and the performance started.

The Duchess smiled then thought to herself, 'I cannot get over how much my eldest son has changed in a short time of knowing Laurentia. Being in love agrees with him, and he is more relaxed and happier.'

Duke whispered, "My dear, is that smile for me?"

Duchess whispered back, "Sorry, darling, I'm watching Jasper, he is truly happy, and it warms my heart to see him that way."

"Yes, he does love her. The play starts; let us en-joy it" he kissed her cheek.

At intermission, the duke stood up, put his hand out for his duchess.

"Let's stretch our legs, shall we, my love?"

"Yes, and I would like a glass of wine. I do enjoy the burgundy Drake brought over from France, and I wonder if they have it here."

Louisa said, "Charlton, let's go too; I would like a glass of wine."

Charlton stood, "Johnathan and Fantina, are you coming too?"

Johnathan said, "I am right behind you, Brother. Come, darling, let us take a walk." He put his hand out for Fantina to take and to stand.

Fantina fluffed out her gown as she stood, then said, "I remember the burgundy wine that you served us a week ago, your Grace. Was that the one you mention now? It was delicious."

"Yes, it's now my favorite. Lord Drake has made sure my wine cellar is stock with the lovely burgundy, every new shipment."

"As you know, being French, the wine reminded me of home. I do hope they have it here. I must speak to Lord Drake and have him supply my home too."

Charlton says again, "Ladies, we need to hurry; the line shall be a mile long by now."

The duke stood at the entrance of their box. He turned back to his family.

"We do not have to rush, dear family. You almost make me laugh for not remembering that service is granted at once when I enter any room. Being a duke has its privileges, so do come along." Conrad put his arm out for his duchess. Everyone left, but Jasper and Laurentia.

"I have noticed that is how things work for you also. High rank seems to have its perks."

"Yes, it has perks, my love. Watching my father in his role is always entertaining enough. Also, I have a new duty to start on Sunday, which shall keep me busy. I believe it's call husband." Jasper raised an eyebrow.

Laurentia smiled, "Ah, I like the sound of that, and wife shall be my new role. Is that right?"

Jasper looked around, seeing how many eyes were watching them, too many, he decided. He stood. "My wife, you shall be, yes." His eyes lit up. "Let's take a walk, my love. We need to find a place where I can hold you and show you what this future husband desires right now." Jasper put his hand out for Laurentia to stand and go.

"Jasper, we must not be seen doing improper things in a public place." Still, Laurentia took Jasper's hand to follow him.

As Laurentia stood, he says softly, "Trust me, my love, we shall not be found."

"I trust you always. Shall we go?"

Jasper looked to see if anyone saw them, then he turned down the corridor the opposite way they came in. They came to a single door. He looked to make sure no one saw them first before opening the door; no one was around. He opened the door fast, pulled Laurentia in behind him, and closed the door. Before them was a staircase that led up.

Jasper, with eager eyes, said. "It goes to the roof. Come, no, shall be up there."

Laurentia followed him up the stairs to the roof. She looked around when they stopped, and he turned to her, taking her in his arms, holding her tightly.

Laurentia looked at Jasper suspiciously, "How many women have you brought up here to do this?"

Jasper smiled at Laurentia, "You are the first, I swear. When I was very young and forced to come to the theater, Leopold and I would escape up here for a while. We thought the plays were boring then. Cross my heart, I have only brought you up here, besides Leopold." He kissed her nose.

Laurentia saw he was truthful. "I like the idea I'm the first. It makes me feel special to you."

"You are more than special to me, you know." He nibbled her lips. "You are my deepest desire, my future, and the new world I cannot wait to explore together. "Jasper took Laurentia's lips in a passionate way that said your mine. He broke free of her lips and kissed down her neck.

Laurentia let him have free rein with her body. "Oh Jasper, all day, I wanted you to hold me like this, kissing me and more."

He stopped kissing her neck and lifted his head to look her in the eyes. "Did I just hear you say more?"

Laurentia nodded her head. "Yes, I did."

"I do aim to please you. We cannot disappoint you, can we?"

Laurentia, playing the game, "No, we must not disappoint me, that would make life most unpleasant for us both. Plus, I do enjoy it when we do naughty things together."

Jasper had that wicked look in his eyes and smiled; she loved so much. He started kissing down her neck again. Her gown was low cut off her shoulder, and he pushed it down further, revealing her creamy flesh. He then went to work, loosening the front lace to her bodice, his eyes lighting up when he freed her breast. His lips went to her left one first, sucking her nipple hard, then he licked his tongue in circles around the nipple, flicking it with the tip of his tongue and continue doing it all over and over again. Laurentia's head went back as she moaned in the pleasure, he was giving her. Then he moved to her other breast.

Jasper was so hard it hurt. He brought his hands to her breasts and flicked his thumb on both of her nipples at the same time as he kissed up her neck to her lips.

"I am so hard for you right now." He took her hand, then put it on his groin so she could feel him. Laurentia ran her hand over his rock-hard cock. Jasper moved them over to the wall, so he can have some support when he took her. Jasper had Laurentia panting with pleasure.

"I need to be inside of you now. We both need this before we go back to our box. When I lift you, wrap your legs around me."

"Oh, my Jasper, I want to feel you inside me, so much pleasure you gave me just now. We need to feel like one." He undid his breeches and pushed up her gown.

"Wrap your arms around my neck, then wrap your legs around me when I am lifting you, and I'm inside you." Jasper did not give her time to think, he lifted her, bracing with the wall to her back, and in one swift movement, he was inside her. She did as she was told and wrapped her legs around his middle. They moaned together with the feeling of fullness and joy.

Jasper said, "You feel so tight and so good, oh, this is heaven, my sweet Laurentia." He did not move for a few minutes, just feeling her warmth, wetness, and tightness around him. Jasper moaned, "So good you feel around me." Then he started to move slowly in a nice rhythm.

Laurentia felt him move slowly at first, and he took her lips, moving faster in a perfect rhythm. Kissing her, moving in and out, so madly wonderful, she started feeling the flutters, the building of an orgasm. "Jasper," she cried out, then she shivered and shook, riding to the edge of pleasure together.

Jasper pumped harder, coming with her. He let out his cry with her, filling her with his seed. He collapsed to the ground with her in his lap, in a pile of the gown over them. They held each other tightly, coming down from their perfect cloud together.

Jasper said, "You are mine, all mine, oh we are made for each other perfectly, my love."

Laurentia lifted her head from his shoulder, looking into Jasper's eyes, "And you are mine too."

Jasper kissed her nose. "Yes, all yours, Laurentia. All yours." He kissed her passionately.

Laurentia felt nervous all of a sudden. "We should go back to the box; they are going to be wondering where we are, everyone."

"I do not care for myself, but for you, we should go back downstairs." He kissed her forehead. Jasper put his hands on her waist, then helped lift Laurentia to her feet. Jasper stood up next and fixed his breeches. Laurentia pulled up her dress back onto her shoulders and laced her bodice.

"Let me help you." Jasper took hold of the lace, tightened it properly, and tied a neat bow for her.

Laurentia watched him do the task quickly. "It looks like you have done this before?"

"No, I haven't. I'm very good at unlacing but never helped to tie it back up once again."

"I like that, another first. How do I look?"

Jasper tilted his head, "Beautiful, shall we go?" He put his hand out for her to take, and they went back into the theater, down the stairs, and back to the Devonshire box. The performance had just started as they sat down together. Jasper held Laurentia's hand as they enjoyed the rest of the evening.

The duke and duchess glanced over to them as they sat down.

Duchess whispered to Conrad, "I wonder where they snuck off too? They are both glowing. It seems to me."

The duke looked again, then whispered, "They reminded me of us when we were that young. Remember the sneaking away so that we could embrace, kiss, and the passion we shared, Vivianna."

"Yes, we were quite good at that, sneaking away. I hope they are careful, is all." Duchess worried.

"Darling, we are talking of Jasper. The apple does not fall far from the tree." He smiled at her.

Duchess sighed. "I know he is just like you; that's why I worry so."

"They shall be married in a couple more days, now stop fussing. Let us enjoy the rest of our night." Conrad kissed Vivianna's hand.

Jasper looked over to his parents, whispering back and forth. He could only imagine what they were whispering. Then he thought, 'my lovely bride-to-be is as adventurous as me. I know our marriage shall be very spicy and never dull. They would always share the same bed-chamber; he would not have it any other way.' They finished watching the play holding hands, and ever so often, Jasper raised her hand to his lips, kissing it tenderly and lowering it back to her lap, not letting go of it all evening. Laurentia felt truly cherished by her beloved future husband.

Chapter 36

Friday Morning, Countdown till Wedding Day

Laurentia sat at her dressing table in her bedchamber while her maid, Sandra, pinned up her hair, leaving the back down to hang in ringlets.

Sandra said, "my Lady, why do you look so blue this morning? It is a lovely spring day."

Laurentia sighed, "you do know Jasper comes to me here every evening and stays with me till dawn. Last night he did not."

"Did you have word last night at the theatre, my Lady?"

"No, we had a lovely time."

"Then what has happened, my Lady? There are only two days left till your wedding day." Sandra finished Laurentia's hair and stepped back. Laurentia spins around in the chair so she can face Sandra as they talked.

"We believe the duchess might know; Jasper had been coming to me every night. So, we are stopping that, trying to be more discreet until we are married. It is truly wonderful to sleep in the arms of the man you love, I missed that last night, and it has made me feel blue, is all."

Sandra tries to cheer Laurentia up by saying.

"Two more days, my Lady, and you shall marry Marquess Bellator and become his Marchioness. If you do not mind me saying, he is most handsome, a real catch, I say."

Laurentia smiled, "Yes, he is and wonderful in so many ways."

Sandra asked, "Would you like to have a tray brought up to you, so you may break your fast up here to have some time alone. You do have a busy day of activities planned for today. Her Grace has a list a mile long for you."

"I shall go down to the dining room. Jasper has been coming here every morning to dine with me, and I'd hate to miss seeing him."

Laurentia stood, walked over to the looking glass, checking her appearance before leaving her room. She touched her hair, then walked to the door to go downstairs.

In the hallway, she saw Aurora leaving her room. "Good morning. Where is Amara?"

"She went down earlier; I prefer not to hurry to dress today." Aurora waited by her door so that Laurentia could walk with her. Laurentia caught up with Aurora, and they descended the stairs together, talking about the wedding plans and her bow to Queen Charlotte later that afternoon.

Aurora said, "I would be excited to meet the Queen. I have heard she is a fine lady."

Laurentia said, as then walk into the dining room, "I'm not scared of meeting her, just nervous that I shall fall flat on my face doing my curtsy in front of her, trying to be perfect as a future Marchioness."

Aurora laughed then said, "I have watched your curtsy; you have an exceptionally graceful way."

Jasper was sitting at the table with his parents and Amara eating, he stood when he heard Laurentia enter the room. Jasper walked to her, "Good morning, my love. I trust you slept well?" He took her hand, turned it over, and kissed her palm, looking into her eyes.

Laurentia smiled, remembering the time last night on the theater rooftop.

"Yes, I had and dreamed of you."

Jasper, still looking into her eyes, said, "As I did of you, my love. Come." He escorted Laurentia to the table, pulled out a chair for her next to his seat, and pushed her in. Jasper motioned for a footman to bring Laurentia's morning tea.

When the footman came with her tea, Laurentia said, "Toast and jam would be lovely, and some eggs." Meanwhile, Aurora helped herself to the food and took a seat by her sister, who was finished eating and sat sipping her tea.

Duchess said, "Good morning, Laurentia and Aurora. We have a lot to do today. First, we shall make a few calls this morning, and then we shall go to Buckingham Palace this afternoon. I believe you shall do well and not fall on your face as you said when you walk in."

Jasper, making light of the subject, said, "Whatever happens, I shall still marry you on Sunday, so not to worry."

Amara said as she laughed at Jasper's remark, "I think you have this Laurentia, and my brother said he shall still marry you."

Laurentia said, poking Jasper, "Thank you all for your support."

"Lady Laurentia, is that a proper way to behave

toward your future husband?" Jasper had an impassive look on his face but was laughing inside.

"It is when he makes light of the subject and is not being supportive like he should be. When I am truly nervous."

Jasper turned toward Laurentia, took both her hands, and made her face him. "You are one of the most confident persons I have ever met; it is one of the qualities I adore about you. Darling, I know you shall do brilliantly with this task. I have seen you curtsy many times; you shall charm the Queen."

Laurentia smiles, "Jasper, that does mean a lot to me to hear you say those kind words to me. Thank you."

Duke said, "We all believe in you, dear girl; it shall be a piece of cake for you today to do your bow. You shall see, and I speak for myself and my Duchess." They both nodded and smiled at Laurentia.

"Thank you; now I feel that I can take on the world, with all your kind words." Laurentia smiled her most brilliant smile to them all.

After they finished their morning meal, the duchess said, "We shall leave in an hour." Jasper asked Laurentia if she would like to take a walk in the garden before leaving for the day.

Laurentia answered, "I'd love to." They walked out the side door to the terrace and down the steps, holding hands as they walked into the garden. When they were out of view, Jasper pulled Laurentia into his arms, kissing her madly.

Laurentia broke the kiss saying, "I missed having you with me last night in my bed. But, one does get used to being held all night long. I was quite blue when I woke this morning."

"I told you, once we share a bed, you shall not like sleeping alone anymore."

Laurentia looked up at Jasper with a pouty face.

He then said, "I missed having you in my arms, also, my love."

Laurentia smiled. "What shall we do?"

"I shall come to you tonight after the ball and make certain I'm not seen. We have two more nights before we wed, and then you shall be the mistress of my home and bed."

"The night before we wed, we cannot stay together. You cannot see the bride until you see me coming down the aisle at the church on our wedding day."

"Do not tell me you are superstitious. You believe in that bad luck thing?" Jasper rolled his eyes.

"Why yes, I do, just tonight you may come to me. Then after that, we shall be together at your home as man and wife forever."

Jasper corrected her, "Our home, you mean."

"Our home. I do like the sound of that. Do you know when I saw you this morning in your parents' dining room, I had to stop myself from running to you and throwing myself into your arms. I missed you so much."

Jasper said, laughing, "I would have loved that and had you on the table."

Laurentia said, "I'm serious. I would have if we were alone."

Jasper, still laughing, said, "I'm serious too, believe me." He stopped laughing and took her lips in a toe-curling kiss that felt wonderful. When he broke their kiss, he said. "I do love you, Laurentia, and I'm counting the hours down until you are mine completely. Then I can kiss you any time I wish, well almost, some places can frown on it. To hold you and make love to you as I please. We have a lot of new ways to try and explore together; I'm looking forward to that."

"Ways? what do you mean?"

He smiled his wicked smile for her, "My love, we have not even touched all the possibilities of the art of making love. There is so much more to teach you and do."

Laurentia smiled. "You have been holding out on me. I do like being naughty with you, as you do know."

Jasper nipped her nose then said, "Yes, I'm finding that out, and I do like your appetite on that. I'm looking forward to that time when it is just us."

"Us, I like the sound of that too." Laurentia smiled and wrapped her arms around Jasper's neck. They pressed together, kissing, touching, as much as they could do with keeping their clothes on. A half-hour later, they walked back to the house hand in hand, talking and laughing together as lovebirds do.

When they were back inside, standing at the bottom of the stairs, Laurentia said.

"I need to go up to freshen myself up to go out for the day with your mother, sisters, aunts, and cousin.

"I do like your hair down like this." Jasper ran his fingers through her ringlets, hanging down her back when he pulled her close. "I shall come back here an hour before dinner is served and take you to our engagement ball. I have been told that Aunt Louisa and Aunt Fantina have been orchestrating the whole event, and this ball is the biggest one of the season. The most important people of the ton shall be there, all the Raventon family and friends. Tomorrow night here, Mother is having a dinner party for the family and some very close friends. The Raventon family always goes big on parties and special occasions."

Laurentia put her arms around Jasper's neck and leaning into him, looking into his blue eyes. "Yes, your mother has been telling me of all the pre-celebrations we are having, it is a bit much, but she said she had the same before marrying your father. I do love you so much."

"We are perfect together, and I love you too." Jasper kissed Laurentia long and demanding, so she'd remember it all day long. They broke the kiss, and then he kissed her forehead before he was letting her go.

Laurentia sighed, "See you this evening, my love." She turned to walk up the stairs to change for the outing.

Jasper smiled as he watched Laurentia walk up the stairs and said, "I am looking forward to it." When Laurentia reached the top landing, she blew Jasper a kiss and gave him a little wave before walking down the corridor.

Jasper turned to walk out the front door. Wesley was there to open the door for him. Wesley said to Jasper as he was walking out.

"If I may, Lord Bellator, I have not wished you congratulations yet. I wish you and Lady Laurentia the best, and you make a handsome couple, my Lord."

"You may Thank you, Wesley, until this evening." Jasper whistled as he walked down the steps to the drive, where a groom was holding Lucifer. Jasper mounted his horse, then decided to take a long hard ride in Hyde Park before returning to his residence.

Entering the park, Jasper decided to ride down the carriage trails that led to the park's back; they were less busy this time of day. He rode Lucifer hard down the tracks, flying, and then he saw Drake and Leopold riding toward him. They stopped when they reached each other.

"Good morning, Brother," Drake said.

Leopold said, "Cousin, you missed a good fight last night. They went five rounds before a knockout."

Jasper said, "Good morning. You are riding late today. Tell me, who won last night?"

Leopold looked Jasper over, then said, "Snyder, of course, he went one more round than I predicted, but I still made a few pounds. You made a few bets that you should collect on too if you can take the time to collect from your busy schedule, that is."

Looking pleased, Jasper said, "Yes, I did. But, Drake, you need to pay up."

"I shall have to pay for you tonight at dinner. I'm not carrying enough on me."

"That shall be fine. It looks as if the trails are empty, which should make for a good ride. Where are you two heading?"

Drake said, "We are heading for Whites to have a bite and then go to Kelly's rifle range. Do you want to join us?"

"I need to give Lucifer a workout. I shall meet you at the rifle range. What time are you going there?" Jasper pat's Lucifer neck.

Leopold said, "About one, Jesse, Kelsey, and Sterling are meeting us too. You don't have any wedding things to do that shall stop you from joining us, do you?" sounding sarcastic.

Jasper could see that his getting married was unsettling to the men; they saw him as their pack leader.

"No cousin, the women do all the planning. I just have to show up for the event. The way I like having things done, that suits me."

Drake said, "It shall be great that you join us. See you there, dear Brother." Jasper nods, yes.

After they'd gone, Jasper thought, 'about how Leopold had been acting. Perhaps he felt Laurentia was replacing him. I better talk with him later, alone, and reassure him that he is my best friend besides my cousin. No one can replace him.'

Jasper kicked Lucifer and took off down the trail like lightning. 'This workout is for both of us to clear my mind and body from stress,' he thought as he rode. Jasper rode two times around the trails and decided that was enough of a ride today for them both and headed home for a spell before meeting the men at the rifle range for some male bonding time with the Raventon pack.

Chapter 37

Spending Quality Time

Jasper dismounted his horse in Kelly's gun range stables; he noted that his family's horses were already here, plus Leopold's coach as he handed Lucifer's reins to a stable lad. He walked out of the stables to the front entrance of the rifle range, and he felt as if someone was watching him. Jasper surveyed his surroundings; nothing of concern caught his eye. So, he continued to walk in, nodding to a few acquaintances as he passed by. Finally, Jasper saw Drake talking to Kelsey and headed over to them.

Drake saw Jasper coming, "We just arrive ourselves. Leopold is checking in for us, Lord Bellator."

Sterling and Jesse walked up behind Jasper and joined the circle; they were still talking about the previous night's fight.

Jesse said, "Bellator, you missed a good one last night. Hopkin was holding his own till the end of the fourth round, and when the fifth started, Snyder knew Hopkin was losing his drive then knocked him out cold."

Jasper said, "There shall be more fights to see. Lady Laurentia needed to be seen out with me last evening since we were gone right after our announcement in the papers. The ton was starting to think we had broken the engagement, and we had to prove it otherwise."

Leopold joined them and heard what Jasper said, "That is why I'm not interested in that institution. The ton shall be watching every move you make and wagging their tongues. No, thank you!" The rest nodded in agreement.

Jasper said, "You may say that now, but when you find real love, you shall be singing a different tune. So, mark my words on that one, you shall see."

Kelsey said, "I'm too young for that talk. I like my life as it is."

Sterling said, "I am with you on that. I'm not going to answer to anyone as long as possible."

Jasper said as the leader still, "Let's go shoot and make some wagers on our shots."

Leopold said, "We have three ranges, numbers five, six, and seven."

Jasper led the way as always to their spots on the field. He was showing them he still was the same, that nothing had changed with him. They all fell into their usual selves again, laughing, making bets, being men. Jasper stood with Leopold talking, watching Sterling show off his skills as the best shot in the family next to Jasper, of course, as Jesse and Drake kept trying to beat him.

Jasper said, "Today at Hyde Park, I notice some sarcasm in your tone toward me, Cousin. Is there something that is bothering you that you would like to share?"

Leopold looked at Jasper, then motioned to walk away from the rest so they could talk in private. They walk over to the side out of the hearing range.

Leopold sighed, then said, "I did sound that way

earlier and maybe some here. I guess it hit me that things shall be changing for us, and I'm not too fond of it. I must admit, dear Cousin." He shrugged.

"We've been together all our life, Leopold, you only being three months younger than I. The only thing that shall be changing is taking a wife and starting a family soon after. But, you and I shall never change. You are the one I know who always has my back first before anyone, as I am for you. We have been through everything together, from learning to walk, running to riding a horse, going to Eton, then the University, and now I am the first to marry. Our kinship is like a brotherhood, and I love you as one."

Leopold was looking into Jasper's eyes and saw the sincerity of his words. He thought for a moment, started to say something, then stopped and shook his head before saying, "You are right. I've been an ass to think otherwise. I felt as if you were replacing me with Lady Laurentia. You're not, and you are just taking a wife. I'm not replaceable." Leopold had a look on his face, like a new revelation.

Jasper said, "Hell no, you're not!" They pulled into a hug, patting each other's back and stepping back.

"I love you too, Cousin." Leopold, now laughing, with relief from their talk.

"I knew that, but it is good to hear, Leopold. Now let's get back with the others to see how much Sterling is winning."

They walked back over to where the rest were shooting, both feeling better they'd had this talk. When Jasper and Leopold returned to where they were shooting, they saw how they were shooting bottles instead of targets. Drake was taking a shot and hit the bottle off the pole.

Drake laughed with joy. "Brother, did you see that I shot the bottle right off the pole. On my second shot, this time." He looked to the rest as if saying, beat that.

"Not bad, Lord Drake, now let me have a go at it." Jasper picks up a musket to shoot.

A tall young gentleman walked into the rifle range, and he has been standing back watching the Raventon party interact with one another. He watched as they laughed, joked around with each other, having a good time. He saw when Lord Bellator and Leopold took a short walk to the side, discussed something of importance, then embraced and walked back to join the rest again. The gentleman noticed that all the men in the party had similar features, but one. That one must be a good friend as he fit in with the rest of the Raventon's.

The gentleman was still watching them; he asked one of the workers, "The men over there, are they the Raventon?"

The man nod, then said, "Yes, sir, they are. They come here quite often."

The gentleman said, "Yes, I have been told that they do. Which one is Lord Bellator?"

The man answered, "That's easy, for everyone knows he wears black all the time. He is the one about to shoot now. But, let me warn you, Lord Bellator is not someone you want to anger unless you want a death wish."

The gentleman said, "Thank you for that advice. I shall keep that in mind." The worker nodded and went on his way. The gentleman thought, a death wish. Bellator has one now of his own when he killed my elder brother. I shall take my revenge, for there was no justice served when he died. No one is taking action to make things right, so I must kill the man who killed my brother. He was consumed with a vengeance.

Jasper hit the bottle dead center, and it shattered off the pole. He swung around, saying, "Top That," with a grand smile on his face. Suddenly, another shot rang out when Jasper spun around, hitting him in the shoulder by someone standing about five feet away. He had no idea that someone aimed a musket at him until the ball from the gun made him lose his balance and feeling slight pain. Jasper stumbled backward but did not fall, looking down to his shoulder, seeing the blood running down his coat, and he then looked back up with murder in his eyes. Jasper looked to see a man with a musket still in hand, smoke coming from the barrel, and lowering his weapon.

Jasper's adrenaline was pumping hard; his features changed in seconds to a warrior. He pulled his sword and charged the man who shot him. In three significant steps, he swung one hard blow to the man's neck, and down he fell to the ground. Jasper stood over him with his sword still in hand. While Leopold was right behind him with his sword drawn, waiting to see if anyone else was coming at them. Drake, Jesse, Kelsey, and Sterling had loaded muskets in their hand, ready to take on their assailants.

Jasper thundered, "For what reason did you shoot me?" Looking formidable

The man on the ground choked on his blood as it ran out his mouth and down his body. "You killed my brother Gerald Hughes, and I take revenge on you, Lord Bellator," then he died saying his last words.

Jasper looked up from the man on the ground. "I believe I shall need medical attention now." Jasper fell backward into Leopold's arms, making him drop his sword to catch him. Drake helped Leopold, so Jasper did not hit the ground.

Leopold yelled in distress, "We need to get Bellator home, and we need a doctor." Jasper was unconscious, blood pouring from his left shoulder.

Jesse took his coat off, saying, "We need to put pressure on his wound, here use my coat to aid the wound." Drake took the offered coat and pressed it to Jasper's shoulder

"Let's get my brother out of here. Come, Leopold, I need help carrying him out of this place." Sterling and Kelsey also helped in taking Jasper out of the shooting range.

Leopold said, "I knew there was a reason I brought my coach here. I did not dream we would be transporting Bellator with a gunshot wound today or any day to speak of." They put Jasper in the coach, Leopold, and Drake rode with him, while Kelsey rode for the doctor, and Sterling rode to Berkeley Square to tell his parents and Laurentia of his fate.

Jesse stayed at the rifle range to handle the situation there. Jesse watched as the coach was riding down the road, worrying for his friend's life, realizing he was losing a lot of blood. What amazes me is how Bellator was shot in the shoulder, and he stilled pulled his own sword, charged the man who shot him, and killed him. Well, maybe, I should not feel surprised. After all, Bellator is no man anyone should ever try to fight against in any way, never a good outcome for his opponent. He shook his head on his last thought and turned to walk back in the rifle range.

Sterling was not looking forward to telling Jasper's loved ones about the shooting. The duchess's coach was sitting in the drive, which told him they have just arrived home from their outing. It was good the coach was still harnessed with the horses and ready to go for when he shared his bad news with them. He rode into the drive, one of the grooms took his horse, and he told him he wouldn't belong, to keep his horse here. He knocked on the door, and Wesley answered immediately.

"Good afternoon, Wesley. I must see the Duchess and Lady Laurentia at once."

Wesley said, "Good day, sir. Her Grace is in the front parlor having tea with Lady Laurentia, Lady Amara, and Lady Aurora. They just returned from the palace. I had heard Lady Laurentia's bow to the Queen went splendidly. This way, I shall announce you."

Duchess was surprised that Sterling was popping in for a visit mid-afternoon, and she tensed when Sterling came in looking nervous.

Sterling bowed to his aunt, "Your Grace, I have bad news to share."

Duchess said, "Sterling, if it is bad, you must tell me at once."

Sterling looks over to Laurentia, sitting in a wingback chair sipping tea, and turned back to the duchess.

"Lord Bellator was shot. Drake and Leopold have taken him to his townhouse, and Kelsey is on his way to retrieve the doctor."

Laurentia shot to her feet, sitting her teacup down on the side table. "I must go to him at once. Your Grace, are you coming with me?"

The duchess said. "Sterling, that had to be difficult for you to bring us that news. I thank you. Lady Laurentia, I am going to message Conrad to come home, that we have an emergency. You may take my coach to my son's residence; the girls shall go with you. That shall suit the ton having them with you, as you are not married yet, to enter Bellator's residence chaperoned."

Laurentia did not care about what was proper at this moment. All that she could think about was she must go to Jasper's side at once. Now!

"Yes, we must go now. Come along, Lady Aurora and Lady Amara."

The duchess followed them to the front door. "I shall follow when His Grace arrives home. Tell Bellator we are on our way to him shortly.

Laurentia said, "Yes, Your Grace, I shall see you there soon."

Laurentia rushed out the door to the coach with Amara and Aurora in her wake. When Laurentia entered the coach, she saw the driver running from the stable; the twins entered and took the opposite seat. Sterling mounted his horse, then yelled to the driver their destination and led the way to Grosvenor Square.

Arriving at Grosvenor Square, the coach stopped in front of Jasper's home in a rocking motion. Sterling dismounted his horse promptly to open the coach door for Laurentia and his cousins. Laurentia

stepped down from the coach, taking in her surroundings. "Which one of these homes is Lord Jasper's?"

Aurora said, pointing to one, "The gray one is his
there." Laurentia picked up the bottom of her gown
and proceeded to run up the walk to the front door.
She pounded hard on the door, feeling frantic about
Jasper's injury and thinking the worst thoughts. Finally, the door opened to reveal Jasper's butler, Mr.
Everett's.

"May I help you, madam?" Aurora and Amara
just came up behind her after he spoke.

Amara said, "Mr. Everett, you're a silly man.
This is Lady Laurentia Sinclair. Lord Bellator betrothed and your soon-to-be mistress of this residence and all his homes."

Everett looked back to Laurentia, then said, "Forgive me, my Lady." Then he bowed to her.

Laurentia said, "There is nothing to forgive; you
had not met me yet."

Aurora said, "Well, let us in. You do not think we
came here just to stand on this doorstep. Did you?"

Everett, still surprised seeing ladies on Lord Bellator's doorstep, said, "Yes, come in. his Lordship
was indisposed with a dreadful gunshot wound when
he arrived home not so long ago. The doctor is with
him in the front parlor. You may wait here in the
second drawing-room this way." He stepped aside
and let the ladies in the front door as Sterling came
up the steps behind them.

They walked into the foyer, and Laurentia, losing
her patience, turned to Everett, saying, "Mr. Everett,
which of these rooms is Lord Bellator in? I shall see
him at once."

"My Lady, that is no place for a lady to be at this moment. Come this way, and I shall have some tea brought to you as you wait in here." He waved his hand to a door just down the corridor.

Laurentia saw she was not getting anywhere with this butler, and tea was the last thing on her mind. She viewed the area they were standing in and decided which door would be the front parlor, then went for that door in one swift move.

Everett yelled from behind her as she opened the door wide, "My Lady, you cannot go in there now. That is not how things are done."

Laurentia immediately saw Jasper lying on a chaise with Drake, Leopold, Kelsey, and she presumed the doctor was standing over him. However, they all turned when Laurentia entered the room. She walked quickly over to the chaise where her beloved lay.

"No one shall keep me from the man I love, and do not try doing so, any of you," Laurentia said fiercely

Drake said and moved aside when she reached the chaise, "Lady Laurentia, come, the doctor is finishing patching Bellator's shoulder. Everett, you may go. She shall be fine."

Everett stood in the doorway, looking unpleased, but he nodded and exited.

Laurentia stood over Jasper; she had tears in her eyes as she saw her love lying there. She fell to her knees, taking Jasper's hand. "My darling, what happened? I came as soon as I heard of this," Tears ran down her cheeks. Jasper opened his eyes, hearing Laurentia's voice. The doctor was still sewing his shoulder.

"My love, don't cry. I assure you I am fine. A gun-shot wound to the shoulder shall not kill me. It shall take a lot more than that to finish one off as I. Pleased, my love, stop crying, all is well." Jasper reached up with the hand Laurentia held to catch her tears from falling and wiped them away.

"Jasper, what shall happen to us next? We have been through so many obstacles since we met. It seems we have been doomed with misfortune. And you are the one hurt, yet I am the one crying and babbling on so. And you are the one trying to console me. That is not right, and you're the one hurt, not I. I'm an awful person." Laurentia lowered her head. The doctor finished sewing his left shoulder. Jasper sat up some and winced at the pain as he did. Laurentia's eyes grew large, watching him do so, and he sat up all the way.

"See, my darling, I shall be fine, and you are not awful for crying or anything. You are perfect to me, and that is all that matters."

"But—"

Jasper cut her off, saying, "No, perfect! You know what shall make me feel better is your lips on mine." He smiled at her.

Laurentia smiled back, then reached up and kissed his lips tenderly, "You are incorrigible, and I love you."

"Yes, my reason for living is you, my sweet."

The doctor said, "Lord Bellator, if you shall let me bandage your shoulder, I am through."

"Yes, finish your work here, as you must." Jasper said, looking irritated.

Laurentia stood to watch the doctor do his work, then asked, "What kind of injury has Lord Bellator received in the shoulder, Doctor?"

The doctor says as he worked on Jasper, "He is a fortunate man the ball went straight through, not hitting any main arteries or breaking any bones. A little bed rest, and you should be fit in no time, my Lord."

The duke and duchess walked in, hearing the doctor's verdict on Jasper's injury. The duchess said, "We shall have to postpone the wedding so you can recuperate."

Jasper said sternly, "No, we are still marrying on Sunday. Come hell or high water, no one is stopping us, and that is final."

Duke said, "Son, you have been shot, let us be sensible about this. Tell me what happened. Who shot you? I shall finish them myself in taking their head."

Leopold cut in, "I shall tell you of what happened." He proceeded to tell them about the ambush.

Duke said, "I am not surprised by my son taking care of his shooter as he did. But, why, and who did it?"

Drake says, "The man said he was Hughes's brother and was taking revenge on Bellator for killing him a few days ago. Those were his last words before dying."

Jasper said, "That is how it happened, yes,"

The duke, still irritated with someone trying to kill his son, "Damn it, is there any more of his family we have to worry about? This has gone too far."

Drake said, "Jesse was left at the shooting range to answer questions and to see to matters, he should be here soon."

Duke rumbled, "This needs to be the end of this,

and I shall make sure of it. Damn, criminals think they can come after my family. They're wrong, and I won't have it."

Duchess patted his arm, saying, "Calm down, my love, all shall be handled after this. Just thank heaven Jasper shall be all right." She stepped forward, kissed Jasper's forehead, then hugged Laurentia seeing she was upset about this whole ordeal too. Then his two sisters came forward, kissing Jasper's cheek and saying they were so happy he was okay.

Jasper said light-heartedly, "If it's this easy to get all this special attention from the Raventon women, I shall endeavor to get hurt more often."

They all said together, "No, you shall not!"

Charlton and Louisa came in, and soon after. Victor arrived, saying he missed all the action, being he could not spare the time from the art gallery today. Jonathan, Fantina, and Gabrielle came in next, seeing to Jasper's condition as well.

Louisa said, "Should I put a stop to the ball tonight, being my nephew was shot today?"

Jasper snapped, "No, everything is still going as planned, dear Aunt Louisa."

Duchess said, "Jasper, a few days shall not hurt to delay things."

Laurentia said, "I agree with Jasper, as long as he is sure he can still do it and all."

Jasper took Laurentia's hand, then kissed it. "You heard my betrothed, and I say the wedding is not changing. The ball tonight, tomorrow's dinner party, and then Sunday we are marrying as scheduled. No gunshot wound shall keep me from marrying the woman of my dreams. It shall take a lot more than that to stop me."

Laurentia kissed him tenderly, then said, "We must get organized here, for it is four o'clock as of now. Darling, can we have dinner here instead of the Berkeley Square Mansion? I shall help organize things and have my gown brought here. I shall not leave your side, and I am going to take care of you." Laurentia smiled down at Jasper.

Jasper liked the idea of Laurentia not leaving his side. He did not hesitate to say. "Yes, that is a wonderful idea, as I have heard. Dinner this evening shall be here before the ball to celebrate our wedding. Everett, where is that man when I need him," he bellowed.

Everett heard his name just outside the door; he listened to all that was being said in the room. Being the butler to his Lordship, he had to know what was happening in this house to keep it running correctly.

Everett popped in, saying, "Yes, my Lord?".

"I know you heard all that is conspiring this evening. You need to set the staff on fire and see things are done. Lady Laurentia is staying to organized everything. You shall start respecting everything she says is to be done; she is the new mistress of my homes from this day forth. Tell all my staff and introduce her. Do I make myself clear?"

"Yes, my Lord, as you wish," Everett bowed, then left to stir the staff to get the things started as ordered.

The duchess said, "We need to go home; I shall have your gown and Sandra sent over so that you may stay here. I could have Bridget come with some of my kitchen staff; they were working on the dinner all day that was to be served at my residence this evening. I would say the food needs to come here. If that is alright with you?" Jasper looked to Laurentia to answer, for she was starting today as the mistress of his homes.

"That's a lovely idea; then it shall not be so hectic on short notice for my household to have things ready when you return for dinner. Thank you, my Grace."

Duchess said, "Then we need to be off, so I may have things rolling smoothly for you. We shall return at half-past six. Conrad, I'm ready to go."

"Yes, my dear. Come, girls, your mother has spoken." Duke winked to Jasper and Laurentia as he escorted his duchess out. The rest of the family said they are off too, and they shall see them at the ball held at Lord and Lady Charlton's home that evening in their honor. The doctor took his leave also, telling Jasper not to overdo it, and he shall check on him tomorrow morning.

When it was just the two of them in his parlor, Jasper said, "I'm sorry, my love, for all of this, I would have preferred your first time here under better circumstances than to be my nursemaid."

Laurentia walked around the room, looking at the furniture and a few knick-knacks he had positioned on various tabletops. She saw he had excellent taste and purchased only the finest money could buy, but it was obviously a bachelor's home.

"This room and most likely the others shall need a woman's touch, I see."

Jasper watched Laurentia walk around and liked the way she was touching everything with her fingertips.

"I have mentioned to you already that you may decorate all my homes as you desire when we wed."

Laurentia walked back to him. "Yes, you have; I

am looking forward to seeing all your residences soon. There is no reason to be sorry about being shot. If I remember right, you sat beside my bed for hours when I was thrown from the carriage a week ago, and we were not even betrothed yet." She sat on the edge of the chaise, looking into his blue eyes. Jasper reached up with his right arm and placed his hand on her face, tracing his thumb along her jawline and pulling her close to kiss her tenderly.

Laurentia pulled back, "It was nice all your family came to check on you. It makes me realize how truly close you all are."

"Yes, we always unite when there is an emergency with a family member. Let us say something happens to Kelsey. I, too, would go see if there was anything I could do and check his wellbeing."

"That is wonderful, and you are all so close. How many bedrooms does this home have?"

Jasper played with a loose strand of her hair. "Four, but next year, I shall buy you a bigger home than this one, with a ballroom, much larger dining room, and gardens. Then you may decorate it to your heart's desire."

Laurentia said, "What about this place? It needs my touch badly."

"I have lived alone here for many years; it had suited that period in my life. I plan to take you for an extended honeymoon and travel to those places you told me you would wish to see. When we return, we shall go to the country. The season shall be almost over with, and I want you to myself. We have plenty of time to socialize later; I believe the term I should use is we are honeymooners, and we shall have the whole castle to ourselves for a few weeks."

Laurentia nibbled his lips, then said, "Yes, I would like that. When shall we leave?"

"The day after we are married, Monday, I have planned it all out for us."

"But now you have a bad shoulder. Oh Jasper, what shall happen to us next?"

"Nothing has changed. We are still going as planned, do not worry, my love, all shall be well. How was your bow to the Queen? I say you were perfect, and Queen Charlotte was highly impressed with your poised"

"The Queen said I have a lovely posture and grace. Have you met Queen Charlotte?"

"Yes, on a couple of occasions, I find her most pleasant."

"As do I. Queen Charlotte talked with me for a few minutes and then dismissed me. Your mother said she does not usually talk with too many ladies. You curtsy, she looks you over, and you're gone."

Jasper pulled Laurentia forward to kiss her lips softly, then said, "I am not surprised. The Queen knows when someone is special as you are, my love." He kissed her again. There was a knock on the parlor door, and Jasper yelled, "Enter," not happy he was being disturbed.

It was Everett. "My Lady, I have informed his lordship's staff of you being with us now. If you wish, I can take you around to introduce you and get started with your dinner plans for this evening."

"That shall be lovely, and when I am gone, you can get some rest, my Lord. Mr. Everett, have a couple of footmen help Lord Bellator to his bedchamber so that he may rest till dinner." Jasper raised an eyebrow at Laurentia ordering and not asking if that was what he wanted to do.

"Right away, my Lady," Everett bowed and went out to fetch the footmen

Looking at Laurentia quizzingly, "What if I do not wish to do so?"

"You shall go and have some rest. The doctor said you need to. Besides, you would be more comfortable in your bed, so no arguments," Laurentia said, looking like a true force of strength.

Jasper gave her a half-smile. "I adore this feisty side of you. I have missed it. Come with me to my room?"

"No, I have a lot of things to do. If you remember, your father, mother, brother, and sisters are coming for dinner. I need to familiarize myself with your servants and home. Too much to do. Let's say when we return from the ball, and I shall give you a rain check." Laurentia smiles and stood.

Jasper looked up at her, "My little vixen is back." He thought to himself, 'my room tonight, what could a man want more.'

The two footmen came in to help Jasper to his bedchamber, but Jasper was too proud to accept their help. They just walk behind him up the stairs. His valet, Farrell, could help him when he reached the confinement of his room.

Laurentia just shook her head when she watched Jasper go up the staircase, not letting them touch him at all, so proud he was. She sighed and then followed Everett to the dining room to start her new role as head of this household and smile as she went, loving every minute of it.

Chapter 38

The Dinner and Ball Must Go On

Laurentia spent her time familiarizing herself with her new home and staff. Meanwhile, Sandra had arrived with her gown and some other belongings. Bridget arrived with two more of the duchess kitchens staff and the large dinner already prepared. Jasper's cook Ellie was pleased to see them not having the proper timing to put together a dinner party meal.

Laurentia was in the dining room giving orders of how she wanted the table set; she was happily surprised Jasper had the correct linens, china, and stemware for a lovely dinner party. When she saw it was five-thirty, Laurentia gave her last orders of what needed to be finished for the dinner party and then went upstairs to change for the evening before all her guests arrived. She walked up the stairs feeling giddy from all she accomplished in a short time. This was her first time in the hostess role for a dinner party, and she was having a grand time doing so.

Walking down the corridor to her room, she knew her room was beside Jasper's. She stopped at his door first to listen and did not hear any noise from inside. She thought, maybe Jasper was sleeping, I shall not bother him now, I shall dress for the evening then check on him afterward.' As Laurentia strolled into her room, she saw Sandra organizing the dressing table. She only had come up here briefly, not noting everything in this room was new

Sandra said, "Lord Bellator has done a grand job with your room here; everything is new. I know it is, my Lady."

Laurentia was looking at all the furnishing, "Yes, I believe you're right. Seeing all the beautiful things he has put in here for me tells me how he cares for me. Lord Bellator has excellent taste and only has the best of everything."

Sandra said, "Look at the beautiful drapes, the bed linens, the carvings on the poster bed."

"We also had fine things at Berkley Square."

"Yes, but this seems more special. You have to see it as I do, my Lady."

Laurentia's heart warmed, for Sandra was right; this room was impressive, and she wondered if Jasper had done all this himself, she would have to ask him later.

"Sandra, we must get me dressed for the evening. I want to be ready when the family arrives, and I need to see if his lordship is alright."

Once she was dressed, Laurentia knocked on Jasper's bedchamber door and listened to hear him call out, but she heard no sound from the other side of the door.

Finding the door unlocked, she walked in then said, "Jasper, are you here?" No answer.

Laurentia walked further into the room; she looked around the room; it was substantial with a large bed with a red curtain that was close. She walked to the bed, then pulled back the curtain, finding Jasper asleep in the middle of the bed wearing only breeches. Laurentia stood there, watching him sleep. He looked so handsome and peaceful, lying there with his eyes closed.

"Jasper, my love, wake up." She wondered if she should let him sleep more. Jasper's eyes opened, and he turned his head to find the most beautiful woman at the edge of his bed looking down at him.

He smiled, "I must be in heaven, for I see a beautiful angel looking down at me." Jasper sat up, wincing from the pain he felt in his shoulder.

"Oh, my darling, I can see the pain you are feeling. Are you all alright? What can I do for you?"

"Not to worry, my love, it did hurt some when I sat up. I should be fine once I'm up and ready for the evening of festivities." Jasper edged off the bed.

Now standing before Laurentia, with his right arm, he pulled her close. He bent down to kiss her lips softly, then said, "What time is it, love?"

"Quarter past six. Did you have a good sleep and rest?"

"I suppose I had; I never sleep during the day. You look lovely in your new gown." Her gown was baby blue with a plunging vee neckline with crystals sewn into it. Her hair was up on the sides and top, with ringlet curls cascading down her back.

"What do you think of my bedchamber and yours, my love?" He walked over to pull the bell cord for Farrell to come.

"My room is lovely. Is the furniture new in there?" Jasper walked back to her, kissed her forehead.

"Yes, I only wanted the best for you, and I picked

the color purple to match your eyes."

"I'm pleased with my room. Thank you, knowing you chose the décor warms my heart. Now your room is huge and has a massive bed, does it not?"

The corner of Jasper's lips twitched. "I would have you in the middle of that bed right now if we did not have dinner guests in fifteen minutes. And yes, it is a large bed, a lot of room to play in, also new this week just for you and me. As I said, if we had more time and you did not look so perfect right now, I would have you on that bed trying it out with you for the first time."

Farrell came in with a bow, "My Lord, are you ready to dress? That nap you had seemed to have made you look more chipper."

"Let's not start with that again. In case you are wondering, the angel you see before you is my future bride, Lady Laurentia Sinclair. My love, this is my valet, Mr. Farrell. He sometimes is outspoken and prides himself on making me look my best in all I wear."

Farrell said, "I am delighted to meet you, my Lady. Maybe with you getting married now, you may start to wear more colors, my Lord. Give me more to work with, and I have tried for years."

Jasper shook his head. "I am perfection, and I have no need to change. Farrell get out a formal suit with tails, I need to look my best, and I need a shave."

Laurentia smiled and said, "It is nice to meet you, Mr. Farrell, and you do a splendid job in styling, Lord Bellator. I shall go downstairs now to greet our guests. I shall tell them you shall be down shortly. I love you." She walked to the door and blew Jasper a kiss.

As Laurentia walked out, Farrell said, "You are a lucky man, my Lord. She is beautiful, and I know now why your mood has changed to happier of late."

"Yes, she is my life now, and no turning back. Now go get my clothes, and I shall sit here to wait for my shave," Jasper said, the last part clipped with losing his patience waiting.

"Yes, my Lord." But he mumbled under his breath, "So testy at times."

Laurentia walked down the stairs finding that Drake had arrived first. He walked to the stairs and took her hand as she descended the last step.

Drake kissed Laurentia's hand, saying, "You look adorable tonight. If things do not work out for you and my brother, I would be more than happy to take his place, my Lady." He winked, so Laurentia knew he was only jesting, and she was getting used to his humor.

"I shall keep that in mind, my Lord." Then Laurentia laughed.

"Oh, how you wound my heart with your laugher, Lady Laurentia." Putting his hand on his chest, and he laughed also.

"Shall we go into the front parlor? Jasper shall be down shortly."

They walked into the parlor; one of the maids set up a sideboard with wine and a few liquors. Drake walked over, and he poured himself a brandy.

"Would you care for some wine, Lady Laurentia? I see Jasper has a white and red."

"Red would be lovely to sip on, for now, thank you."

Everett entered with a bow then announced, "The Duke and Duchess of Devonshire, Lady

Aroura and Lady Amara." He stepped aside to show them in.

Looking irritated, the duke said, "Everett, I believe everyone knows us here, and you may go."

Duchess walked across the room, greeted Laurentia, kissing her cheek and then Drake's. She wore a deep purple gown this evening.

Duchess asked, "Is Jasper unwell? Should I go to him and check on him?" Feeling worried, not seeing him in the room.

Laurentia answered, "No, he has just woken up from a nap. I woke him myself before coming down. He is dressing and shall be down shortly. He has reassured me he is alright to join us. Would you care for some wine or something stronger to drink?"

Duchess said, "The red shall be lovely. Is it your imports, Drake?"

"Yes, it's the burgundy you been enjoying of let, Mother," Drake pours a glass and hands it to her.

The duke came over and helped himself to brandy.

Amara was wearing a pale pink gown, and Aroura was wearing pale yellow. They both look lovely and very grown-up. The twins were allowed to go to this ball, because it was a pre-celebration of their brother's wedding.

Amara said, "Mother, may Aroura and I have some white wine, please?"

Duchess nodded. "Yes, but you need to sip on it."

They said in unison, "Oh yes, we shall," obviously excited to have some

Jasper walked in, and everyone watched him move as he entered. "Good evening, everyone, I trust your ride here was pleasant." He walked to Laurentia and kissed her cheek.

Duke said, "The night is cool; it shall be good for a ball this evening. How do you feel, Son?" Everyone was quiet as Jasper answered.

"I am a little stiff, but I should be fine for the evening." But he thought to himself, 'I hurt like hell, but I shall not let this ruin the night for Laurentia. Her happiness means too much to me.'

Duchess came over to him and pressed her hand to his forehead to check his temperature for fever. "You are not hot, that is a good sign." She reached up to kiss his cheek. She continued, "I do worry for you, as I do for all my children, so do not roll your eyes at me, Jasper." Then she went to a chaise to sit.

Jasper said, "Thank you for the concern, Mother; it is duly noted."

Everett announced that dinner was served, and the Duke and Duchess led the way, then Jasper escorted Laurentia, and then Drake put out both his arms for his sisters to take as he escorted them. The dining room in Jasper's London home had a table that sat ten people comfortably; tonight, it was seating seven. The food was served, and they made a light conversion throughout the meal. After finishing dinner, the family went back into the parlor for a brief time to wait for eight o'clock to go to the ball.

When it was time to leave, Jasper said, "We should be on our way, my love. To be fashionably late is my general statement, but seeing we are the honorees for tonight's ball. Aunt Louisa and Aunt Fantina would prefer we come at the start to be a part of the receiving line.

Laurentia said, "I am ready to dance and start to celebrate." She stands, smiling and highly excited for the ball.

Duke said, "Darling, are you ready to go celebrate that our firstborn is tying the knot."

Duchess said, "This ball is the highlight of the season. Louisa and Fantina have worked ever so hard all week at making it wonderful for their nephew's upcoming wedding celebration. All the family shall be there in their best, and the list of guests goes on a mile-long that are invited tonight."

Drake said, "I take it we are riding in two different coaches tonight?"

Jasper said, "Laurentia and I shall share my coach. You may ride with us, Drake, if you wish."

Duke said, "Sounds right. Your sisters shall ride with your mother and I."

Drake said, "Sounds like a plan lets us go by all means,"

Jasper kissed Laurentia's hand, then escorted her out to the awaiting coach. Laurentia had not seen Jasper's coach till now, for he preferred to ride a horse to most occasions if the weather was fine. She stopped to look it over a few feet away.

Jasper asked, "Is something wrong, Laurentia?"

"No, your coach is just so beautiful; it is so shiny. I'm sure I could see my reflection upon it."

"I only have the best, my love. I had Leopold build this for me last summer. He assured me it is one of the top models and has the most luxurious ever built."

The coach was black with a high gloss finish, with the family crest on the door. The interior was royal blue, with two brass lamps lit for the ride. A team of six black horses stood at the ready.

Laurentia was still taking in luxury before her. Finally, Jasper said, "Darling, we should step inside so that we may go."

"Yes, sorry, I just sometimes forget how wealthy you are. Let us continue."

"We are wealthy, is what you meant to say. Once we're married, everything I have shall be yours as well."

Laurentia smiled, "It can be overwhelming sometimes. I was raised well, but your wealth is beyond my experience."

"Is that a problem I may have to worry about, Lady Laurentia?"

She gave her grandest smile. "No, never, I love you so much; nothing could come between us, nothing. I shall get used to your wealth, as I have with your overbearing ways." She reached up and kissed him lightly.

Jasper stepped over to the coach and opened the door, saying with a grin, "Your chariot awaits, my love."

"Why, thank you, my Lord," she stepped in, still smiling.

Drake was waiting for the lovebirds to finish with their folly and wondered if he should ride his horse instead of riding with them.

Jasper saw that Drake was feeling uncomfortable. "Are you coming, dear Brother?"

"I'm giving a second thought of to taking my horse. Seeing this new side of you can be a bit much, Bellator."

Laurentia peeked her head out from the coach, "Lord Drake, we shall behave. Come and ride with us."

Jasper looked at Drake, "You would not want to disappoint Lady Laurentia. Come, we shall restrain ourselves with the short ride." Jasper stepped in first and sat by Laurentia taking her hand, and then Drake stepped in next, sitting across from them and closing the door.

Riding the short distance to Hanover Square took little time. Looking out the window, Aurora said, "Mother, look at the line of coaches in front of us. I bet there are at least twenty, and it is early."

Amara said with excitement, "Look behind us, Aurora; the line doesn't end."

Duchess said, "Now girls control yourselves, please. Tonight, is going to be a huge event, and I shall expect you to be on your best behavior."

Smiling most innocently, they said together, "Yes, Mother, we shall."

Meanwhile, in Jasper's coach, Laurentia looked out the window to the line in front of them. "How many people do you believe are coming tonight?"

Jasper said, "Over two hundred, something like that."

Drake said, "I could get out and walk to the door before we would arrive in this coach. This waiting one by one is a complete bore, and they need to move faster."

Jasper said, "You had better stay put. Mother would not be happy to see you walking by and not make an entrance with the rest of us. You know how she loves to shone with pride."

Drake sat back, "Damn family pride, gets in my way sometimes."

Smiling, Laurentia said, "Five more to go, and we are there. Then, all shall be well."

Jasper squeezed Laurentia's hand to say thanks for calming Drake and, she looked up and smiled; you are welcome.

Duke's coach was first to unload; he stepped out first to survey his surroundings and then turned back to the coach to hand out the Duchess and then his two daughters. They step forward to wait for Jasper, Laurentia, and Drake so that they could walk in together as a family.

The twins were restless, waiting to go in. The excitement was much to hold in; the Duchess gives them a look to please restrain themselves.

The next coach pulls up, Jasper's coach; he steps out first and helps Laurentia out next. Laurentia stepped a couple of feet from the coach to fluff her gown out, and then she looks up to see Jasper watching her with a smile on his face.

"You are perfection, my love. No one shall outshine you ever."

Laurentia smiled back, "Thank you, my Lord, for your kind words. I am ready to enter now."

"Lets' start the show, family," Drake said, grinning now in a much better mood from being out of the tight confined of the coach.

Duke turns to his duchess. "Parade time, my Darling."

Duchess said, "This never gets dull to do, not even after so many years."

Duke whispered to her, "I hope our children shall always feel the same." They walked on, nodding to the people of importance as they traveled to the front door. It was wide open so all the guests could pass through until they reached the butler, who announced each party or individuals at the staircase's top landing. The duke gave the butler a nod that he was ready to be announced with his duchess and daughters.

"The Duke and Duchess of Devonshire, with daughters Lady Aurora and Lady Amara."

They walked down the stairs to greet the host and hostess at the bottom. The duke shook his brother's hand, then said to Louisa, "This evening looks to have a grand start, Lady Louisa."

The duchess, right beside him, chimed in, "I agree, my Lady, everything looks lovely."

Louisa says, "I cannot take all the credit, as Lady Fantina and I worked together on all this. We are so pleased you let us have Lord Bellator and Lady Laurentia pre-wedding celebration ball here."

Duchess said, "I shall note to tell Lady Fantina when I see her too. I know my son and Lady Laurentia do appreciate all this tremendously, thank you."

Louisa smiled and said, "You're most welcome, your Grace."

Jasper and Laurentia were waiting to be introduced. Everyone was taking notice, for this was the first time, besides the ride in Hyde Park and the theater to see Lord Bellator with Lady Laurentia on his arm since the announcement in the papers.

The butler cleared his voice and announced, "I may present to you, Marquess Bellator and his betrothed Lady Laurentia." They stood together shining, looking like perfection.

Laurentia was beautiful, with her golden blonde hair cascading in ringlets down her back; the crystals down her skirt glittered as she walked. Jasper, with his raven black hair that touched his shoulders, plus his handsome polished features, was her perfect match. He wore an evening suit with tails, his only color of choice black, and a waistcoat in black with a subtle brocade paisley pattern with red silk thread, a crisp white shirt with white cravat perfectly knotted that enhanced his physique.

Jasper whispered, "Are you ready, my love, for all eyes are on us this evening."

Laurentia whispered, "Yes, I'm so thrilled about this."

"As am I, my love." They stepped down the stairs together in complete union as the new power couple, the one that would keep the ton's tongues wagging for years. As they stepped off the last step,

Charlton stepped forward to welcome them. "Ah, Lord Bellator, I'm glad to see you up and about, with what happen earlier today."

Jasper said, "I would never let Lady Laurentia down and miss the wedding celebration, and with all, you have done here to honor us this evening."

Louisa said, "You make sure you let me know if you need anything. I mean it."

Jasper kissed his aunt's cheek. "Yes, dear Aunt, I shall, not to worry."

Laurentia said, "Your home looks lovely tonight, thank you for all this."

Louisa said, "I love to entertain, and this is what family does, so welcome to the family Lady Laurentia."

Laurentia said, "Thank you. Would you like for us to join the receiving line here?"

Charlton said, "You may go in and enjoy yourself; this line shall go for some time."

Laurentia looked up to Jasper, then he said, "Come, my Lady, you have many to meet this evening." Jasper nodded a thank you to his uncle and aunt. Then, Jasper escorted Laurentia into the half-filled ballroom with the London ton and with more to come.

As they walked into the ballroom, they could hear the orchestra tuning their instruments on a stage to the room's front left. Jasper surveyed the room, seeing so many familiar faces, then he saw Leopold and Sterling walking toward them.

Leopold said, "Bellator, you look dapper tonight, and a little color I see in your attire. Very nice. Lady Laurentia, you look stunning." He took her free hand, bowing over top of it and kissing.

Laurentia said, "Thank you. The ballroom looks wonderful, does it not?"

Leopold answered, "Mother and Aunt Fantina have been here working for two days or more. They can accomplish any task at hand so easily."

Sterling bowed and kissed Laurentia's hand, saying, "I'm glad the earlier tragic event that happens today hasn't stopped this evening celebration here. Mother and Aunt Louisa would have perished in disappointment if this night did not go on as planned."

Jasper said, "It shall take more than a gunshot wound to stop me from marrying this weekend."

Leopold said, "In here, they are serving wine and champagne. In the card room, I could get you something stronger for your pain, Cousin."

Jasper said, "I shall keep that in mind for later if I need it, thank you." His honest thoughts, 'I could use that now, but I must keep a stiff upper lip.'

Laurentia looked around the room, and she saw Fantina and Gabrielle coming over. Fantina said in her heavy French accent, "Lord Bellator, how do you feel? Is there anything I may get for you? Lady Laurentia, your gown tis exquisite just as you are."

Laurentia said, "Thank you, and everything looks so wonderful in here. I do like the color violet you use throughout the room and flowers."

Fantina said, "That was Lord Bellator's request for you."

Looking impassive, Jasper smiled down at Laurentia then said, "Looking into your beautiful violet eyes when we first met was when I knew we were meant to be. So, I suggested the color."

Gabrielle said, "No, you demanded that is to be the color of the ballroom décor, as I remember right, my Lord."

Laurentia laughed lightly, for they did not hold back at each other, regardless of rank in this family.

Jasper raised an eyebrow at Laurentia, laughing. "Are you laughing that they do not care about my rank and are bold to call one out on the matter of simple words, my love?"

Laurentia tried to stop laughing, "Yes, my love, it is amusing, is it not?" They all laughed together but Jasper.

"Believe me, only my family should get away with bad etiquette when I am the jest in this case," Jasper said, still not looking amused.

Leopold said, smirking, "Yes, no one dares otherwise. It is true."

The dowager duchess walked over, wanting to know what was so funny, her companion Miss Evans beside her. Gabrielle kissed her grandmother's cheek then told her the jest on Jasper's account.

The dowager duchess said, "Bellator, my dear boy, loosen up some. Laughter is a wonderful tool, even when the joke is on you."

Jasper said with an impassive face, "Yes, I can see

that. Thank you for enlightening me."

The dowager duchess asked, "How is the shoulder faring now and do not patronize me, Grandson."

Jasper said with his stern stance, "There is a hole through my left shoulder; it does hurt like hell if you must know the truth of it."

Dowager duchess looked Jasper over, "Huh, so you are telling me the reason you are here is for your beautiful bride, and you are not letting her down."

"Precisely, we've been through too much to stop our plans to be together, end of the story."

Everyone in the circle was used to Jasper's bluntness, and grandmother Raventon had the same personality as him. So that is where he has received most of it from; they all realize that years ago, and his grandmother admires it.

Dowager stepped forward and reached out to touch his face. "Bellator, you have made me truly proud with all your accomplishments throughout the years. It warms this old lady's heart to hear you found love, and you shall make a fine Duke one day, I know it. The music is going to start soon, do enjoy these times."

Jasper kissed his grandmother's cheek, "Thank you, Grandmother, that does mean a lot to me. I do wish Grandfather could be here tonight with us. I know he would approve of Lady Laurentia as my bride."

She nodded, then looked to Laurentia and said, "Our Jasper resembles my late husband, Randolph, and I know he has the same heart as him. God rest his soul. I can see the love in your eyes for my grandson, and I do approve of your two unions. Shall we start celebrating?"

Laurentia said, "I say we are both lucky women to have found the perfect gentleman and love. I shall take care of Lord Bellator, not to worry."

The dowager said, "Good to hear, child, and now I see a nice cushion chair over there. You children need to start dancing. Miss Evans, shall we move on?"

Miss Evan says, "Yes, Your Grace, I am right behind you." They walked to the other side of the room to the chair, set up for her comfort.

"I adore your grandmother. She reminds me of someone dear to me." Laurentia said, smiling up at Jasper.

"It seems she likes you too, which means a lot to me. The first dance shall be a waltz, and we were told to start dancing. Shall we, my Love?"

"How could I say no, for if I do remember right, you have told me once that all my waltzes belong to you."

Jasper smiled, "Yes, that is true, and that shall still stand, even after we are married, my Love."

Laurentia smiled back, "You do the waltz divinely, my Lord. As long as that does not change, I shall be good with accepting that."

Jasper put his arm out, and Laurentia took it. They were the first on the dance floor, waiting for the music to start.

Leopold said as he watched Jasper and Laurentia walk away, "I do hope I do not turn into that someday."

Gabrielle said, "Whatever do you ever mean, dear Cousin?"

"Those two. Do you not see it?" Leopold said, gesturing his hand in Jasper and Laurentia's direction.

Gabrielle said with a smile, "I do, and it is lovely."

Leopold saw over his cousin's shoulder, his mother heading his way with a young lady by her side. He thought fast, then asked Gabrielle, "Would you care to dance the first set with me, dear Cousin?"

Before Gabrielle could answer, Leopold, grabbed her hand, then said, "Good, let's go." Pulling her onto the middle of the dance floor as many others walked out and around them.

Once on the floor, Gabrielle said, "What was the hurry about, Leopold? I was going to say yes."

"My mother was the realization to hurry. She was heading this way with a young lady to try to push her on me again."

Gabrielle looked over her shoulder in the direction Leopold was looking. "Oh, that is Lady Evalena Patterson. It is her third season, and her father is an earl."

Leopold said resentfully, "She shall be number three I had to derail so far tonight. Just because Jasper is marrying Sunday, mother thinks it is my turn next. I am not ready for that any time soon. No, thank you. I like my life as it is, and I do not understand why others think differently. I am too busy with my company and so on."

Gabrielle said, "Just tell her that then."

Leopold said, "That's like telling a young child that there is no more cake for you, and they keep after you for some more. Get my picture, Gabrielle? God, help me, please." Then, the music started, and they took a turn around the floor.

Gabrielle said, "I do not know what to say, but you are safe this time."

"Thank the heavens. Let us set fire to the dance

floor, shall we, and I shall figure out later how to handle mother." They glide across the floor. One thing was for sure, all the Raventon men and women could dance divinely.

Jasper was holding Laurentia close as the music started. "Is this hurting your shoulder to hold me and dance? We could sit out, and it is alright if we do." Laurentia looked up at him, hoping for a true answer.

Jasper looked down into her beautiful violet eyes, "It hurts me more when I am not holding you, my Love."

"Please be serious. I do not want to be the cause of your pain."

They moved on the floor as the music started. "Darling, I'm fine as long as I have you close; my pain goes away, breathing in your scent. You are my healer."

"Promise you shall tell me when you need to rest or sit down a spell. I mean it, Jasper; I want you well."

Jasper put his index finger under her chin to make her look up at him, "Laurentia, I shall tell you if I need a rest. Stop with the worrying, please."

"You worried me earlier telling your grandmother you hurt so. Is it true, the pain?"

They glided around the floor, some more. "Yes, I hurt, darling. I did get shot today, but I do have a big pain threshold. I am fine right now. Come, let us show all how well we dance together." Jasper spun Laurentia around and around until she giggled, and that was music to Jasper's ears.

The music stopped in the ballroom, and the first

set had finished. The Duke of Devonshire with the Duchess stepped onto the orchestra stage, and the room fell silent.

"My Duchess and I want to welcome everyone for coming this evening to help celebrate my eldest son, Marquess Bellator, and Lady Laurentia Sinclair's upcoming wedding that shall be held on Sunday." Everyone looks at the couple and claps their hands.

Duke continued, "I also want to thank my two sister-in-law's Lady Louisa and Lady Fantina, for putting this ball together to honor my children. Thank you." The two women nodded their heads in acknowledgment.

All at once, trays of champagne were carried out by servants; everyone in the room was to take a glass. The duke looked around the room to make sure all-in attendance had a drink.

Duke continues, "I now want to make a toast to my son and his betrothed Lady Laurentia." He raised his glass. "I wish them both a long, happy marriage, to have many children and to have an heir. It makes my Duchess and I proud to know they have found true love as we have. To Marquess Bellator and Lady Laurentia." He and the duchess raised their glasses and took a drink as everyone followed.

Jasper took a sip then said, "Thank you, Father and Mother."

Duke then said, "Let the music start again and the dancing to continue, enjoy all." He took the duchess's hand, and they stepped off the stage together.

Jasper and Laurentia walked over to his parents as they stepped down from the stage.

Jasper said, "That was well-received. Thank you. I now want to walk around and introduce Lady Laurentia to all. If you shall excuse us."

Duchess said, "Have fun, my loves. Conrad, I see a few people I must say hello to over there. If you would excuse me, I shall catch up with you later."

The duke was left standing alone, thinking that his family would never change, and then again, he thought he would never want them to. He then felt a pat on his shoulder. "Devonshire, it has been a long time. How are you?" It was his longtime friend Marquess of Dorset. They had been friends since their days at Eton together.

Duke said, "Yes, it has. Where have you been hiding yourself these days? I am pleased you have come this evening." They chatted, catching up with new and old news.

Jasper and Laurentia were stopped every two feet as they moved through the crowded ballroom. Jasper introduced her to all that she had not met yet to congratulate and well-wares on their upcoming wedding day.

Lucas appeared, "Ah, dear Sister, I thought I would never reach you before the night was done. I do not think you could fit another person in this residence. Good evening, Lord Bellator."

Laurentia kissed Lucas's cheek, "Yes, it seems that all the ton has come here tonight, quite a crush, as one would say."

Jasper said, "We are glad you came; do enjoy yourself."

Lucas said, "Thank you, have you seen your cousin Victor or your brother Drake about? I am hoping they would introduce me to a couple of ladies so that I could dance a few sets."

Jasper decided to help him; he saw a lovely young lady he knew moving her way through the crowded room near them.

Jasper stopped her, "Lady Rowena."

She stopped and smiled. "Yes, my Lord. Oh, I have not had the honor of meeting your betrothed." She curtsied to them.

Jasper said, "No, you have not. Lady Rowena, this is Lady Laurentia, and my love, this is Lady Rowena Seymore; her family has an Estate near mine in Kent.

Laurentia said, "It is a pleasure to meet you, my Lady."

Lady Rowena said, "And you. You are the luckiest lady of the ton, for so many hearts have been broken knowing Lord Bellator is off the market."

Jasper cut in, saying, "Lady Rowena, I like you to meet Earl of Berwickshire; he is Lady Laurentia's only brother. Plus, he is a new face among the ton. I thought perhaps you would be so good to introduce him around, being you know so many of our friends here tonight."

Lucas took her hand, bowed over it as he kissed it, "I am charmed to make your acquaintance, my Lady."

Lady Rowena's eyes lit up, being also charmed. "I am delighted to meet you, my Lord. It would be my pleasure to introduce you to a few of my friends. So, you are new to London, being we have not met before?"

Jasper led Laurentia away from them. "He shall meet at least half the ton tonight through Lady Rowena. She is such a chatter bug if one likes that."

Laurentia smiles at Jasper, "Thank you for doing that. What title does her father hold?"

"Her father is an earl also, a nice family and good neighbors."

Drake walked over with Kelsey and Leopold, and they formed a circle.

Drake said, "Lady Laurentia, would you honor me in the next dance?"

Laurentia said, "I would, shall we?"

Drake put his arm out for her to take, and then they went out onto the floor together and waited for everyone to take their place for the next set to start. The others found their partners, leaving Leopold along with Jasper.

Leopold said, "Thanks to you; mother is on this crusade to bring all the eligible women to me tonight, parading them to me as she thinks I should be marrying soon too. Which I am not, Cousin."

Jasper smirked, "Sorry, it was not my intention for that to happen to you."

Leopold sighed, "No, you probably did not. So how is your shoulder faring now?"

"Not that bad."

"Sorry, Bellator, I never saw that coming today."

"Neither did I. I never saw the man before today."

Jesse walked over to join them. "Who had you not seen before?"

Jasper answered, "The shooter today."

Jesse said, "When you left the range, I found out that the shooter was Hughes's younger brother. He had been hanging around there, asking about the Raventon family and mostly about you."

Jasper said, "Too bad, and we did not know this

sooner. I could have been spared a hole in my shoulder, and I would not have killed the man today."

Leopold said in alarm, "It's time for me to go. Mother is heading this way again with another chit for me to meet, see you later." Leopold dashed away, going the opposite direction of his mother as she was coming near.

Jesse asked, "What was that about?"

Jasper answered quickly, "Aunt Louisa all evening has been trying to introduce the eligible ladies of the ton to Leopold tonight, believing he is ready to marry. Which you can see he is not."

Jesse laughed, then said, "Poor chap." Then they laughed together, watching Leopold escaping his mother once again. They stopped laughing when Louisa reached them.

Louisa asked, "Where did Leopold just go off to? He was just here talking with you both."

Jasper said impassively, "Leopold said he had an urgent matter to take care of and went through there," waving his hand in the direction, Leopold fled.

Jesse said, "Leopold was in the most hurry to correct his problem, my Lady." Meaning his mother.

Lady Louisa looked in the direction that was indicated, then back to Jasper and Jesse. "Urgent matter, huh, I'm sure. I do not know why he has been dodging me all night. Come Lady Noleen, and we shall go around this way. Leopold is a delight once you meet him." Louisa looked back over her shoulder as she walked away, not amused with the answer she received from Jasper and Jesse.

Jesse said, "Glad, it's not me in Leopold's shoes right now. Is that your two sisters dancing over there?"

Jasper looked in the direction Jesse indicated, taking his eyes off Laurentia, gliding around the floor.

"Yes, her Grace, let them come this evening for it is my wedding celebration. Next year they shall make their formal come-out."

Jesse smiled. "They sure look most grown-up tonight, lovely if you ask me. What are they, fifteen now?"

Jasper said menacingly, "They are my sisters, Jesse. Watch yourself, and yes, they are fifteen."

"My apologies, I just have not seen them for a while. They are too young for me, and I would never step over our friendship for them."

"Good to hear that. I hope none of these gentlemen here tonight do think it is alright to call on them tomorrow. Father shall have some heads rolling, for they are not out yet."

Still watching them dancing, Jesse thought, 'the twins shall definitely be breaking gentlemen's hearts next year.'

Laurentia came back after her dance set with Drake, her cheeks flushed.

Jasper said, "My love, it looks as if you could use something cool to drink. Shall we go into the refreshment salon?"

"That would be lovely, and maybe we could find a place to have a seat and rest." But, of course, the rest part was for him, but she would not say that out loud.

They journeyed into the next room, finding a large table set up with little cakes, biscuits, and an array of different beverages. As they walked up to the table, Jasper saw someone he was hoping to see this evening.

"I would like you to meet a friend of the family." They walked up to a slender woman with brown curly hair around her face. She recognized Jasper when he walked to her beside the long table.

Jasper greeted her, "Miss Jane, I am glad you join us this evening. I would like you to meet my betrothed. Miss Jane, this is Lady Laurentia. Lady Laurentia, this is Miss Jane Austin."

Jane curtsied to Jasper and Laurentia, saying, "I am pleased to meet you, my Lady."

Laurentia said, "How wonderful to meet you. I have read your books, and I enjoyed them tremendously."

"Thank you, I am glad that you like them, and they bring joy to your life."

"Lord Bellator had mentioned when we first met that he knew you when he saw I was reading one of your books, and the next day, he gave me his copies of the ones I have not read yet. He did not know then how I enjoy reading as a pastime, that giving books is better for me than receiving flowers." Laurentia laughed at the end part she said.

Jane laughed too, then said, "I believe I would like a book rather than flowers as well, my Lady, how true."

Jasper felt lost in their laughter. "Lady Laurentia, what would you care to drink?"

Laurentia caught her breath from laughing, "I would like champagne since we are celebrating getting married on Sunday."

Jasper handed a glass of champagne to Laurentia, gave one to Jane, and picked one up for himself. He toasted, "Here is to the start of a long, wonderful life together with my love."

Laurentia clinked her glass to Jasper, saying, "And many years of loving marriage bliss."

Jane lifted her glass, "I drink to the new couple that I see before me; I wish good health, happiness, and longevity together."

Leopold came from one direction, Drake, Victor, and Jesse came from another direction. They all said in unison, "Here-here, I shall drink to that too." They lifted a glass also, and they took a drink together. Kelsey, Sterling, and Lucas came into the room next, seeing the group gathered near the refreshment table.

Lucas said, "What have we missed? It looks to be something of good spirit."

More people gathered around them, Gabrielle, Aurora, and Amara.

Laurentia said, "We just made a toast to us."

Lucas said, "Well, I have one for you then. To my lovely sister, Lady Laurentia, and her betrothed Lord Bellator. I wish you many years of contentment and love." They all toasted to that and drank.

Jasper said, "Thank you, everyone, for your toast to us. I know I speak for both of us, saying we are truly blessed for having a supportive family and friends like the ones I see before me." The group was laughing and talking together, almost forgetting the ball was in the other room, still going on at full speed. Then, finally, the duke and duchess walked in together.

Duchess said, "I was wondering where the Raventon children had all made off to."

Duke said, "I had a feeling they were in here, from hearing all the laughter they created when you are gathered together."

Drake said, "Yes, we do have a jolly time together."

Leopold said, "I did not get a toast in earlier. So, I'm going to make this toast to all of us. May we stand strong as a family forever and a jouissance life." So, they all toasted to that.

Duchess said, "Leopold, your mother was looking for you not long ago. She said it seems you are avoiding her. Those were her words."

Leopold said casually, "No, Your Grace, I have not. I believe we just have not crossed paths tonight, is all.". Jasper, Jesse, Drake, Victor, Sterling, Kelsey, and Gabrielle all laughed together, knowing the truth behind what Leopold just said.

Laurentia whispered to Jasper, "What is so funny that I'm missing?"

Jasper bent his head to the side, then whispered back, "The jest is that Leopold has been running scared all night from Aunt Louisa. She wants him to marry now because I am. Whenever you see my Aunt, she has an eligible young lady on her arm trying to hunt Leopold down. It has been like a cat and mouse game all night for Leopold, and he is the mouse, no doubt."

Laurentia said, "I have been missing this. It is funny, I can tell by the look on Leopold's face."

Jasper laughed. "Yes, very much so. He has been going quite insane about it this evening."

"He has not found the right one, is all. Give him time."

"Raventon, men like to do their own hunting for a lifetime mate, you cannot push us, or we shall dig our heels in the dirt and not be moved an inch."

"Poor Leopold, he does not seem ready for that next step."

Jasper kissed Laurentia's hand, "Exactly right."

The supper bell rang, then they all walked in the correct order to the next room that had been set up with a buffet of food. Knowing how much Laurentia enjoyed Jane Austen's books, Jasper arranged it with his aunt that the author would be seated next to Laurentia.

They dined and chatted at a large table, and laughter was all around them. After the supper hour, Jasper and Laurentia walked back into the ballroom, where the orchestra was ready to play again. Jasper was starting to show he was in pain; Laurentia could see the strain on his face.

"My Lord, we may leave now if you wish. I can see the pain you are feeling."

"Perhaps a shot of whiskey from the card room would soothe the pain I'm feeling now," Jasper suggested.

Leopold said, "I shall go to fetch that for you and be right back, dear Cousin."

Laurentia said, "Thank you, Leopold." Jesse and Victor stayed with Jasper and Laurentia, just if he needed assistance, but they knew he was too proud to ask for help. The music started again; the floor was filled with couples dancing.

Jasper said to Victor, "You have not danced with Lady Laurentia yet."

Victor said, "No, I haven't. Perhaps Lady Laurentia, would you care to dance?"

Laurentia looked to Jasper, wanting to stay by his side, but he nodded for them to go. Then, looking back to Victor, she said, "Yes, I do like this tune they are playing. So shall we take a spin on the floor?"

Victor put his arm out for her to take, and they

were off onto the dance floor.

Jasper said to Jesse, "My pain level is quite high; I do not want Laurentia to worry."

Jesse said, "We all can see you are not at your best right now. Is there something I could do for you?"

Jasper shook his head no. Leopold came back with a bottle and three glasses; he gave one to Jasper and Jesse. Leopold poured the whiskey.

"I thought we could all use some as well. Cheers." They clinked their glasses together and drank it down fast, feeling the burning as it hit their stomachs.

Jesse said, "Thanks, that hit the spot."

Leopold asked Jasper, "Would you like another shot for the pain you are feeling? You look as if your pain has spiked." Leopold knew Jasper well, and he could tell what he was feeling and did not need to ask, just as Jasper could do the same with Leopold.

Jasper said, "I could use one more glass, thanks." Leopold poured another for Jasper and him, plus offered more to Jesse, but he declined.

Jasper drank it down in one big gulp. "That should do the trick for now." He put his glass on a tray as a servant was walking by, as did the others. The night spun on, with the celebration and dancing. Jasper never let on about his pain to Laurentia; he would not let it ruin the night's fun and to let her worry. So, he worked harder on his facial expressions to not let his shield fall anymore that night. He had years of training at the craft.

At one in the morning, Jasper and Laurentia traveled back to Grosvenor Square. She would be staying there and did not care what the proper etiquette was for a gently raised Lady. Jasper was hurt; she would remain by his side.

Laurentia yawned, "That was quite a night we had and so much fun." Laurentia sat on Jasper's right side; he had his arm around her holding her close.

"I'm glad you enjoyed the evening, my Love. It certainly was a crush. My two Aunts shall be the talk of the ton for weeks to come." He kissed the top of her head.

The coach stopped in front of Jasper's residence, and a groom jumped down from the coach to open the door for them. Jasper stepped out first, surveying his surroundings before he helped Laurentia out of the coach.

Everett opened the door as they hit the top step. "Good morning, my Lord and my Lady."

Jasper said as he walked in with Laurentia, "Is there anything I need to know about before I retired for the night?"

Everett answered, "Just a reminder that Mr. Turner and Earl Berwickshire shall be in your library at ten for a meeting you have scheduled. Everything in the household is running smoothly, my Lord."

Jasper said, "If that is all, Everett, you may retire yourself."

Everett bowed, "As you wish, my Lord." Then he was off down the corridor, leaving them alone.

Jasper said, "Shall we go to bed, my Love?"

"Yes, I'm ready; it has been a long day."

Her words were music to Jasper's ears as they went up the stairs together. He would love to be able to scoop her up and carry her to his room as he had dreamed for weeks, but this damn wound in his shoulder says that was not happening today.

Laurentia said when they stepped to the top landing. "I shall go to my room first to take my gown off and send Sandra to bed. Then I shall come to your bedchamber afterward, my Jasper."

He grabbed her tightly, then kissed her demandingly, hinting at what would come next when she came to him. He then trailed kisses down her neck and then back to her lips with so much passion.

Jasper broke the kiss, then said, "Do not keep me waiting long."

Laurentia tried to catch her breath from Jasper's seductive embrace and kiss. "I never, my love."

Jasper kissed her one more time before he released her, and they walked to their rooms. When Laurentia shut the door, she laid against the closed door to steady herself.

Sandra came out of the dressing room and saw her mistress standing there. Sandra stepped closer to Laurentia, holding a candle to see if she was alright, then asked. "How was your evening, my Lady?"

"Simply wonderful, so many people wanted to meet me, the ballroom was decorated so beautifully as the rest of the home too, and we laughed, danced, and drank so merrily. I shall never forget this night."

"How did Lord Bellator do this evening with his injury?"

"He kept telling me he was fine, but I knew better he was hurting. He made it through and now wants me to come to him in his bedchamber. So, let's get me out of this gown, shall we?"

"Come, we should not keep his Lordship waiting long."

Twenty minutes later, she was sitting at her dressing table. Sandra had just finished taking her hair down and brushed it out, and Laurentia dabbed a little more perfume on before leaving her room.

In just her shift, she stood then said, "You may go to bed now. I shall see you in the morning, Sandra."

Laurentia took a deep breath for courage, for she had never gone to a gentleman's chamber dressed in only her undergarments on. She picked up a silk robe, put it on, and tied the belt around her. That's better, she thought, just in case she crosses paths with someone else in the hallway. Picking up the candle left on her dressing table, she walked to the door, opened it, and looked out to see if someone is out there but saw no one. She walked to Jasper's door, wondering if she should knock or just go in. She opted just to go in, as maybe someone would hear her knock beside Jasper. Turning the handle, she pushed the door open then only stuck her head in to look around first. There was no movement in the room nor no one standing around. Good, she thought Jasper must have sent Farrell to bed as she has with Sandra.

Laurentia now walked into the room and saw Jasper lying on his massive bed that he said he just purchased for them. He was lying there nude with only his shoulder bandage with a bit of blood seeping through, with the covers pulled down, waiting for her. Laurentia just stared down at him, thinking, 'God has made a masterpiece before me, and he is all mine. I still cannot believe Jasper had made it through the evening by looking at that bandage the way it looks and telling me it does not hurt, he's okay. My warrior.'

Laurentia wet her lips, "Darling, I'm here." Nothing. His eyes did not move at all. She said louder this time. "Jasper, my love, I have come to you." Nothing again, not even a twitch. So, she put the candle on the night table beside the bed then crawled onto the bed. She sat beside him though, 'I do not believe I took that long to come to him. He looks peaceful, sleeping like an angel, but I would not say he's an angel to his face when he is awake, that is.' She giggled and caught herself from laughing, not to wake him. Tonight, must have exhausted himself because she knew well Jasper would have wake up right now with her sitting in just her shift in his bed-chamber on his bed. She bent down to kiss his fore-head, still no movement. I shall just snuggle in and get some sleep. She reached down, pulled the covers up over them, and laid down beside him. She snug-gled right up to him, laying her head onto his good shoulder, then said, "Good night, my Love," and went to sleep, pressing her body to his warmth.

Chapter 39

Jasper woke up to feeling a female's warm, soft body pressing against him. He could smell her honeysuckle scent and thought, 'my Laurentia all warm and sweetness beside me.' He heard the clock on the fireplace mantle chime to 6:00 am. His thought's still turning in his head, 'I must have fallen to sleep before Laurentia came in, damn it to hell. Our first time in my bed, and I fall asleep before she came in. I dreamed of this since the first time I kissed her in the garden. Oh, how I must have disappointed my Laurentia when she came to me. Well, that can be rectified right now.'

He rolled her gently off him and lay her onto her back. She made a soft sigh but still slept. Jasper moved over the top of her, kissing down her neck, pushing her shift up her body so he could feel her skin next to his, then dragged it up over her head and tossed it to the floor. Laurentia woke up, letting out a sound like the coo of a dove.

"Good morning, my love. I did love the feeling of finding you asleep beside me when I woke up this morning. But now it is my job to make up for falling asleep on you before you came in."

Jasper kissed Laurentia, deep and demanding. Then he trailed his tongue all around the inside of her mouth then licked her bottom lip.

He whispered in her ear, "I am going to pleasure your body and make you beg for more, my Sweet." He considered his words, then corrected himself, saying, "No, you should never beg for anything, my love, just tell me what you want, and I shall give it to you always." He smiled against her ear, feeling more satisfied with his words, and kissed down her neck.

Laurentia's body was singing with lust for him, from hearing Jasper's seductive words. "I am all yours. Take me to paradise, my Jasper."

Hearing his name from Laurentia's lips has fueled Jasper on fire, even more, to give her the paradise she asked for, and he knew just how to take them there. His hands were on her breast, and he cupped one perfect globe. Then with the tip of his tongue, he licked her nipple, gliding his tongue around and around, flicking the nipple and then sucking it hard between his lips. That about raised Laurentia off the bed, making her pant and grab the bed sheet beside her. Jasper moved to the other breast, doing the same, licking, sucking, running his tongue all around her nipple again and again. He liked her response from that; he trailed kisses down her ribs slowly to her navel. He stopped there, circling his tongue around it. Jasper said in his sedative voice,

"Your skin is so soft and sweet-tasting; now I need to taste your womanhood, my love."

Jasper went down between Laurentia's legs, pushing them wide open, so he could make her yell with pleasure and make her whole body shiver by the touch of his very talented tongue. He spread her with his fingers, then inserted one finger inside her to feel her wetness for him, and pulls it out. He liked that she was wet for him, so he took his tongue and tasted her, running his tongue all around inside her and sucking her juice like it was nectar from a peach.

"Oh, Jasper," she cried as he made his magical moves on her. He licked her little nub over and over, making her pant even more. She moved her head side to side, feeling the building up of the flutter below. He licked and licked, Laurentia yelled out.

"OOOOH JASPER Yessss." And her body came hard for him, as her body quivering and shaking in bliss.

Jasper moved quickly on top of Laurentia and looked into her eyes. Then, in one swift plunge, he was inside of her and stopped, feeling her tightness around his rock-hard penis. He loved the feel of them as one.

"My love, you feel so good with me inside of you, so tight you are. You are mine only, mine to love and touch."

Laurentia sighed, trying to make words from what he just did to her and now feeling the pleasure of them as one. "Yes, I am yours, my love, only yours, we are as one. Take me over the edge, Jasper. Oh, how I need you."

On that command, Jasper took her lips, kissing wildly. He moved slowly at first so they could feel each other smooth and slow. She was still so wet they could feel and hear it as he moved in and out. The rhythm was sweet and so good. Jasper moved faster, pumping. He was holding on till Laurentia was ready to come with him again. She had her legs wrapped around him as he rode her hard.

"Come with me, Laurentia. Let's take that edge together."

She felt it building, and the building then yelled out in ecstasy. "Oh Jasper, I'm There Let Us Fly...."

Jasper pumps more; he fills her with his seed, he yells. "I'm With You Baby All The Way So So gooood," He collapsed on top of her, patting.

Jasper then rolled over to his back, taking Laurentia with him, so they were lying in each other's arms, patting in a pool of sweat.

Laurentia giggled in delight, hugging him.

"I do love your delightful little giggles, knowing I made them."

"Oh, you definitely made them, and that was so wonderfully good. How long before we can do that again, my love?"

Jasper lifted a little to look down at her but did not pull out of her yet. "You are a little minx." He kissed her nose and smiled.

Laurentia smiled back, then said, still smiling, "Well, how long?"

"Laurentia, a male body, needs some time to recharge, but with you not long, not long at all. We both have a lot to do today, for our big day tomorrow. To think finally one more day, and you will be my Marchioness Bellator. I do like the sound of that."

"I would never have guessed by coming for a job interview; I would have met the man I am to marry and spend the rest of my life. But, if I remember correctly, I did tell you I had other plans, and here we are."

Jasper laughed. "Yes, after we made love the first time, I do remember you were telling me that was nice, and you were thanking me. Then you told me your plans for traveling when you receive your trust at twenty-five. You should know I have written into our marriage contract's paperwork that you shall keep the trust fund money and do with it as you please. I have more than enough money for us to live on in a grand style, which I'll share with you before. The rest of your endowment shall come to me, and later we shall set that up for our children to have a future income."

Laurentia smiled, "That was bad of me to try and dismiss you after we made love. I thought you were just dallying with me, is all."

"Oh, I was not going anywhere. I knew you were the one, and I wanted to marry you. So I had to continue seducing you and make you mine."

"I am glad you did; I do love you."

"I love you." He kissed her tenderly. "My love, do you like the plans I made for your dowry and trust fund?"

"Yes, that sounds lovely for the endowment, being your heir shall receive all your wealth, that our other children shall have money from me. Do you know the amount I'm receiving from my trust?"

He said with an impassive look, "Yes, I do."

"It is a lot of money. You do not want it?"

"No, you may shop with it or even donate some to charities if you wish. Darling, between what I have made in personal investments through the years and profits from my Estates, I'm a wealthy man. We have plenty to live on in an exceptionally grand style.

"I never have asked you how wealthy are you. May I ask?"

"With all my Estates, stocks, and other investments, I have."

Laurentia cut him off, "You may stop there. I believe you; it sounds like more than enough, as you said. You seem to have done well with investments you made, and with your Estates, you are rich."

"We have enough is the correct answer, and I am ready again to make love to my very future wife." He had that wicked smile on which she loved so much.

Laurentia smiled, kissed Jasper tenderly, "I too, I'm very ready. future husband." She giggled then said, "It's about time."

Jasper said, laughing, "So demanding are we." They kissed long and passionately and did not roll out of bed until half-past eight.

Later that morning, Jasper and Laurentia walked into the dining room together to break their fast. Laurentia said, "It seems strange for just the two of us to share our morning meal and not have the rest of your family here with us."

Jasper took the chair at the head of the table then said, "I think this is quite nice, just the two of us, Darling." He lifted her hand, kissed it, then leaned over and kissed her lips tenderly.

Laurentia said, "Mmmm, I see your point now, and I do like it too. I am worried we might have hurt your shoulder earlier, doing you know. Although I must admit, I had forgotten you were wounded yesterday when you overwhelmed me with your special skills."

Jasper thought it was cute how she was talking of their lovemaking upstairs minutes ago with servants around.

"My love, I'm faring much better than yesterday. I believe with the good night's rest I received last night made a world of difference for me. Plus, waking up finding delectable you beside me in my bed was better than any remedy, believe me. Stop worrying, my love, please." Jasper kissed her hand and smiled into her eyes. Laurentia nodded yes, gazing back at Jasper.

Once they had their food, Jasper asked, "What time shall Mother's coach be picking you up this morning?"

Laurentia sipped her tea, then answered, "Ten, we have many last-minute tasks to do before tomorrow, our big day," she smiled.

"I can only imagine how much you have to do, my love. I have a meeting with your brother and my secretary at ten. Then I have some last-minute errands to do myself this afternoon."

"Sandra and I shall stay at your parents' home tonight, after the dinner party. I shall leave most of what was brought here yesterday."

Jasper frowned, "My love, I prefer to have you here with me. I adored how you took on the task yourself and changed my bandage to my shoulder this morning. Do not tell me you believe in bad luck if I see you before our wedding." He shook his head in disbelief.

"Of course, I do. I shared that with you the other day. After tomorrow we shall have the rest of our life together. And do not come to me through the wall tonight, either."

Jasper bit his sausage, then chewed unhappily. "I suppose one night shall not kill me to be apart from you. It was only that this morning waking up and having you beside me in my bed was true happiness."

Laurentia tried not to laugh at him, for he was almost pouting like a little boy. "You shall survive tonight without me." Laurentia finished eating and was now sipping her tea.

"I guess I shall have to, and it may be lonely." Laurentia could not hold back anymore, and she laughed at him for sounding in such despair.

Jasper raised an eyebrow. "Are you laughing at me, Lady Laurentia?"

Laughing still, "Yes, my Lord, I am. You are very much acting like a child not getting his way."

Jasper sat up straighter in his chair then said, looking smug, "I do not think so. You shall miss being in my arms tonight, and then we shall see who is laughing, my dear."

Laurentia stood, "It is one night, and then we shall be together for the rest of our life. I have to go now and get ready for your mother to come and fetch me." She bent and kissed him softly on the lips and walked out of the room, not looking back.

Jasper watched her go. 'Laurentia is feeling extremely comfortable around me now to be so bold. I like her being that saucy, and it is definitely arousing.' He watched her hips sway as she walked down the corridor.

Jasper finished eating then went to his library, still thoughts on Laurentia. I shall have to bring her wedding present to dinner tonight and hope we can have a moment alone when I give it to her.

When Jasper entered the room, he found Turner already there going through paperwork.

Tuner looked up, then stood and bowed, saying. "Good morning, my Lord. I trust you slept well. How is your shoulder faring this morning?"

Jasper went to his desk and sat. "All is well this morning, Turner, thank you. My betrothed's brother should be here any minute now, and we can finish the dowry business in hand. Then if you have anything else of importance to go over estate's matters and so on, we shall do that next after I excuse the Earl. After tomorrow, I shall be gone for two weeks on my honeymoon, so let's make the most of this meeting."

"Yes, I have all in order here what we need to go over, my Lord."

"Good, I have a few calls I must attend to when we finish."

A short time later, Lucas arrived with his secretary Gibbs in tow just as the clock chimed ten times outside the library in the corridor.

Jasper said, "You are on time, have a seat." He indicated the empty chairs in front of his desk with a wave of his hand.

Lucas and Gibbs took the empty chairs, then Lucas pulled out the paperwork from a leather attaché

"My secretary assures me all is in order now, with the final change we made on my sister dowry." Lucas started to hand the papers to Jasper, but Jasper waved his hand for Turner to take the documents to read over.

Lucas said, "On pages five, eight, and ten, you shall find the corrections made." Turner skimmed through, noting the changes.

"Yes, it is all written as you dictated, ready for yourself and the Earl to sign, Lord Bellator." Turner handed the contract to Jasper, who took it and laid it in front of him on the desk. He read through the pages one by one until the last page. He looked up to Lucas when he finished.

"Everything is in order now. I am pleased to sign it." Jasper picked up an ink pen, dipped it into an ink well, and signed the papers before handing them to Lucas. "We need two witnesses to sign. Turner, you may sign, and your secretary Gibbs shall be the second one. I take it, that is why you brought him today."

"That and for the purpose if we needed to make other changes. I am happy it's final now." Lucas dipped the pen and signed, then handed the pen to Gibbs.

Lucas said seriously, "I have only one request from you, Lord Bellator; that you make Laurentia happy and take good care of her, she is all the family I have, and she deserves only the best life can offer her."

"I shall make it my life's mission to see to her happiness; you have my word on that."

Lucas nodded, "Your word I shall take. Thank you."

Jasper stood then walked around the desk. "Thank you for coming. My secretary here shall file the paperwork. I need to call this visit short, for I have too many things to finish today before the wedding tomorrow."

Lucas stood, "Then I shall see you this evening at your parents' residence. Until then, my Lord," he bowed

As Lucas and Gibbs left, Lucas said, "Gibbs, I do not ever recall being dismissed from anyone so quickly."

Gibbs said, "No, neither can I, but in London, things do move faster than the country."

"I can see your point, but Lord Bellator is a force I would not want to challenge ever. He was shot yesterday, and I do not even see any fatigue whatsoever." They stepped up into Lucas's coach and rode away, still talking about Lord Bellator and how remarkable he was.

Later that morning, Laurentia was in her bedchamber at Berkley Square, trying on her wedding gown that had just arrived with a modiste to take care of anything not perfect with the gown, and then the woman would alter it right on the spot. Laurentia stood in front of a looking glass.

"Have you ever seen anything more beautiful in your life, Sandra? The gown is perfect." She spun in circles, feeling giddy. A knock sounded on the door. Laurentia called, "Enter." In walked the duchess and the twins

As the duchess came in and walked around Laurentia, seeing the whole gown, she said. "Lovely, the gown came out more beautiful than one could have predicted."

Amara said, "Jasper is going to love it; you look stunning, Lady Laurentia." She stood behind Laurentia as she gazed at her image in the looking glass.

Aurora said, "I hope my gown is as lovely as yours on my wedding day. You are truly

beautiful."

Laurentia said, "Thank you. I feel beautiful in this. Aurora, when it is your wedding day, you could wear a burlap bag and still look beautiful, both of you." They all laughed at Laurentia's jest.

Duchess said, "I do not think the gown needs any last touches anywhere. So, what do you think, Laurentia?"

Laurentia smiled, "I believe you are right. I am so happy as it is, your Grace." Duchess waved her hand, dismissing the modiste.

Laurentia said, "Sandra, help me out of this and hang my gown in my dressing room, please."

Duchess said, "We shall go down to the front parlor to wait for you there. Come, girls, let's give Laurentia her privacy to change." They exited the room leaving Laurentia still admiring herself in her gown with Sandra.

"My gown is so lovely. I hate the thought of taking it off at this moment. But, I better do it, to not wrinkle it any more than need be. I'm ready, Sandra, let it be done." Sandra helped her out of the gown, and she then slipped into the dress she had on earlier. Sandra took her wedding gown to the dressing room for tomorrow's big day.

As Laurentia walked down the main staircase, she heard several different female voices coming from the front parlor, and one voice she heard sounded familiar to her, almost like her mother's voice. She walked into the room, finding her aunt, Countess of Angus, sitting by the duchess in a wingback chair chatting. Laurentia's eyes lit up with happiness, and she rushed to the aunt she had not seen for years with open arms. The countess stood quickly when she saw her niece coming toward her; they embraced and kissed each other's cheek and hugged again.

"Aunt Renee, it has been too long since I've seen you, oh how wonderful you are here."

"I do agree with you. Let me have a look at you. Yes, you are a true image of your mother. God rest her soul. She would have been so proud of you to see you now and marrying tomorrow to a Marquess, perfect child." She patted Laurentia's hand as they stood face to face.

"He is, and I do love Lord Bellator with all my heart, as he loves me too."

"That's even better news to my ears, for your parents were madly in love."

"I do remember, and I would not settle for any man unless he did love me. I want what my parents had, love, and more." Laurentia smiled.

"We have a lot to catch up on in these next couple of days."

Duchess said, "I have rung for tea, do have a sit. We have a few more details to go over for tomorrow." The twins, Gabrielle, Fantina, Louisa, the Dowager Duchess, and Miss Evans, were in the parlor. They had assembled to help with the last-minute details that need to finish, the Raventon family way.

Jennell rolled the tea cart in, with finger sandwiches and small cakes. The Twin served everyone to practice their proper etiquette, and the Duchess smiled, then nodded well done when they finished and took their seats once more.

Laurentia sat near her aunt, she asked. "Where are you staying in London? Is Uncle Maxwell with you on this trip and Cousin Philip and Harvey?"

"We are staying with Lucas, and yes, Maxwell and my sons had accompanied me. The three and Lucas were going for a ride on horseback through Hyde Park and then have lunch at that Whites Club of theirs. We have only arrived early this morning. It has saddened me that we missed the ball last night; your new family here was telling me the highlights of the evening before you came in."

"It was quite a celebration, and lovely, yes. You shall come tonight to the dinner party this evening here at Berkeley Square, shall you not?" Laurentia said, then looked to the duchess to ensure that it was alright with her, as it was her home.

Duchess said with a warm smile, "It would be welcome to have more of Laurentia's family join us this evening."

Renee said, "We'd be delighted to come, and may I say, Your Grace, you do have a beautiful home here."

"Thank you, this home has been in the family for a hundred years or more. However, I do enjoy decorating, and my gardens are my true passion. Perhaps Lady Laurentia shall take you out for a walk in them later."

Renee said, "That would be lovely, thank you, Your Grace."

Duchess nodded, then said, "Let's finish our light lunch, then we shall go over the last-minute tasks for tomorrow's wedding, and I shall send out with my staff to see that things are correctly done and executed. Not to worry, Lady Laurentia, you and my son's special day shall be unprecedented and the talk of the ton for years to come."

That afternoon, Jasper walked into White's after picking up a wedding gift for Laurentia and finished his other errands so they could leave the following day to go on their honeymoon. He saw Leopold and Jesse talking in the lounge, speaking in a deep conversation when he strolled up to them.

Jesse saw him over Leopold's shoulder. "Good afternoon, Lord Bellator. This is your last day as a single man. Come and have a drink with us."

Leopold turned, then said, "Because of you, all last night, I had to play cat and mouse with my mother and the ladies she had on her arm to meet me. You have made my life a living hell. So I am leaving London the next morning before dawn after your wedding to the country to get my sanity back. I have been telling Jesse here."

Jasper tried not to laugh at his cousin dramatics, but then Jesse started laughing, and Jasper laughed with him.

Leopold said, "Ha-ha, the jest is on me. I hope your mother starts on you next, Kingsley. Then we shall see who is laughing."

Jasper said, sobering, "Cousin, do not be so cross; love is not so bad of a thing."

Leopold, still growling, said, "Not to forget, you were not too happy when your father told you it was time to tie the knot, as I remember right. So, give me some due and stop laughing. It's undignified."

Jasper said, "My apologies, Leopold. Unfortunately, when Jesse broke loose with laugher and with you looking so pitiful, I could not help myself."

Jesse said, "My parents have not started that yet, but I do imagine they shall soon. Being I too have to have an heir someday."

The men decided to have lunch and journey to the dining room together.

Leopold asked, "How is your shoulder faring? You do not look to be in pain; most people would be in bed healing, dear Cousin."

Jasper said with an impassive face, "My shoulder is fine, as long as I do not use that arm. To make things clear for you, I am not like most people."

Jesse said, "That is true, and I, for one, am glad you are well. On the other hand, I would hate to lose you as a good friend."

Leopold chimed in, "I feel the same. I hate to admit it, but life would not be the same without you around, most likely dull."

"One of you shall have to be the leader of the small pack we have when I'm gone on my honeymoon." Jasper laughed, then went serious. "Both of you mean a lot to me also; we have been through a lot together. Have we not?" They all nodded heads in agreement.

At the dining-room door, they heard a loud group of gentlemen coming in, and it's the rest of their Raventon pack. In came Drake, Sterling, Victor, and Kelsey. When they saw the seated gentlemen, they immediately walked over.

Drake asked, "Is this a private party, or can we join you?"

Jasper said, "Bring that other table there over, and by all means, join us."

Drake said, "You heard him; let's grab that table and chairs." They pick up the table, bunt it to the other, and then there was room for all of them. Jasper motion for the server to come back over

Once they were all settled and had their drinks, Jasper raised his glass then said. "To the Raventon's and you, too, Jesse, you are one of us. Let's celebrate my joyous upcoming union tomorrow."

They all raised their glasses, saying, "Here-here."

They laughed and joked around the table for a couple of hours before that night's dinner party. Anyone looking at the Raventon men would see a group filled with integrity, loyalty, and honor.

Chapter 40

Prewedding Celebration Dinner

Prior to the dinner party, Laurentia was soaking in a hot tub of water. She was very much enjoying a leisure bath after a long day of activities, and Sandra had just left after finishing washing her mistress's long blonde hair. Laurentia closed her eyes, lying back in the warm water, and thought about Jasper. 'Since I left my love in his dining room this morning and having the last word. I have not seen him and how I miss my Jasper when we are apart.' She giggled, then her mind wandered, 'He is so handsome, wonderful, intelligent, brave, and all mine.' She giggled again, then sighed, remembering, 'the lovemaking session they'd had shared that morning.'

In Laurentia's ear, she heard a whisper of an all to a familiar voice saying, "You look deliciously beautiful in that tub before me, and I hope your delightful giggling, and that sigh was something to do with me." Jasper nibbled on her earlobe.

Laurentia did not jump or move with Jasper on his knees behind her, seeing her naked and bathing.

Laurentia casually said, wetting her lips. "If you must know, I was thinking about you, my love."

Jasper was kissing her neck. "Mmm, do tell, you

have my full attention right now." He had already taken his coat and sword off before coming over to her.

Jasper was at the back of the tub; he had rolled up his sleeves, his hands were on her shoulders before running them down her arms and over to her breasts.

Laurentia sighed at his touch. "I remembered the lovemaking this morning, our first time in your bed. Why have you come into my room here at your parent's residence? You should not be in here, Jasper."

Jasper, still kissing her neck, said, "I have missed you. I hoped to be alone with you before the guests arrive and to give you a wedding present."

Excited by the word 'present,' Laurentia sat up fast in the tub, sloshing some water over the side. She turned to look over her shoulder to see what he had for her and saw only him.

"Careful there, I do not have a change of clothes with me." Jasper stood to avoid the water on the floor.

Laurentia looked disappointed, not seeing a gift. "I thought you said you have a wedding present for me. I see none."

Jasper tilted his head, looking down at her beauty, "It is in my coat pocket. You look adorable with your pouty face right now. Would you like to have your gift, my sweet?"

Laurentia nodded and stepped out of the tub, smiling and dripping wet, "Yes, besides the books you gave me and my engagement ring, this shall be my third gift from you."

Jasper grabbed the towel for Laurentia and wrapped it around her helping to dry her off, and then he bent to taste her lips before walking over to his coat, lying on the bed. He picked it up and pulled out a jewelry box from his inside pocket. Laurentia's eyes lit up as he walked back to her.

Jasper opened the box, saying. "I am told diamonds go well with everything you wear. I do hope you like them, my love." Jasper placed the box in her hands. She looks down to see a necklace of diamonds shining brightly at her. Laurentia looked up into his blue eyes.

"It is beautiful, Jasper. I have never seen anything so breathtakingly exquisite. Besides the ring you already gave me."

Jasper took the necklace out of the box, and Laurentia turned around, holding her towel still so that he could put the necklace on her. Jasper fastened the chain of diamonds around Laurentia's neck then said.

"A beautiful necklace for my beautiful lady, perfection if you ask me. Do you like your gift, my love?"

Laurentia touched the necklace on her neck then turned around, beaming up at Jasper. "What is there not to like? I love it." She ran over to her full-length looking glass to see what they looked like on. The necklace had an enormous pear-shaped diamond in the center, at least ten carrots or more, and round-shape diamonds that went all the way around her neck to the back latch.

"Oh, Jasper, I have never had anything so lavish in all my life. It must have cost you a fortune. I love it, I do." She turned around to look at him smiling. Jasper walked over to her, and she got on her tiptoes, putting her arms around his neck and looking into his eyes.

"Thank you for my present; I do love it as I love you." She kissed him long and passionately.

Jasper broke the kiss, then said, "If this is the response, I receive giving you jewelry, I shall do it more often." And kissed her deeply.

Breaking the kiss, Laurentia said sweetly. "We do not have time to make love right now. I must get ready for the dinner party. I shall have to thank you properly later, I promise."

Jasper smiled down at her, "I shall hold you to that promise, my sweet Laurentia," he kissed her nose.

Sandra walked out of the dressing room, saying, "My Lady, we must get you out of that tub now, so you don't prune." Sandra stopped when she saw her mistress in her betrothed's arms in front of her. Then, putting her head down, "I am sorry, my Lord and Lady, for I did not know we had company."

Laurentia let go of Jasper's neck, then grabbing her towel so it did not fall off. "No, you did not. His Lordship was leaving now, so we may have me ready for tonight's party."

Jasper tilted Laurentia's face back up with his finger and bent down to kiss her one last time. "I shall see you downstairs shorty, my love."

He strolled to the bed, rolling his sleeves down, and put on his dinner coat and his sword back on. He then proceeded to the door and walked out, shutting it behind him. You could hear Jasper whistling as he happily strolled down the corridor.

As Jasper walked toward the staircase, he saw his mother coming toward him from the opposite direction.

"Good evening, Mother. You are looking lovely

for the soiree." He seemed to be in a chipper mood that was not typically his persona.

Duchess looked in the direction he came from and back to him.

"Do I want to ask where you came from, my Son?" She did not look at all pleased with her arms crossed.

"My betrothed's bedchamber. I just gave Laurentia a wedding gift, that is all. After you, Mother." Jasper waved his hand for her to descend the stairs first.

"I should not be surprised with you coming up here to Laurentia's room like this, for I am sure with her spending the evening at your home last night." Duchess's voice trailed off.

Jasper almost laughed at his mother's discomfort, then simply said. "Laurentia shall be wearing her present when she comes down. I am quite sure."

They walked into the front parlor together, finding the twins already there chatting away about the ball last night and who their dance partners were.

Jasper walked to the sideboard to pour himself some wine then asked, "Would you care for some wine, Mother? There seems to be the burgundy here you enjoy."

"Thank you, that shall be lovely, my dear." She took a seat in a wingback chair across from the twins, who were sharing a chaise. Jasper walked over to hand the glass of wine to his mother, then walked to the terrace door, looking out and hoping Laurentia did not take long to come down.

A few minutes later, Drake and Kelsey came strolling in together. Drake smiled, then walked over to his mother to kiss her cheek.

"Good evening, Mother; I see you are enjoying the wine I had sent over for you and Father."

"The wine is my favorite now, and I thank you, my darling." Drake smiled and nodded your welcome.

Kelsey greeted the Duchess, kissed her cheek, said hello to the twins, and walked to Jasper. "Cousin, not too many hours left till you are a married man."

Jasper turned to face the room. "Yes, you are right on that. This time tomorrow, I shall be a married man and genuinely happy."

Kelsey said, "You seem pleased with that, and I am happy for you. I am not so against marriage as the rest of our pack. However, I shall still wait a couple or more years, just to make sure my finances are on par before asking for a lovely lady's hand."

Jasper said, "That is honorable of you, but you are the one who knows how to make money on investments. So I see no problem in that category for you."

Drake came over to join them, "How is the shoulder? You look as if nothing happened to you yesterday."

Jasper answered, "I'm fine, not to worry. The pain is mostly gone."

The duke came in barking at Wesley, telling him, "This is my home. I never need to be introduced." Duke shut the parlor door, then walked over to his duchess, kissed her hand. "You look beautiful, my darling."

Duchess smiled up at him. "Thank you, and you look most dashing yourself in your royal blue suit."

Lord and Lady Charlton were announced, and

Louisa glided over to the duke and duchess with Charlton beside her.

Duke put out his hand for Charlton to shake. "Can you believe my eldest son is marrying tomorrow? It only seems as if it was yesterday; our two eldest boys were in the cradle."

Louisa picked up on that, saying, "I do not know what happened to Leopold last night. I had a few gently bred ladies last evening to meet him, and he practically ran from me all night long."

Duchess said, "To tell you the truth, I thought Leopold would marry before Jasper. Leopold is so charming, and Jasper was a sybarite. But I have to say since Jasper met Laurentia, he has softened around the edges, and you can see the love in his eyes when he looks at her. I am proud of him."

Louisa said, "I feel helpless with Leopold right now."

Charlton said, "Give him time; Raventon men like to do their own hunt when it comes to finding a mate for life. You need to let him be, Louisa."

Duke said, "That is true; I have to agree with my brother here."

Lord Johnathan, Lady Fantina, and Lady Gabrielle arrived shortly after the dowager duchess and Miss Evans. Gabrielle joined the twins, while the others joined the duke, duchess, Charlton, and Louisa.

Duchess walked over to her mother-in-law to welcome her. "Good evening, Your Grace. Come have a seat with your granddaughters, and I shall see to having a glass of wine brought to you before we have dinner."

The dowager said, "I'd like to see my grandsons first. I know my way. But you may send the glass of white wine over and one for Miss Evans."

"Yes, I shall see to that."

Lord Kingsley, Leopold, Victor, and Sterling were the next to arrive. They walked to the sideboard to help themselves to a glass of wine, then joined Jasper, Drake, Kelsey, the dowager duchess, and Miss Evans.

Earl Berwickshire, Earl and Countess Angus and two sons arrived, and the duchess greeted them., "Welcome to my home. It is nice to see you again. Lady Laurentia has not come down yet. Would you care for some wine?" She motioned for a footman to bring a tray.

Duke walked over to Lucas. "Good evening, Berwickshire, and who do we have here?" Lucas introduced his uncle, aunt, and two cousins to the duke and duchess. Then excused himself to talk with the younger gentlemen. The dowager had now taken a seat with her granddaughters, Miss Evans beside her.

The room filled up with the family, and Jasper wondered what kept Laurentia as it was nearly half-past seven. Just as that thought entered his mind, Laurentia glided eloquently into the room. Jasper froze for a moment, watching her come in. She looked so beautiful in her rose-pink gown and Jasper's wedding present around her neck. He was pleased she was wearing it. Jasper met Laurentia in the middle of the room, making eye contact with her. He then took both her hands and raised them to his lips, kissing tenderly.

Still looking in her eyes, he said. "I am the luckiest man in the world to have found you and to make you my bride tomorrow. You are beautiful, my love, and you take my breath away."

Smiling up at Jasper, Laurentia said, "Thank you, and I too feel I am the luckiest woman in the world to have you also, and I adore you." It seemed as if the world stopped turning. They stood there looking into each other's eyes, forgetting everyone around them. That seemed to happen quite often with them. Finally, Jasper snapped out of the trance.

"Darling, would you care for a glass of wine? We should mingle with our guests here."

"Yes, white wine would be lovely," Laurentia said as she looked around the room, noticing all were watching them. "Tis rude if we just stand here and not acknowledge the family."

Jasper nodded to a footman to bring a glass of wine to Laurentia. She took the glass from the tray, and then everyone started to come over to them to greet Laurentia. Duke and Duchess came over first to Laurentia and Jasper. Duchess's eyes lit up, seeing the large diamond necklace around her neck. She remembered Jasper saying he came upstairs to give Laurentia a wedding gift.

"That is a lovely necklace you have on this evening, Lady Laurentia," Duchess said with a smile.

Laurentia touched it, remembering it there. "Thank you; Lord Bellator gave it to me this evening as a wedding gift. It is a little overwhelming, but I do love it, Your Grace."

"My son does have an eye for the extravagant things; it is charming. The necklace shall also go well with your wedding gown, and I have the perfect pair of earrings to match your gift, which you shall wear tomorrow. Then you shall have something borrow and something new."

Duke greeted Laurentia, saying, "Beautiful gifts

for a beautiful woman." He winked at his son with approval.

Lucas came over and kissed his sister's cheek. "Mother and Father would have been thrilled with you marrying into this grand family. I am also pleased and that you found love, dear Sister."

Laurentia kissed Lucas's cheek, "Thank you, Lucas; I feel blessed." She looked up at Jasper and smiled. Still holding her hand, Jasper raised it to his lips, kissed it, and then smiled at her.

Laurentia's uncle, aunt, and cousins came over, and she hugged them one at a time. Laurentia turned to Jasper, saying, "This is my mother's sister Countess Angus and her husband, the Earl of Angus. Also, their two sons, my cousins Lord Philip their heir and Lord Harvey."

The Earl put his hand out to shake Jasper's hand. "I am Uncle Maxwell, and this is Aunt Renee. After tomorrow we shall be family, we might as well end with the formalities."

Jasper shook his hand. "I am Lord Bellator; I am pleased to meet Laurentia's family. I know to have you here with us this evening to celebrate our nuptials, which means a lot to my bride. I thank you for coming."

Lord Philip said, "I remember you from Eton. You were a few years ahead of me. But everyone knew whom you were, for being most brilliant in all the art of sports. It is a pleasure to meet you, Lord Bellator."

Jasper said, "Thank you for the compliment. Although most tasks come easy for me to exceed, I perhaps may held a few records throughout the years at the school.

Harvey says, "Forgive me in budding in, Lord Bellator, but you still hold those records, you are a true highflyer in my book, and it is a pleasure to meet you, and to boot, you shall be family marrying my sweet cousin here." He stepped forward and kissed Laurentia's cheek. "It is good to see you again, Lady Laurentia."

"As it is lovely to see all of you again, I am genuinely pleased you came on short notice to my wedding, thank you, "Laurentia said, with her heart filled with joy.

Aunt Renee said, "I was delighted that we received the invitation to come and see my niece being married. Lady Laurentia's mother was my elder sister by four years. We had an elder brother Lord Alfred, who was killed a few years ago serving the king in the Napoleon war. Our Laurentia is the image of her mother, from her hair to her eye color. As you may see, my sister was lovely, and to look at my niece warms my heart, for I see that my sister lives on in Lady Laurentia, and I hope in your children to come."

Jasper said, "I, of course, would like a son first, but when we do have a daughter, I have no doubt that she shall resemble Lady Laurentia and your sister, her mother. That would please me."

Renee said, "Very much so, my Lord." She turned to Laurentia, "I have brought something for you." She opened her reticule, pulling out a blue embroidery handkerchief. "This was your mothers. She made it as a young girl, I want you to have this, and now you have something blue plus something from your mothers as well."

Holding the handkerchief in her hand, Laurentia

could feel her mother's presence in the room. She opened the cloth and ran her fingers over the delicate stitching of embroidery. Along the edge of the handkerchief was an elegant rose pattern with leaves, and in the left bottom corner was her mother's name, Esme. Laurentia looked up to Renee.

"Oh, Aunt Renee, this is beautiful. Thank you ever so much and have something of my mother. I can truly feel her presence here this evening and with Father. Thank you." Laurentia embraced her aunt, then turned to show Jasper the handkerchief.

Jasper looked down at Laurentia's gift from her aunt. "It is lovely. Your mother's needlework is brilliant, and she must have enjoyed doing embroidery."

"Yes, she did, and I remember Father teasing her, saying 'if you had not married me, you could have been the personal queen dressmaker and done all your fancy stitching for her.' Then Mother would say, 'No thank you, I love my life as it is, and you.' Then they would kiss. They were very much in love."

Lucas came over, for he heard the story Laurentia just told. "I do remember that as if it were yesterday. They were wonderful parents to us." Lucas kissed his sister's cheek. Then Lucas saw the necklace on his sister's neck he had not noticed before and thought to himself, 'No wonder Lord Bellator did not want Laurentia's trust fund. Bellator most certainly has enough of his own money, buying my sister excessive pieces of jewelry like that. My kid sister shall be alright with her choice to marry.'

Wesley came into the room then said a few words to the duchess before exiting. Duchess said, "I have been told our dinner is ready to be served. We may journey into the dining room."

Two footmen opened the doors that led to the dining room. The duke put his arm out for his duchess, saying, "Shall we?"

"By all means." Duchess took his arm, and they led the way.

Next in line were Jasper and Laurentia. "To think my first dinner here was a few weeks ago, you led me in like now, and here we are about to marry tomorrow. I still pinch myself, wondering if it is all a dream." Laurent said with a smile.

Jasper replied, "You are my dream, and I plan to live it to the fullest with you." He bent his head to kiss her cheek as they strolled down the corridor to the dining room. Drake escorted his Grandmother Raventon, Jesse escorted Aurora, Leopold escorted Amara in. Then Earl and Countess Angus went next with Philip and Harvey in their wake. Lucas asked Gabrielle if she would walk with him, and she accepted. Next in the order went Charlton and Louisa, then Johnathan and Fantina. In the rear, Kelsey escorted Miss Evans, then Sterling and Victor walked together.

As they all sat, Laurentia saw that the duchess had the table decorated in the most elegant silver, crystal, china, flowers, and the beautiful Devonshire crested candelabras. Duchess nodded, and four footmen filled the wine glasses around the table and went back to their posts by the wall.

Duke stood with his wine glass. "This evening is just for the family and soon-to-be family." He looked at Laurentia's family then moved his gaze over all of them. "I shall never get tired of saying this; I am proud of my heir, Jasper, he has always overachieved in everything he set out to do, and that includes finding a bride." He looked down at Jasper and Laurentia and raised his glass. "I toast to my son, Jasper, and soon-to-be daughter Laurentia. Best wishes on this wonderful journey as you build your new lives together." He took a drink as all followed him in his toast. Then he said before sitting, "My Duchess has planned a wonderful meal and evening. Let's celebrate, shall we? Enjoy."

Duke took his seat, and the duchess nodded for the first course to be served. They had a feast big enough for a king, starting with cream of watercress soup, roast boar, roast pheasant, potatoes, vegetables, cheese from France, bread, and some of Jasper's favorite desserts Bridget made special just for him to finish a perfect meal. They ate, drank, laughed for hours, and the duchess had music to entertain them throughout the meal and evening.

Shortly after elven, they were saying their goodbyes to their guests at the front steps. Coaches were filling, then heading down the drive, and the duke and duchess stepped inside with the twins.

Jasper faced Laurentia, holding both her hands in front of them. "I shall miss your warm body next to mine tonight. I shall keep good on my promise not to come to you tonight."

"The next time you see me, I shall be the one in a white gown walking down the aisle at the church toward you. Shall you meet me there, my Jasper?"

"Yes, you know I shall. Do not be late; I shall not have any patience waiting for you. Since our first kiss, I have wanted you for my own, and I shall count the hour to the minutes when you are finally all mine, and nothing shall keep us apart ever again, my love." Jasper took Laurentia into his arms, kissing her lips deeply and passionately, a promise of what would come in their future life together.

When they broke their kiss, Laurentia said, "I love you. Goodnight, my Jasper."

Over Jasper's shoulder awaited Leopold's coach, plus Lucas's coach with all the single men from the dinner party and some on horseback.

Drake yelled out, "Bellator, let us go already. The night is ticking away."

Laurentia frowned, and Jasper quickly explained, "They want to take me out one last time as a single man; I had better go. Do not worry, my love, no other woman shall ever do once I have had you. I love you." He kissed her again and walked down the steps.

The men cheered and carried on like boys as he walked toward them. Jasper looked back before he entered Leopold's coach to see Laurentia watching. She waved goodnight, and she turned to walk inside with the door closing behind her.

Jasper turned back, saying, "Alright, you animals, let us go." He stepped into the coach and closed the door. Leopold tapped the roof of the coach, and they were off. Jasper's last night of being a bachelor, the Raventon pack had made unique plans for him for a barmy time tonight with the boys.

Chapter 41

The Wedding Day

The following day, Jasper woke up in his bed alone, and he felt as if he'd just fallen asleep moments ago. It was four in the morning when his head hit the pillow; he remembered drinking a lot, playing cards, and laughing it up with his brother, cousins, and friends last night. Now sitting up in bed, Jasper ran his hand through his hair, got out of bed, put on a red velvet robe, and walked over to pull the cord to summon Farrell. He continued over to a wingback chair near the fireplace to wait.

Jasper looked at the empty chair across from him, though, 'Laurentia should be sitting there with me, sharing our morning meal in private together. Instead, he pictured her long blonde hair, messy from their morning lovemaking, and her lips slightly swollen from his passionate kisses. Starting tomorrow, she most defiantly shall be here, and every morning after that, Laurentia shall be all mine.'

When Farrell came in, he said, "We shall start with a hot bath, you smell of cigar smoke, and some coffee, my Lord. I shall be right back."

Not giving Jasper a chance to say anything, Farrell walked back out to give the order for the bathtub to be filled with hot water and a tray with coffee and pastry sent up to his lordship's bedchamber at once.

Farrell came back into the room. "It is your big day to marry the lady of your dreams, and you stay out all night, like a young hellion. I have my work cut out for me today to make you look perfect for your future marchioness." He walked over to the window and pulled back the curtains to let the sunlight come in.

Jasper sat there, watching, and listening to his valet ramble on, then he barked. "Where is my coffee, Farrell? I do not need to hear your opinions on my last night's outing. I want the tub in here by the fire where it is warm. Do you have my new suit for my wedding press and ready?"

Farrell stopped in the middle of the floor with some towels in his hand, looking straight at Jasper. "Thank god, you have your wit about you today. I was thinking—"

Jasper cut him off, "Never underestimate me, Farrell. Now stop with your babbling and do as I ordered."

A knock sounded on the door, and a footman came in carrying a tray with a pot of hot coffee, a cup, and a plate of cinnamon rolls. He placed the tray on the table beside Jasper's chair, poured the black coffee into the cup, and handed the cup to his lordship. Jasper glared at the footman to leave before drinking down half the cup before setting it down on the table beside him. Next, he picks up one of the rolls, he ate one and another and drank more coffee. Jasper was starting to feel better than he looked now. Moments later, buckets of hot water were being carried in by his footmen; Farrell had managed to bring the tub by the fire as Jasper ordered. After several water buckets filled the tub, Jasper stood, walked to the tub, dropped his robe, and stepped in.

Farrell came over to Jasper and first took the bandage off his shoulder. "Your wound is healing splendidly, my Lord." He washed Jasper's back with a sponge, and Jasper took the sponge to wash his front himself. Farrell shaved Jasper as he leaned back to relax and finished washing his hair last before leaving the tub. Now done, he stepped out of the bath as Farrell handed him a towel. Jasper dried off, wrapped a towel around his waist, and headed back to his chair to have more coffee and rolls.

After more coffee, Jasper said, "I feel much better, Farrell. I need to be at the church at ten-thirty. Laurentia shall come down the aisle at eleven. Ah, this shall be a new beginning for me to start, and I am ready for this new chapter in my life." He looked out the window, wondering what Laurentia was doing at this moment. He missed her, her scent of honeysuckle that filled his senses, that told him she was nearby. He sat and dreamed of her as he finished his coffee.

Early the morning of her wedding, Laurentia went out for a walk; she felt restless lying-in bed without Jasper. Yes, he was right; she did miss him beside her and in his strong arms. But she would not admit it to him. As she walked into the Devonshire mansion dining room for the last time as Lady Laurentia Sinclair, the duchess, greeted her.

"Good morning, Lady Laurentia. I hope you slept well. It looks to be a lovely day out."

Laurentia sat down at the table, "Yes, it is. I just came in from a morning walk."

Duke said, looking concerned, "You had a Footman with you, did you not?"

"Yes, Your Grace, the footman Gus, accompany me this morning. He still felt badly for what had happened to me before. But I reassured him, it was out of his control, the way we were ambushed, and I have no ill feelings toward him. Jasper had hired an extra footman; his purpose is just to guard me when Jasper cannot be present with me. I must say, having two strong men walking behind me, two feet away this morning. I must have looked like a site."

"Good, excellent, we still need to be careful out and about. After all, between your kidnapping and Jasper shooting only a couple of days ago. I do not want any more incidents to happen to this family. I am not sure yet if that Hughes had any more siblings to worry about coming after us." Duke rumbled.

"Darling, we shall all take care not to worry you and take precautions," Duchess said and patted his hand to calm him down with a warm smile.

The twins came walking in arguing, then they stopped when the duchess raised an eyebrow at them as they took their seats at the table.

Duchess said in an even tone. "Good morning, Aurora, Amara. We have a long day ahead of us. Is there a matter you wish to discuss this morning before breaking your fast?"

Amara said, "Aurora thinks Leopold shall be leaving the season early. I said he would not."

Aurora said, "I overheard him talking to Victor at the ball, saying he shall."

Duke said, "Nonsense, the season has just begun. Leopold always enjoys the London entertainment and is well received."

"That is what I said, and he loves the ladies as well," Amara said with a nod.

Duchess snapped, "Amara, that is not a proper topic for you to talk about."

Amara said, "Sorry, Mother," with her head down.

"Your Father is right; the season has just begun. Leopold shall stay in town. Let's talk about today's event and not worry about your cousin."

The twins glared at each other as they sipped their morning tea, and they still felt right about their belief on the subject.

Duke stood and kissed the duchess' cheek. "I need to do a small amount of work in my library before we head to the church. I shall ready myself in plenty of time." Then he exited the room.

Laurentia asked, "What time shall we leave for the church, Your Grace?"

"I think half-past nine shall give us plenty of time. How are you doing on your packing?"

"Sandra is wise in packing, and between us both, we have it all organized."

Aurora asked, "Where are you going on your honeymoon?"

Laurentia smiled, "I know we shall be traveling for at least two weeks or more. Jasper is not telling me the first destination. But I am pretty sure we shall be traveling through Europe."

Amara said, "Wherever you go, Jasper shall only have the best accommodations for you, knowing my brother."

Aurora said, "That's for sure; even if it is Jasper we are talking about, it is very romantic that he wants to surprise you on this."

Laurentia laughed, "Under his hard exterior, he is a big softy, really."

Duchess said, "I have noticed that with you in his life, he is calmer and happier. I heard him whistling yesterday and thought it was one of our footmen until he came closer to me in the corridor, most surprising indeed."

Amara said, laughing, "Jasper whistling, now that is a sight."

Laurentia said, "You make him to be a beast sometimes. I have seen and known his stern and arrogant side, but still, to me, he is perfect in all ways."

Duchess smiled, "I am glad my son found you, Laurentia. You complete him, and that pleases me."

"I better go up, have a bath and start getting ready for the church, and make sure all is packed correctly." Laurentia stood and went up to her bedchamber one last time at Berkley Square.

When Laurentia walked into her bedchamber, she saw a massive bouquet of red roses in a vase on the dressing table. She walked to them and smelled the beautiful fragrance they had. She counted at least three dozen of them and saw a note in Jasper's writing. She reads the card:

My love, we are marrying in a few hours. I never saw this day coming to life until I met you. You bewitched me in my parents' front parlor the first time I looked into your beautiful violet eyes. If you remember, my first words to you were, 'you are beautiful.' I was leaving that afternoon and not staying for your interview, but I knew that I might never see you again if I did not stay. I was not about to let that happen. You know how that interview went and how I sent for your belongings.

That evening when we took that walk in the garden alone, we chatted a bit, getting to know each other, and I kissed you by the fountain. I could feel your passion from that first kiss, and that is when I told myself you are the one.

I Love You, Lady Laurentia Sinclair. When you come to the church today, and when it is time for you to walk down the aisle, I shall be the gentleman in black waiting for you at the altar with a smile on my face. I believe you are my soulmate, and I am ready to share the rest of my life with you. I shall see you at the church soon.

Love, Jasper

Tears ran down Laurentia's cheeks, this is the first love letter Jasper has written to me, and it is so beautiful.

Sandra came out of the dressing room with more things to put in the trunk for her mistress honeymoon. "My Lady, I did not hear you come in. I shall ring for your bathwater now. After that, we should start getting you ready for the church. It won't be long till you are a married lady." Sandra noticed Laurentia standing by the roses with her letter clutched to her chest and tears running down her cheeks.

Sandra rushed over to Laurentia, alarmed, "My Lady, what is wrong, has something happen to Lord Bellator? Oh, please tell me all is well, and no more awful events had happened again."

Laurentia shook her head no, and she said calmly, "When did these flowers arrive, Sandra?".

"Not too long after you left for your walk, my Lady." Sandra was still not sure what was wrong with her mistress with all the tears.

"The flowers are truly lovely, and Jasper wrote me the most beautiful love letter I have ever read. I cannot wait to marry him, and my tears are tears of joy. Let's get that water up here, Sandra, I have a wedding to go to, and I am the bride!"

"Right away, my Lady, as quick as lightning." Sandra rushed out to see that things are done fast, and there was no time to waste.

Laurentia stood in her wedding gown before the full-length looking glass in her bedchamber, admiring her dress plus the new necklace she had on that Jasper had given her last evening. A knock sounded on her bedchamber door, and Laurentia called, "Enter."

The duchess wearing a jade green gown that enhances her green eyes walked in. Duchess held a small box in her hand. "You are a vision of loveliness. Your Sandra never disappoints; your hair looks beautiful, Laurentia,"

"Thank you. I think I am about ready to go now. I do not want to sit and wrinkle my gown too much." Duchess handed Laurentia the box she is holding.

"Here are the earrings I mention last evening to you that shall match your lovely necklace. His Grace gave them to me when Jasper was born, and he said, 'A gift to you, my love, for giving a gift to me, an heir.' It is something that shall match Jasper's wedding gift to you."

Laurentia took the box then opened it finding two pear-shaped diamond earrings that looked to be at least three carats apiece. Laurentia looked up at the duchess smiling at her. "Your Grace, they are beautiful, and you are so right they match the center stone in my necklace."

The duchess helped her take them out of the box, and Laurentia put them on. She walked over to the dressing table to pick up her mother's handkerchief and tucked it in front of her gown over her heart, out of sight.

Duchess said, "Now you are ready. We shall go."

"I am quite nervous, but yes, I am ready, Your Grace."

"To be nervous is a part of the whole picture in front of you. I never met a bride who was not. Come, the coach is waiting for us and the duke. His Grace does not like being late."

They walked downstairs together; the twins and the duke were waiting for them in the foyer. Sandra walked behind them as they descended the stairs.

Duke says when they hit the bottom step. "My dear girl, you are truly lovely; my son shall be pleased when he sees you. Let's not keep him waiting."

Wesley opens the front door for them as they all walked out. Two footmen helped carry Laurentia's fifteen-foot train so it would not get soil from the grown.

Duke turned to the ladies then said. "We are using both coaches today. Laurentia, you shall ride in the duchess's coach with your maid. That coach shall take you to the back of the church entrance so that you are not seen until you come down the aisle."

Duchess said, "I shall come to you after we make our entrance in the front of the church to help with last-minute details, if any. Then your brother shall walk you down the aisle."

Laurentia nodded yes, "I am ready, all nerves, but ready to go."

A footman opened the coach door and helped her

in as Sandra assisted her with her gown and train, ensuring it did not wrinkle any more than needed. The duke helped his duchess in the other coach and his daughters. When they took their seats inside, he stepped in, sat down, and tapped the roof to go. The duke's coach was first down the drive, with the duchess's coach riding behind. Both coaches had the Devonshire crest on the doors, so when anyone saw their coach arrive at any venue, they knew who was riding inside. All heads would turn to see them step down from the coach and watch them walk into any venue they chose to enter. One would say the Duke and Duchess of Devonshire were as popular to watch as the King and Queen.

Jasper was in a side room at the church's front, pacing the floor anxiously. Finally, he said to Drake, who kept him company until it was time to go out.

"Is Laurentia here yet? The time is getting close. She has to be here, and I had mentioned to her last evening I am not a patient man to keep waiting." Jasper looked up at Drake when he passed for the tenth time or so.

"I am sure she is here. You are going to wear a hole in the floor if you don't stop pacing."

Jasper stopped, looking up at him, and snapped, "If I do, I shall pay to have it repaired as if that is something important." He shook his head and started pacing again.

The door opened, and Leopold came in, saying, "The ducal coaches have arrived."

Drake said, "It won't be long before we start, which is good. Jasper, here, is pacing like a caged animal ready to attack."

Jasper stopped. "You are exaggerating, as usual,

Drake." He started pacing again. Drake looked at Leopold and raised an eyebrow to indicate who was right on this.

Leopold said, "Jasper, you could still back out of this now if you wish. You look as if you are unsettled right now."

Jasper stopped again then looked Leopold in the eyes. "I have no patience in this waiting game. I never have and never shall." He groaned. Drake shook his head to Leopold to let him be, not to stir him up anymore.

Leopold shrugged, "I shall go out and then come back to let you know when it is time to come out into the altar, dear Cousin."

Laurentia waited in the back room in the church for the guests to all take their seats as Sandra fussed over her. Laurentia noticed Jasper's coach in the front of the church, which meant he was here. 'I wonder if he is as nervous as I am.'

Lucas knocked on the door and stuck his head in asked if he might come in.

Laurentia said, smiling, "Yes, do come in Lucas, Sandra is just touching up my hair."

Lucas walked over to her. "You are a vision of loveliness, dear Sister. I believe it is almost time to take your walk down the aisle."

"Thank you, Lucas, for your kind words. I feel Mother and Father's presence here today at St. Paul's; it is a beautiful church."

"I too can feel their presence, and they would be pleased with your choice to marry here today."

A knock sounded, and the duchess came in. She greeted Lucas, then said, "It is time. Are you ready?"

Laurentia stood. "Yes, as ever one can be, Your Grace."

"You look perfect. I shall let them know you are ready and take my seat." Duchess said and smiled at Laurentia before leaving.

"I guess this is it, Sister. Shall we?" Lucas put his arm out for Laurentia to take. Laurentia smiled and took his arm, and they walked out the door together.

The duke came into the room where Jasper was waiting. He could see the impatience in his son's face. "I am told it's time, Son."

"Father, this is a new chapter in my life. I believe Laurentia shall be the perfect marchioness. She does make me happy."

"Do you love her, Jasper?"

"With all my heart."

"Then she is perfect; let's go and get you married today." Duke smiled with pride.

Jasper, Drake, and the duke walked out of the room to the altar. The duke took his seat by his duchess and took her hand as she looked up at him and smiled. Drake took his place, too, leaving Jasper standing alone with the priest on the altar.

Jasper saw Laurentia with her brother at the door of the cathedral. He took a deep breath and told himself, 'There she is and perfection just as I knew she be. Laurentia's beautiful blonde hair shining, her gown is stunning, and there is a glow that is coming off her as she smiles at me.' All of Jasper's fear disappeared, and he felt calm as he took another deep breath.

Laurentia saw Jasper waiting for her down the long aisle at the altar. She wanted to run to him and land in his strong arms, but she knew she could not. Laurentia knew it was essential to take this walk, an elegant one, as everyone's eyes were on her and her brother.

Laurentia took a deep breath, then whispered to Lucas. "Let's show the ton; we Sinclair's are proud and proper like all of them before us."

"I say we outshine most, dear Sister." Lucas squeezed her hand, and they glided down the aisle together, both looking magnificent.

Jasper locked eyes with Laurentia when she made her way to him, and he put his hand out for her to take when she took her last steps. Lucas took Laurentia's hand and placed it in Jasper's when they reach the altar. Lucas kissed Laurentia's cheek and stepped back.

The priest asked, "Who gives the bride away today?"

Lucas loud and clear, "I, her brother the Earl of Berwickshire."

The priest nodded, and Lucas took his seat. Jasper and Laurentia held hands standing in front of the priest.

Jasper said to Laurentia, "You look beautiful, my love."

Laurentia said to Jasper, "You look very handsome." She smiled, looking into his eyes.

They looked at the priest, who cleared his throat to get their attention. Jasper nodded for him to start now.

The priest asked, "Is there anyone here to give just cause, why the two before me may not marry here today?" The church was silent. The priest said, "We may start; I shall read scripture first from the Bible."

Then the moment the two had been waiting for. "Jasper Edwin Raventon Marquess of Bellator, do you take the Lady Laurentia Kathleen Sinclair as your lawful wife. To have and hold from this day forward, for better or worse, for richer or for poorer, in sickness and in health, to love and cherish until death do you part?"

The church was quiet, then Jasper said, "I do with all my heart."

The priest then said, "Lady Laurentia Kathleen Sinclair do you take Jasper Edwin Raventon Marquess of Bellator as your lawful husband. To have and hold from this day forward, for better or worse, for richer or for poorer, in sickness and in health, to love and cherish until death do you part?"

Laurentia smiled up at Jasper then said, "I do, with all my heart." Jasper raised her hand to his lip and kissed it gently.

The priest said, "May I have the rings?" Jasper reached into the inside pocket of his coat and pulled out two wedding bands. One was in gold with diamonds that went all the way around the band for Laurentia, and the other was solid gold with a smooth finish for Jasper. The priest put his bible out for Jasper to lay them there.

The priest blessed the rings then said to the bride and groom. "You have opened your heart to one another, declared your love and friendship. You shall unite yourself with the exchanging of rings. Lord Bellator, you may go first and repeat these words to your bride: I Jasper Edwin Raventon, Marquess of Bellator, give a ring to seal our vows from this day forward, amen, and slide the ring on."

Jasper picks up the ring; he put it on the tip of

Laurentia's ring finger. Then, looking into her eyes, he said the words. and slid the ring down Laurentia's finger.

Laurentia picked the other ring up, put it to the tip of Jasper's finger, then repeated, "I Lady Laurentia Kathleen Sinclair give a ring to seal our vows from this day forward, amen," she slides Jasper's ring down his finger.

The priest said, "For as much as Lord Bellator and Lady Laurentia have consented together in holy matrimony, and have pledged their love and loyalty to each other, and declared the same by the joining and the giving of rings. Therefore, with the power vested in me, and as witnessed by family and friends, I now pronounce you husband and wife. You may now kiss the bride." Jasper did not hesitate; he wrapped his arms around Laurentia's waist, pulling her close; Laurentia's arms went around Jasper's neck, leaning into him. They kissed so passionately everyone's mouth just about fell open. Jasper did not care for one minute; he showed his love for his bride and wanted all to know and see.

Duchess was in some shock watching the display as her son kissed his new bride so vulgarly.

The duke broke the silence saying, "Well, my darling, our eldest son is married and watching them kiss right now. I believe there shall be an heir in no time at all."

Duchess replied, "You would think he wait for private to show one desire."

Duke laughed, "Have you already forgotten how we were at that age? If I remember right, we were caught in each other's arms quite a few times before our wedding vows were said."

"That was many years ago, and I do remember. It was exhilarating, passionate, and sometimes naughty of us." Duchess whispered the last part.

"Ah, you remember now. Jasper is just like me in many ways. Later, we shall have to reminisce about those memories. What did you call them?"

Duchess answered softly, "Our naughty ways."

"Yes, my love, and we have mastered them, haven't' we."

"Conrad, sssh, we are in church, but I shall look forward to playing later." Duchess smiled.

"That's my girl," and he winked at her.

Jasper broke their kiss, "You are all mine now. That has made me a happy man."

"As you are mine, also, I think we are to leave. Everyone is watching and staring at us. We have a wedding banquet to attend at your parents' residence next."

Jasper whispered, "I wish we could just go home and make love all day and into the night."

"A few hours at the wedding party, and then we can go home and not come out of the bedchamber till morning. I like that word I just used, 'home.' Our home." Laurentia said, smiling.

Jasper smiled and squeezed her close again. "Yes, our home Marchioness Bellator." They kissed once again passionately.

Jasper kissed Laurentia's nose before saying, "Shall we take our first walk as man and wife, my Marchioness?" He put his arm out for her to take.

"Yes, my husband, that sounds like a wonderful idea." Laurentia took his arm, and they walked off the altar together as husband and wife smiling to all. They did not move fast; all attendance from the ceremony were greeting plus congratulating them step by step as they walked down the aisle, and when they reached outside, Jasper's coach was pulling up at the front door of the church. Standing on the front steps, they looked out at the crowd that had formed before them. It was not just the guests from the church, but it seemed most of London was there wanting to see the heir to the Dukedom of Devonshire marry and his new bride and future duchess.

Still standing on the top steps, Laurentia said to Jasper, "There were not this many people in the church minutes ago. Jasper, it does look like half of London is here. Why would they come like this?" She sounded alarmed.

"They wanted to see you, the one who won my heart, to be my wife, and have my love. Remember, darling, you are a future duchess, and that always draws attention. I am used to it, for it has always been my life and this way."

"I love you, and if this is what I have as a future thing, one shall have to smile and deal with it," Laurentia said and squeezed Jasper's hand.

Jasper turned toward Laurentia, smiled, "That's my girl, and I love you even more." He kisses her long and hard. That made the crowd cheer, seeing the future heir kiss his new bride, and they loved it. After the kiss, the groom and bride walked down the stairs and to the coach as the crowd continued to cheer. One of Jasper's grooms held the coach door open for them, and Jasper helped Laurentia in and stepped into the coach, taking a seat beside her. Jasper tapped the roof, letting the driver know he could go. Laurentia waved to all the people in the street as they rode by, then she sat back in her seat and saw Jasper watching her.

"Dear husband, you look quite amused watching me wave to the people," His bright eyes were shining.

Jasper leaned back in his seat, relaxed. "Yes, I am. London, or should I say England, seems to love you. Not as merely as much as I do, but close."

Laurentia said seductively, "Could you show me how much this love you say you have for me, perhaps now?"

Jasper's expression changed to that wicked smile she adores so much, and she knew all too well what happened when it appeared. She was anticipating what would come next. Jasper closed the curtains on his side of the coach, leaned over to Laurentia's side, and closed them. Jasper tapped the little door on the ceiling where the driver sat.

It opened, and the driver said, "Yes, my Lord, is there somewhere else you like to go?"

Jasper answered, looking into Laurentia's eyes, "I would like to take a couple of rounds of Hyde Park before we go to my parent's resident, slowly."

The driver said, "Yes, my Lord, as you wish."

Without breaking eye contact with Jasper, Laurentia said, "This time of day, it shall take over an hour to ride that."

Jasper reached under Laurentia and put her on his lap. "Yes, it shall; I am counting on it. You did ask me to show you the love I have for you. Since I saw you walk to me down that long aisle in the church earlier, my desire has been growing for you, and not having you in my bed last night and this morning has made my hunger for you have grown even more."

"Hunger, did you say? I like the sound of that, as

I too have that same feeling for you." Laurentia wrapped her arms around Jasper's neck and kissed him deeply. Jasper's hands were on her breasts; he had managed to slip one out the front of her dress, and his lips are on her nipple playing and arousing her more.

"How are we going to do this with all my gown everywhere?" Laurentia sounded distressed.

Jasper raised his head slowly. "Darling, relax; you are going to be on top. We cannot take all our clothes off." He took her lips in a deep kiss, teasing his tongue around her mouth. Laurentia wrapped her arms around his neck and melted into his kiss. Jasper undid the front of his breeches to ready himself, and he then broke their kiss.

"You are going to straddle me, like in the chair in your room, remember? Your gown shall stay on. Are you ready, my love?"

"More than ready. I need you, my Jasper."

That fueled him even more, always from her lips to hear his name, and she knew it too well. He lifted her to put her facing him, then placed her on her knees over him, and he pushed her gown around them like a tent. He put his hand under her dress to find the slit in her pantaloons. Jasper was hard as a rock, and he was working fast to remove all obstacles in the way. When finished, he lifted her over his penis and lowered her down slowly, so they could both feel the fullness of becoming together as one.

"Grab hold of my shoulders to help yourself to ride me, my sweet. I shall also help by lifting you, keep on your knees, and we shall do this together."

Laurentia nodded, then took Jasper's lips. He put his hand on her hips, raising her, then lowering her down all the way. They both moaned. They had a nice pace going, with Laurentia doing most of the work riding him once she got the hang of it. Jasper held back so they could come together in this delicious feeling of the lust they had for each other. Laurentia moaned against Jasper's lips as she rode him hard, and she hit her particular spot, which spiraled into an orgasm that felt like waves of sheer bliss going through her entire body. Jasper came hard, filling her with his seed, moaning, and wrapping his arms around Laurentia to hold her still as they came down together. Laurentia lay her head on Jasper's shoulder.

She sighed and spoke, "That was so wonderful, and I like it this way on top, husband." She lifted her head off his shoulder to look down at Jasper, smiling up at her.

Jasper nipped her lips, "My little vixen, you are learning fast how to enjoy a different way to pleasure the body. I do agree with you that it was incredibly wonderful." He kissed her long and with passion. Jasper broke their kiss, then opened a small door on the side of the wall and pulled out a couple of small hand towels. Jasper handed one to Laurentia, then lift her off him and sat her on the seat beside him. Laurentia knew what to do with the cloth, she put her undergarments to the right again, and Jasper did the same. Sitting side-by-side, Jasper wrapped his arm around Laurentia's shoulder and pulled her close.

Laurentia sighed with contentment, "We need to arrive at our reception soon. They shall be wondering where we are by now. Is my hair a mess?"

Jasper kissed her forehead, "No, I made sure not to touch your hair so that no question shall be asked on our appearance. But, for our whereabouts, I simply shall say London's people demanded to see my new Marchioness, so we rode about the city to not disappoint them is all I shall say, my love."

Laurentia sighed again, "That is quite clever of you, the story. I do hope our flame never goes out of our need to make love so spontaneous. I do have to say it is exciting and wonderful."

"Not to worry, my love. I shall always crave to make love to you; breathing in your lovely scent of honeysuckle always arouses my senses and desires for you. And now, hearing you declaring to me you share the same desires too. That flame shall always burn bright for us and extremely hot."

When they arrived at Berkley Square, Jasper said before the coach door open, "We shall drink, eat, and celebrate with our family and friends for a few hours. Then Lady Laurentia Raventon Bellator, our honeymoon shall start once we return to our home. After that, we shall retire to our bedchamber and not come out until morning."

Laurentia smiled at Jasper, "That sounds like paradise, my dear husband."

Epilogue

The morning after their wedding, Jasper and Laurentia broke their fast together in the master bedchamber at their now residence on Grosvenor Square, as man and wife. They were enjoying the comfort of a fire in the vast fireplace to take the early morning chill out of the room. Sitting in the two over-stuffed wingback chairs, they both wore only a robe. Laurentia sipped her tea, as Jasper drank coffee.

Jasper said, smiling, "Darling, I believe married life agrees with you, for you are showing a lovely glow this morning."

"Husband, I have to agree with you. Between the many times of making love last evening and waking up in your warm, wonderful strong arms this morning, I do feel cherished." She sighed with happiness.

"I do cherish you, my love, and I have something for you this morning."

Laurentia lit up, looking around the room for a gift box. "I do not see anything anywhere."

Jasper stood and walked to the night table by the bed, and he opened the drawer, pulling out a jewelry box. He walked back to Laurentia, placing the box in her hands before sitting back down in his chair. Laurentia looked down at the box, and she beams a smile at Jasper.

"What is in the box, dear husband?"

"The only way you are going to find out is to open it, my love." Jasper raised an eyebrow at her and smiled inside.

Laurentia opened the lid, took in a breath then said, "Oh Jasper, it is beautiful. It matches the diamond necklace you gave me for a wedding gift." She pulled from the box a diamond bracelet that sparkle at her.

"Did, I not say I would spoil you, my love? This, my love, is the start of that promise, and you shall learn in time I always keep my promises, especially when it comes to you, my sweet Laurentia." Jasper tilted his head to the side, and his corner lips were twitching to smile.

Laurentia stood then leaped into his lap, throwing her arms around his neck, kissing his lips, cheeks, nose, before moving back to his lips and kissing him deeply this time. She broke the kiss.

"You are the most wonderful husband."

"So, I take it you like your little gift?"

"You're a silly goose; you know I do. I love it, and I love you." Laurentia smiled, cheek to cheek. "Can you help me put it on, please?"

Jasper took the bracelet from her tiny hands and put it on her wrist, then said. "It fits perfectly, as you are a perfect fit for me." He kissed her nose and smiled.

"We are a perfect fit, and if this is how you are going to start spoiling me, I am going to have to show you how much I love it in so many ways, my dear husband," Laurentia said in a seductive voice, like a purr of a cat.

Jasper's groin was starting to grow hard beneath

Laurentia. "Oh yes, my love, that is the whole fun of spoiling you. I shall receive your handsome rewards, and I intend to enjoy every minute of it tremendously." Of course, Jasper's wicked smile appeared.

Laurentia asked, "What time does our boat leave today?"

Jasper laughed, "My naughty wife that I love and worship, we need to be on board at eleven, and we sail at noon. Is that enough time you seek?"

"Yes, plenty. Now carry me to bed so I may reward you and show you how much I love my husband and my new bracelet."

Jasper stood and carried Laurentia to their bed. She placed her arms around his neck as he walked over. He put her down in the middle of the bed and climbed over her like a panther. Laurentia wet her lips.

"I do love married life and you. I want you, my Jasper, to take me now hard and wild. I was hoping you could take me to that almost out-of-body feeling as we shared the last evening. Being on a honeymoon is most desirable, you know."

Jasper kissed her long and hard before saying, "Laurentia, I am so pleased I found you. You are the most perfect woman I have ever met, and now you are all mine. Come, my love, we shall fly together as one." He took her lips, and they were off to paradise once again and forever together.

At dawn that same day, even before the sun fully rose, Leopold was in his carriage heading out of London with this dog Mick by his side. He saw no one in the streets as the cold air hit his face, and he shook away the feeling of being trapped by the unwanted introduction his mother kept trying to force on him. The Introductions are the young ladies of the ton seeking an eligible gentleman with high income, like himself, to marry well. The word marriage sticks on his tongue like a bad taste one cannot shake out of one's mouth.

Leopold thought, 'Yes, Jasper has found love, and I am genuinely happy for him. I do like Lady Laurentia, and I believe they shall be happy together. However, I am not ready for that commitment yet, and a Raventon man must do that hunt of his own free will. That is the way of it'.

Leopold was on his way to the family estate in Devonshire, for he knew his family would be standing in London as the season was in full swing, and they would not return to the country for at least six to eight weeks. He could go to his own estate north of London, but Leopold opted for a change in his surroundings. Quiet and seclusion were what he sought, and he would get a lot of work done. Plus, there was something that Leopold felt that was calling for him to return to his childhood home again. It has been many years, and to see his old haunts would be well received.

Leopold looked now over his shoulder when passing the city limits. He had only told a couple of his cousins he was leaving and his brother Kelsey, so there was no big fuss when he departed. His valet Nigel and a few of his servants would follow behind him shortly in a couple of his coaches, and they would be bringing Magnus, his stallion, to enjoy some riding in the countryside. Yes, this is what I need, some time away from London. Away from all the ton and my meddling mother. I do love my mother, but she can be impossible at times, and this is one of those times. I am not ready to marry yet, and my father is not helping to derail my mother onto another project that is not me. So, goodbye to London for now, I shall return soon.

Coming Soon, Raventon Collection Volume 2 and 3

Made in the USA
Monee, IL
12 January 2025